WILDFIRE

"I wonder how much you can stand," he muttered. His hands tightened on her wrists, then, hard and demanding, his mouth covered hers.

Her mind howled defiance, even as her treacherous body betrayed her to his touch.

Their burning ache mounted, sparking into needles of scarring, despairing heat. Then wildfire flared, untamed lightning that turned their passion to smouldering ash . . .

"Say what you like," he whispered huskily. "*I say you're mine.*"

Other Avon Books by
Christine Monson

RANGOON
STORMFIRE

Surrender the Night

Christine Monson

AVON
PUBLISHERS OF BARD, CAMELOT, DISCUS AND FLARE BOOKS

AVON BOOKS
A division of
The Hearst Corporation
1790 Broadway
New York, New York 10019

Copyright © 1987 by Christine Monson
Published by arrangement with the author
Library of Congress Catalog Card Number: 86-91026
ISBN: 0-380-89969-8

First Avon Printing: March 1987

AVON TRADEMARK REG. U.S. PAT. OFF. AND IN OTHER COUNTRIES, MARCA
REGISTRADA, HECHO EN U.S.A.

Printed in the U.S.A.

K–R 10 9 8 7 6 5 4 3 2 1

*For the Toths and Mad Hungarians
of All Nationalities,
Particularly, My Big Racer
and Our Little Racer Chaser*

Dragonflies that mate do burn
  in jewelled, shivering silence;
A whisper spent,
  a hovering sun glimpsed among
Narcissus.

Prologue

The Gilded Snare

Northern Italy: March 4, 1847

Eliza's panic soared to the shrieking point. Her small face was set, her golden eyes dilated with tension in the darkness of the coach that hurtled toward a place, a man, she'd never seen, never wanted to see. With Lake Como and Prince Miklos Sztarai only minutes away, Eliza was trapped like one of the frantic birds that had begun this whole adventure. She blamed no one but herself, not even Princess Elizabeth von Schmerling, who steadily watched her from the opposite carriage seat. With open eyes, Eliza had walked into the sly princess's gilded snare, step by step . . .

Chapter I

The Terrier and the Clam

Newport, Rhode Island: New Year's Eve, 1846

"Now let the heavens yield their happy choristers!" trilled Mrs. Lucia Packer, fluttering her plump, beringed fingers skyward. A dead wren struck Princess Elizabeth von Schmerling's powdered shoulder. In startled bemusement, she looked up and saw a deluge of tiny, feathered corpses plummet from a gold silk canopy stretched across the Anderson Packers' ballroom ceiling. The birds that survived suffocation in the airless silk exploded against the Italian frescoes and ponderous chandeliers with a smash of crystal. As the trapped birds wheeled and darted about their heads, the guests scattered, pawing and swatting. Shrieking women fainted among the inert ornithologia on the parquetry floor.

Newport in December; now this! Determined to make her social mark, Lucia Packer gave her winter ball in off-season Newport, where it would not compete with more prestigious New York balls. Three hundred guests had been invited; one hundred seventy-five of the desperate arrived.

Including me, Princess von Schmerling reflected irritably. The Vanderbilt and Astor Christmas affairs weren't enough; like a vulture, I *had* to prowl every parvenu ball just to be sure . . .

With a snort of exasperation at the confused melee,

Princess von Schmerling elevated her fan above her tiaraed, silver head and stalked through the squealing throng as if reviewing a battalion of hopeless troops. As she passed the orchestra dais, with sharp accuracy her grosgrain-shod foot sent a stiff little corpse flying from the floor to flatten against the hysterical Mrs. Packer's back. At the woman's ascending screech, the princess smiled in grim satisfaction.

With a twitch of her silver tulle skirts, Bette von Schmerling advanced swiftly toward the rank of Venetian doors locked to prevent icy drafts. A pale-haired young woman she was soon to know as Eliza Hilliard reached the doors first. For a few moments, Eliza wrestled with the ornate door handle, then, with an awkward, determined strength Bette would not have expected from so small a person, seized a flower stand and with a scattering of roses swung it against the stubborn lock.

Reaching her side, Bette said briskly, "Bravo, my dear. Lend a shoulder." The two threw their combined weight against the damaged lock. With a splinter of wood, the doors burst open. Out into the harsh, December night stumbled the Austrian and young American. With them escaped several birds, quickly followed by more, some tearing their wings against shattered glass in the wind-buffeted doors. Huddled against the biting Atlantic wind, Eliza Hilliard watched the birds' dark, winged shapes disappearing into the night toward the beach's sandy parapets. "They'll freeze now, most of them," she muttered, "all because of that silly woman's vanity."

"Are we not all a little vain, my dear?" The princess smiled without humor. "Come, we can do nothing more now for those wretched creatures. The best and luckiest of them will survive." Her hand firmly closed over Eliza's. "I want some of your American coffee with a good dash of Anderson Packer's vile cognac. It should be unguarded for the moment."

Eliza followed her to skirt the still frantic crowd under the bird-beaded chandeliers. Several women had fainted. The settees were clogged with befuddled, pale-faced guests. Fans beat the air and tempers were raw. Nearly every breakable object in the room was broken; porcelain shards, bird feathers, dung, and bodies littered the floor.

Once in the deserted study, Bette went directly to the liquor carafes and as she poured observed to her young companion, "You're something of a little cat, aren't you, Miss . . . ?"

"Hilliard. Elizabeth, but usually Eliza. Why do you say that?" Under thick, level brows, Eliza Hilliard's eyes were guarded, tawny gleams of amber in a thin, angular face with wide cheekbones. The nose was small, the chin cleft. Though she could scarcely be eighteen, she looked like a dancer worn out long before her time. Her expensive dress was a brutal purple meant for a brunette of forty. Diamond and tortoise combs sagged in fine hair knotted at her nape. Her pallid skin had goose bumps.

Bette studied her with the leisure acquired by birth and experience. "I meant you appear to be able to quickly find your balance, no matter how extraordinary the situation." She added coffee to the cognac and handed Eliza Hilliard a cup. "My name is also Elizabeth. Are you from Boston?"

"New York." With a shiver, Eliza peered at the coffee.

"You've more the look of Boston."

Eliza's pale head came up, golden eyes flat. "Miss . . ."

"Princess," the older woman corrected amiably. "Elizabeth von Schmerling. I'm Austrian, so you must forgive my preconceptions." Comfortable as a lazy terrier, she settled on a curved, Lawford sofa before the walnut-paneled fireplace. "Of course, I'm wrong. No Bostonian would assault a door with a flower stand." Her glacial face turned impish. "Come here, child, and sit beside me. You and I may shortly be in a great deal of trouble with the Packers over their doors, so we may as well get to know one another." Deliberately, as if Eliza's agreement was unquestionable, she ceased to look at her and began to stir her coffee.

The princess shrewdly considered her choices as Eliza warily approached. Just possibly Eliza might do, unlikely as she looked. Bette was tired of searching. For her purposes, beauty would be pleasant, but unnecessary, within reason. Even by the harsh, uneven glare of the gaslight chandelier, Eliza was not bad. With that antique gold hair, her darkish brows and mahogany lashes were an odd contrast, but striking. A trifle less chin and a trifle more nose might be in order, but the mouth was good: generous and firm. She'd have to get a look at her teeth. Whether Eliza's resemblance to Loise was in her favor or not also remained to be seen. "Has your family lived long in New York, Miss Hilliard?"

"Not yet a generation, Princess." Eliza sat down but still made no effort to drink her coffee. Bette sensed she was less prim than unsure, unused to a European accent, also to aristocracy; yet her manner held no trace of subservience.

"And do you like the city?"

"Tolerably well. As you observed, Your Highness, I am adaptable."

And as much clam as cat, I suspect. Just as well. Clams are never without a niche. "Yes, resilience can be a great advantage. So often it's gained by travel. If so, you must have been much abroad," Bette suggested, virtually certain Eliza had not.

A small, amused smile touched Eliza's lips. "I have seen New England, ma'am."

The princess laughed. "I daresay."

At that moment, the study door burst open to be filled with a large-boned, redheaded woman upholstered with pink flesh and yellow taffeta. "Eliza! How many times have I told you to stop creeping . . ." Bette's diamonds registered. Yellow charged forward, a plump, beringed hand extended with the invitation of a bayonet. "I am Mrs. Dorothy Hilliard, Eliza's mother. I don't believe I've had the honor . . ."

Bette bestowed the honor and watched the round face unfold in delighted awe, refold in a pearl-toothed simper. "Why, what a delight! Lucy's guest of honor! My goodness, Princess, you are sweet to take time with Eliza. She's such a shy thing. I can hardly get a word out of her."

I don't wonder, thought Bette. One might better converse with a bellows. "I'm sure you can be quite persuasive, Mrs. Hilliard." As she spoke, she eyed the woman's coquettish, lace-festooned taffeta and awesomely expansive crinolines. "I see you must help Miss Hilliard select her wardrobe."

The inference rolled past Dorothy Hilliard. "Why, of course. Eliza can't pick an apple by herself!"

As the woman chattered on, the princess came to another conclusion. If one judged by Mrs. Hilliard, Eliza had no breeding: only recent money, a low, tenuous place in an often gauche society. Unless her father proved to be a very different creature from his wife, Eliza was a plow pony saddled with a perfect ass of a mother.

Only Eliza hadn't a common look. Somewhere along the line, she had acquired patience of steel; otherwise, her character would have been ground into dull dross like her mother's. Given the flower stand incident, she had the nerve to smash her way to what she wanted, but if that capability was unpredictable and uncontrollable, she might be more dangerous than useful.

Showing no sign of embarrassment or apology for Dorothy Hilliard's behavior, Eliza was serene, her mind clearly a million miles away. Where *is* that mind of yours, girl? wondered Bette. Just how far would you like to go? Shall I turn your dull world upside down and cannon you into the stars?

I won't. Not just yet. The stars may not be dull, but they can be cold. I'm not at all sure yet whether you can stand that terrible cold.

After inviting Mrs. Hilliard to join them, Bette adroitly slipped in her own questions. In ten minutes, she knew the embellished history of the Hilliards. They were Ohioans, import–export dealers expanded to large-scale department store owners. Uninterested in bourgeois merchandising, Bette shortly tried to divert the conversation to Eliza's history.

"Eliza? Oh, she's a very usual sort of girl, aren't you, Eliza? Now, Your Highness, do tell me about Austria! It must be fascinating . . ."

"But I'm sure your daughter is fascinating, too. What are your greatest interests, Miss Hilliard?"

"I paint."

Bette smiled encouragingly. "That's wonderful. How else do you pass your time?"

"I spend most of it at the New York City Library." With an innocent air, Eliza surreptitiously tested her brandied coffee. Bette suspected she'd never had liquor in her life, but couldn't resist tweaking her impossible mother. "I should love to see your artwork before I return to Europe, Miss Hilliard."

Now Bette had Eliza's full attention, laced with an additional element that coolly glinted in her eyes: suspicion.

Eliza's coffee cup lowered. "My efforts are quite ordinary, Your Highness; surely nothing that would interest you after your experience of Europe."

"Eliza, don't be impertinent!" interrupted her mother, who then somewhat comically became caught between irritation and the desire to cajole, for by now she reluctantly realized Bette's interest was solely in her daughter. "Your little pieces are very nice, Eliza. Certainly you're too modest to presume the princess's taste. We should love to have you to tea upon your return to New York, Your Highness. You're not neglecting our fair city, I hope."

"Oh, no, but I fear my next visit must be brief. I sail from New York to Italy Friday next."

Mrs. Hilliard looked flustered for a moment. At Eliza's brief, hard look at her mother, Bette surmised the family plans for Newport had just been wrenched awry.

"Oh! Then Monday certainly . . . if that's convenient. At four?"

"That should fit beautifully." Bette turned to Eliza. "And you need not fear I shall be disappointed in anything you do, Miss Hilliard. I'm quite sure very little about you is ordinary."

Eliza was startled. For an instant, her cheekbones stained rose in her pale face, and the princess thought again, no, not bad at all.

"Well, my dears . . . ?" came a low, hesitant voice from the doorway.

The women's heads turned. "Oh, Willy." Dorothy Hilliard sounded disappointed. "Princess, my husband, Wilson Hilliard."

As Wilson Hilliard shyly bowed, his wife added importantly, "Willy, I want you to meet our new friend, Princess von Schmerling. She'll be coming to tea Monday next."

Hilliard's eyes widened, then he nodded nervously. "That's nice. We're greatly honored, ma'am."

"Your Highness, Willy," came his wife's chilly admonishment.

Wilson Hilliard flushed. "I'm sorry, ma—Your Highness. I haven't met much royalty, you see." He was a man who looked smaller than he was, thanks to years of long work hours and Dorothy Hilliard. His faded flaxen hair had paled to whitish gray at the temples and disappeared altogether at the crown. Behind their gold-rimmed spectacles, the brown eyes had dulled: Eliza's eyes once, but without their tawny intensity.

"How do you do, Mr. Hilliard," Bette said kindly. Whatever else the man was, he was unpretentious, and after his wife, a relief.

"Won't you join us, Papa?" Eliza Hilliard's voice was soft, her eyes reassuring.

"Oh, no, no. I just wondered where you were. Been helping clean up the mess."

Dorothy Hilliard gave him an impatient glance. "Willy, Anderson and Lucy have servants to handle janitorial services."

Hilliard flinched, then said uncertainly, "Yes . . . well, I didn't really think. Everybody was running around complaining and Mrs. Packer looked so . . ."

Bette caught Eliza's look of pity as he fumbled. So she has compassion, reflected the princess, not just for easy creatures like those pitiful birds, but difficult ones: the kind that don't go away, but wear one down with their flaws and needs. If she has no escape from the cold—Bette

flexed the weight of the heavy diamond on her left hand—
she just may be able to endure it.

"Oh, Willy," Dorothy Hilliard was saying impatiently,
"you never think . . ."

Eliza stood up, interrupting her mother without a sound.
Impassively, she studied the pink, porcine face. "No, of
course, Papa wasn't thinking, Mama; he was being thought-
ful." Leaving Dorothy Hilliard to ponder the difference,
she held out her hand to her father. "Why don't we look
for the Packers together, Papa. They might welcome a pair
of friendly faces."

In that moment, Bette decided. This little clam's the
one. I want her and her hard shell with its soft center.
Then, with a sharp pinch of dismay as Eliza went to take
Wilson Hilliard's outstretched arm, Bette noticed for the
first time that she was a cripple. Her careful movements
virtually concealed the flaw: uncertainty in an occasional
step, an awkward stiffness of the right leg. For a fleeting
moment, Bette envisioned Miklos's body. No. No, this
poor Hilliard girl would never do . . . and yet . . . she had
everything else. Her parents would pose no difficulty.
They were plums, ripe for plucking. And time was running
out.

Eliza turned, her arm linked in her father's. "Mama,
Princess, if you will excuse us."

As the pair left, Dorothy Hilliard caught Bette's expression.
"Is something wrong, Princess? I hope Eliza hasn't . . ."

Bette's eyes shielded. "No, of course not, Mrs. Hilliard.
I think your Eliza's very nearly perfect."

She couldn't have been more wrong. Bette had gauged
Eliza Hilliard fairly well, but she was not clairvoyant. She
had already made several disastrous mistakes in unearthing
the "little clam."

New York: January 5, 1847

For tea with Princess von Schmerling, Eliza was decked
in maroon silk swagged like a curtain and enough jet
jewelry to fringe an undertaker's parlor. She didn't mind.

She had long ago ceased to mind, even notice, her mother's taste. So long as she was left alone with her books and sketchpads, Eliza would scarcely have minded if the rest of the world disappeared.

She had already seen a good deal of that world: its vitality, cruelties, inequities, elegance, and griminess on the New York streets. As her parents had no expectation for her to marry, they'd let her go about the city much as she pleased, both of them presuming that what she pleased would be unimaginative and appropriate. For years, she hid her slum and foreign ghetto sketches: the charcoals of overcrowded flats and sweatshops, the stubborn life and energy and unexpected beauty that battled grinding poverty and fatigue. The power of her artistry was beyond her years, its pain beyond her years, for the pain of her injury had been her constant teacher.

As for Wilson Hilliard, Eliza loved and understood him, but was uncomfortable in his company. The dull knell of his misery and defeat tolled through every word he uttered, every look that never quite focused on anyone's eyes. So, here they were, with all their foreseeable tomorrows filled by the devouring, matriarchal pinkness of Dorothy Hilliard.

The ebony shine of an approaching carriage gleamed under the elms. Yellow spokes blurred, reversed briefly, and halted as matched bays were pulled up in front of the Hilliard gate. The hack jumped down to open the carriage door. A darkly handsome young man in a beaver hat and green talma cloak stepped from the carriage, glanced with distaste at the granite, Gothic house, then turned to assist Princess von Schmerling. As her escort bade the hack to wait, the princess, in a Turkish cashmere turban and sable scarf to set off a fitted, ink blue carrick coat, came briskly up the walk.

Eliza wearily recalled the hasty packing and harried train journey back to New York dictated by this determined-looking Austrian. The princess, she conjectured, hadn't the remotest interest in viewing her artwork. Most people, particularly socialites, had no interest in her at all. This she matter-of-factly attributed not to her clownish mother, but

to her own lame leg. Whether or not they had ever met
Dorothy Hilliard, people rarely lingered in Eliza's company once they noticed the lameness.

Damp weather always made her leg ache. Absently, she
rubbed her thigh as she watched the dark man come up the
walk to join the princess at the door. He looked as beautiful as a bit of bait. What *did* the woman want?

"Marriage?" Dorothy Hilliard's fleshy jaw dropped as
her teacup bounced on her parlor carpet. "With Eliza? But
Eliza's . . . you can't mean . . ." Her hope that the
princess meant the proposal jumbled with shocked amaze-
ment and a quick, furtive suspicion that the princess was
less than she seemed. She would dearly love to be rid of
Eliza, but not to a fortune hunter. She shot a satisfied
glance about her Gothic Revival parlor. She'd be hanged if
she'd support some dingy, titled beggar. Yet . . . "You
say, *Prince* Miklos Tis—Zis—"

"Sztarai. Eliza would be a princess with even more
privileges than my title allows. And you would enjoy the
social triumph of the season."

Eliza's eyes had narrowed in exasperated disbelief.
"Mother, this is a joke."

Dorothy Hilliard waved her to silence. "What sort of
dowry had you in mind, Princess?" Her voice had all the
caginess of an Ozarks horse trader.

"You may wish to issue a modest block of stock of your
mercantile concern to Eliza to assure yourself of her future
security; however, this is simply a suggestion for your own
peace of mind. The prince is more than able to support a
wife." Stoically, Bette ignored the glass-domed, stuffed
marmoset in the center of the table. "My nephew has
estates not only in Hungary, but in Austria, Switzerland,
and France. His paternal aunt, Princess Gertrude von Zusen,
was first cousin of the Empress Maria Louisa of Austria.
The blood of the Hapsburgs runs in his veins; through that
line he is related to most of the royal houses of Europe. The
Sztarai line itself goes back more than two thousand years."

"Most impressive, certainly, Princess," murmured Dorothy Hilliard, becoming more bewildered as to why this paragon should bother with Eliza.

Eliza had several ideas and liked none of them. Either this prince was a frog or the princess had a malicious sense of humor. With a sweep of crinolines, she rose from the settee and went to the fireplace, where Wilson Hilliard fidgeted with his watch. "Papa," she said firmly, "surely *you* see this is impossible. You must tell them."

Catching his wife's warning look, Wilson was reluctant to be so blunt. He poked his watch out of sight. "The prince, er, Princess, what sort of fellow is he?"

"I must say with all respect"—Bette's escort, an Italian named Enzo Rossi, intervened easily—"the princess is not the person to fairly describe Prince Sztarai. She is far too fond of him." At the princess's little shrug of mock reproof, Rossi's white teeth gleamed in an unrepentant smile. "Still, I assure you the prince is not at all repulsive. He is strong, healthy, and only a few years older than myself." His arms expanded as he strolled over to Eliza. "He went to Sandhurst and graduated with honors from the military academy at Weiner-Neustadt." Again came the grin. "Like me, he is very polite." As if in admiration, he stroked a blown glass, bloated pug dog on the mantel.

"I'm beginning to think the prince has more than one relative in this room," impolitely retorted Eliza, having completely lost patience with the whole charade.

"Eliza!" snapped Dorothy Hilliard.

"Quite right, *Signorina* Hilliard. I am his highness's cousin." The Italian sobered. "Like you, *Signorina*, I have no title or great eagerness for one. I am simple Enzo Rossi of Milano. My father is a banker. I went to the University of Padua and am following his footsteps more or less seriously in the family business."

"Then you will forgive a more or less serious question." Eliza eyed him as if he were still fishing with the wrong fly. "Why should so eligible a personage as Prince Sztarai want an obscure, dowerless wife he has never seen?"

Dorothy Hilliard gave a sigh of exasperation, though she had been dying to ask the same question.

"My cousin finds himself in a bizarre predicament, Miss Hilliard," Rossi replied somewhat sheepishly. "He is obliged to choose a bride, yet cannot without causing a great deal of trouble."

"What Enzo means is that Prince Sztarai's marriage with a Hungarian or Austrian young lady of birth will cause political animosity among the rejected families. State affairs in the empire are exceedingly complex just now, rivalries extreme. A French or Italian bride, in view of French ambitions in Italy, would be anathema." Bette waved at Eliza. "Therefore, an English or American wife seems appropriate. As for what you call obscurity, Prince Sztarai does not want a wife who will give herself airs that will antagonize his family and friends. Many American women who marry into aristocracy become insufferable snobs." She did not look at Dorothy Hilliard. "I think you, Eliza, have too much sense for that. And as for dowry"—her head tilted with a twinkle of diamond earrings—"the prince is quite able to support himself." She smiled faintly. "I do not pretend this arrangement will be easy, Eliza. You will find it a daily challenge, and your New York Library a very long way from Hungary." Then slyly, "Your mother, too, will be out of reach."

Eliza's tawny eyes accessed her, then flicked away toward the fire.

"What do you think, Mr. Hilliard?" asked the princess negligently.

He looked startled, as if he'd never dreamed his opinion would be asked. "Why, Eliza ought to do what she likes, I suppose, after she and the prince get to know each other."

"That, I'm afraid, Mr. Hilliard, is a luxury Eliza and Prince Sztarai will not enjoy," the princess said briskly. "Prince Sztarai must marry within the next few months; this unfortunately allows no time for courtship. I expressly came to America to find him a bride. I should not care to have to come again." She watched Eliza. "If Eliza agrees, she will be married to the prince by proxy this Friday and sail with me the same day. Enzo will stand in for the prince. If upon their meeting, the prince does not wish to take her as his wife, which I cannot imagine, Eliza will receive a substantial settlement for her trouble.''

"But, with all respect, ma'am, what if it turns out she doesn't care for your nephew?'' Wilson Hilliard protested.

"Then the marriage will be quietly annulled. No one need know it ever took place.'' The princess gave Eliza a mischievous smile. "Eliza will be free to simply return to her usual life with a fair settlement.''

"Oh, Eliza would love being married to your nephew, I'm sure," Dorothy Hilliard said hurriedly. She was hardly eager to face the prospect of her daughter's return once the idea of being rid of her set in her mind. Besides, one way or another, they couldn't lose. She'd make sure the settlement was not only fair, but fat, or the Sztarai clan would have faces as red as turkey wattles.

Just as the princess shrewdly guessed Dorothy Hilliard's train of thought, she also guessed Eliza's. For the first time, Eliza was tempted, not only by the idea of getting away from home, but by the prospect of never having to return, whatever the outcome of this marriage. Of taking her settlement and going the opposite direction from Dorothy Hilliard. Frog or no, Prince Miklos Sztarai now intrigued Eliza. Most certainly, he would demand an immediate annullment; with enough money from the settlement, she could live the rest of her life in peace and independence. She could find a quiet apartment in Paris near the Sorbonne, attend art school, and observe the riotous student life. Wouldn't that scandalize her mother!

"In view of the situation," announced Dorothy Hilliard firmly, "there ought to be a marriage contract, oughtn't there, Willy?''

Her husband was again startled. "Why, yes. Most definitely, but . . .''

Dorothy Hilliard overran him. "Have your lawyer call tomorrow morning at ten o'clock, Princess. Our lawyer will draw up the papers.''

"I haven't agreed, Mother," interrupted Eliza coolly.

Whatever the prince's possibilities, she had no intention of being railroaded.

"You will agree," said her mother with a bland look that suggested life would be living hell if she were disappointed.

After Princess von Schmerling and Rossi left, the fire-works exploded. Wilson half suspected his daughter re-sisted her mother's blandishments just to perversely watch her rant and rave. Soft soap was not Dorothy Hilliard's strong point; like a well-wet pig, she slid through it to her forte: browbeating. "How long do you think you can drift around with your nose in a book and live out of your hardworking father's pocket? Just how many offers like this do you think you're going to get? How many offers, period?!" As she stalked about the parlor, her temper soared at her daughter's studied indifference. "Who do you think you are? Let me tell you, I've protected you too long because of that twisted leg!" Like a true harpy, she fed off the spark of pain in Eliza's eyes. "You're spoiled rotten; that's the trouble. Your father's been soft, not wanting me to make you face up to things." Ruffles pouched as Dorothy Hilliard planted herself in a narrow chair. "Well, no man wants a gimp."

"That's enough, Dot," cut in Wilson Hilliard sharply.

Dorothy Hilliard folded her arms. "It's time it was said."

"You don't have to go to Hungary, Eliza," Wilson said quietly. "You're not a burden to this house, but a bless-ing. As long as I'm alive, you'll want for nothing."

"So long . . . humph!" Dorothy Hilliard's eyes nar-rowed. "I've known these past five years about your strumpet and brat up in Albany." At his guilty start, she shot a triumphant look at Eliza. "Didn't know your father kept a trollop, did you?" She rounded again on her hus-band. "Well, if you know what's good for you, you won't be telling me what to do. I'll raise a stink that will reek from here to San Francisco."

"I'm sorry to hear you say that, Dot." Wilson was waxy pale. "If you try to embarrass them, I'll go directly to the New York District Attorney and confess I'm a thief.''

Eliza stiffened in disbelief as Dorothy Hilliard spat, "What are you talking about! That's absurd!''

"Nobody will think so when they find the spare ledgers I've contrived to avoid this kind of unfortunate confrontation." He smiled faintly. "I'll go to prison, Dotty, but you'll lose every dime.''

Dorothy Hilliard's face was now as ashen as his. "You're bluffing! I don't believe it." Her eyes narrowed. "You haven't the stomach to face prison.''

"I've faced you for twenty years. Prison can't be a lot worse.''

At that, Eliza came to an abrupt decision. If she continued under her parents' roof after this savage confrontation, life would be unendurable for all of them. She knew now her father would never feel free to leave and make his own life unless she did. In the end, Dorothy's malice would destroy him. "Neither can Prince Sztarai be very much worse than prison, Papa," Eliza said quietly, picking up the fireplace poker.

"You mean you want to . . . ?''

"No, not particularly. I could be just jumping from the frying pan into the fire"—she gave the dulling coals an ironic prod—"though that may provide some relief from the Hungarian winters; they're probably as bad as the Russian ones.''

"I don't know." He was partly relieved, partly uneasy. "Rossi and that Schmerling woman might be just a pair of shysters.''

"The princess is authentic," snapped Dorothy Hilliard. "I telegrammed a detective agency from Newport to check on her. By tomorrow morning, they can review her finances." She turned to Eliza. "Well, have you made up your mind?''

"Yes, Mother.''

"Well?!''

"It's yes, Mother. Yes to you, to Prince Charming, to

the fairy godmother and her beautiful Italian rat. Trot in the parson.''

The parson was a priest, resplendent in white and gold robes. Eliza wore the most unbecoming, sallow ivory satin gown Dorothy Hilliard could find. In his part of proxy, Rossi squirmed, giving the impression that his feckless spirit found being married to any woman, even in pretense, an experience of horror. Dorothy had huge sheaves of calla lilies arranged about the parlor. Fat candles oozed wax and tepid light, which played moodily on the priest's robes, Eliza's tallow-toned satin, and Rossi's perspiring face. Due to the embarrassingly short notice, no guests had been invited. When Eliza had set down her little dog, Coriolanus, on the upstairs landing before going down for the ceremony, she held out her hand to him. "Like a sniff of the stiff in this bloomin' wake, laddie?"

With a wistful smile, Eliza watched the small dog tenderly lick her hand. How she loved Cory. How she might have loved a man, given half a chance; now she was marrying one coldly for money, and she felt sick inside. If she loved Miklos Sztarai, money would matter not at all. Like Cory, she would follow him anywhere. Limping. She closed her eyes. How foolish to imagine he would linger for her to keep up with him.

As Eliza descended the stairs, even Princess von Schmerling looked a trifle tight-faced. Dorothy Hilliard wore a permanent, manufactured smile; Wilson, who escorted her, none at all.

Eliza barely listened to the unfamiliar Latin. She had halfheartedly agreed to take instruction in the Church, as stipulated by the princess in the marriage contract; the only other royal requirement was that any male children born of the marriage would be raised in Hungary. Like Coriolanus, Eliza reflected absently as the priest droned through the lengthy ceremony, I am, if not trained to amuse, reliably housebroken.

While also politely housebroken, Coriolanus was a great thorn in Dorothy's side. On her way to the library one day,

Eliza had found him half-drowned in a muddy carriage rut left by the iron wheel that had crushed his hip. She had taken the sodden creature into her father's immaculate offices. Wilson immediately wrapped Coriolanus in his cashmere scarf, then sent a clerk to summon a veterinarian. Dorothy raised holy hell when the pair brought Coriolanus home, but for once her tantrums made no impression on Wilson. Eliza, who was desperately gripping Cory, had never been permitted a pet since the pony on which she had been injured had been sold.

So Eliza had gotten Cory . . . and now she had Miklos Sztarai.

The Manhattan wharves were crowded with Europe-bound passengers, their chatter and nervous excitement carrying under rain-pelted umbrellas, their luggage growing sodden as it was hauled up the gangways. Wilson Hilliard's face was doleful as stevedores heaved Eliza's trunks onto a cart. He hunched into his beaver-collared greatcoat, sneezed, whipped out a handkerchief and blew his nose. "Remember," he muttered to Eliza as the princess and Rossi said good-bye to Dorothy Hilliard, "you don't have to stick it out any longer than you want, honey. I went over that marriage contract with a fine-tooth comb. Once out of your mother's reach, you'll be free as a bird."

"Don't worry, Papa. I don't think Mother will reach for me," her voice softened as she affectionately turned up his collar against the damp, "or you, if you want to leave badly enough." She dug into her reticule. "Give this to Teddy . . . my brother, for me." She pressed a toy fire wagon into his gloved hand. "It isn't new. You know Mother and pocket money. I found it stuck in a storm drain."

The brass steamship whistle shrieked. She looked at the sooty, wooden ship rubbing the piling buffers, took a hard breath, and handed Wilson Cory's leash. "Look after Cory for me, will you? I think he'll answer more happily to a western drawl than Hungarian. Teddy will like him, I think."

His chocolate eyes reproachful, Cory flopped on his side and groaned. She wanted to snatch him up and run for Timbuktu.

Wilson bent to scratch the dog's ears. "You sure about this, honey?"

"Yes." Her throat ached terribly; she must be getting a cold.

He looped the leash about his wrist. "Well . . . thanks. Teddy'll think it's turned Easter and Christmas." He started to put the fire wagon in his pocket, then realized Dorothy had turned from the Europeans and her attention was on the toy. Anger and pain twisted her face, then dulled to stiff resignation. As the princess and Rossi crossed the wharf toward Eliza, Wilson dropped the fire wagon into his pocket. "I'll write you from Wyoming," he said softly.

Chapter 2

Don't Dance at My Wedding

The Britannia: *January 12, 1847*

By nightfall after leaving New York, the eastbound *Britannia*, transatlantic steamer of the Cunard Line, was well into the nebulous, treacherous world of the North Atlantic. A damp winter fog closed in to thickly bank a sluggish churn of sea. The few passengers slowly walking the deck were hushed, yet their murmurs were exaggerated and thrown back by the fog, so that like furtive children at some mischief, they constantly darted looks at their fellow shadows, their voices lowering to near whispers.

"The gray shades of Valhalla must wander the sea here," murmured Eliza, curling her cloak hood high about her face as she and Enzo Rossi leaned against the rail.

Enzo laughed. "I've been imagining myself as Dante searching the murky abyss of Hades for my Beatrice." He sighed. "The poor devil, to feel his lady always so close, yet ever beyond his reach."

This Enzo's very aware of his good looks, Eliza mused. He uses them as a musician uses an instrument: all for effect, but a pleasant effect. He resembled a Renaissance prince with his black, tousled cap of glossy curls. Tall, slender, he wore his modish clothes gracefully without being foppish. Oh, Enzo Rossi was the stuff of maiden's dreams, indeed. She couldn't resist tickling his assurance.

"Come, *Signor* Rossi, what would you do with Beatrice if you had her?"

With dreamy lechery, he perused the vague, billowing expanse of dripping canvas above their heads. "Oh, I can think of several things."

"Better then your Beatrice be safely married to someone else. I have observed the confinement of legal *amour* fairly puts you into a cold sweat."

He blinked, shocked at her unmaidenly bluntness.

In spite of herself, Eliza colored. "I may be shy, *Signor* Rossi, but did you really think me demure? Only a creature made of either mush or metal could agree to marry a total stranger. I rather doubt the princess chose me because she thought Prince Sztarai could squeeze me through his fingers."

Enzo had thought exactly that. He would not have chosen her for Miklos in a hundred years. Reluctantly bowing to his aunt's reliable intelligence, he had helped wheedle Eliza into acceptance, then dismissed her existence as he invariably did with women he had persuaded to do one thing or another. Indeed, he had barely noticed her except to pity his cousin for her colorless seriousness and awkward gait. Now he had a glimmer of understanding of his Aunt Bette's bridal choice for Miklos. Still, while Eliza might not be demure, as she admitted, she knew nothing about attracting men and less of how to flirt. Despite similarity of coloring, she and Loise were unlike as day and night. Careless, lovely Loise had been like an innocent, voluptuous child. This Eliza was skinny, knowing, with eyes that made him think of an old woman who had seen too much, yet somehow were younger than Loise's.

"You must not be afraid of Miklos," he said impulsively. "He's not an easy man, but . . ."

"*Mein Gott!* This is miserable weather for a saunter about the deck," came Princess von Schmerling's voice behind them.

Enzo turned, wondering how long she had been there. "Why, hello, aunt! Haven't I seen you climb the Jungfrau in worse fog?"

Bette gathered her sables about her throat. "I was younger then, and first cousin to a goat. Eliza isn't used to this damp. I don't want her down with a cold all the way to Southampton."

"I'm not as frail as all that, Your Highness," said Eliza quietly.

"I daresay you're not, but if you catch cold, I shall end up with it in that close cabin, then likely Enzo will begin to sneeze." She linked their arms. "Come, join me for tea in that nasty little salon. We've scarcely had a chance to talk since Newport."

Under the dim timbrel lights, the cramped dining salon showed mildew, the linen on the few tables needed rebleaching, and the crockery was chipped. Eliza dismissed such shoddiness as an inherent part of the passage; Princess von Schmerling was less lenient. She sent her maid for monogrammed porcelain, a samovar, silver, and an Italian shawl to cover the stained tablecloth. The steward was graciously allowed to provide hot water for the samovar; the maid brewed tea.

Eliza, who had never seen a samovar in use, watched the maid prepare a strong diffusion of pungent tea, pour it into each cup, then dilute it with boiling water. No lemon and milk was used. The princess smiled in approval at her interest. "Your observation of our ways will stand you in good stead, Eliza. Also, as we are both princesses now, you need not address me by my title. Bette will do. Enzo calls me *Nene* Bette."

You will never be cozy Aunt Bette to me so long as I live, thought Eliza as the maid served. Still, she considered it best to be polite for the time being; no doubt family relations would soon grow hot enough. "*Signor* Rossi tells me you are Hungarian, not Austrian, Bette."

"Yes, I am a Sztarai like Miklos. I went with my family to the court of Emperor Joseph II at Vienna when I was only five. At fifteen, I was married into the Schmerling family." Something in the princess's eyes told Eliza the older woman understood her present mood better than she might like. Bette sipped her tea. "I returned to Budapest after Willi died. That was only four years ago." Her eyes twinkled. "So you see, we shall discover Hungary together."

"What is it like?"

"Like no place on earth you have ever been. Our children sing, 'If the earth is the hat of God, Hungary is the flower on it'." Teasingly, Bette twirled her muff. "As you see, we Hungarians can be very vain, very arrogant, very charming. We have grand moods, grand passions, grand appetites. Everything is black and white; nothing is gray."

Still idly playing with the muff, she gazed across the narrow salon as if she envisioned fields and mountains. "As for customs, I suppose they appear Russian to the uninitiated. The dances and festival costumes are somewhat similar." Bette's forefinger traced the silver chasing on her teacup handle. "Is there anything in particular you wondered about?"

She means the prince, thought Eliza. "Where shall I be living?"

Enzo and Bette exchanged glances. "The family estates border Lake Balaton in southwestern Hungary," answered Bette, "but you will meet Miklos in Italy. He is holidaying at a Lake Como villa belonging to the king of Piedmont-Sardinia."

A flicker of melancholy entered Enzo's eyes. "Balaton and Como are something alike, though not enough to suit Miklos, I think."

"What sort of things *do* suit him?"

Again he looked at the princess, then smiled easily. "Oh, horses, dogs, hunting." As if Eliza might view all that as too jolly squirish, he added, "He's also a patron of the arts."

He sounds perfectly useless. Eliza drank her tea.

That night an icy gale ripped down on the ship. As Eliza lay in her stateroom bed, she listened to the timbers creak and squeal, the wind hiss and howl. Although the bed was bolted to the floor, it lurched as the *Britannia* wallowed

into troughs, soared, and rolled. Eliza, finding she liked the
unpredictable motion, hummed softly to herself. In the
opposite bed, Bette was sound asleep. At length, Eliza
noticed an odd ticking from the porthole; so cold its creton-
draped, ice-glazed glass clicked in the wind. Silently, she
slipped out of bed to peer out. By a faint moon, the waves
were black, moving mountains; terrible, unpredictable, and
grand. She clung to the porthole fittings until the glass
became so ice-distorted she could not separate sea from
sky. Shivering, she pulled on a cloak over her nightgown
and put on her warmest shoes. Then she went on deck.

Minutes after Eliza departed, Bette knocked at Enzo's
door. "She has left the cabin. See to her."

Enzo couldn't find Eliza. The deck was treacherous with
ice; the sailors were fairly skating on it, and seasoned as
they were, brutally falling against the searing boiler and
cabin housings. The moon was blotted behind storm clouds
so he could only sense, rather than see, the monstrous sea
about them. He slithered toward the bow, jammed his
wrist against the hull side, and swore.

For a quarter hour, Enzo stumbled about the deck, but
saw no sign of Eliza. Becoming sickeningly certain she
had fallen overboard, he hurried back to the cabin hatch to
tell Bette. Then he saw Eliza, crouched just aft of the
hatch with her hands wound about a stanchion. She was
looking at him, must have seen him when he first emerged
from the hatch. He felt uncomfortable, aware she was
playing games with him, that he and Bette were not quite
in control of her. Her wet face was pale, exhilarated, and
proud. "What are you doing?" he demanded harshly.
"Don't you see how dangerous the storm is up here?"

"Yes," she replied breathlessly, "I see. The sea's not a
mill pond, is it?"

Is she crazy? he wondered. "You must come below.
Now"—he caught her hand—"come."

She pulled away. "No. I've spent enough time in beds."
Then quietly, "They're not as safe as you may think; only
dull."

You've never been in my bed, Enzo considered ironically. Ennui was his personal plague, particularly with women. Then he was surprised that the idea of Eliza Hilliard in his bed had even occurred to him. He saw now she was not demented, but out for an adventure; with that he could sympathize. "Would you like company?" He didn't really want to give her company; he wanted to go to bed.

"No, thank you," she replied pleasantly. "Good night."

Bette will kill me, he thought. He kissed Eliza's hand and left her to the storm.

Once in bed, Enzo found he couldn't go to sleep. A small, intense blonde with great, topaz eyes imperiously brushed away his need to sleep. Eliza Hilliard, you're a strange girl, he decided, and you're going to cause a damned lot of trouble.

The Arcadia: February 3, 1847

The weather cleared off Southampton, with bands of sunlight sifting through the gray to glitter the still steely sea. A week later, Bette, Enzo, and Eliza boarded the Arcadia for Albano, Italy. Spain, the African coast, and Gibraltar's lonely bulk had passed in a driving sweep of rain over snarling seas. Enzo still wondered that Eliza had habitually ranged the salt-crusted decks in the lightning's glare as if she were part of the storms that lashed the Mediterranean.

"Don't trouble to understand her, Enzo. She's not the sort of girl you're used to," coolly advised Bette as she strolled on his arm.

He laughed shortly. "At times I feel she might explode. A quiet, unpredictable bomb."

"Oh, she's predictable enough, darling. Just leave her to me."

He tilted his hat down, then glanced back at Eliza, who was ensconced in a stern deck chair with a book. "What about Miklos? She isn't his style at all. He's going to be furious. You may be able to handle her, but no one has ever been able to handle him."

Bette shrugged. "Miklos is a man like any other. He
has weaknesses, and for all her simplicity, Loise found
them all. To have used them would never have occurred to
her; it will occur to his new Princess Sztarai. She must
become deeply attached to him, through his own charms
. . . or yours." She eyed him through the veil wrapped
about her feathered toque. "Do you understand?"

He frowned. "Are you saying I'm to seduce the bride if
the groom doesn't appeal to her, or more likely"—he
shielded his eyes to peer at Eliza's serious face—"vice
versa?"

Bette wandered toward the bow. Determined to take
advantage of the sun, most of the passengers were topside
taking turns at the telescope to view the rugged Spanish
coast and play deck games. Doggedly, the crew worked
around them and dodged shrieking children gone wild after
weeks of confinement. Bette paused by the telescope. "I
don't want you to bed her, Enzo, except as a last resort.
Just show her how to attract him . . . and other men."

"I'm not a street pimp," he hissed angrily, "and that
tiny-titted girl couldn't make an Arab jealous."

"Scruples have no place in politics, boy," snapped
Bette, turning toward him. Then, watching Eliza's fair hair
whip in the sunny wind, she patted his arm. "Many will
pay with their lives to overturn our unsteady world. Eliza's
loss will be nothing to theirs."

"And Miklos?"

A stab of pain raked through her voice. "Either way it
goes, God help him."

Hadrian's Villa: February 28, 1847

Despite Enzo's assiduous attentiveness in Majorca and
Rome, Eliza didn't trust him. He said nothing untoward,
yet hung on her every, rare word; he complimented the
sunlight on her hair and lyonesse gold of her eyes. Never
had she received so much attention from a man, far less a
young, attractive one, and she found his behavior exceedingly strange. Her mind fidgeted as, unused to lazy picnics

with Italian pastry, she drowsed fitfully on a blanket amid the sun-soaked ruins of imperial Hadrian's country villa. Bees droned among the first crocus and dandelions patched among low, tumbled stone walls of the old villa. Across from her, Enzo was half-asleep in a canvas sling chair. He batted a fly from his cheek; it settled again. Bette slowly waved a lazy fan, her still beautiful profile and needle sharp mind tranquil under a shell pink umbrella.

They might look disarming, Eliza decided, but something was odd about this pair. Consider that they had avoided the shipboard passengers, even those of their own class. Their behavior at the Castiglione ball in Rome last night had also been peculiar, although they'd predictably guarded her from awkward questions about her marriage. Eliza knew not a word of Italian, but she did know Latin, and such questions as "How did Miss Hilliard and the prince meet?" "How long have they been married?" "Where is the prince these days?" were fairly recognizable. Eliza was amused to hear herself described as a New York socialite of distinguished family who had met the prince while touring the continent with her mother the previous year. She had extended her stay to become betrothed and wed quietly in London. Eliza lazily waved her fan under a bland, uncomprehending smile. Either the prince had spent the last few months in London or Enzo thought a wedding there more respectable than one, say, in Paris. I should like to see London, she thought wickedly. To think I passed my honeymoon without viewing the outside of my hotel.

What were they guarding against, besides gossip about a hurry-up marriage?

Also, Eliza noted that while Bette rarely spoke to anyone, she seemed much discussed, judging from the stares directed at her, muttered conversations, and discreetly turned shoulders. Bette seemed not to notice; indeed she appeared a trifle bored and more autocratic than usual, though several of her pert remarks about various guests made Eliza duck her head to hide a burst of laughter.

She had to fight that impulse to duck when she had been

announced as Princess Sztarai. While she was unprepared
for such public exposure in a role she had scant intention
of maintaining, she was dismayed by the shocked faces
throughout the crowd. Well, to the devil with them! She
might be an untitled, lame American, but she was not a
monster! Even as Enzo's hand reassuringly tightened on
her arm, she was more confounded to see the spectators'
gapes in the crowd fade to sympathy and naked pity. Lord
help her, was Miklos Sztarai the monster?!

After the ball, Eliza tried to thrust back her misgivings.
Rome and this lazy, bee-browsed meadow were pleasant;
New York and her mother were unpleasant. While unpleasant Miklos Sztarai might be, were he Prospero's
Caliban, several benefits were attached to him. She expected to pay a certain price for her freedom, but free she
would be. While Bette might believe parading her as
Princess Sztarai would sew her into this marriage, Eliza
had an idea or two that would rip the stitches.

Northern Italy: March 1, 1847

Eliza was less cavalier about encountering her groom as
she and Bette, leaving Enzo behind, rolled out of Rome
the next day and north through the flat, khaki vineyards
and olive groves of central Italy toward the mountainous
Piedmont. The roads were deep in spring mire, Eliza's
thoughts sunk deeper in trepidation. The marriage contract
subtly stated consummation would be completed upon mu-
tual agreement between its parties. She was not to be
leaped upon willy-nilly, and despite Enzo's attentiveness,
she doubted if his cousin would be moved to a grand,
Hungarian passion at the sight of her.

Then again . . . a contract might be a contract, but her
lawyer was in New York. She could squeal "nay, nay,
foul fiend" until kingdom come for all the dent it would
make in the princely prerogative.

Sztarai. What would he be like? Dark, probably. With
heavy jowls and endless eyebrows. Barrel-chested with the
beginning of a paunch. Rossi said he was a sportsman. A

jolly-fellow-well-met, then, with a taste for the bottle and unbound women. Then again, perhaps he was so toadlike no woman with a choice would have him. Her ruminations were covered with warts, resounded with oaths and belches. She closed her eyes. No doubt he was enjoying equally pleasant daydreams of her. No doubt he was doing it in tortuous Hungarian because he was unable to say *boo* in English.

Yet, from first mention of the marriage in New York, a nagging, contrary hope had threaded stealthily under all her misgivings: a hope so tiny, so terrible, she could hardly bear to admit it. What if Miklos Sztarai were a man she could love, but a man who wouldn't want a plain cripple for a wife?

No, she was in no hurry to reach Lake Como. She had hurried only twice since her accident. The first time, she tried to run when some cousins had come for Christmas three years after the accident. She was as well as she would ever be, the doctors said, and when a Christmas Day relay was declared for purses of sweets, she wanted to know how well that was. "Well" was a lurching, clumsy stumble that she had not repeated until four years later upon spotting Cory lying broken in the street. In the relay, she cared miserably about her body being seen in so unnatural a way. With Cory hurt, she had not cared. Somehow since, holding the idea of going to Cory, a creature who needed her, the only creature who needed her, made it easier to ignore how she looked getting where she had to go.

Lake Como: March 4, 1847

The carriage reached Como just after nightfall. A few stars haloed silver-rimmed clouds shadowing the lake. A witch's fingernail of a moon cast a dim, ghostly glow about the pines and rolling, irregular shoreline where scattered villa lights shone over flat, pewter water. The carriage turned off the lumpy main road into a smooth, graveled drive through a pine stand and halted at a high,

wrought iron gate tipped by flame-shaped spikes. Torches
blazing from its posts revealed the royal Piedmont-Sardinia
insignia. From a stone cottage emerged a dark-clad figure
who spoke briefly to the driver, then opened the gate.
Unexpectedly, the gatekeeper was armed with a crossbow.

By now, Eliza, with the black mitts on her hands soaked
with perspiration, was more concerned with the possible
need of a weapon of her own. Blessedly, the princess had
made no effort to soothe her with idle chatter; Eliza sensed
Bette was almost as tense as herself.

The carriage rolled along a drive winding through fanci-
fully shaped boxwoods and pines scattered among geomet-
ric flowerbeds. Then a fountain jetted a dim spray of
silver. Light gleamed from long windows beyond a sprawling terrace bounded by stone balustrades and huge urns
cascading rain-flattened, red cyclamen. After passing Ca-
nova statues of Diana, Apollo, and Hermes, which studded
the terrace, the carriage stopped. The driver jumped down
to drop the dismount step. Her hands knotted in her lap,
Eliza waited for Bette to descend, then, feeling clumsier
than usual, followed.

The royal villa was smaller than most Newport mansions, but even by marginal, rain-drizzled moonlight, lovely.
Finished in salmon stucco trimmed with floral garland re-
liefs, the villa had a tiled roof and feminine lines where
Eliza had expected Roman marble and masculinity.

With the driver bearing an umbrella over their heads,
the princess led the way up stone steps to the terrace, then
to double doors opened by a knee-breeched lackey. His
powdered periwig and pourpoint coat could have done
service during the American Revolution. Eliza had seen
servants in similar costume at American society balls, but
this man did not look costumed. She might have gone back
a hundred years since entering the steel-flamed front gate.

Inside the door, her eyes widened. Luxuriating beneath
a vast, Venetian chandelier, gray silk walls were covered
with very ungray, richly curved female nudes, several of
them pearl-skinned wonders by Titian and Rubens. Squares
of olive, Ferrara marble gleamed underfoot. The doors

lining the foyer were closed and the house seemed deserted. Then Eliza noticed a crack of light beneath one of the doors. Bette noticed it, too. "The prince is in the library, Your Highness," murmured the lackey.

"*Grazie*, Vincenzo. See that our rooms are ready."

After Vincenzo had gone, Bette turned to Eliza. "Well, my dear, just remember even Adam and Eve did not meet by choice. Whether or not that meeting was disastrous may be debatable, but the results were far from dull." She smiled mischievously. "Whatever other reactions you and Miklos may have, I very much doubt that you will bore one another." Her hand lifted. "Your husband awaits, my dear." She headed for a curving green marble stair.

Eliza stared after her in disbelief. "But . . . surely you intend to speak to your nephew, to introduce us . . . !"

"No, no." Bette replied lightly over her shoulder. "Trust me, it's better to dispense with formalities on this occasion."

Eliza glared at Bette's departing back. The damnable woman! After baiting me from my burrow, she coyly trots away when the fur is likely to fly! With mingled anger and fright, she fidgeted before the library door. There was no getting out of it. Short of being struck flat on the spot with plague, she couldn't duck the prince—warts, wizened, or witless. With a hard lump in her throat, she advanced to the door and opened it.

No one was in the mahogany-paneled library; an aging wolfhound snored before the low fire in the fireplace. A gold-shaded sinumbra light burning on the empire desk left the room nearly dark. Beyond open Venetian doors, rain was beginning to steadily fall again in the garden. Vastly relieved she could delay meeting Prince Sztarai until the next morning, Eliza had half turned to go to her rooms when, in a lightning flash beyond the windows, she briefly saw someone in the rain-sheeted garden. A man crouched on his knees among tall, wind-buffeted pines. Given the guarded villa gate, he was unlikely to be some prowling thief. Stealthily, she crept to the open door. Was he in prayer? Then his head reared back as if he were howling at the elements and she knew he was beyond

prayer. Sickened, she knew he was Sztarai. Mad? Dear
God, *was* he? Was this why they'd brought her here?

With mounting apprehension, she ventured across the
terrace, then down toward the pines on the rain-swept,
silver sweep of lawn. In fury and pleading, Sztarai was
shouting something against the wind. Hearing her nearing
footfalls at his back, he stiffened like a wolf with rising
hackles. She froze. Then, with a slight shiver, he unexpectedly relaxed. "Go to bed, Vincenzo," he murmured
lucidly in low, husky Italian. "I want nothing else tonight."

Eliza swallowed, then heard a tiny voice. "Would you
consider a wife, sir?"

Sztarai's Alexandrian, cropped, blond head shot up.
He whirled, poised. His gray eyes widened, then narrowed
under a pale-browed frown. If Eliza had looked for Roman masculinity, this was it. By the rain-silvered light,
Sztarai's lean, tanned face had the hard planes of a battle-
worn gladiator. His curved, predatory nose had been long
ago broken, shoved out of line over a wide, flat-lipped
mouth too precisely shaped to have the coarse brutality one
might have expected. His neat, flat-eared head was set
high, and went higher yet as he swiftly rose until his full
height was silhouetted against the night sky. Good God,
he's a giant! she thought in alarm. He was not, she realized an instant later, *quite* that tall, but he was well over
six feet. Even in a simple Austrian soldier's undress breeches
and tunic unbuttoned at the throat, which were revealed
beneath his cloak, he was magnificently impressive, though
not precisely regal at the moment; he was too startled.

Indeed, he'd whitened as if he had seen a ghost, but
whether the ghost was beloved or horrible, she could not
tell. For a long moment, he stared at her small, scared face
in the shadows and through his gray eyes stormed pain,
grief, yearning, as if he would reach out to her.

If Eliza knew little of men, she knew loneliness and
torment. As if it were the most natural thing in the world,
she put out her hand to him. Sztarai hesitantly touched her
fingers, slid his hand to her wrist. Then she was in his
arms and his mouth was moving over hers, whispering

words she couldn't understand, didn't need to understand when he kissed her. She became part of the rising wind, the rain-crushed flowers, the lightning playing across the sky, the sting of the pungent pines. Became part of him as if she had been fragmented, an unfinished riddle now at last complete.

The storm enveloped them both. Miklos Sztarai's mouth on hers grew fierce, his hand sweeping away her hood to tangle in her hair. His lips burned down the arch of her throat as her head fell back, her senses racing with fearful excitement and wondering anticipation. As he sought her mouth again, for a breathless moment his lips hovered over hers and he gazed down at her as if to reassure himself he had not indeed met some enticing wraith. The pine shadows wove their mauve and black tracery in a delicate Pierrette mask against the luminous pearl of her cheek and earlobe. With her tumbled hair shimmering like a live thing in the wind, she clung to him, harkening to this man who made her know her body's helplessness and strength.

He touched her face, then his expression altered from longing to uncertainty. His fingers beginning to tremble, his hands dropped away to hover in indecision at his sides, leaving her suddenly bereft and lost. She sensed he badly wanted to enfold her in his arms again. Oh, please, why didn't he?

Hoarsely, he blurted something in Hungarian, then, as if just realizing he'd ardently kissed a total stranger, asked breathlessly in unaccented English, "Who are you?"

Her heart seemed to stop. Feeling the stiff drag at her leg, she backed into a long block of light from a villa window. She halted hesitantly, then stated with all the firmness she could muster, "I am Elizabeth Hilliard."

A stunned look replaced the confusion in his eyes, then angry, flat disappointment. From the rusty flush in his cheeks, she knew he was more than angry, he was furious. Their passionate, ephemeral intimacy blew away like a dead leaf. Eliza could practically see his claws beginning to flex. Her worst expectations of his reception realized, her heart turned to stone. "You need not keep me, sir," she said expressionlessly. "My father's business policy affirms that a dissatisfied customer may return merchandise."

Embarrassment flicked through Sztarai's eyes, then was replaced by exasperation. "Please, come into the house."

Upon reaching the villa, he ducked through the study door. After brushing through his dripping hair, he threw off his military cloak. She took a hesitant step forward and the dog, coming dimly alert, let out a low growl. Sztarai silenced the dog with a glance. "Where is my aunt?"

"Fled."

"Ah." The gray eyes studied her with new appraisal in the gold-shaded light. "Yet you advance, Miss Hilliard."

She'd gathered her wits on the way back to the study. Her sharp sense of loss was receding, her alienation mounting. Her claws might be short, but she knew where to plant them. "I merely hold my ground, Your Highness. Still, I do not fight pointlessly." She lifted his quill from its inkwell. "You may free us both at the stroke of a pen."

Like her, Sztarai had quickly steadied and Eliza wondered if he'd endured as much practice. Watching him now, she could scarcely believe he was the same man who had railed in the wind's teeth, the same man who kissed her as if he'd found his soul. In the darkness, he must have mistaken her for someone else. Now, like her, he was trying to forget anything had happened. Although a faint odor of brandy lingered about him, he was almost unnervingly lucid. Seemingly lazy now, the lion was mentally prowling about his threadbare mate. "I also have certain habits, Miss Hilliard, which I hope you will indulge" —while Sztarai's tone was smooth, it suggested his being indulged was mandatory—"and the hour is fairly late." He retrieved his quill from her fingers and returned it to the inkwell. "I presume you have dined?"

"In the town of Cantù," she replied evenly. My nappies have been changed, my ears washed, and I can trot up to bed without being told.

The wolfhound rose to warily sniff her as his master grimly studied her shedding rabbit neck scarf and limp

mustard traveling outfit that smelled of mildew. "Back to
the fire, Max," ordered Sztarai. "Lie down." After the
dog resettled, he said absently, "You must be weary, Miss
Hilliard. Would you care for brandy?"

She was surprised. "Yes, of course." She didn't want a
drink; she wanted to inspect him. He poured brandy only
for her. His movements were precise and military now.
She suspected he was no quibbler; more likely he laid out
decisions in planned attacks. She wondered what it would
be like to have his teeth buried in her neck.

Sztarai indicated a medallion chair. "Please sit down."
Another tacit order. When she was settled, he handed her
the brandy balloon. His long-fingered hands about its fragile globe were strong enough to crush a human skull; Bette
had been wise to keep hers out of reach. He sat on the
edge of his desk, but instead of grilling her as she
expected, stared thoughtfully into the guttering fire in the
black marble fireplace. She could not read his face, but
undoubtedly he was debating how to be most easily rid of
her. No questions meant he knew about her all he wished
to know. Suddenly wanting to be done with the whole,
pointless ordeal, she drank the fiery brandy too fast and
choked.

He glanced at her. "Perhaps you would prefer sherry?"

"Thank you, no. I much prefer the brandy. It's . . .
vivid."

Seeing a hint of amusement curve his lips, she defiantly
tossed down a gulp. With watering eyes and seared gullet,
she sat stiffly, daring him to be patronizing.

"Princess von Schmerling's letters gave the impression
you were about eighteen years of age, Miss Hilliard,"
Sztarai said dryly. "Are you eighteen?"

"Closer to seventeen." She flipped the sagging rabbit
scarf over her shoulder.

"In six months?" he suggested wearily.

"Eight."

He leaned across the breadth of her crinolines and firmly
took the brandy away. "Good night, Miss Hilliard. Vincenzo
will see you to your rooms."

She wanted to slap him. Who did he think he was? Prince Charming! He was the beast! "I am not ready to retire, sir."

"Yes, you are. You're completely worn out," he corrected flatly. He rose, rang the service bell, then went to a shelf and idly selected a book. "Try this." A fat volume of Gibbon's *Decline and Fall of the Roman Empire* dropped heavily into her lap. "You should be asleep in ten minutes."

Gibbon was propelled back at his midriff. "I've read it, also its precedents and antecedents."

A blond brow lifted slightly. After letting her support the volume until she thought her wrist would crack before he relieved her of it, Sztarai gestured toward his collection of books. "Then choose."

Why were the choices he offered never choices? Eliza wondered irritably, yet went to scan the shelves. Petty arguments at this point would avail nothing. Thanks to Bette's lack of formality, she and Sztarai had been in each other's arms, and in a moment at each other's throats. She felt his attention follow her uneven stride. Be civil, sign the annulment, collect the money. Then the prince could order a princess stitched to order for all she cared.

Taking her time, she looked over the shelves. The morocco-bound book collection, full of rarities and classics, was priceless, though rarely in English. Should she chose something for pleasure or to impress? Pleasure; he would see through the latter. Voltaire's *Candide* came down.

"Ça va, lisez vous en français?" His French had a strange, attractive accent; not quite French, but perhaps the Hungarian that didn't echo in his English.

"Enough."

"Et bien parlez-le?"

"Badly." She slapped on a Vermont twang.

"So you do not try. What other things do you do badly?"

She flushed, assuming he obliquely referred to her lameness. "Is there nothing you do badly?"

He seemed to gauge her mute pain and anger. "Yes.

Occasionally, I am too direct. It's a soldier's fault." His half-apology lacked apology and she was not altogether sure whether he referred to kissing or insulting her. He escorted her to the door. "Good night, Miss Hilliard."

"Good night," she answered coldly. Let him think as an American, she refused to use his title. He had not once addressed her by her married name and title, doubtless because he had no intention of letting her use them.

Feeling damp and cold and shriveled, she left him to find Vincenzo patiently waiting outside the library door.

"This way, *Signorina.*"

Naturally, the servants would follow their master's lead.

Miklos Sztarai glared into the dying fire. A flush still scorched his face when he remembered kissing Eliza Hilliard. Before his lips ever touched hers, he realized she was a stranger. A devil, an angel, she seemed in the shadows . . . until humiliating sanity overtook him. One minute, he had been yelling like a maniac, then making love to her. He had *known* she was not Loise, but he'd been wild with hopeless frustration that had been mounting for months. Discipline, exercise, women, liquor: nothing eased his desperation. Tonight the villa walls pressed in like a vise. He had flung himself out into the rain, fallen to his knees, and screamed.

How long before he *did* go mad? Before he wanted a bullet instead of the brandy he downed tonight? He may have been somewhat drunk and demented when he kissed Eliza Hilliard; it wasn't the first time he had made love to a woman he scarcely knew, but he'd never thrust himself on one out of hand. Besides, she was no woman; he first dimly realized her youth when she was in his arms. She was small and fragile, the naive witchery of her kiss never meant for a hard-bitten reprobate like him. He'd felt such a clear spring of peace that he could have gone on kissing her forever. Then that spring had been stirred by desire, so deep and turbulent it unsettled him. Now, like him, she was probably regretting their rash embrace with a passion!

He had covered well enough with her, considering the shock, but now . . . she was his wife! Wife?! Was Bette

demented! God knows what tortuous connivance between
her and Enzo produced this pathetic farce! No wonder
Bette hadn't written since New York. Why waste more
lies? No; evasions, omissions. She and her damned Enzo
had matched him to a crippled child! And believing he
could trust no one else, he had been fool enough to trust
them.

Bette had declared Eliza Hilliard was a tolerable-looking,
bright, respectable girl with a sense of humor. Tolerable to
him? The chit ought to be; she looked enough like Loise.
Bright? Like a hard diamond. And respectable? God, if he
hadn't kissed her, he would think her starched in the crib;
scarcely out of it, to boot.

Miklos didn't know whether to feel sorrier for himself
or her, with her look of a drowned sparrow with those
great, golden, ancient eyes that for all their careful wari-
ness could not hide when she hurt. Dumped out of her safe
nest by that sly buzzard, Bette, and into a disastrous
marriage! What was he to do now? Send her home, pay
her off? If Bette thought he was going to dutifully bounce
into his new bride's bed tonight, she was in for a start.
Hell, he'd give her one!

Eliza, half asleep in her bedroom, heard yelling. Roaring was more like it. Sztarai's furious baritone drowned
his aunt's placating, higher pitch in her rooms across the
hall. Gradually, Bette's note altered from placating to
penetrating. An ironic half-smile curved Eliza's lips. The
royal lawyer would likely be fetched by cockcrow.

Chapter 3

Burning Roses

Lake Como: March 5, 1847

Eliza slept long past cockcrow. Lingering abed was not her habit in America, as Dorothy Hilliard did not permit such self-indulgence, but she was more fatigued from the journey and tension than she had realized. Besides, in Italy, laziness did not matter and she no longer had anyone to please but herself. Better to displease everybody and be sent on her way the sooner.

Drowsily, she slithered over on the satin sheets in the canopied bed to feel the sun warm on her back. The yellow Empire suite with its frieze of capering, diaphanously clad nymphs was never designed for a virgin. What would it be like to awaken some morning with a man? A great, golden wolf of a man like Miklos Sztarai? Her eyes slitted open. She wasn't sure why she thought of him, but that moment when he had looked so desperate and alone, the memory of his kiss, still troubled her.

She tried to forget Sztarai. He had proven he was hard and autocratic and didn't want her. She mustn't be foolish and weak. After all, why shouldn't he linger in her mind? He was extraordinarily attractive, broken nose and all. Discounting a few stevedores as broad as they were tall, he was the most man she'd ever seen in one piece. She recalled his lean hips, the unprudish fit of his breeches. Her eyes closed, then abruptly opened again. From their sylvan glade, the nymphs seemed to smile mischievously. What if Sztarai thought this dallying in bed was an invitation?

She flung out of bed, into her ugliest black dress, and down the stairs. Miklos Sztarai was nowhere in sight. Only a few studiously incurious servants were cleaning the splendid rooms. Vincenzo, the manservant of the previous night, found her wandering uncertainly about the cream silks and ivory Florentine marble of the drawing room. "May I be of service, *Signorina?*"

Beneath the vast unicorn tapestry, she turned quickly as if she were the maiden startled while secretly baiting that puissant beast. "I . . . was looking for *Principessa* von Schmerling."

"The *principessa* breakfasts in her rooms, *Signorina.*" Flavored with the harsh, local dialect, Vincenzo's English was labored, and he looked as if he devoutly wished she would strain it no further.

"I should also like breakfast, Vincenzo."

"Then, if you will follow, *Signorina.*" He led her to the dining room. At a lace-clothed table capable of seating sixty guests, she was served her solitary breakfast. She was not altogether uncomfortable. The room's size was made more intimate by terra-cotta walls with gleaming gilt moldings. Lemon trees were placed between long windows that faced the palm-clustered terrace and morning sun of glittering Lake Como. Beyond the forested far shore with its pastel villas, soared the snow-capped Alps. The natural magnificence of the view was counterpointed by the room's Della Robbia medallions and a Medici-commissioned battle scene by Uccello that hung along the western wall. As she was looking over the minor paintings and having a final cup of *cappuccino*, the dining room's double doors opened.

Miklos, in white uhlan uniform, squinted through the sun-streaked gloom. "Ah. There you are," he muttered. The door closed.

A few minutes later, Bette, with an air of agitation,

opened the door. "You're wanted, dear. Gird up your loins."

Recalling her waking thoughts that morning, Eliza stiffened in startled alarm. Gird up her loins?! If Miklos Sztarai had any silly, forceful notions, she'd armor plate them!

As Eliza and Bette entered the study, three men stood: Miklos, in uniform; an impeccably suited, courtly Italian; and a small, paunchy Italian in a straining frock coat. The lawyers, Eliza supposed. Sztarai must have had them brought in by racehorse.

"Aunt, Miss Herriott," Miklos said blandly, "may I present *il Duce* di Bellaria, Emperor Ferdinand's representative, and *Signor* Antonini, the family barrister."

Why not just order up artillery? thought Eliza. I really don't have to be blown out of here astride a cannonball.

Sztarai, with a glance of sardonic amusement, met her eyes as the duke bowed over her hand. *"Principessa,"* murmured Bellaria, "my best wishes for great happiness in your marriage. I cannot express the emperor's delight that Prince Miklos has chosen a bride." His felicitations had the smoothness of a machine, and as much warmth. Especially as she looked more like a widow than a bride in her black silk clanking with teardrop jets.

The lawyer was oilier, more hurried in his address. "So good to meet you. I am particularly fond of Americans."

"Grazie, gentlemen." Briefly, Eliza considered a curtsy, then remembered that if only for the moment, she outranked both men. "How considerate of you to have come so far to congratulate us."

"And so promptly," dryly added Sztarai, studying his seemingly oblivious aunt.

"Oh, no difficulty," hurriedly muttered Antonini, his clothes rumpled as if he'd spent half the night in a coach. "I happened to be in Cantù when I heard the news."

The duke's expression tightened a fraction; apparently, he expected a dowdy, American nobody to be more impressed with him. "Fortunately, my villa here at Como is even more convenient than Cantù.'' His glance flicked to the prince. "But indeed, all Rome rejoices. I fear your honeymoon may be interrupted by many well-wishers.''

For a split second, the eyes of "bride and groom" met over Bellaria's trap. If they weren't careful, they could find the way out of their unwanted arrangement cut off by public assumption of its finality. Flatly, they said as one, "There's been a mistake . . .''

"The honeymoon was in London, my dear *Duce*,'' Bette smoothly interrupted. "I presumed everyone knew Miklos was there at Christmas.''

"Everyone doesn't share your interest in my quiet life, Aunt,'' Miklos said briefly, his eyes expressionless as a pale sheet of slate.

Eliza had the impression he could have cheerfully tied her and Bette's necks together in a knot. He wanted this marriage no more than she.

"Ah, but everyone does share that interest, Your Highness,'' offered the duke. "Your uncle, Emperor Ferdinand, has already sent felicitations to His Majesty, Charles Albert. What news have you from his imperial majesty?''

"That his hay fever is worse.''

The duke of Bellaria was clearly not here to annul the marriage. Who was he? wondered Eliza. Cowed by Bellaria's assurance and prestige, Antonini was visibly squirming, as if he had been beaten to the quarry. Antonini was tongue-tied, but in Bellaria's every third sentence lay a snare. Bellaria seemed bent on confirming the marriage, and if so, he was Bette's man. That was it! No wonder Prince Miklos looked grim. With Bellaria's backing and the imperial relative's approval, Bette meant to seal the marriage before Miklos could end it.

Eliza could not allow that seal to set. She'd not yet had time to reach an annulment agreement with Prince Miklos. She might gain the upper hand in bargaining for a generous settlement if she relieved Bellaria's pressure; she could increase it any time she liked. For the moment, she and Miklos were reluctant allies.

Eliza took a deep breath. "My dear gentlemen, won't

you please join us for luncheon? You've been so kind"—
she timidly laid her hand on Bellaria's sleeve—"I trust
I may ask you a small favor."

As her eyes widened pleadingly up at the duke, both
Bette's and Miklos's eyes narrowed.

"If it lies in my power," guardedly replied the duke.

"Oh, you may be sure it does." Eliza's small arm
appropriated his. "Miklos, would you ask Vincenzo to
serve on the veranda? It's more friendly than the dining
room." Bette's and Miklos's expressions grew a trifle
owlish as she drew Bellaria toward the veranda doors.

Bellaria neatly swallowed his lemoned perch. "Excel-
lent. Absolutely fresh." So, too, was the scent of the
garden that surrounded the balustraded terrace, making
Eliza glad of her decision to move the gathering out of
doors. The garden, much larger than she had anticipated,
spread with a swirling calligraphy of boxwoods and ciner-
aria flowerbeds to the lake and for some two acres on
either side of the villa. Beyond tapered pines spaced along
balustrades garlanded with climbing roses, cypresses winged
over six fountains that jetted high into the sunlight to spill
rainbows in their spray. The clouds were puffed, the lake
blue, the day perfect. Bellaria sipped a bit of wine. "And
now *Principessa*, what is this small favor?"

Eliza lowered her head as if to hide a blush. "I . . .
well, you see, it's a delicate matter."

"Perhaps it should wait, child," put in Bette warningly.

"Oh . . . no, I'm certain the duke is well aware of the
weakness of women." Fingering her jet lozenges, Eliza
gazed at him innocently. "You have a wife, sir?"

"Ah . . . yes. Yes, I do."

She nodded as if greatly relieved and took up her wine.
"Your honeymoon . . . it was pleasant?"

"Eliza!" Bette admonished as Miklos sat back in his
chair, his face quizzical, edgy, fascinated.

"Um, yes," answered the duke warily. "Pleasant."

Eliza took a long draught of wine to bolster her nerve
and gazed sadly at him. "Mine was not."

Miklos let out his breath with a choked sound.

Her empty glass made a slight wag at Vincenzo and hastily he refilled it. "You see, sir, for the whole time, *every* time I looked at Miklos, I was perfectly nauseated."

As Eliza peacefully ignored the stony, stupefied stares of her newly acquired relatives, the duke carefully put down his fork. "Madame, are you sure . . ."

"Oh, quite." Her pitch descended as had the level of her wine. "Quite, *quite* green." She smiled at Miklos's grim face. "It isn't Miki's fault, of course. He's been so sweet, so patient, but I've had such a delicate upbringing. Of course, I shall get over it"—her smile shifted again to the duke—"if Miklos and I are permitted to extend our honeymoon without a great deal of distraction. Perhaps if you were to suggest to well-wishers that they postpone their visits for a time?" She cut an impish, sidelong look at Miklos. "With such a considerate husband, I'm sure I shall not remain a bride forever."

For a moment, she thought Sztarai might burst out laughing, then he grinned at his irritated aunt. "You must admit, Aunt, my . . . beloved may have a point." He lay a finger against his lips. "Quiet. So much better."

"Yes," agreed the duke bemusedly.

"Oh, yes," eagerly put in Antonini.

"So you will keep our little secret, gentlemen, and play our cupids?" entreated Eliza prettily.

The duke seemed to wake up. "Oh, you may rely on it."

"Of course."

Peacefully, Eliza returned to her scarcely touched fish. Though her stomach was still full from breakfast, she had a surge of appetite. Gossip of Sztarai's marriage might have spread like wildfire, but that it had yet to be consummated? The chatter would have the crackle of a cannon!

"I suppose I ought to thank you." Sztarai had followed Eliza to a carved stone bench in the garden after Bellaria and Antonini had retired to play cards with Bette in the solarium. "Still, you've placed me in an embarrassing position."

"I confess I had no thought of anyone's position, sir," Eliza said bluntly, "except my own. You signed to me a legal choice of either marriage or settlement in the event of your dissatisfaction with this arrangement. I believe I am not wrong in judging you dissatisfied." She rose from the bench. "So, shall we conclude matters as quickly as possible?"

He ran his thumb over the bark of the overhead cypress. "It seems I'm to be offered nothing but cold fish this morning. What makes you so certain I mean to send you packing?"

"I'm too young for you."

He quizzically regarded her cool, astute little face and bulky, rattling dress. "I'm beginning to doubt that." He gestured carelessly to the bench. "Please, sit down."

Feeling half his size standing up, Eliza didn't want to sit down. "I would rather walk, if you don't mind." She waited for the involuntary drop of his eyes to her feet. She wanted that moment, to have that barrier, their final separation, established.

"I don't mind." His eyes held hers. "Do you like amaryllis?"

"I've never seen one."

"This way, then."

Hup, right. Yes, sir, General. Eliza stretched to match his long, unhurried stride along the palmetto-fringed walkway.

Sztarai's hands folded martially behind his back. "How old do you think I am?"

Her eyes cut to his irregular, granite profile. He might have been an Alexander who had unwillingly outlived the zenith of his victories to find his winning dross, his allies treacherous. "Forty." He was nothing like that age, of course, but she wasn't in a conciliating mood.

He laughed shortly. "Twenty-eight."

She was startled. He didn't look *that* young. Aside from sun creases at the corners of his eyes, his face was stretched smooth over its strong bones where endurance of many changes, climatic and otherwise, had pared its planes to spare, unyielding essentials. Pain and pride and hate had scraped and howled across that face; she knew it, just as she knew the forces that had shaped her own, beyond nature. "So, twenty-eight and barring precocity, I concede you are not quite old enough to be my father. And"—she stopped abruptly by a chestnut hanging over a still, hedge-framed pool—"you are not old enough to be unduly concerned about finding a wife. Why then does everyone seem to be waiting with bated breath for you to marry?"

He plucked down a chestnut leaf and pleated it, his fingers slow as if he were debating his answer. "The day I wailed into the world, everyone, as you put it, was waiting for me to marry. Commoners have certain advantages in obscurity."

"Still, those advantages don't explain why you would pick an obscure commoner as a wife."

"My aunt chose you," he replied with a tinge of self-mockery, the leaves arrowing shadows about his face. "I had little to do with it."

Eliza's chin advanced. "You must want little to do with a wife if you cannot be bothered with which one you get."

He flipped a scrap of bark from his fingers into the ivy dark pond. "Were you so forthright with my aunt when you agreed to her proposal?"

She flushed. "My consultation was the last thing anyone thought necessary . . ."

"Yet you presume I dictated my matrimonial requirements to my aunt and sent her off like a terrier to fetch . . . you?"

"Hardly me. I think you might have been happier with a long-buried bone. Your patting her on the head was audible all over the house last night."

His lips curved wryly. "Quite right; you're not what I expected, but then, am I what you hoped?"

The pale luster of his hair made the gilt braid of his uniform seem tawdry. *He* made everything around him seem less. "I don't hope for anything," she said quickly.

His eyes narrowed. "Nothing?" The mockery returned

to his mouth. "No title, no fortune, no children . . . no man?"

Her flush burning brighter, she turned away. "Nothing. If I don't suit, let me go."

He shrugged and looped his arm about a branch. "I have an investment in you, and you have traveled a long distance. A few days of consideration won't matter much one way or the other, particularly as our comical boudoir frustration will soon be public." His easy drawl made her feel as if she were a mouse squirming between his adroit paws. "Unless you've an immediate appointment elsewhere."

Careful, Eliza, her instinct warned. If he finds you're just after a settlement, you're in trouble. She faced him. "I've no plans."

"Good." He gestured in the general direction of the central garden. "The amaryllis circle the Dial. If you need anything, Vincenzo will see to it." He bowed slightly. "Good afternoon, Miss Hilliard." With that, he strolled off toward a towering grove of California sequoias south of the villa. Eliza heard him whistle at the garden's edge. The wolfhound's tail flashed, then man and dog disappeared into the wood.

Miklos was less complacent than he looked as he strode through the wood to the stable. He didn't know what to make of Eliza Hilliard. She was wily as a ferret and as skittish. Her eyes had been level as she lied in her teeth about her aspirations, her back stiff in her staunch effort to keep up with him. She was so young to be so old. He had a premonition that if Eliza ever enraged him, that if he reached out to quell her impertinence, he might find his hand turning, turning . . . to caress her cheek so she might never be afraid, never have to lie again. Only gentleness and patience had been a total waste with Loise, and after his coldness last night, Eliza would shy away. Also, if he showed any softness now, she would use it against him. She was up to something, although she certainly didn't seem to be playing Bette's game.

He hadn't foreseen Bette's gambit, but he at least had

taken the precaution of having the easily manageable Antonini stay in the neighborhood in case he needed to be immediately and quietly divested of his new bride. If Antonini's coach hadn't broken an axle, the absurd match would have been annulled by breakfast. Instead, Antonini's coach limped into the villa gates after Bellaria's *barca* docked at the boathouse.

The marriage contract involved a settlement, but Miklos wasn't about to pay it without knowing Eliza's motives in making the agreement in the first place. Why be gulled just to fatten her purse, then left with a shoddy scandal? He'd had a gutful of women who tried to use him, and waiflike Eliza had shown herself as wily as any of them. When the fat landed in the fire this morning, Eliza neatly cooled its sizzle; indeed, thanks to her, his amatory reputation would shortly be as cold as frozen cod.

But Eliza, clever as she might be, had outsmarted herself. For one thing, she'd shown she was too clever to be let go without his finding out what she was after. Calculating women could cause vastly more trouble than men, he'd discovered; certainly, Miklos found them more intriguing, and if nothing else, Eliza was intriguing. Just now, though, he wanted a companion deft at thawing cod.

Miklos didn't return until the following morning, after Antonini and Bellaria had left. Eliza heard him whistle to his dog outside her bedroom window. Scarcely had he entered his bedroom when Bette pursued him. Giving the princess a few minutes, Eliza drifted after her to linger outside his bedroom door. Eavesdropping might be a bad habit, but one developed over years of being discussed in whispers. Snatches of the princess's flaring anger drifted into the hall. "Miki, you're mad to offend the *duce!* Don't you want to go home?"

"Vienna? Paris? Capri?" drawled Sztarai's voice.

"Don't play games with me. I know what goes on in your mind, what you want . . ."

"Do you, Aunt?" Sheets rustled as Miklos turned over.

"Is my cold-eyed waif of a bride representative of your perspicacity?"

"Don't judge her too soon, Miklos," the princess snapped. "There's more to her than you think."

"But I'm not being hasty, Aunt. Surely you've noticed she's not perched atop her luggage on her way back to Rome. Yet. And what more there is to her is not something I'm sure I want to find out. It promises to be unpleasant."

Not unpleasant, just expensive, Eliza thought ironically. With a quick glance down the hall to make sure she wouldn't be seen by a servant, she pressed closer to the door.

"Don't forget Eliza can make a great many things possible for you, Miklos." Bette paused. "Unless you're afraid you can't deal with her any better than Loise . . ."

There was a silence, then Miklos Sztarai's reply came low and wolfish, "You're treading on thin ice."

"And so are you. You've spent last night trying to freeze your brain and your . . ."

He laughed sardonically. "I was hardly cold."

"Weren't you? When will you realize that trollop can only fire your lust?" Eliza hurriedly backed, hearing Bette step toward the door. As she hastened down the hall, she missed another muffled remark, then, safely inside her room, heard Miklos's door slam.

With an unexpected jab of jealousy, Eliza sat on her bed. So Miklos Sztarai had a mistress. Of course. Then she held her breath. Bette was knocking on her door. Eliza waited. Another impatient rap came, then silence.

That afternoon Eliza had lunch brought to her easel in a shady, out-of-the-way part of the garden where she hoped she would not be bothered. She was not bothered. She had a feeling no one even thought of bothering her.

At dinner, Miklos and his aunt were preoccupied. Silence like a soiled table cloth depressed the dining room. Just as well, Eliza considered resignedly; the less said the better. With relish, she applied herself to the chicken pepperoni, only to notice Miklos watching her. Specifi-

cally, he was watching her eat as if her appetite under the
awkward circumstances interested him. Ah, she was too
blithe, too cheerful. He was suspicious. She began to pick
at her food, refused the entrancing, cream-dolloped des-
sert. His mood changed to amusement. Sensitive to ridi-
cule, she was annoyed. With rare revulsion, she wished she
weren't wearing a gown the sickly off-white of pigeon
dropping. "You seem to be in fine spirits, sir," she
observed with wicked innocence. "I trust last night af-
forded you some relaxation."

Bette's head shot up and Sztarai looked startled, then his
lips twitched. "Quite the opposite, I assure you. No less
than full attention was demanded; however, in your company, I find myself completely at ease."

Bette choked. Eliza, divining she was the butt of some
double entendre, but unsure of its nature, prickled. "May
I ask, sir, whether in your easeful state, you have decided
what to do with me?"

Bette seized a rose crystal water goblet as Miklos's
regard turned sleepy. "Why nothing. You may please
yourself."

"You mean . . . I may go?"

"Do you wish to go?"

"I do not wish to stay where I am unwelcome," Eliza
countered carefully, mistrusting his apparent indifference.
In black formal clothes and eggshell silk cravat, he merely
seemed sheathed. Attilan cheekbones didn't mesh with
English tailoring.

"Do you feel unwelcome?"

She hesitated. "No, but . . ."

"Well, then?"

"Why," she parried, "do you wish me to linger, for
'inspection,' as it were, if you are elsewhere?"

"Would you like us to spend more time together?" His
attention deliberately shifted to her slim shoulders, her
throat modestly guarded by a battalion of ruffles.

Involuntarily, her fingers fanned across the ruffles. "Not
. . . necessarily, but don't you think it would be best to
get everything . . . over with?"

"Everything?" he asked mischievously. "You mean as in bed you or boot you out?"

"Miklos!" rasped Bette, slapping down her goblet with a spatter. "Don't be crude!"

"Miss Hilliard has a proclivity for plain speech, Aunt. Don't you, Miss Hilliard?"

Eliza had gone scarlet. "Naturally," she ground out with an effort, "I want to know what you plan for me."

"Then you've no need for concern. You may be sure whatever I plan will happen . . . naturally." The tinge of Eliza's complexion deepened to vermilion.

"Miklos, stop tormenting the girl!" admonished Bette. "She's kept her part of the agreement."

Sztarai's strong fingers wound casually about his glass stem. "Why?"

"Why?" echoed his puzzled aunt. "What do you mean?"

"I mean . . . what does Miss Hilliard want? She says nothing." His eyes lingered dreamily on the gold candelabra ranked down the table, the radiant silver and crystal, the Della Robbias, the priceless Uccello. "One does not travel thousands of miles for nothing." His attention flicked again to Eliza. "Shall I send you away with nothing, Miss Hilliard?"

Unable to evade a confrontation now, Eliza stoically braced herself. "You will send me away with a substantial income, sir. Paragraph 4, clause *b* of our marriage contract. Unless you want me on your hands until Kingdom Come."

His eyes turned eerily cold. "Given my reputation, that is a singularly reckless ultimatum." He rose abruptly. "So it's money. Why didn't you say so? Five minutes after you got here you could have been on your way."

"With nothing."

"Exactly."

She rose. "Oh, no, sir. I am fully prepared to meet my obligations." Her hands clasped behind her back to stiffen the bluff. "Yours is the forfeiture. And if you cheat on the bargain, I shall contact my lawyers."

His chest and shoulders blocking her view of everything

else in the world, he towered over her. "May I point out you are a long way from a telegraph."

She reared to her tiptoes. "May I point out that, despite the remonstrances of the duke of Bellaria, you may shortly expect visitors. Won't all Rome, the emperor and pope in particular, be delighted to learn our marriage has been *consummated?*"

"So you'd sing one tune as quickly as another." His jaw neared hers. "Suppose I let you warble it in some solitary nest out of universal earshot."

Eliza's hands clenched tighter. "Don't you think my disappearance would be awkward under the circumstances?"

Again came that strange, wintry glow in his eyes that chilled her marrow. "Disappear," he whispered. "Now. To your rooms. The less I see of you the better."

Only a fool would have ignored that warning. She disappeared.

"You have done brilliantly, Aunt," gritted Sztarai. "A scorpion for a mate could suit no better."

Miklos went to the study, jotted a quick note to Antonini, made a copy, then forced his anger aside and had an espresso before he summoned Vincenzo. If, in a temper, he sent the note to Antonini tonight, Eliza, with an un-avoidable but probably short storm of gossip, would fol-low. Given his family connections and well-placed bribes among the cardinals, he could disavow consummation, citing Eliza's own remarks on her virginal state. He would win an annulment if he packed her out of the villa *now*.

If he waited, he was risking all hell. While a quiet, private separation was vastly preferable to a public cat-fight, its negotiation would take more than a few days. Eliza had enough nerve to stand up to him even when she was shaking in her shoes.

Still, while he didn't want to turn rough, a week or so could give him a chance to prove premeditated extortion. More leniently, he might make friends with Eliza, appeal to her better nature, although he wasn't altogether sure she had one under her iron shell . . . unless, perhaps he might crack that shell. He could scarcely blame her for resenting his virtually rejecting her on sight. She had once kissed him, whether in pretended passion or compassion for his miserable distraction, he didn't know. She might now as easily poke him in the teeth, but he was tempted to chance a bit of investigative poking of his own.

Eliza must have been desperate to marry a total stranger. If she hadn't married for position, had she been pushed by her gargoyle mother into fattening the family coffers? Thoughtfully, Miklos slid his espresso cup across its saucer; instantly, it balked at the curve's subtle rise. No, Eliza didn't push. This marriage gambit was probably her idea, possibly because she wanted to be rid of tyrants like him and her mother in her life. If so, she was pursuing a future that left her real needs unanswered.

How was he to handle a gold digger if she wanted not gold, but freedom? As he poured a second espresso, he considered Eliza's vulnerable points. She felt unlovable; he sensed that from the first. She wasn't unlovable, just intolerable anytime she could contrive it. Also, despite her sturdy efforts to be boring, she wasn't. Her mutinous, fiery independence under its thin camouflage challenged him more than beauty could have done. Sometimes the calculating little witch was even charming in a peculiar way. And just now, she depended on him in a way she didn't want, he didn't want.

So, audacious Eliza, I must have a pry at your shell . . . though you may well end as turtle soup. He tossed the note to Antonini into his desk drawer.

Uncertain of Miklos's mood, Eliza spent the next morning in her room. When no one summoned her, she decided to make an appearance lest he think her cowed. She made a great show of setting up her easel in the most frequented part of the garden. And for the rest of the afternoon, saw not a soul.

Sztarai was not at dinner; his aunt was. "My dear, you make a grave error in defying Miki openly. Not only is he royal, but he was a colonel in the Austrian army. He's

used to giving orders and having them obeyed. If you wish
to bring him around to your way of thinking, a little charm
may ease the matter. He has a good deal of it himself
when he cares to use it.''

"I've never learned charm," stated Eliza, glancing at
Sztarai's empty chair. "However, I have learned to ignore
being ignored.''

"Yes, I've noticed your lack of curiosity," Bette retorted. "You set up that easel daily in the garden. The
same places, every day. You see the same things and paint
them minutely. How narrow you are! Don't you ever
wonder what might be beyond your tiny imagination?''

"Nothing is lacking in my imagination. How do you
think I lived as I did for so many years?''

"You're afraid to live." Her diamonds flashing, Bette
thrust impatiently to her feet. "If Miki pays you, you'll
make another narrow prison and paint it minutely, repeat-
edly. You won't be free and you won't be alive.'' She
gripped her chair back. "Miki's a wonderful man, a remarkable man. If he liked, he could move mountains,
nations. He can bring you alive! He's the key to the future,
if you're not too stupid to seize it!'' She jerked the chair
out of the way. "I'm beginning to think you are!''

For a long time after Bette left and Vincenzo had taken
away the untouched courses, Eliza sat watching the candles flicker. Singly, they burned much the same, dripping
sooty puddles on the lace cloth; when she grouped all the
candelabra, their flames played and writhed together, unpredictable in proximity, with the air they burned creating
strange, beautiful effects. A haloed ecstasy of light in the
darkness. The lace began to char; before her eyes blazed a
tracery of roses and lilies in an intricate, scarlet web.

This web is the bright, dangerous, beautiful world far
beyond the narrow limits I have known, Eliza thought.
This is the world I want: wonderful, terrible, so filled with
life it brushes the edge of death. And Bette thinks Miklos
Sztarai, a mere mortal man, can give this to me.

The cloth hissed as a tear struck it.

Outside, she heard gravel scrape as Miklos rode away

from the house. She poured the contents of the water pitcher on the lace.

The next day, Eliza explored the park beyond the garden. Great sequoias reared from tumbled, ivy-draped rocks, which were shadowed by twisted pines and Japanese cryptomeria. Among alpine plants thrived cactus, aloe, and mimosa. Elephant ear, banana, and Spanish bayonet clustered around the mossy stone boathouse with its roof garden and slippery steps to the lake. Nothing was normal here: not the plants, not the mild weather within sight of snow caps. Not her situation.

And Miklos was not at all what she'd expected, only exploring him was not so easy. He seemed remote as an ice-clad tundra. Determined to know her enemy, she began to mark his habits, but after a few days soon realized if she were to know them all, she must rise at a much earlier hour and stay up later than she liked of late. Around luncheon, he usually took his wolfhound, Max, and went fishing. During the afternoons, he either rode or sailed. In the evenings, if he did not visit his mistress, he stayed in the study with the door closed. Although he seemed on fair terms with his aunt, he appeared to have forgotten Eliza existed.

She debated how to bring matters to a head. She would have to corner him privately; that would be tricky. She was afraid of Max, who snarled if she got within five feet of Miklos, and in the middle of a lake Miklos was difficult to reach.

That night, Eliza left her door slightly ajar so she might hear him get up. All the same, the next morning she almost missed his silent stride past her door. From her window as she hurriedly dressed, she saw Miklos, wrapped in a cape, head with the wolfhound toward the lake. The pale moon was still visible through the pines on the horizon across the water.

Quickly, she descended the stair and followed his footprints across the dewy grass into the damp, spongy turf of the sequoia and pine grove bordering the lake. From the

rhododendron undergrowth along the bank, she watched
him walk out on a crumbled stone jetty jutting from the
boathouse. He whistled to the dog, who had drifted after a
ground squirrel. As the dog loped toward him, Miklos,
with a long, graceful gesture, skipped a stone across the
still water. The dog scrambled to the edge of the wharf,
sailed out after the stone. A moment later, to her horrified
fascination, Miklos shrugged off the cloak, and naked,
arched out in a clean, flat dive across the water. Eliza
crouched, still frozen in shock. Aside from statues, she'd
never seen a naked man, and when she would have turned
away, a vision of burning flowers in darkness held her
still.

Don't be afraid to look, she reassured herself. He's just
a man.

And so was Michelangelo's *David*, she reconsidered
abruptly, her eyes widening as Miklos heaved himself up
on the jetty. Marvelous as he was, David was a boy.
Miklos Sztarai was Joshua, golden Saul. He seemed more
than a man. Perseus might have looked so, poised upon
the Gorgon rock after slaying Medusa. And Hector, pensive among the mists of Troy. Shoulders and arms that
could have challenged a Minotaur tapered to slim, flat
flanks and buttocks. His legs were long, straight, his
carriage erect, with the grace of a practiced athlete.

Miklos crouched to help Max scramble onto the jetty,
the dog's wet, gray pelt a dark blotch against his master's
tawny hide. A rich laugh came across the water as the
shaking dog sprayed him. Then, before Eliza realized the
danger of her position, the dog galloped up the bank. His
head swung around when he caught her scent; his neck and
body stretched after it as he loped with a low growl toward
her.

She scrambled backward, scratching for a possible weapon
to fend him off. Her fingers closed on a tough root,
yanked. The root came free and she toppled backward,
clawing mud. With a yell, she felt icy water slap her
spine, its jade lid close over her head. She writhed like a
cat trying to land on its feet, kicked, felt her slipper ribbon

snag on something and hold. Panic ripped through her mind and she opened her mouth to scream; it flooded. I'm drowning! Can't anybody see I'm drowning?! Miklos, help me. For God's sake, help me! Her arms flailed out. He's not . . . he's not going to . . . Her nails roweled something; it twisted away. A hand jerked hard at her hair, made her choke in pain when her snarled slipper strap, her scalp wouldn't give. Bubbles swirled and her mind blanked as she was shoved aside into murk. A large hand gripped her trapped leg, yanked at the strap; it gave and she was hauled up against a bare, powerful body. Her head cracked against the jetty as she was tossed stomach down on it.

The lake's dark water followed her. It filled her mouth and eyes, lay leaden in her chest, on her spine. A blow came sudden, sharp. Made her gasp and choke. Again on her spine. The old injury stabbed, making her leg twitch. She tried to cry out to make the blows stop, but all she could do was choke. They kept coming until finally she caught her breath. "Stop it!" she gasped. "Are you trying to kill me?!"

"I've considered it," came Miklos's dry reply.

"Then please pick another spot to make up your mind. I'm not a settee!" He slightly eased up from astride her and she wrenched weakly over . . . to find herself practically nuzzling another male portion she'd never seen before. Her jaw dropped. She squeaked; a small, stifled sound that made his mouth crook.

" 'And the brave, young soldier saw a monstrous dog with eyes as big as mill wheels guarding a chest of gold . . .' "

She squeezed her eyes shut. "Will you please cover yourself!"

His blond hair glittering in spikes, he leaned forward so that a waterdrop from his nose dripped onto hers. "You're shy for a spy. You must have wanted to see something. Now you see everything: every little bit."

"It isn't little," she stammered, bewildered, then was mortified. "I mean, you aren't . . ."

He studied her pale blue face, her childishly shaking

mouth. "You're right. I'm a great, hairy beast and you're
not big enough to stalk me. Open your eyes."

She shook her head.

"Open your eyes or I'll twist your scheming head off,"
he advised calmly.

"You won't," she muttered.

"Oh, yes, I will"—his mouth hovered over hers—"or
something worse."

In case she had doubts about the something worse, he
undid a button on her bodice. Then another. On the third,
she screamed, loud, long, and scared.

Her eyes opened, dilated with fright, as he drawled,
"Come now, wife; you said you were willing to do your
part."

Her gaze instantly focused on his navel. "Not here . . .
not . . . now."

"Why not?" He sleeked her gold-streaked hair, teased
the waterdrops from her nose. "We're alone."

"Someone might come."

His lips twitched. "Ah, yes, someone might; but I'm
afraid you must make do with me. I seem to be the only
one up at this hour."

Feeling a slight movement against the cleft of her breasts,
she realized what he meant by up. Her cheekbones went
white. "Don't . . . please. I've never . . ." Her eyes
lifted, pleading, desperate now. "Don't hurt me."

Then Miklos saw the real fright in her. Her willing kiss
the first night they'd met might have been pretense, he
thought with disillusionment. What *had* driven her to marriage, if she was so afraid of men? Suddenly, with a jab of
anger, he wondered if she had reason. "You're a virgin?"
he asked abruptly.

"Yes." Her lips were still tight.

He felt an unexpected sense of relief. Still, hadn't he
been waiting for a soft spot in her armor? As she shivered
between his thighs, he was sharply aware she was all soft
spots: a flat, wet, sheathed middle he could span with his
hands; small, pointed breasts, and scared mouth. For an
instant he was tempted to mold her mouth to his, warm it

until she lost her fear of him. "What do you think it would be like," he murmured slowly, "not to be a virgin?"

Wild to get away, she jerked spasmodically against him and forcibly, he was reminded seduction was not his best tactic; worse, it could be treacherously double-edged. He had to make her dance to his tune.

His hands closed on her shoulders. "It's all right. I'm not going to rape you . . . but just remember, by law, so long as you're married to me, I can do what I like to you, and it won't be rape." His mouth lowered briefly to hers again. "If you try to force me, I can force you."

"I won't leave with nothing"—her voice was shaky, but determined. "You can do what you like."

"Careful," he breathed. "You don't know what I might like." He grabbed the wet collar of her dress and dragged her to her feet. Dangling soggily by the scruff, she was ready to kick and claw. He casually dropped her. "Go back to the house and change before you catch distemper."

Her fists clenched. "You great bully! I'm not some stray cat!"

He studied her skeptically. "I wasn't aware you came with a pedigree."

Her lips trembled. "You damnable, complacent snob! You think brains and courage require *papers?*" She whirled and stumbled along the jetty. The wolfhound guarding the bank lowered with a snarl.

When she ignored the dog, Miklos ordered, "Max, down!" He watched her climb awkwardly up the bank. She had hurt her leg. Her limp was more apparent at some times than others, particularly when she meant to hold someone at bay; this time she wasn't pretending. He caught up the cloak and jogged after her. Before she had time to protest, he threw the cloak around her and scooped her up. She pushed at his damp chest. "Don't! I can walk, damn you!"

He ignored her. "You can also swear, and threaten, and bluster, and play at blackmail. You're going to learn better manners before we part company."

"Not from you, you naked ape."

"Oh, yes, from me. And a few other lessons, if I decide you need them."

She started to snap a retort, then realized they were beginning to cross the garden below the villa. Her fingers knotted in his chest fur. "Put me down! We'll be seen!" Then, as another thought struck her, her fingers tightened. "They'll think we've been . . ."

He grinned. "Only if you don't scream." While she silently fumed, he carried her into the house and upstairs past a round-eyed maid, then into her room. He dropped her on the bed. "Shall I help with your buttons?"

"Get out," she gritted.

He waited.

"Please."

He bowed slightly and headed for the door. "There may be hope for you yet."

Behind him, the door closed to be smacked by a slipper.

Chapter 4

An Elusive Fish

Lake Como: March 10, 1847

A fishing rod shadow extended across Eliza's easel. Startled, she looked up to see Miklos, dressed in worn breeches and unbuttoned shirt, blocking most of the sun. His sudden presence was like a pillow slapped over her face. With his tall frame haloed by the light, his careless masculinity was awesome, making her feel overwhelmed and defensive. Strung over his shoulder was a wicker creel. "Care to join me?"

"At fishing?" she asked incredulously, lowering her palette. "I don't know how to fish."

"Then you can watch me"—he smiled—"while we talk."

She didn't trust him. He hadn't wanted to talk for days. Why now? With an unsteady hand, she wiped a daub of cobalt paint off her nose, unwittingly smearing it onto her cheek. "Where's the dog?"

He indicated the wolfhound, dispassionately panting a few feet away in the shade.

"Is he coming?"

"He won't harm you." He caught her dubious look. "I promise."

Eliza was more concerned over a possible assault from Miklos than from the dog. She stared at the uncompromising paint strokes that shaped the villa's outlines on her

61

canvas. For practical purposes, she *had* to trust Miklos, but how far could she trust him? Slowly, unwillingly, she got to her feet. She dreaded another confrontation with him, but her father's letter this morning made it necessary. The postmark was from Saint Louis. His and Dorothy's divorce had been quick and quiet. He and his new family were headed west. Cory was fine; they were all happy and excited. Now, unless she wanted to involve her parents in another court case, she was on her own. "Is it far?"

Miklos stifled an inward sigh. "It's not far."

Eliza followed him into the sequoias. As they threaded through the rocks to the pine grove, sunlight played through the trees like subtle variations in a symphony. Pools of light drenched the cool forest floor, glittered in the breeze-swept needles of the pine tops. The underbrush rippled in deep, glossy greens and tallows, honey and lichen grays. Shortly, Miklos discovered Eliza's concern for distance was not completely due to a tepid constitution. In less than a half mile under the dappled shadows of the pines, her face showed the strain of her damaged leg. He wiped the paint off her nose and cheek with a leaf, then picked her up. Predictably, she protested, "Stop packing me about like this."

"Then learn to manage on your own." He continued down the rock-strewn path. Miklos was always startled at how light she was in his arms, as if he were holding a small, wild thing. She was stiff and her heart was battering against his ribs. She even smelled like a forest creature where pollen had dusted her thick, fine hair. He had to stop himself from brushing his cheek against its perfumed, silky spill over his shoulder, from scenting her as some predatory male wolf might a helpless rabbit . . . or his mate. Instantly, he shoved that last idea out of his head. For now, he needed to calmly talk to her, not complicate their impossible relationship and frighten her.

Her voice came tight as she pushed at his chest. "Put me down. I want to go back."

"I don't. And you can't, alone. What happened to your

leg?'' he continued matter-of-factly, ignoring the prods at his breastbone and ribs.

Forced to give up the idea of denting him, Eliza really hated him at that moment. Hated his strength, and assurance, and merciless complacency. Hated the way he made her heart race when he touched her. In exasperation, she stuffed her hands under her armpits. "None of your business."

"But it is. A simple matter of taking inventory." Reshifting her weight as casually as if she were kindling, he stepped over a fallen log. "As a merchant's daughter, you should understand."

"Your goods were damaged by accident," she spat, "and in case you mean to apply hammer and nails, irreparably."

"When?"

"I was seven," was the sullen reply.

As if concentrating on the steepening descent, he was silent for a few moments, then observed expressionlessly, "More than half a life."

"One can become accustomed to anything," was the flat reply, "in more than half a life."

This time he said nothing for several minutes until the path leveled into new-leafed lindens fluttering in the shoreline breeze. Then he commented, "Yes, I see you've become adjusted to your condition. Perhaps too adjusted."

She stiffened. "What are you suggesting? That I'm pretending?"

"I'm suggesting the injury occurred a long time ago. Perhaps you've gotten used to more than you ought. When did a doctor last examine you?" He sat her down on a lichen-encrusted log and dropped his creel. "We're here."

Eliza relaxed a fraction now that he was no longer touching her; when he did, her brain knotted. She must keep her wits. Despite their clinical interview, the intensity in his eyes hadn't quite matched his dispassionate voice. Judging by their secluded, lovely surroundings, if Miklos didn't intend to molest her, he meant to soothe her into letting down her guard. She looked about the green glade bordering a lake inlet that wandered into a cascading brook. Down the hill the brook spilled through undergrowth. Enormous, lacy ferns capped glistening, charcoal rocks and shadowed the eddies over clay-bound, water-worn stones. The rushing water tugged at the ivy netting its banks, in some places fraying tough threads bare. Rhododendron and wild strawberry plants grew thickly about the brook, thinning as they spread into the pale-barked lindens. Max wandered off through the bracken as Miklos strung the rods.

"How long since you saw a doctor?" he asked again.

Rebelliously, Eliza stood, ignoring the ache, and began to walk around the sun-dappled glade. "When I was ten, the doctors decided no more could be done. That was the end of it."

He handed her a pole. "And what had they done?"

She told him; the account came out less in words than in pulleys, plasters, bindings, casts, and operations.

Three years, Miklos thought. Three years of medical torture, most of it probably useless. No wonder her eyes are old. "Are you in pain?" He kept his tone flat.

Hers was equally so as she tinkered with the rod. "The worst was over when they gave up."

"And you were relieved."

"Wouldn't you be relieved to stop being part of a pulley?" She held out the rod. "Here. I don't know how this works."

"I'll show you."

"I don't want to know. I don't care for fishing."

"You've never tried it." He left her holding the rod, sat down on the bank and began pulling off his boots. "Take off your shoes," he ordered, then pulled off his belt and tossed it to her. "For your skirts."

"You know I don't swim," she objected, confused.

"You don't need to swim"—he waded into the stream that spilled about his calves—"unless you're a dachshund."

"Listen, I'm not . . ."

"Can't hear you over the rush of the water."

She gritted her teeth. To talk to him, and she didn't

want to, she would have to literally angle after him. If she didn't talk to him, she could probably look forward to another week of being dangled. She wrenched off her shoes, belted up her skirt, then gasped as her feet met cold water.

While her attention was on her footing, Miklos watched her with her skirts hiked about her knees, awkwardly lurching toward him across the white-foamed rocks. She was favoring the good leg; the bad one was a trifle under-developed, both were thin. When she reached his side, he showed her how to manage her line, let it draw out with the water's flow. Reluctantly, she obeyed.

In silence, they cast flies into shaded pools and rippling depths with only the water's song running in the stillness, the occasional call of a bird, and crackle of Max roaming through the brush. Sunlight filtered down on their heads and Eliza, with an odd sense of growing tranquillity, watched Miklos's hair flash white-gold as he shifted to an unshaded eddy. Suddenly he yelped. "Your hook"—he plucked swiftly at his back—"the devil, I can't reach it."

Embarrassed, Eliza realized she'd absently let her hook drift in the air. Stammering an apology, she worked at the sun-warmed cloth at the small of Miklos's back, its hard ridge of muscle brushing her knuckles. The hook didn't give way and she fumbled at the damp cloth where perspiration had molded the shirt to his broad shoulders and the long groove of his spine. He smelled pleasantly male, faintly musky and tangy and powerful. She was reminded of the scent of cedar, but not the kind men bore from armoires. The men she knew never perspired; she strongly doubted if they bathed nude in misty lakes. Finally, the prong worked loose.

"Thank you," he said dryly.

"Thank you"—her lashes lowered—"for saving my life off the jetty. You could have solved your problem by turning your back."

Surprise filled his eyes, then mischief as if he guessed the unmaidenly thoughts that inspired her belated gratitude. "No naked knight worth his salt would turn his back on a helpless damsel."

Flushing, Eliza glared fiercely at her pale toes under the water. "You couldn't have hoped to be rewarded for your trouble."

He was silent for a moment, then gently lifted her chin, and in his eyes she saw an unexpected sadness. "I mistrust debts. Accountings. By now you must know that." His forefinger traced her jaw. "But I doubt you will ever know what I hope for."

Eliza found herself held by those clear, light-filled gray eyes. She could still feel the ghost of his touch against her face, remember the more insistent ghost of his passionate, mesmerizing kiss that first night they'd met. The brief tantalizing promise of a mysterious magic that they would now never share. So much had gone so wrong between them . . . but then, had mates so misfitted ever really had a chance? "You think me greedy and selfish," she murmured. "I don't really want to hurt you . . . anyone. I just . . .," she faltered.

"Just . . ."

She shook her head, backing away. "Nothing."

She stumbled against a rock and he grabbed at her hand, making her flinch. "Look out." He righted her. "This 'nothing' you want makes me feel irrelevant." His grip was tight on her arms, his voice husky.

"Being needed is important to you?" she asked uncertainly.

He looked puzzled, then his eyes shielded as if he'd said more than he intended. He smiled disarmingly as he released her, then lifted her hook. "Just now, not being taken for your first trophy is my main concern." He turned her away from him. "Come, it's time you learned to cast properly."

His big, warm body moved against her, his arms guiding hers to flick the rod. The fly landed exactly where he wanted: a dark pool in the mossy overhang of the opposite bank. She stood still, liking the warmth of him, yet, as if she could feel the rush of his blood, mistrusting his masculine vitality. The firm shape of his manhood rounded just below the scar of her last operation.

His breath was lulling on her neck, stirring the wisps of her hair across it. That soft breath was life; that now lazy, indifferent power between his thighs was life. Simply by touching her, he was making her know it; in a way, share it. He could have mountains, nations, Bette had said. And susceptible, foolish women, her logic warned. You dare not play the fool for him.

Then his manhood subtly hardened, increased in pressure and weight and heat. His breathing stopped altogether. Eliza was bewildered, yet felt a strange excitement. What was happening to him? To her, that she was suddenly breathless too, her heart beginning to pound?

The line snapped taut and she let out a startled cry, nearly dropping the pole. "Hold on, hold on!" Miklos's hands tightened over hers, then let go. "Let him run a little. Hear the line? That's it . . . not too much."

She gripped the rod, her mind half numbed by nervousness and excitement. Somehow the moment with Miklos and the pursuit of the fish were swirling in her mind. The fish ran hard, then, after letting her think he was subdued, tore against the line on a new tack. "Help me," she whispered, hardly aware she had done so.

"Claim your trophy?" Miklos laughed softly. "Shouldn't I be on the side of the fish?"

Eliza didn't understand, didn't have time to puzzle. As its struggles grew more brief, she began to reel in the fish. More. More. Glimpsed silver. Shrieked in triumph and dragged him up. Thrashing, the fish slapped her cheek. The blow was wet, slippery, sensuous. Startled, she grabbed at the sting.

"Careful of the hook!" Miklos warned as her hand clamped down on the fish's head. Quickly he twisted out the hook, leaving a stream of blood down the fish's belly. "Thrust your hand in the gill. Hurry!"

Her hand went in, felt a cold, bony fan beating against it. She squealed in exultation. "I did it! I got him!"

"And now that you have him, what will you do with him?" came Miklos's soft murmur.

She realized vaguely he'd backed away from her. "Why . . . I don't know." She gazed enraptured at the fish's diamond scales. "He's beautiful, isn't he?"

"Yes."

She noted the heaving gills. "But out of his element, he won't live long . . ." She let him go.

When she turned to Miklos, his face held an odd quietness. "A tender heart can mean an empty belly, Miss Hilliard."

"The next one I'll eat."

His pensiveness turned into a wry smile. "A sensible decision, if a next one comes along."

"You're tired of fishing?" she blurted, disappointed. He was standing with a strange tension as if he'd grown impatient, yet his eyes were alive with a glow she couldn't define.

"Not unless your feet are cold."

"They're not," she lied. He might not bring her again. To her surprise, she did not want the afternoon to end. In Miklos's arms, in catching the fish and letting it go, she knew an excitement she had not known since before the accident. She felt alive.

"All right." Miklos's line snaked out.

By the time they left the stream, five fish were in the creel, Eliza's feet were frozen and the sun had lowered over the trees, the dusk breeze spangling the lindens. She noticed Miklos look up from wrapping the fish in moss to pensively gaze into the frail leaves as if they were part of some holy window: some sweet, sad, faraway memory. Wondering where his mind had drifted, she sat on the fallen log and rubbed her feet. Although he hadn't touched her again after she had caught the fish, the afternoon had been easy, as if they had been friends, even lovers, rather than antagonists. While he had not pried, she had freely allowed him more than a glimpse of herself. In return, she had been given no glimpse of him: only sensations she might have stolen, yet something in his spirit had been lent to her. Again, he was reaching to her . . . for what?

The sun set like a Renaissance rose that flushed the distant snowcaps before the sky purpled into a jeweled veil of stars. They roasted the fish over a fire with Eliza's feet nearly shoved in the coals. With a chuckle, Miklos swatted her toes. "Not cold, eh?"

She gave him a quick, shy smile. "I'm all right. New York has cold winters."

"Do you miss it?"

Her face lost its animation. "No."

"Not your family?"

Suspicion entered her eyes. "Why do you ask?"

"You don't write many letters."

She tucked her toes under her. "Hilliards have never been regular correspondents. Still, I haven't complained to Mummy, Daddy, or the solicitors . . . yet. Beginning to worry?"

"If I were worried, I could always have a letter written for you." He turned the roasting spit. "You would sound safe, well, and happy."

Studying his eagle profile carved like a gold coin against the flames, she could imagine Roman standards buffeted by the rising smoke. She wondered how unscrupulous Miklos might be, though tonight she *felt* safe, well, and if not happy, closer to it than she could easily remember.

Suddenly, his head turned and his gold-fringed, pale eyes seemed to look through her. "Would you like to return home?"

"No!" Stunned and appalled, she unthinkingly fought to her feet. "I won't go! Nothing, not you, not God himself can make me go back there!"

He gravely turned his attention back to the spit. "Sit down, Miss Hilliard."

"No." Their warm, comforting intimacy had chilled into a threatening frost. Feeling colder by the step, she backed away from the fire. "You've brought me out here just to trick me, put me off guard."

"Doesn't that guard sometimes become heavy?" he asked gently.

"Not as heavy as the blows I've not been quick enough to duck." She started into the woods, saw how black they were. Feeling the old rage at being helpless rise again, she spun about to see that Sztarai had followed her. His tall form blocked out the firelight.

"I may not keep you, but I'll not send you back," he said quietly. "Come have your dinner."

White-faced with disillusionment, she didn't move.

"Staying hungry won't make you any quicker at ducking." He put his hands on his hips. "I'll offer a truce; but if you choose the woods instead, I won't look for you."

He probably meant it. Shivering in the dark until dawn would gain her nothing. Again he was giving her a choice that assured him just what he wanted. She would take great pleasure to one day be in the unlikely position of denying him what he wanted most. Yet . . . whatever his motives, he had given her today. Her face lost some of its stiffness. "What sort of truce?"

"We negotiate. Hopefully, each of us gets something he requires."

"You haven't said what you require."

He was silent, the distant firelight framing his dark shape, and for a moment, she sensed uncertainty in him. *I wonder if he knows what he's after?*

"Dinner," he said finally, "at the moment. I'm hungry; aren't you?"

She had been; now she wasn't sure. The magic had gone from her accomplishment in catching the fish.

He seemed to guess what she felt. "I *am* irrelevant. What you did today, you did. You needn't give me anything you want to keep. But decide." He turned away. "In five minutes, I will have eaten your fish."

In five seconds, she went to claim her own.

This time, when he carried her back to the house, she made no comment. He might have been a pack mule, so detached, so sure of his untiring strength did she feel. Only the insistent pulse of his heartbeat against her side was not to be ignored. She had glimpsed her future through Miklos Sztarai and her future had the shape of a fish, loose and liquid in a stream.

The next morning, Eliza hung about the boathouse wharf at the usual hour Miklos took out the sailboat. She doubted if he would ever guess the turmoil she'd experienced during that hour she'd waited alone on the steps in the morning mist seeping up from the lake. Mysteriously, the mist curled about her as if tempting her to venture into an unknown, secret dimension: Miklos's world, which she might be unable to leave if she advanced too far.

At the top of the boathouse steps stood an earthy, rough-planed, stone satyr. The satyr's ivy-shadowed smile was alive, intriguing, as if a pagan spirit haunted it and the lush, surrounding wood. Twice she stood to return to the villa, only to settle uneasily again with the lake lapping at her feet. Sitting stiffly under the satyr's insidious gaze, she knew if she pursued Miklos's company, one thing could lead to another. Now he was probably baiting her into a false sense of security. With an exasperated growl, she propped her chin on her forearms. She might sniff the bait, but he'd find himself with an empty hook. Only she'd better be careful; he'd shown himself an adroit fisherman.

A smile flickered across Miklos's lips when he saw Eliza's bulldog expression, her skirts stained from sitting on the mossy steps. He was not vain enough to presume she wanted his company. Given one heady taste of achievement, she was bent on another. If she knew how far his desire had been primed yesterday, she would have been racing back to the villa. Wet, stubborn, and naive about men, she caught at his heart with the appeal of a lost pup, yet intrigued him as a courageous, clever woman who had left childhood far behind and was made for loving. Another man's loving, his logic sharply reminded. "So you want to learn something new today?"

Her chin came up. "On a boat, you needn't carry me about."

Wearing the same fish-scented outfit of the previous

day, he twitched loose the mooring lines. "Sailing is a bit more complicated than fishing."

"I can do it."

"All right. We'll give it a try."

Sailing *was* complicated. She could cope with complexity, but she wasn't quick. The sailboat was twenty-four feet long and she couldn't seem to move fast enough across the deck to respond to Miklos's orders. As the wind was unreliable on most parts of Como, he headed for the blustery Lecco arm of the lake. He saw her eyes grow larger than they ought to have been, her movements clumsy as she tripped over her skirts. While the bright-awninged, tourist-laden *barcas* provocatively danced across their course, he told her to stay put and hold the jib. She held the jib line until her hands cramped. Miklos's hands closed over hers. "Cleat it," he said quietly, and showed her how. Realizing she should have cleated the line in the first place, she felt like a fool. He wouldn't bring her again. She knew it.

Defeated, she watched spray spring from the bow's cut through the rushing, sunlit sheet of Como, with its streaks of clouds and hovering gulls. Her skirt, her hair, her skin were damp. She dreaded being dull and dry again.

When they docked, Miklos let her climb onto the boathouse jetty by herself. "Tomorrow, we'll have to get you out of skirts."

"You didn't think I was dreadful?" she said faintly as she tried to balance on the slimy stone.

"Abysmal." Tactfully refraining from retying her square knot in the stern line, he secured the bow. "I've yet to see anyone crew worth a *lire* in crinolines."

Relief was flooding over her when he straightened. "And as we're on the subject, your daily wardrobe is unsuitable."

So already, he was tampering with her! "Unsuitable to what?" she inquired icily.

"To the Italian climate, to your age, your coloring, fashion for the last decade, and good taste in general," was the mild reply. He fanned out her sticky, ruined skirt. "Have Bette call in a seamstress."

She flicked the skirt out of his fingers. "I'll dress as I please . . ."

"Miss Hilliard, I won't have my household depressed by a resident vulture."

"You have no right . . . !"

"The contract you signed gives me the right. I'm captain, and so long as you wish to sail with me, you'll be crew."

"You don't want a wife," she sputtered. "You want a swabbie!"

He grinned. "That, too. I'm dry-docking the boat next week. You're going to help me scrub her hull."

She glared at his departing back. Her? Scrub? A boat? She'd never done physical labor in her life: cooked a meal, made a bed. The man could afford a small navy and he expected her to *scrub* a boat? She marched back to her easel. So much for sailing!

Next morning, as Eliza lay glumly abed writing a falsely cheerful letter to her father and another to ward off a grilling from her mother, the maid brought in her breakfast tray two hours early. Folded over her arm were a boy's green knee breeches, a blue shirt, a loosely woven vest, and Tyrol jacket.

Miklos gave a slow nod of approval when Eliza, looking uncomfortable, ventured onto the boathouse jetty. The boy's clothes were a shade big; Eliza had cinched the breeches about her middle with a drapery cord. Taking his time, he strolled around her with a speculative air that made her fidget. He seemed altogether too preoccupied with her unbound breasts and the curve of her bottom. "Good," he drawled at last. "Now you look more like a bluebird than a vulture. Only one thing." He flicked loose the tight knot of hair at her nape.

She caught angrily at the pale skein of hair that spilled down her back. "Why did you do that?"

"Buns remind me of fur balls." Deftly, he braided her hair into a long pigtail. She wondered whether his skill was due to his practice with ropes or with women. "Better," he judged. "How do you feel in breeches?"

"Conspicuous."

He laughed. "You were more so in purple widow's weeds, believe me."

Although Eliza was sharply aware that Miklos's fascinated gaze rarely left her, the sailing lesson that day went better. She was quicker without skirts, and to her surprise, almost as much mentally as physically. In Miklos's perverse way, he had removed another barricade she had scarcely noticed. She could reach farther, stretch, nearly dream of doing the impossible, even run again as she had so long ago through the meadows of Springfield.

Miklos set course for the lake's single island, Comacina. Among the ruins of Rome's last stronghold in northern Italy, they lunched on Genoa salami, goat's cheese, and fruit in the long grass. Her appetite at full peak, Eliza unabashedly ate almost as much as Miklos, whose accounts of colorful regional history, comic Italian folktales, and mildly wicked jokes soon had them both laughing over their wine. She supplied pithy, crackerbox anecdotes he found hilarious, declaring one of them was similarly told in Hungary. Miklos was an altogether winning companion, so long as she didn't forget he meant to win their settlement conflict.

With feline contentment, she lay back with her arms over her head in the grass and stretched. Giving a pleased little chuckle at nothing, she turned her head to look at Miklos lying beside her. She wondered what making love with him in this deep, breeze-rippled grass might be like. To have him caress her, kiss her. To make her dizzy, and longing, and willing to yield him anything, so long as he made her again part of that turbulent force within him. Once, his kiss had promised her something . . . left her still confusedly craving it.

The sun was high now, hot; the clothing that had seemed too little, now was too much. The Chianti, too heady. Miklos, too near.

Wondering why she was suddenly restless, Miklos

watched Eliza as a big, golden lion would the stirring of his young, sleek mate. The gray glints under his lashes belied his indolence, for he was intensely aware of the brush of grass against Eliza's skin, of the rise of her small breasts. The sun-touched tint of her flesh was intensified by the pale blue shirt and her golden eyes. Loosened from her braid, wisps of hair clouded pale about her face, and her lips, stained pomegranate with wine, were soft and full and inviting. He imagined burying his face in that cloud of hair, kissing her, tasting the pink, inner softness of her mouth. How easily he could pluck free those few buttons that kept her breasts a mystery.

Eliza's eyes were closed now with a slight frown puckered between her brows. Easy to guess her thoughts might be wandering, if more shyly, the same wayward paths as his. Innocent as she was, she couldn't imagine what came next. Miklos's lips curved as his own eyes closed. I'll take us both there, sweeting. To that forbidden place we will never explore together.

Mentally, with a delicious languor that tantalized them both, he unbuttoned her shirt, then eased off her breeches. In his mind, the swelling peaks of her nipples were tawny rose, exquisitely sensitive under his fingertips. Her long legs were wondrous and entwining; the fluff of gold between them a tease against his lips.

Under his lashes, he saw Eliza's body stir as if she felt his touch. Her hand slipped to her throat, trailed restlessly between her breasts. Somehow, at that point, his playful mood too quickly evaporated. His mind and body blurred into desire; he felt naked, hard, his body aching to join hers. Though he and Eliza were not touching, the shadows of the olive trees laced them as if they were bound together. Eliza's arms were enveloping, her breath quickening, as her body welcomed his. As he poised, she eagerly arched beneath him, her slender thighs parting, her face embroidered with flowers. Then horribly, in a single, terrible moment, her face so near his became another's, mocking and cold and filled with hate. A discordant mazurka clamored in his ears. A pistol thrust at his belly and fired.

His eyelids flew open as he gasped, his face pricked with sweat. He lay still, letting the vision pass, his heartbeat slow. His attention flicked to Eliza as he slowly sat up. She was lying quietly, her lips slightly parted, her body curiously rigid. As his shadow crossed her, she became aware of him.

Why is Miklos looking at me with such confusion? wondered Eliza, startled and bemused. Does he guess I've been daydreaming of kissing him? At my disappointment that I still haven't learned that man–woman secret he promised? Hastily, she reclosed her eyes. He couldn't possibly know what she'd been thinking. She sensed he was back in Hungary, and probably with some other girl.

Remembering his homeland made Miklos pensive. He had never spoken of Hungary before today, did not now, but she could tell he was thinking of it. Unseen people joined them in the ruins: people who made him detached and moody. When he shortly suggested they continue their exploration of the lake, she was sorry to leave Comacina, much less so to leave his ghosts.

But leave them, Miklos did. As if by force of will, he resumed his light, lazy role as her guide. As they sailed around the lake, Miklos pointed out lovely Villa Pliniana and its hillside cataract described by Pliny 1800 years before. Along the sunny Tremezzina shores were ancient Guelph and Ghibelline fortresses, convents, churches, and villas set like pearls in glorious gardens, cypress and olive groves. At the center of the three great fingers of Como curved the town of Bellagio with its graceful bell tower. Everywhere was loveliness and romance, nature and antiquity. Despite her uneasiness about Comacina, Eliza was in her element.

Her hands were blistered by day's end, her eyes sore from squinting at sun on water, her skin burned, but she wouldn't have traded a twinge. When she was free, she'd have a small boat she could sail herself and she'd wear nothing but breeches and the slippers of a dancer. She'd look as healthy as tanned Miklos in his fisherman's cottons and be just as bossy.

Only she would never again lie in the long grass with him. Never know that secret . . .

"Miki, you're marvelous," commented Bette in the drawing room after watching Eliza reluctantly head upstairs to change for dinner. "The girl's confused enough. Must you addle her sex as well?"

"Would you rather see her stalking about like a grave digger's wife?"

"When you put it like that, no. She looks well enough in an eccentric fashion, but don't you think her outfit lacks something?"

"Gypsy earrings?" he teased.

"A cork vest. I'll warrant the child won't be able to swim a stroke if she tumbles overboard."

"No vest."

She looked startled, then her lips tightened. "Miklos, whatever are you thinking?"

He gave her an ironic look. "Aunt, whatever are *you* thinking?"

Eliza was hurrying downstairs to join Miklos at the boathouse next morning when Vincenzo scurried into the foyer from the drawing room. *"Principessa . . . Signorina,* you have a guest. *La Contessa* Bellaria." He looked unaccountably nervous, and as Eliza entered the drawing room, she gained a shrewd idea why. Her caller was a stunning, opulent brunette born for every experience Eliza had never had, particularly in the realm of seduction. La Bellaria was the sort who liked vulgar sex, and Eliza could guess who she had been liking it with.

With startled appraisal of Eliza's breeches, then a smile as brilliant as the rubies in her ears, the woman extended her hand. "I have so looked forward to meeting Miklos's bride, *Principessa.* You met my uncle upon your arrival. I am Vanda di Bellaria, your neighbor."

Not the sugar-borrowing kind, Eliza judged: just one who's after a half cup of husband.

With amused condescension, Bellaria gripped Eliza's small, unenthusiastic paw. "What a daring fashion you're wearing. I admire a woman of courage."

"As do I, *Contessa*. That silk *is* a remarkable shade of green." As Bellaria's eyes involuntarily dropped to her dress, Eliza, with deliberate boyishness, pumped her hand. "But how good of you to call. Had Miki and I known you were coming, we would have invited you to go sailing with us." She noticed Bellaria's smile become a trifle set. Her own was innocent. "A pity you aren't suitably dressed."

"Yes, next time I shall manage better." Under her peacock-feathered hat, Bellaria's eyes turned feline. "As we've been friends for some ten years, Miki and I stay in close touch."

"That's remarkable," Eliza exclaimed in admiration. "Ten years ago, I was still wanting a bedtime story." She pumped Bellaria's hand again. "Until we meet again, Countess. I'm so sorry, I must run. Miki's waiting and you may have guessed how impatient he can be"—she laughed conspiratorially—"about so many things."

Bellaria gave her departing back a look that would have melted lead.

"What's wrong, Bluebird?" Miklos asked patiently in midlake. "You've left your mind in your nest today."

Have you forgotten? Eliza wanted to retort. I haven't a nest at the moment and I want out of your fouled one as quickly as possible. Impatiently, she gave her snagged halyard a yank. It freed suddenly, tripping her backward. As she lost her footing on the wet deck, the flimsy rope rail gave under her weight. Frantically, she grabbed at it. The rope scraped her palms, vibrated free. For a horrible instant, she remembered nearly drowning off the jetty, then Miklos grabbed her around the waist and dragged her upward. With a choked sound, she clung to his neck.

"It's all right . . . you're all right."

Her heart pounding against his ribs, she buried her face against his throat, blocking out everything but his safe strength. Hesitantly looking up, she saw his eyes were soft; he might have been comforting a child. Gray glimmered beneath shadowy gold as if sunlit mists were parting after a storm. Her arms tightened about him and the sunlight grew brighter, blinding until she caught her breath. Then gradually, she realized what she was doing, what Vanda Bellaria and God knows how many other women must have done when Miklos held them. Still trembling, she put her hands against his chest and pushed him away. "I don't need . . . please, thank you." Her knees failing, she sank down on the deck and hooked her arm over a gunwale.

For a long moment, he was silent, then with his shirt ruffling in the wind, he hunkered onto his heels and took her hands. "No more sailing lessons unless you learn to swim."

He might have suggested she try to fly. "I don't want to learn to swim. Can't I just tie on some sort of float?"

"You'd still have no idea of how to maneuver." He waved at the lake's two-mile width. "If I didn't see you go overboard, you could drown." Step by step, he had tempted her to learn one new thing after another to stretch her limits. He had brought her to the point where she must explore new medical help in order to continue past the confines of her present abilities. Shoved against her limits, which way would she jump?

She gazed dejectedly over the sun-sequined, blue water. "You don't understand. I *can't* swim."

"Your injury?"

She was silent, her fingers tightening on the gunwale.

Miklos wanted to take her into his arms again. Against his cheek, he could still feel the light, alluring lash of her wind-ruffled hair. When he'd held her, her eyes had gilded, been dazzled as if she had stumbled from bleak darkness into a lovely summer noon. For that unwary moment, he had been tempted to forget tepid Comacina daydreams, push the future away, and make love to her in reality; yet in her present distraction, he knew better than to touch her, even in reassurance. He mustn't be seduced by her growing trust. There were degrees of loathing; if she came to care for him, she might yet discover its arctic zone.

"You see now you need a medical examination?" he said softly. "In a matter of days, I can have a Milan specialist: one that doesn't rely on Chinese torture."

"Don't you see there's no *point?* I was dissected to everybody's satisfaction years ago." Seeing the Chinese patience in his eyes, she wanted to cry.

Dr. Tinetti arrived the following week. Though he was as gentle as Miklos promised, his testing the limits of Eliza's flexibility, reflexes, and endurance summoned echoes of pain she had hidden far back in memory. Stiffened muscles screamed and once, so did she. Inwardly, dreading the diagnosis, she cursed Miklos and all his kind.

Miklos was as tense as Eliza. He'd won. He had persuaded her to take her first painful step into independence; unless she endured it and all those that would come after, her bright spirit would be sharply dimmed by her physical limitations. In the world's eyes, she must appear inadequate. Inadequate! To call Eliza inadequate was like underrating a lurking typhoon. Though it might cost him, he wanted to see her loosed to storm and wreak havoc as she would.

Tinetti's diagnosis was brief; Eliza's original surgery had been botched. Atrophy, scar tissue from bungled surgery, calcium buildup on weakly rehealed, sacral vertebrae, had crippled her. Also, several nerves were either pinched or dead. Eliza had known scarcely a waking hour without some pain. Surgery, while not free from risk, would correct certain problems and relieve the pain. Without surgery, swimming would do little good to increase her mobility; anything more strenuous was out of the question.

Miklos debated. Having taken the possibility of destroying Eliza in his hands, he longed to cast it down. She was as treacherous as a cornered mink, but for all her slyness and bared, tiny fangs, she had inveigled him into being deeply protective of her. She hadn't meant to do so, he was sure. She didn't even know she had done it.

And now he could not refuse the stakes for her future. Like him, she was no gambler by nature, but she could bide her time, weigh the odds, and when the long chance came, coolly take it without a quiver. She'd gambled when she married him. He wasn't going to let her win *that* pot, but he wouldn't see her leave the table empty-handed. When she was healed again, both in body and spirit, he would let her go. That would be her marriage settlement. In her heart, she would judge it fair. She would lose the whole game now, though, if he gave her a chance. She would never agree to another operation.

"You smell of liniment," Miklos teased Eliza.

Rigidly sitting in her shapeless flannel robe on her bed, she wouldn't look at him.

"Do something about it before coming down to dinner, will you. We've having a delicate grouse." He sauntered toward the door.

Her head slowly swiveled. "What did he say?"

He turned. "As much damage may have been done in surgery as in your accident."

Her lips trembled, then set. "So . . . there's no hope."

"You may be surprised. How much do you want to stop being a partial invalid?"

I don't think you could comprehend how much, she thought, though you've certainly known how to make me feel dreadfully what I've missed. "I want it."

"Remember that," he advised with a strange smile. "And please, don't wear black to dinner."

Eliza stared wonderingly at the door that closed behind him. He was maneuvering her into something again. She was like a donkey petted and swatted at the same time, yet so far, Miklos had only led her where she was secretly tempted to go. In a bizarre way, she had begun to trust him, though he was a man dangerous to trust.

She wore amber jewelry and brown taffeta to dinner; brown did something for her eyes and hair, and despite her lingering suspicion of Miklos, she was more animated than at any time since coming to Italy. Nervous from exhilaration, she scarcely noticed her food and spoke eagerly of visiting the Pennine range, which Bette had described.

"Might we go to the Pennines?" Eliza asked Miklos. "The mountain meadows must be covered with flowers now."

"We can go as far as Mont Blanc if you like."

From her seat beside Dr. Tinetti, Bette gave him a speculative look. "That would be nice, Miki. You've been hibernating here like a bear. A holiday might do us all good."

"Then we'll plan for midsummer." Almost dreamily, Miklos watched Eliza sip her drugged broth. "A few matters must be put out of the way first. Even bears cannot wander at their absolute whim."

"I daresay you mean the French problem," Tinetti observed. "Mont Blanc is right on the border."

And the imperial problems, reflected Bette wearily. Two emperors to bait one chained, bored, wretched bear . . . who is in a deuced odd mood. "We ought to celebrate our holiday," she said aloud. "Miki, why don't you play your balalaika for us?"

He eyed her with a glint of something like dislike, then silently crooked a finger at Vincenzo. When the balalaika arrived, Eliza thought Miklos was loathe to pick it up. If he didn't like to play, why had he agreed?

When he finally did play, he took Eliza to another world. Took them all. Miklos was a poet. Those fingers that could destroy life could also create it, and a beauty she never dreamed he could understand, far less form. She had rarely heard Hungarian, but now he sang it in a husky baritone that recalled centuries of passion, sorrow, sweetness, and savagery. This was not the music of Europe, but of a world that had come before and lingered yet.

Miklos sang of love and death and dreams. Forgotten wars and remembered tears. For Eliza, he sometimes sang in English; for Tinetti, Italian, but Eliza liked the haunting Hungarian best. While Bette and Tinetti danced, she wan-

dered to a window to gaze at the moonlit lake. She was
melancholy, drowsy, as if melting in the music. She drifted
so far away she hardly noticed when Miklos ceased to play
and only his voice still wove its spell. He came to the
window and held out his arms. She moved into them
without hesitating, without thinking, without remembering
she could not dance. They drifted about the floor. Leaning
her head against his shoulder, she began to hum.

When her head finally dropped back across his arm,
Miklos stroked loosened strands of fair hair back from her
face. Now, for once, she looked like the child she was in
years, but had never been in reality, all because she could
not take a step without consideration, without feeling crooked
and criticized. He had drawn from her years of suspicion,
made her believe in a possible fairy tale. "The clock has
stuck twelve and you are still at the ball, *Principessa*."
Reluctantly, sadly, he picked her up. "Now your prince
must turn back into a scuttling rat." His voice lifted.
"Dottore."

Eliza awoke the next morning in her bedroom to a
nightmare, her oldest one, of pain she'd prayed she'd
never know again. Only moments passed before she realized he'd done it. Miklos and that shy, fiddling doctor had
cut her again. If she had the knife they'd used, she'd have
plunged it into Miklos's hard, treacherous heart.

Suddenly, she saw his heart was in reach and her
eyes blazed as she tried to get to it, but pain bound
her down and she could only look at him with pure
hatred.

"You said you'd do anything," he said softly. "Remember?"

"Anything but this," she breathed harshly.

"Only this would do. By midsummer, you'll walk the
slopes of the Pennines, and limp only if you let yourself."

"How sure you are," she choked. "Do you think you're
God? I should love to watch you make a mistake!"

"But you wouldn't like it *this* time . . . would you?"

"As soon as these stitches heal, I want *out!* Do you hear

me?'' When he said nothing, she fairly screamed at him, ''When, *when* are you going to let me go?!''

Miklos found himself at a loss for an answer. In the face of her blistering rage, he saw he had made a destructive error in underestimating Eliza's terrible resentment. His betrayal had hit her harder than he had ever thought possible. She despised him. If he sent her away like this, she would go on despising him, perhaps distrust all men because he had encouraged her fragile trust, then shattered it. Had he merely turned her from one cripple into another?

No, he saw grimly, his responsibility to Eliza was not yet done; for both their sakes, he prayed it soon would be.

Into the early summer months, Eliza worked with Miklos. Did the tiresome, aching exercises. Did her utmost to get on her feet again so she could point them south to Rome to get an annulment. She wrote her father and mother; she wrote the pope. She snapped and snarled at Miklos, who saw that her letters went as far as his fireplace. Bette collaborated with her nephew more than he might have wished by also intercepting two letters from Eliza's parents. No word came from anybody and Eliza stewed. Why should Miklos go to all this trouble of making repairs unless he meant to keep her? Keep her. *Keep* her!

Though she knew Miklos must guess the extent of her desperation, he gave no sign of it. His patient, false oblivion made her frantic, in time suspect her letters had been appropriated. As she had been.

Chapter 5

The Satyr Smile

La Mer de Glace, Courmayeur, Italy: July 1, 1847

Eliza no longer believed Miklos's promise of a holiday. In a way, she believed it less when confronted by the awesome, glacial cataract of *La Mer de Glace* poised in ponderous, frozen suspension below the rocky Tacul Massif. Heavy streams of water burst through the glassy shell to spill down the rift. Slipping from her donkey cart to venture onto the lower Leschaux glacier, she shielded her eyes from the glare of the torrential, rotting ice. "It *is* a sea of ice. How tremendous!" she breathed. "I never thought I should see anything as impressive as Niagara."

Miklos tethered the donkey to browse among the daisies and snow flowers that pelted the slope. In rough, mountain garb, he resembled one of the tall, fair, Italian guides that ranged the Pennines. He belonged in the mountains as certainly as a strong, clean-limbed fir. "One day, you must visit the Dolomites. For now"—he took Eliza's shoulders and turned her eastward—"do you see that snow-capped mammoth across the valley? That's Mont Blanc. You'd have to go as far as the Himalayas to find its rival."

"One day I mean to go that far," she said softly, then hearing Bette's yodel, waved at her and Vincenzo. They were down the mountain incline picking Alpine daisies, buttercups, and avalanche lilies while the guide set up a picnic from the cart. Due to French unrest, Miklos thought better of taking the train from Chamonix to Montnevers along the glacier. They stayed in Courmayeur and Eliza and the food rode up the mountain from the village; everyone else walked, picking their way with sturdy staffs. "I want to see it all," went on Eliza, shifting her gaze to the sun. "Everything." Her eyes were as brightly impertinent as black-eyed Susans, her upturned face was determined. "You may have stolen my letters, but you can't hold me against my will. No court will make me stay with you after what you and Tinetti did."

Miklos gave a weary sigh. Before Eliza realized what he was doing, he firmly turned her around and his arms closed about her. "It's time you learned, Miss Hilliard, I can hold you as long as I like . . . and pretty much do as I like." His mouth plummeted down on hers, taking her breath, her certainty. The glacier's cataract seemed to have completely melted and crashed about her ears. Her temples began to pound and she couldn't catch her breath. His tall frame was so hard she might have been battered against a rock face, yet the searing sensuality of his mouth sent rivulets of sensation surging madly beyond their narrow bonds to a high, raging torrent. Her lips felt slack and bruised; her naiveté fled. Besides fright, Miklos's knowing, dizzying embrace left her with a racing pulse, a raw temper, and a ferocious tingling in her stomach. When his head finally lifted, she tried awkwardly to kick him and he laughed. "You won't get to Tibet if you muck up Tinetti's work."

When she pulled away with an angry cry and stumbled down the mountain, Miklos stayed where he was. His eyes were narrowed with desire; his body's readiness was quick and strong and wild. Eliza was right to run, for the turbulence within him was reaching a storm flood that would be hell to check.

The Cristallo Inn, Courmayeur, Italy: July 1, 1847

That night, severely shaken and uneasily wondering if Miklos's proprietary kiss might impel him to assert a more irrevocable claim, Eliza sat by her inn window, where she

alternately watched the narrow main street and started at
every footstep in the outside hall. The isolation of Como
made it a virtual prison, but her current situation in
Courmayeur was not much better. She should take her case
to the town magistrate, but how? Her room was on the
inn's top floor, three stories up; two knotted sheets would
dangle her just far enough to be severely damaged.

Sometime after midnight, when the gayly thronged terrace at the rear of the inn became deserted and the floors'
creaking ceased, Eliza crept to her door. Thank heaven,
Miklos was too complacent to take the key. As her key
squeaked in the lock, she held her breath. She peered into
the dim hall. Vincenzo peered back. "What are you doing
here?" she demanded, anticipating the answer.

"Good evening, *Signorina.*" He straightened in his chair
opposite her door and waved to the two doors on either
side of her room. "I am here to see the family is not
disturbed." His foot shifted as if to nudge the boy drowsing at his feet. "You need something? Shall I have the boy
fetch the innkeeper?"

I need wings and a trumpet, Eliza decided blackly: one
to get out of here and the other to fetch the devil to haul
Miklos Sztarai down to where he belongs! "I should like a
bottle of wine." She wanted to get wildly drunk.

Vincenzo nodded, tapped on the door to her right. After
a moment, a blond head poked out. In Italian, Vincenzo
relayed her request to his master. *El maestro* smiled
sweetly, shook his head, and went back to bed. She slammed
her door.

Though during the next several days Miklos did not
attempt to kiss her again, Eliza was slow to relax. What
was she to do? His kisses left her with the brains of a
rabbit. If he hauled her to bed, nothing would be left of
her but flying tufts of fur!

Miklos would have been intrigued to know the cart
donkeys made Eliza almost as uneasy as he did. Only
stubborn craving for adventure impelled her to tolerate the
pillow-packed wicker cart that bounced along the moun-

tainsides. To climb or ride sidesaddle like Bette so soon
after her surgery was out of the question, and she would
not have attempted riding if her life depended on it. As
reward for braving the cart, she was able to walk, if not
run, in the mountain meadows as she had dreamed of.

The pain, though now equally distributed in both legs,
was no worse than before the surgery, so she could be
grateful Dr. Tinetti had done no more damage. Midway
through the holiday, the pain gradually lessened.

After dinner every evening, they all sat on the inn's
terrace to enjoy the brilliant stars and a vigorous band of
green-waistcoated musicians who had a great capacity for
wine and cheerful racket. Eliza refused to go to bed early,
but due to the altitude, her eyelids invariably drooped
during the third course.

She actually fell asleep once, then drowsily found Miklos
carrying her to her room. She was too exhausted to do
more than mutter at him when he laid her on the bed.
Taking longer than she thought he ought, he slipped the
pins from her hair, skeining it out over the pillows. In the
uncertain moonlight, she had an impression, brief as a sigh
of wind in lindens, that his hard face looked sad, as though
he were losing something he would never have again. His
eyes had darkened as if night had closed on a high, hidden
valley filled with roaming, wild creatures who left no trace
of their passing save whispers and small cries. Loneliness
crept through that night, luring her to follow. A flicker of
pity must have shown in her eyes for he abruptly left her
alone. Possibly, he had gone to a black-eyed servant girl
who'd been brightly flirting with him. After that, Eliza
stayed awake over dinner.

With great good luck, the mayor and his wife, and the town
magistrate and his daughter were among the town officials
present at a party at the Cristallo the evening before the
Sztarais' return to Como. Eliza made a beeline for them,
only to have her arm commandeered by Miklos before
she'd gotten six feet across the lantern-lit terrace. "One
word and you won't get a *lire*," he murmured.

"You never mean to settle," she retorted, straining to break his hold. She might have tried her strength against a steel manacle.

"I haven't decided," he purred, his gray eyes narrowing, "but I do dislike being rushed, and yonder bourgeois will dislike being put into an awkward situation." As if ardent, he drew her inflexibly toward him until the top of her head nearly touched his cravat. Sharply, she lifted her chin to stubbornly meet his eyes. "I am in Italy," he went on, "at the behest of the Emperor Ferdinand of Austria, who is an awesome fellow to embarrass, even a bit more awesome than Charles Albert, whose guests you and I are. That fat mayor, his inept magistrate, Ferdinand, Charles, and I will cheerfully paint you as a lunatic rather than allow you to cause us an ounce of trouble." His lips brushed her ear. "Do you understand?"

"You can't keep me a prisoner," she hissed. "This is the nineteenth century and I'm not your property!"

His complacent smile was insufferable. "The degree of your being property is indicated merely by the degree I am disposed to pamper you. Like it or lump it, nineteenth century liberalism has rarely uttered a peep in behalf of wives."

"I'm not your *wife!*"

He fingered the plum ruffle at her shoulder. "In ten minutes, given a flight of stairs, I can remedy that."

Eliza couldn't read those opaque gray eyes. If she made a fuss now, the magistrate couldn't force her to stay with him, even by Italian law. At worst, she'd be stranded penniless for months, then have to go back to New York. At best, she'd have to hold out a few more weeks, months . . . years? Could she really bear to wait until Miklos finally made up his mind?

Surely if he meant to keep her, he'd have said so by now. Unless he was trying to bring her to heel. Surely, kisses could be nothing to him, could be only meant to tease and keep her off balance.

Besides, in spite of the surgery, perhaps because of it, he knew she had never been so well off in her life;

whatever his motives, she could now walk virtually without pain. He was like a falconer, letting her fly from his tower because he was certain she would return. One day she would surprise him!

"I see the stairs. What if I should agree to be remedied?" she purred, her lashes sweeping up over topaz eyes glittering in challenge. Her bluff got instant results.

He recoiled, his eyes narrowing with suspicion quickly erased by his usual, laconic smile. "Perhaps I don't relish feeling like a prisoner any more than you"—his smile curved ironically—"still, I could make love to you, then lie about it later. The doctor's examination didn't include the state of your virginity." Seeing she longed to slap him, he laughed. "Don't worry. I'm satisfied your chastity is intact." His voice lowered teasingly, "As to what remains to be satisfied, we may discover that together. We do have a truce, do we not?"

"The truce ended the night you let Tinetti carve me up," she replied flatly.

"So, all's fair now, is it?" His forefinger looped through the velvet ribbon around her neck.

"Neither of us has ever had any intention of being fair. My position doesn't allow it and I doubt if you know the meaning of the word."

The glitter in her eyes brightened with defiance, making him wonder for a moment if she would be so fiery in bed. Whether he could make that taut body, that fierce spirit, yield to him. She'd been too startled, too angry, to kiss him on the mountain, but he'd stirred her. She was as much afraid of herself as him. Only he had never wanted her to be afraid. He wanted her to be bold and confident and demanding of him. Kissing her was like taking a storm in his arms. Being inside her . . . He thought of her lying on the bed in the moonlight, her darkening eyes as he had looked down at her. Love between them would be soft, hard; never without the magnetism inexorably drawing them together. She was warily watching him now, uncertain what wickedness he was thinking. Sweet wickedness, my virgin bride, that we must never taste together, lest it precipitate our craving and destruction. His finger reluctantly disengaged her ribbon. "Ah, how sadly you misjudge me. Go, *Signor* Potbelli the mayor and his minion await thee. Embrace the *signor's* chubby knees and tell your tale."

Eliza had seen conflict in his eyes, but misread it for political machination more than desire. She reviewed the well-fed *signor* and his equally comfortable wife and daughter. "No, thank you. You've made your point about his awe of emperors." Her head cocked. "What are you doing in Italy for Ferdinand?"

Miklos almost laughed. He might have known that balked on one track, her energetic mind would quickly jump to another. His fingers light on her arm, he strolled her toward the punch table. "Very little, really. I rate among his more insignificant affairs of state."

"You're a diplomat?"

Her mild skepticism didn't surprise him. His Parisian, dark blue suit might suggest a diplomat; his darkly tanned, Magyar face and broken nose didn't. "In a quiet sense." His lips quirked sardonically. "The less I do, the happier Ferdinand is." He poured a cup of punch for her.

"But no one comes to the villa at Como. Aren't diplomats at least expected to charm the citizenry of their assigned country?"

"Don't you like the peace and quiet?" He handed her the cup.

"I don't like being cut off from the world."

"But you may leave Como any time you like." He chose a salmon canape. "The one thing you may not do is return."

"Why would I?" she muttered defiantly.

His eyes glinted impishly over his cup. "Perhaps for another kiss."

Her "Ha!" sounded strangled.

Lake Como: August 3, 1847

The next day, Eliza returned to her twenty-eight room honeymoon cottage at Como. Homecoming was not warmed by her husband visiting his mistress on their first night home.

When Miklos went up to Vanda's bedroom, she was in dishabille, pulling on her stockings in her dressing room. He knew the stockings were timed for his knock. She kissed him lingeringly. "Umm, playing mountain goat never takes the goat out of you." She stroked his shoulder, then offered him a humidor of cigars. "Playing with that little boy you married doesn't either . . ." Miklos's hand altered its course from the humidor and applied a firm swat to her satin-covered rump. The humidor lid snapped shut. *"Bastardo!* That hurt!"

"Become a bit plumper and it won't. My 'little boy' hasn't your weakness for pasta." Miklos reopened the humidor with apparent disinterest. "Just when did you make Eliza's acquaintance?"

Her black hair tumbling about her face, Vanda gave him an arch look. "Some time ago. She didn't tell you?" Selecting a cigar, he didn't answer. She laughed with mocking amusement. "Then your little boy has guessed about us. I thought so."

So that's why Eliza was so distracted that last day on the boat, Miklos realized. "I'd forgotten she mentioned your inspection. First week in March, wasn't it?" He seated himself in a deep chair and nipped off the cigar tip.

Studying his face, she lit a match from the astral lamp, expertly held it below his cigar. "I know I promised to stay away, but you were such a clam, darling, and you haven't visited me for so long. I couldn't stand not knowing any longer."

"Knowing what?" He drew on the cigar.

"What do you think?" She sat on his lap and rubbed her bare shoulder against his. "Miki, you can't be bedding her. She's still in braids!"

Suspecting she had jealously spied on Eliza and him

from the boathouse garden, he smiled peacefully. "I plait rather well."

Her eyes rounded. *"You!* Surely those clothes aren't your idea, too?"

"Marvelous little derriere Eliza has." His eyes became dreamy. "A man can imagine only so much under crinolines."

She glared. *"Dio mio!* You *are* bored!"

"On the contrary. I can't recall a single night that Eliza has been boring."

Furious, Vanda snapped to her feet. "Then why are you here, sneaking into my bedroom while my uncle is gone to Rome? Why are you not *there*, *boring* her?"

Miklos had considered bedding Vanda again to relieve the mounting difficulty of keeping his hands off Eliza, only he had ceased to want Vanda, had scarcely thought of her since Eliza had come into his life. Not that Vanda would be terribly hurt. She was a mercenary as much as any Swiss guard, except her battlefield was spread on satin sheets, and she took her pay in influence and rich gifts. He patted her cheek. "Would you rather have me say goodbye in a note? We've shared many amusements, *cara*, but now we must go our separate ways."

With a practiced, delectable pout, she shook her head. "So you've got a fresh little wife who's temporarily amusing; that ends so quickly. You and I have entertained each other for a long time. Don't torment me by staying away all these months, eh? Since this whey-face came, I never see you." She teased his ear. *"Caro*, we've always understood one another. Why didn't you just marry me and do as you like? I wouldn't have complained about a dozen women."

"As you do now about just one."

"You could have had a match of your own standing, estates, more titles . . ."

"More trouble."

Her eyes flashed. "Why, what do you mean?"

"Your Aunt Sophia's portrait downstairs bears a certain resemblance to Lucrezia Borgia."

Her voice cooled. "Don't be insulting. We Bellarias were poisoning unwanted mates before Lucrezia cut milk teeth."

He grinned. "That gives one such a sense of confidence."

Slyly, she shrugged. "Just remember, if you ever want to be rid of your skinny little wife . . ."

Abruptly, he caught her chin hard. "Don't you think I can manage it?"

Sourly, Eliza envisioned Miklos as a lecherous satyr among her bedroom nymphs. One of his hands adroitly caressed a milk white breast as the other stroked a pouting belly. Cheerfully, he grinned at her own disapproving face.

Nibbling a strand of hair, she imagined Miklos and Vanda making love, then hastily tried to unimagine them. The idea of Miklos naked, caressing another woman's body, created a strange fluttering in her belly and hot fury in her heart. She went back to sucking her hair and sizzling.

Bang, bang! Sharp raps on her bedroom door jolted Eliza upright in her bed. The door opened a handspan and a blue lump of cloth sailed into a chair. "Swimming lesson at seven o'clock!" called Miklos smartly.

How dare he perform for Bellaria all night, then show up as frisky as a seal! "I haven't had breakfast," growled Eliza.

"After you flail a yard or two."

"Didn't you get enough exercise last night?" she retorted acidly.

Miklos was silent for a moment, then thrust the door open and strode to her bed. "You ought to have your bottom spanked for listening at keyholes." Clad only in knee-length briefs, he was all blond fur and muscle, and the bedroom walls seemed to evaporate.

"I don't have to listen at keyholes," she lied, grabbing the covers up. "I could have heard you eagerly pounding out of here last night if my head were stuffed under a pillow."

His bare hide earthy and immediate, Miklos bent over the bed with his hands barricading her. "Perhaps I enjoy moonlit rides."

Her chin lifted impudently. "Whatever you're riding, I'll wager it doesn't have four feet."

His chin neared hers. "You're not in a position either to wager or comment upon my habits"—his eyes scathingly raked her high-necked, flannel gown—"and speaking of habits, I'd like you to be out of that one and into that bathing suit in ten minutes; otherwise, I shall go to the lake and sail hereafter without you." He patted her cheek and left.

She wasn't about to give up sailing, not after being rearranged by Tinetti and doggedly exercising every day. And didn't Miklos just know it! She threw back the covers.

When Eliza looked at herself in the skirted bathing outfit, she nearly flinched. She looked tiny and pale and bony. Then she grimaced. Even Vanda Bellaria's curves would look silly festooned in this middy. And Miklos would hardly be encouraged to "exercise" with a balletic penguin.

He laughed. When he saw Eliza march out of the house in her overlarge, laced bathing shoes with the lank middy bow hanging aflop like a sick bird, Miklos threw back his head and laughed. "Forgive me, Eliza mine, but I'm not responsible for the quixotic priggishness of women's dress. Tomorrow we'll find something else." Still chuckling, he waved her to the jetty.

Miklos was a good teacher. Patient and firm, he understood Eliza's fears of the water at the same time he ignored them. She whined, she whimpered, used every trick she'd learned in childhood to avoid being humiliated by venturing beyond her depth. As if deaf, Miklos prodded, teased her past the point where she could rely on any footing beside his, on anything but her own nerve and capacity to learn. The cold water made her newly healed muscles ache; under her breath, she swore at the cold and him. The only thing she did not do was cling to him any more than necessary.

The next morning, Miklos was true to his word. Going through her lingerie drawers, he hauled out a cotton camisole and pantalettes. "Here. Better indecent than depressing."

With a cautious eye out for the servants, Eliza emerged from the house. Her skin was a pale shade of blue. Every bone still showed, but to considerably more advantage than in dank woolies. Just how much advantage reflected in Miklos's darkening eyes as he eased his robe about her shivering shoulders on the jetty. She flinched, afraid he was naked under his robe, then saw he wore the previous day's bathing tights; they revealed far more than her own attire, which gave her no great ease. The way they clung to him in the water made her begin to be desperate.

When wet, the briefs sagged well below his waist, baring the slope of muscle down his abdomen, the curling hair that changed to gold wire near his groin. There, the dark briefs shaped the long, shadowy outline of his manhood, its promise of invasion and potent dominion. The symmetry of his back, his powerful arms and shoulders, were wonderfully male; only when his lower body was hidden beneath the water, she fancied him the satyr from the boathouse willows. In this still, dreaming dawn, his eyes were pagan, mysterious, bewitched, and bewitching. Gray as the circling mist, they never left her; his hands were slow to leave her when they gentled her nervousness of the water. A treacherous spell was woven about them both.

And what she was thinking was unthinkable. She tried to fight temptation with logic. She'd begun to realize Miklos mistrusted his touching her as much as she did. He had backed off from his threat to bed her in Courmayeur, too. If she need *not* fear his consummating their marriage, she had a strong bargaining leverage in ending it. Eliza took a deep breath to clear her head. Forcing herself to appear relaxed, she edged closer to him. "Shouldn't I learn to float?"

"Probably not," he muttered. "Lie back."

She obeyed, her eyes widening as her neck touched water.

"It's all right; I've got you." His hands pressed against her back and thighs.

Staring fixedly up at the trees, Eliza wondered if water were going to run up her nose; and worse, if Miklos were going to dispense with his amatory reservations. Her eyes flicked to his; they were focused on her breasts as if he thought they might slip free of their nearly transparent restraint. In rising panic, she was about to thrust free of him when he dragged his gaze away to have it involuntarily land on her navel, then quickly to the overhanging willow where her own gaze had been so determinedly placed.

A nervous laugh welled up in Eliza's throat. Her nose went under and she flailed. When Miklos caught her up, she scrambled away, coughing. He looked vastly relieved to have her at a distance. Made braver by that distance, she managed a casual front, then sneezed. She wiped her nose. A tentative, then confident smile began to form in her brain. Miklos desired her, all right, but he wasn't going to do anything about it! Seeming to guess her source of amusement, Miklos eyed her grimly. "Porpoise," he ordered, "blow bubbles."

She went under in a mass of bubbles, came up, and spat a stream of water accurately between his eyes. "Porpoise, Papa?" she inquired sweetly.

Before she realized what was happening, she was crushed into his arms with his flat-lipped, marauder's mouth hard on hers and his big hands firmly cupping her small bottom. She abruptly realized the extent of his arousal. With a frantic squeak, she squirmed, and Miklos's hands tightened, his kiss deepened. His tongue hotly probing her mouth made her dizzy, momentarily distracting her from complete fear by its unfamiliarity, its adroit certainty.

Her head felt hot, her breasts prickly. Trying to twist away only made the length of his sex at her groin seem more unnervingly hard. He was arching her back, his lips trailing down her throat to brush the swell above the lace edging of the camisole, to sear hotly against the cold roused peaks of her thinly covered breasts. Gasping at the exquisite sting, Eliza frantically pulled at his hair. His strong teeth knowledgeably closed on a nipple, his narrow hips fitting to hers until her hands trembled, stilled, tightened in a different, surprised way. Until, although still frightened, Eliza stopped fighting him, her head slipping back as her body moved uncertainly to seek his.

With a stifled sound of exasperated regret, he abruptly let her go. "Tomorrow," he gritted in her shaken face, "wear that damned middy!"

That night, Eliza stared into her mirror as if she'd never seen herself before. Not once in her life had she thought of herself as a young, desirable woman. A scrawny, unappealing girl: yes. A skinny, tight-lipped spinster: yes. A withered, eccentric old woman: yes. All these she had and could dismally imagine, but a woman who could attract Miklos Sztarai? *No*. Perhaps the routine, the boredom of the villa had made him less particular about bedmates, perhaps the mere proximity of a female . . . but no again. She touched her lips. She had never been kissed by any man but Miklos, but she needed no great experience to know his embrace held a hunger that was perhaps more than any woman could appease; yet he seemed to feel she, innocent as she was, could answer that need. How was that possible when Vanda Bellaria, a vision of desirability, had not more than momentarily satisfied it?

Eliza thought of not appearing for the next morning's lesson, but did, to prove to herself and Miklos she was not a coward . . . after she crammed on the middy.

Possibly, she need not have bothered. For the next several days, Miklos virtually looked past her tense head as he matter-of-factly directed her through the intricacies of coordinated flailing. Finally, she relaxed and he thawed. They began to laugh together and she eventually learned to swim to a degree sufficient to pass his standards for sailing again.

"Do you know," she told him in the late afternoon of their first time back out in the boat, "that on the water, you're less grumpy than anywhere else?"

His lips quirked as he eased a sheet. Her sunburned nose was peeling and she looked sixteen in her boy's garb. "Poor Bluebird. Have I been so horrible?"

"Frequently," she admitted, then on reflection, "but not as bad as I thought you'd be."

"So you arrived here thinking you'd be fed to an ogre."

"Bones, beak, et al."

"And now you've decided you can stand me."

"Um." With the wind spilling her pale hair, she idly hung from the halyards. "But I'll never trust you."

He laughed, leaning out against the gunwale. "You trust me every day: not to let you go too far when you swim and to lynch yourself when you sail. Not to"—he shifted abruptly forward—"seduce you."

Her grip on the halyard tightened. "In little things, yes, but important ones, no. I'm not forgetting Tinetti and his knife."

"Then perhaps you'd prefer only a little seduction."

She eased from the halyard back to the bow to fiddle with a cleated line. "Little? An elephant in heat must be more subtle."

"Ah, well, your wet camisole the other day could have set off a whole herd of rogues less impetuous than me." His recollective grin widened.

Settling against the gunwale, she grinned back. "At least you have the grace not to be repentant."

"Not in the least. I often think fondly of that moment."

"So long as your affection is restricted to memory." She dragged her fingers through her damp hair and tossed it back. "That was the last moment you'll ever get."

His grin turned wry. "Pity, isn't it? We did seem to get on."

Yes, she thought with a faint flush as she unwillingly remembered the excitement his bare body against hers had roused; we did and do. He was wearing frayed, white cottons now; she half wanted to touch his tanned skin, half wanted to replace his missing shirt buttons for him. She didn't like to sew and he could always toss the shirt to a servant; yet somehow the knowledge that he had no woman who cared for him to do his mending made her a little sad. Isn't it odd? she reflected. We're like brother and sister at times like these, only at times like *those* . . . God help me, I like the way you kiss, Miklos Sztarai. I don't think I want to know what else I might like.

Miklos didn't miss the softening in her expression, the gentler line of her mouth. Roughly, he wiped the spray from his face. He didn't want to recall kissing her, that slim, unconsciously sensual body in his arms, her last, surprised response he had wanted but not expected. It startled him, inflamed him until he came within a breath of losing control—control he *had* to keep. Until she was gone . . . and he was alone again.

She no longer hated him, but his elation was quickly dulled. The time to let her go had come at last, and that realization made him go numb at heart. "I grew up on a lake," he said suddenly, unevenly. "Balaton. It's wild during storms; the colors are forever changing." He could not keep the longing for home from his voice. "When the surface is peaceful, it dreams of all its sunsets and sighing winds."

Don't make me even think of loving you, Miklos Sztarai, Eliza thought suddenly. Then fiercely, I won't. Don't tell me what you're thinking. Lie and smile and leave me alone.

But she was not to be left alone, nor was he. When they docked, Bette was waiting with a letter. "Well, dears, you've had your honeymoon. We've company."

Chapter 6

The Crow Is Plucked

Lake Como: August 15, 1847

"Miklos!" Enzo Rossi slapped his cousin's damp-shirted back. "You're looking well." His attention fixed on Eliza's tanned face and sun-streaked hair in the golden, garden sunlight. She was surefooted, with wonderful legs; and fit as a colt. Also, she wasn't nearly as flat-chested as he'd imagined. She was damned fetching and Miklos damned jealous of his intent perusal. "Both of you look well. You must be spending a great deal of time outdoors."

Miklos smiled at Eliza as if they shared a private secret. "Not all of it."

Noticing everyone staring at her, Eliza smiled sweetly back. What was Miklos's game this time? They'd barely had time to leave the boathouse when Enzo and his companions from Rome had met them on the walk. Bette made introductions while the stylish visitors took in her unconventional outfit. Now they were positively fascinated with her.

With slightly narrowed eyes, Miklos looked around at Enzo and his friends. "Your coming was quite a surprise. Your letter just arrived."

Dapper in his white linen suit and straw boater, Enzo grinned sheepishly. "If I'd written earlier, you might have put me off again. I confess I've been envious. After all,

I'm the one who married Eliza.'' He put an arm about her shoulders.

With her sunburn and breeches, Eliza began to feel like a mouse being appropriated by two indolent, pampered tomcats. She oozed away from Enzo with an elusive, but slightly forced laugh. ''Actually, I'm not married to either one of you, and I'll thank you to remember it.''

''You don't mean''—despite the gossip in Rome, Enzo managed to look startled—''you two still . . .'' He grinned at his stoic cousin. ''Come, Miklos, this is unlike you.''

''Yes, Miki,'' teased Marianna, the pretty, pink-frocked redhead at Enzo's elbow, ''most unlike you. Such a bad boy to desert so many sad chorines at La Scala.''

There were three of them besides Enzo: Marianna's lover, Paolo Tourni, a young lawyer; Guido Sidoro, a bespectacled journalist; and his artist wife, Bianca.

The press, Eliza thought grimly. *Bête cousin* Enzo brings the press. I smell another Bette behind this one!

For the rest of the day, Eliza clammed. All Rossi's charm, their guests' friendliness, Bette's nudging and Miklos's persuasive patience could not urge her to conviviality. Finally, Rossi and his crowd gave up and Miklos and Bette's exasperation began to show. As soon as possible after lunch, Eliza retired to her easel and paints.

Still, even in the far reaches of the park, she could not completely escape from Bianca, the journalist's darkly attractive wife. ''That cypress sketch is quite good,'' she observed.

With an inward sigh, Eliza looked up. On another occasion, she might have liked to paint Bianca's gypsy face. ''Thank you.''

''Your work reminds me a little of John Constable's.'' With no apparent concern for her lilac lawn skirts, Bianca Sidoro settled on an adjacent rock. ''The drawing is bold for such a quiet young lady. I shall be curious to see if that energy endures into the finished work. Constable sketches bravely, but his paintings often lose something.''

Reasonably certain Bianca Sidoro was less interested in art than prying, Eliza twiddled her charcoal. ''Then I fear you will be disappointed in this piece, for I do not rival Constable.''

"Not yet, no. Still, I should like to see a woman rival the male gods of art. Have you ever tried etchings?''

"I've never thought of it.''

Bianca peered closely at the sketch. "The trick is to forget constraint. Etching can lead one to tediousness.''

Stoicly, Eliza resumed drawing. "Perhaps I should forget etching. I'm a tedious sort of person.''

Bianca gave her an inscrutable smile. "If so, you wouldn't be still with Miki. He can't bear tedium.''

Eliza's charcoal hesitated for an instant. "Then he has chosen a strange occupation. I should think a diplomat's life must be boring to some extent.''

"Miki, a diplomat?'' Bianca paused as if considering a novel idea. "He has diplomatic privileges, I suppose.'' Her black eyes studied Eliza thoughtfully, then her parasol shadow veiled her face. "If I may ask, what did you know about him when you left America?''

"Enough,'' said Eliza shortly. *Signora* Sidoro certainly had no aversion to personal questions.

"Yet you still came.'' Bianca closed the parasol and slowly traced its point along a faint trail of rabbit tracks that marked the damp earth. A few feet away, they disappeared under a moss-covered cypress root. The umbrella point jabbed a paw print, then another that led toward the moss. "You *are* bold.''

Eliza fought strong impatience and growing unease. "Why do you say that?''

"Exile is rarely amusing.''

"Are you inferring Miklos has no choice about living in Italy?'' Though utterly startled, Eliza made Bianca's revelation sound absurd. Miklos had discouraged personal questions, and while curious she might be about his past, she considered revealing too much of her curiosity to Bianca Sidoro unwise. Was Bianca after scandal to feed her journalist husband? Or something more?

Bianca was not easily put off target. "One does not disagree profitably with emperors.''

So Miklos must have needed official permission to visit the Pennines, Eliza suddenly realized: her operation hadn't been the sole delay. And she wagered he hadn't been in London at Christmas; that was Bette's fabrication for the benefit of Roman gossip about the wedding. She turned to Bianca with full interest. "Just what do *you* suppose would happen if he returned to Hungary?"

"He'd be thrown in prison."

"On what charge?" She hoped she didn't sound as shaken as she felt.

"Oh . . . disobedience would suffice."

Then the villa gate confined Miklos as surely as it did her, Eliza perceived with shock. The bowmen were both his protectors and his jailers. Poor Miklos! How a man with his pride and ability must hate being so confined. But why was he here?

Distractedly, she tried to collect herself. Miklos's bride was no more than his cellmate. Sympathy could trap her with him. Those kisses that made her explode inside might leave her just another stick of his and some emperor's debris. With tears stinging behind her eyelids, she pressed too hard on the charcoal; it snapped.

"If I've distressed you," Bianca said quietly, "I'm sorry."

"I'm less distressed than curious about your customs. Americans are unaccustomed to imperial government."

"Emperors are enthroned on habit." Bianca rose and put up her parasol. "Habits can change . . . and so must I for dinner. Are you coming?"

"In a moment. I want the last light."

"A good idea." Bianca turned to view the scarlet sun setting against the pale, hyacinth sky. "We may all soon see the last light of many things. Best to capture it undistorted by memory."

At dinner, Eliza could tell Miklos was irritated with her deliberate dreariness. Not that he was less polite; he was too polite with the martial calm he could assume like a cloak, making himself seem bigger and her smaller. He kept talking to her black dress, not her face, and he hated the dress; that's why she'd worn it. She needed every shield now.

He and Enzo and Bette, even Bianca Sidoro, were all trying to maneuver her, but she wasn't going to budge. She'd gone back to stage one, when she'd known who she was and what she wanted. Even Enzo was daunted by the dress and Bette had finally been squelched. She should have felt triumphant. She felt like a crow.

Next morning, Miklos gave her until midmorning to reform, then prevented her playing the crow again by plucking every feather.

She'd evaded playing croquet with the others by keeping to her room through breakfast and most of the morning. Sitting in her nightdress on the rug, she glumly read *Othello*. By the time she had grimly reviewed Othello's dispatch of Desdemona, Miklos came into her room without knocking. He'd been riding; his boots and breeches were stained and muddy as if he'd bulleted through a marsh. His shirt was sweat stuck to his skin and he'd taken a briar cut across a cheekbone, white with barely suppressed anger the reckless ride hadn't battered out. Ready to fight or run, Eliza scrambled to her knees. Miklos tossed the book out of the window, then went to the wardrobe and in two armloads hauled out every dress, frowsy hat, and wrap. In a grim cascade, they emitted from the window before the startled eyes of the croquet players still considering *Othello* by the third wicket. Was a strangled wife to follow? After the first large dropping plummeted shoes, parasols, then a flutter of grandmotherly lingerie. All accompanied by a long, unbelieving screech.

"You, you *Nero!* You *Prussian!* You . . ."

"I want that nightgown," Miklos interrupted firmly.

Any last traces of sympathy for him scattered to the winds, Eliza scrambled away. "Touch me and I'll bite! I'll scratch those icy eyes out!"

"I am in no particle German but if you don't surrender that nightgown, you won't have a stitch left on your nude, New York rump!"

With a howl of fury, Eliza dove under the covers. A few seconds later, the required object was hurled in Miklos's face.

"I warned you I was tired of carrion couture." He tossed his crow's last feather to the winds and strode from the room.

Ten minutes later, a small figure marched onto the lawn. With a great deal of dignity and tripping, Eliza advanced like a disheveled tart in a toga. Marianna let out a giggle; Paolo, a gasp. "Is that a sheet she's sporting?" Guido whispered to Bianca.

"Nothing but," she replied in wonder.

Eliza skirted Miklos, whose jaw hung slack until it slowly rose and bunched.

"I think I heard his teeth click," murmured Bianca.

Clutching the sheet at her shoulder, Eliza selected a mallet, shuffled to the ball, and gave it a cracking whack aimed at Miklos's skull. With fortunate inaccuracy.

With far more accuracy, he was after her in seconds. Scampering away, she swung the mallet in a wide arc to fend him off, but on the back swing, could not manage sheet, mallet, and Miklos. The mallet went sailing and Eliza, kicking and clawing, went over his shoulder. His jaw leading the way, Miklos hauled her into the house.

"They don't seem to be getting along," mildly observed Marianna.

"On the contrary"—Bette gave the croquet ball a toss in the air—"good head-butting rows are more exciting than billy goat glands."

"Damn!" A fingernail caught Miklos's cheek as he dumped Eliza on her bed. "You weasel-tempered little . . . !" He dodged another swipe. Grabbing her wrists, he pushed her down and straddled his weight across her thrashing body.

She glared up at him in pure fury. "Now they know! Everyone will know this marriage is a farce. That you've married a woman who can't stand you!" The stark pain that lanced through the rage in his eyes shocked her. Uncertain, baffled, she stared up at his unguarded face.

"I wonder how much you can stand," he muttered. His hands tightened on her wrists, then hard and demanding, his mouth covered hers. She jerked, bit. She felt him flinch, tasted his blood as he kept his mouth clamped to hers. Then his hands left her wrists, slid to her armpits, her breasts beneath the sheet; with his determined caress moved fear and excitement. She was beginning to want whatever he was going to do and her mind howled defiance . . . only her damned, treacherous body was supply molding to his hands as if it were melting.

She pushed at his shoulders, caught his hair. Her head flailed as he stroked her nipples, then slid his fingers lower to the liquid warmth between her thighs. She went rigid as a finger slipped inside her. Though gentle in his exploration, his probing moved steadily inward as his mouth continued its maddening distraction. She twisted, gasped at a tiny stab of pain. In that startled moment, his tongue thrust deeply into her mouth. Involuntarily, her hips lifted to evade the pressure, only to find him pressing further within her. The more she squirmed to escape, the more sensitivity he found, beginning to stroke her rhythmically, expertly, until her hands clamped his head, her tongue entangled his as she awaited that next thrust with humiliating urgency. And when it was slow to come, moved to take it for herself. His sex met her eager body, making her gasp at his deception, his velvet hard shaft that invaded her with aching fullness, a desperate hunger that answered her own. The drive of his body quickened, the burning ache of him within her mounting, sparking into needles of scarring heat. Then wildfire flared, an untamed lightning that played over them both to leave their desire still smoldering ash.

Branded with the first, irrevocable knowledge of passion, Eliza dazedly gazed up at Miklos to find his eyes brilliant, intense, his body taut as if restrained by invisible wires. He hadn't planned what had happened, she knew. He'd been as furious and unthinking as herself. His eyes, as her own must be, were still clouded with brooding desire. His mouth was bloodied and she was suddenly aware of a slight trickle of blood between her thighs. His fingers went to his mouth, came away tipped with scarlet. He flicked the sheet away and gently touched her there, mingling his blood with hers. "Say what you like," he whispered huskily, "I say you're mine."

If she denied his claim, all his restraint would snap. He would possess her utterly and nothing again would be as she had planned. He would rule and she would not be ruled. She bit back defiance and tasted his blood.

His lips curved crookedly. "Why is your silence always a lie?"

"Force begets and feeds lies. Surely as a soldier, if not a man, you've learned that."

His cheekbones went white, then the tautness went out of him. "I don't want to go to war with you, Eliza. Always you will lose." His eyes locked hers. "Your body is now your traitor; when I touch you, it will never be faithful to you again. This we both know. What began with force did not end so. Your willing virginity is mine."

He was right. He could use her, then turn his back on her any time he liked. "What are you going to do with me?" she murmured unevenly.

Miklos was unsteady himself as he swung his legs off the bed. Just because they had gone to bed together didn't mean they should stay together. He much doubted if a child had been conceived in a single instance of lovemaking. He should tell her she was free to go . . . only he had a black idea that feckless, womanizing Enzo would feature in that departure, and she would sadly rue any intimate connection with Enzo and his friends. Aside from practical reluctance, he just couldn't frame the word *go*. His mouth crooked in a rueful smile. "I seem forever unable to make up my mind. Maddening, isn't it?"

Still couldn't make up his mind?! Eliza felt a volcanic mixture of pain and rage seethe high. She'd make up his mind for him! "We created a scandal today," she reminded him abruptly. "You with your dictatorial dumping of my wardrobe; me with my mallet. We were better than a Punch and Judy show. I could claim rape and everyone would believe it now; particularly if it reaches the papers à la Guido Sidoro. The marriage contract would be nullified. You'd have to pay.''

He sighed as he stripped off his sweaty shirt. "Money. You are singularly dull about its capabilities.''

"I'm not dull about the realities of being without it, but what would Your Highness know about a poverty of money? Have you ever been poor?''

"Have you?'' Deliberately, he tossed the soiled shirt on the luxurious carpet. Sweat-sheened and bare to the waist, he looked like a magnificent beast.

Refusing to be intimidated, Eliza sat up, tightening the sheet about her. "No, but in New York, I've seen six-year-old children in sweatshops. I've seen ten-year-olds selling themselves on the streets with torn mattresses waiting in dirty alleys. I've seen men and women old at thirty.'' Her eyes dilated with rebellion, she rose to her knees. "If you've trouble making up your mind, I haven't. I don't want to live with you. I'm going to leave with Enzo. If I don't take the contract settlement with me, I'll go to the pope.''

His hip outthrust, Miklos gave her an almost peaceful look. "Take a lesson from my vacillation, you little moneygrubber. Never reveal your plans.'' Then he sauntered out.

No good to fume and give way to her pain, Eliza decided, determined to govern her passions. She'd lost her head and more with Miklos. Desire had swept over them both like an unpredictable storm on the lake. All because she'd been fool enough to lose her temper. Fool enough to want Miklos for a few, mad moments that must *never* happen again. Even as that resolve hardened in her mind, it brought numbing desolation.

She was not given the luxury of recovery. Miklos was scarcely gone five minutes when a quiet peck sounded on the door. Eliza collected her sheet. "Who is it?''

"Bianca Sidoro. Are you all right?''

"Of course." She heard a sound of relief.

"May I come in? I've brought you something I think you may need."

Eliza opened the door. Bianca entered with her lilac dress and crinolines over her arm. As Eliza closed the door, Bianca held out green silk shoes. "Everything's a bit large, but you'll agree that sheet isn't quite the thing this year."

"Oh? I was thinking of wearing it to dinner."

Bianca laughed. "I believe you would. I suppose Miklos deserves it." She held the dress up to Eliza. "He led a wild youth, I gather, but he's not much given to reckless-ness of late."

Eliza caught Bianca's quick glance at the bed's sugges-tive stain. "How fortunate I didn't meet him when he was really impulsive." She relieved Bianca of her offerings. "Thank you for the dress."

"Of course," Bianca replied pityingly as if to add a silent, "poor thing."

Though she wished for her croquet mallet again, Eliza was obliged to indulge Bianca's supposition of rape if she were to maneuver Miklos. She even limped a bit as she went to drape the dress over a chair.

At dinner, everyone stared expectantly at Miklos and Eliza. Miklos stared blandly back as if he were not a rapist: Eliza as if she were not a rapee; the braver she appeared, the more believable her final, reluctant story would be. Enzo was miserable and furious with Miki; clearly he blamed himself.

The trouble was, even by comparison with the elaborate coiffures and silks of the other women, she looked won-derful. The low-necked lilac was the prettiest dress she'd ever worn, and her suntan gave her cheeks a glow by candlelight. The maid had threaded her long plait with vivid pink camellias and pearls. She looked golden and flushed and expectant. Lest that glow become suspect, Eliza turned it on Enzo as if he were a white knight come to her rescue.

Miklos became abrupt in conversation. To hide his jealousy, all his cool arrogance came out. With his rugged, pagan good looks making Enzo's patent leather polish seem effete, he was witty, aristocratic, insufferable as a diamond with too many carats.

Predictably, with tension running high, Enzo shortly picked a quarrel with him. The foil was politics. Like a swordsman, Enzo scampered and pricked from all sides while Miklos patiently held him off with experience and a longer reach.

"Miklos, the liberal cause is on the move," Enzo stated. "Austria and the Piedmont will soon be a battlefield."

"You've been predicting revolt on all fronts for years, Enzo," Miklos returned imperturbably. "Only the French government's like a dog unsure of which political flea to scratch first." With a trace of boredom, he lounged back in his chair. "Austria, Hungary, and Russia haven't had a popular revolution in centuries. Here in Italy, the common people just want full stomachs. Instead, they're fed high-flown treatises in words they don't understand. Intellectuals are a puny minority."

"We're not so puny now," Guido put in, squinting through thick spectacles. Eliza was surprised to hear him say anything; Bianca said everything for him. His lank hair thinned from a high, polished forehead and he had a long upper lip with a thin moustache that reached tentatively for jaw-length sideburns. He was an unlikely match for his vivid wife, but then perhaps Bianca's desire to rival "the male gods" decreed a tractable mate. Guido leaned closer to the candlelight. "The pope himself is behind our liberal cause and so is your mentor, Charles Albert."

" 'Behind' is a good word. Pius IX is inclined to liberalism, yes, but I think he's already in deeper than he wants; the same goes for Charles Albert, who's a monarch, not a republican. If Charles fights here in the Piedmont, it will be to tame his opposition and annex Lombardy and Venice. The locals don't welcome him here."

"Under Austrian protection, *you* won't be welcome, either by the locals or by Charles, if war breaks out." Delicately, Paolo Tourni buttered a roll. He was about Enzo's age, with a modest portion of his good looks. He had a lively sense of humor but, Eliza suspected, little depth and an eye to the easy mark.

"In that event, what would you suggest I do?" Miklos asked mildly.

"Join us!" asserted Enzo. "That may be your only chance. You're wrong about the revolutionary movement and I think you know it. The old ways are tottering; with a hard enough push, they'll collapse."

"My position has been chosen for me, gentlemen. I cannot join you and in honor maintain my diplomatic status, which excludes meddling."

"What *are* your concerns, Miki?" Enzo's olive face was flushed with exasperation. "Balaton and Hungary? With us, you might have all that again, or would you rather rot at heel on Charles's leash?"

"Being leashed imposes less restraint than being hanged." Miklos negligently waved at the fabulously appointed room. "You must concede Charles's kennel has its comforts."

Among them a new bride, considered Bianca. She well understood the lapse in Enzo's customary suavity. When she had informed him about Eliza's stained bed, he had been disbelieving, then furious. She barely restrained him from calling Miklos out. "Something strange is going on between Miklos and Eliza, Enzo. What he does with her may explain what he did with Loise, give us a weapon." She had rested a consoling hand on his arm. "I think Eliza knows less of his past than she pretends. If so, she's curious now, which also gives us a weapon. Gain her confidence; she may come to see you as her best way out of this mess . . ." She pinched his flushed cheek. "Come, be your charming self, eh?"

But, as Bianca resignedly watched him at dinner, Enzo wasn't charming. He wasn't even thinking. Eliza Hilliard had become the sort of conveniently towered damsel he was so fond of mooning after, but the guardian dragon he baited was no easily cuckolded, paunchy dimwit. Besides, Enzo rarely assisted damsels out of their confinement; he merely consoled them.

After dinner, everyone retired to the terrace. Arranging their skirts like false flowers, Bianca and Marianna sat on the padded settee across from Bette while Enzo, Guido, and Paolo moved to the end of the terrace to smoke . . . and mutter. Miklos, disinclined to join them, walked Eliza down to the drive. He looked almost conventionally handsome by the moonlight that silvered his hair and softened his angular features. Just now his face was contained, undisturbed by his argument with Rossi. His sleeve on Eliza's arm was a little rough, warm, and very real. War and revolution seemed unreal to her, particularly with Enzo as an agitator.

"Miklos," she asked as they strolled along the rose- and cactus-lined drive, "why does Enzo want to involve you in sedition?"

"He thinks he's doing me a favor." He toyed absently with her fingers as they wandered across the dew-sparkled lawn under a blaze of stars. "Liberals in all countries want what you Americans have, only in European style, produced by guillotines and gallows, which always leave a nasty mess."

"What about his friends?" She glanced back at the group silhouetted by the terrace windows.

"Paolo is a utopian dreamer, Marianna out for excitement. Guido is ruled by Bianca, who is dangerous."

"Dangerous? An artist? A woman?"

"Why so surprised? Your croquet ball might have cracked my skull today."

"Perhaps that ironclad skull might improve with ventilation," she retorted impudently. "Did it occur to you when you so forcefully displayed your couturial tastes, that you'd left me without a stitch of clothing? If Bianca hadn't lent me this dress I'd indefinitely be stuck with that sheet."

He paused, turned her to him. Night made her soft, hazy as a wayward gypsy star; so elusive she scarcely touched the earth as she came to peep at mortals with secret amusement. "Damn Bianca," he said softly as he wound her flower-woven plait about their necks. "I prefer the sheet." Then, he kissed her.

At first, Eliza started to pull away, then rapidly lost any desire to relinquish his mouth—hard–soft, coaxing, so easily lulling her into pliant complicity . . . until she remembered the guests on the terrace, and the role she was to play for them. Enzo, having seen their embrace, was striding toward them. Breathlessly, she pulled back. Miklos was only further asserting his domination. If he'd guessed her gambit, he might be trying to checkmate her with this public display. Enzo, in particular, looked bewildered by her first, unthinking response.

"Don't!" she said loudly enough for the others to hear as she backed away with a swirl of crinolines. "You can't make me believe you're not going to hurt me as you did this afternoon. Hit me again if you like, but I won't give in!"

Miklos stared at her as dead silence fell. Bianca hurried down the steps and clamped onto Enzo's arm as, bewildered no longer, he furiously quickened his stride. When Bianca firmly reined in Enzo, Miklos's eyes took on a knowing glint.

"Pout all you like, but I won't pay for an all pink wardrobe. And if you ever come for me with a mallet again, you'll think that piddling crack on the rump was a pat!"

Eliza halted and glared at him, but had to stifle a severe urge to giggle. He'd wriggled out of her trap in the blink of an eye. He guessed her amusement for she caught a flick of a grin. "Very well," she informed him meaningfully, "but tonight I'm locking my door."

"*Je suis désolé.*" His voice lowered. "But I look forward to making up."

"Don't go gray waiting," she whispered sweetly.

That night, alone in their room, Bianca and Guido had a low-pitched, vehement argument. "Now, Guido," Bianca finally told her husband flatly. "We'll never have a better chance at him. We must risk it *now!*"

Chapter 7

Life Among the Wolf Pack

Lake Como: The Next Morning

Eliza's nose twitched. Still dreaming, she rubbed it, flopped over into her pillow. Now something scratched her cheek. She squirmed, pushed it away. Heard a laugh. Her eyes flew open and through a barricade of creamy organza, she saw Miklos grin down at her. Sitting up, she swatted the organza away, then realized it was a dress. She was afloat in a sea of dresses that covered the bed. Silks, laces, lawns, organzas. Dainty silk slippers with ribbon laces; tiny, jeweled flowers for her hair. Hats of fine Italian straw. Bright mandarin caps with tassels, airy mantillas, and cashmeres. Outrageous, luxurious pearls of satin lingerie. Clouds of petticoats and crinolines. Involuntarily, she squealed.

Miklos laughed again. "Will this wardrobe last the summer?"

"The summer? It will last until I'm old and gray!" She pounced on a leghorn hat, put it on, then palmed its veil across her face.

The grin softened on Miklos's features as her pale hair tumbled about her bare shoulders. Her eyes, bright and childlike, womanlike and mysterious as they sparkled through the veil, would be little different when she was old. What would his be like when he was gray and she was not there in all her kaleidoscopic moods? To keep that

prospect at bay, he held out a small, brocaded casket.
"These are simple, but they should suit you."

The casket's little collection of jewels *was* simple, but
as she'd never worn any but her mother's ponderous pieces,
Eliza thought them perfect. "They might be meant for a
child." She held up a tiny gold and diamond locket in
delight.

"In a way they are," he murmured.

Not knowing what to look at first, she hardly heard him.
"All these beautiful things can't be meant for me," she
murmured dazedly. "The clothes must have taken months
to have made."

"Dr. Tinetti took your measurements to a Milan
seamstress."

"And he got them while I was still chloroformed."
Laughing, she still had the childlike look. "I shouldn't
accept such a splendid present. I shouldn't trust you." She
let a mantilla slide through her fingers. "But you might
have Tinetti carve on my head, if I don't try on everything
. . . oh, Miki." Her flushed face lifted. "No one's ever
done anything like this for me. I never dreamed of having
such lovely things."

His head cocked teasingly. "But isn't money all you
said you wanted from me? This is what money buys." He
sat on the edge of the bed and temptingly dangled a
slender, pearl necklace. "Which would you prefer, your
limp or oyster droppings?"

Her flush deepened under the gauzy veil. "I don't understand . . . all this, Miklos. You could just ignore me,
whether you decide to keep me or not."

"Mallets aimed at my head are difficult to ignore."

She gave him a puckish look. "Given your medieval
manners, I haven't been unduly unpleasant, have I?"

"You've been more cast iron than cream puff, I admit,
but while cream puffs only grow stale"—he lifted her
veil—"iron can melt."

She watched him uncertainly. His gold-lashed eyes had
taken on a tawny warmth as if, like hers, they were full of

dreams and longing. "Is that what you're trying to do? Melt me?"

"Perhaps." His lips brushed hers. She felt something hard within her dissolve: her fear of him, the urge to keep fighting him. His kiss was sweetly tender, as if he were kissing a little girl. Then, surprisingly, he drew away. "You're radiating heat already. You ought to wear nothing but a hat more often." He wove his fingers through her hair where it met her slender, sun-browned shoulders, let it whisper free to curl about the hollow of her throat.

Eliza had never hoped to have a man look at her as if he'd found a princess of fable. Miklos made her feel rare and lovely, even light-headed. Seeming strangely hesitant, he kissed her again, his tongue lightly probing until her eyes closed. Her lips parted to let him browse until he probed deeper to meet her own tentative, curious little tongue. Her fingers brushed his cheek, the corner of his mouth on hers. As he eased off her hat, her head slipped back against his arm. His lips moved to the softness of her throat, her shoulders, the curve of her breasts with their creaminess translucent in the morning's lambent sunlight. She caught her breath, feeling his nuzzling tease the sheet lower, then heard his delighted sigh. "You've a lovely body, Bluebird; your worthy mother must have deplored every inch of it." When she laughed, he wonderingly stroked the lily curve of her breast to its peak; her laugh turned breathless. "So sweetly soft for iron, so sensitive," he murmured against her flesh. His mouth closed gently on the honey rose crest, luring her, caressing her until, seeking the warm sun of his mouth, she bloomed. Her body arched against him. Then froze, as they both stiffened at a sharp sound.

"Miki? Darling, are you in there?" The rap insistently came again.

Eliza was choked by shock and anger. Her eyes turning to ice, she shoved mightily, if uselessly, at Miklos's broad chest. "You skunk! You could at least keep your floozy from sniffing my door!"

"I didn't invite her here, Eliza," he said sharply, catching her hands.

"Then send her back to her den," she hissed, twisting away from him, "or I'll raise a stink for all the rest of our uninvited guests!"

"Miki!" trilled the voice. "Have I mistaken our room again?"

He let out a short, exasperated sound, then let Eliza go. "Don't threaten me, Eliza. You haven't Vanda's seniority." He rose with a brief swat on her rump. "Wear cream; she's the color of dead kippers in it."

Cream?! She'd like to drown Bellaria in cream! Cottage cheese! Rancid butter! Eliza pitched her hat at the ceiling, then sat drumming her fingers on the satin coverlet. Gradually, boiling fury reduced to a speculative simmer.

Cream, hm? Angry as she was, she'd been invited into a conspiracy with Miklos, but why should he side with her against his mistress? Was he bored with Vanda Bellaria? Had she become too demanding, too sure of herself? The latter seemed likely, given her astounding boldness of a few minutes before. While Eliza considered she couldn't compete with Bellaria's charms, she did hold, if crazily, the advantage of being Miklos's wife. Why not go along with the game? The whole idea stirred her wicked sense of mischief. The day should prove lively; Bellaria was sure to show more fight than a dead kipper.

Had anyone told her she was vain before this moment, Eliza could with justice have flung the accusation in his teeth; however, as she walked into the drawing room where everyone gathered before breakfast, she learned she had lost the virtue of modesty; its reversal had a seductive, unabashed appeal. She *was* vain. She loved the admiration in the men's eyes; relished the startled reappraisal in the women's, particularly the hard stare she and her cream, Venetian lace dress received from Bellaria.

"What a wisp of a bride you have, Miklos," purred the *contessa*, circling Eliza's exquisite tiers of ruffles. With narrowing eyes, she surveyed the peach rose behind Eliza's ear, the coral and pearl necklace about her throat. Eliza's complexion was dew, her hair gossamer, her golden eyes as challenging as those of a proud young lioness confronting a rival sniffing her mate. Bellaria ironically paused under the wall tapestry's horned unicorn; on one side preened the treacherous damosel, on the other gathered the hunters. "Yes, Miki, she's quite a find. So virginal."

"Two husbands have made Vanda appreciative of the art of innocent deception, darling," drawled Miklos, putting his arm around Eliza's tiny waist. "I was just telling her how delighted we are she has called on us at long last; so long, in fact, she appears to have forgotten the location of rooms where she and Charles Albert played as children."

"Surely you cannot put the blame upon time, Miki," Bette wickedly observed. "Vanda isn't much over . . . thirty."

"Ah, yes," agreed Miklos, blandly appraising his angry mistress. "Nefertiti might envy her skills."

"And so might your new *principessa*," sharply returned Vanda. "Expertise is one quality you appreciate."

"Miki is a marvel, isn't he?" Eliza smiled adoringly at her husband. "So easily pleased."

As Miklos gave his bride a fond, if forceful squeeze, his aunt made a stifled sound as if she were squeezed in Eliza's place. "Shall we go into breakfast, ladies and gentlemen?" Miklos returned mildly. "I believe the morning menu features kippers."

No, decided Eliza as they all wandered into the garden after breakfast, life among a "civilized" wolf pack was not dull. Best to escape before the sniffs at her turned to bites. In his current rash, guilty mood, Enzo just might help her get to Rome.

If she did not leave now, Miklos might regard the contract as sealed and keep her. She was a toy to him, relief from the ennui of a country squire. When he ceased to be amused, she would become another indistinguishable, if animate, part of his estate furnishings, his prison become hers. Her hateful diversion would be to have him bed more Bellarias.

Would she be able to forget him? Not likely. He had made his mark on her, whatever his reasons. She understood him far less than he understood her. She poured a second cup of tea at the terrace table. Whether he was a good man or not, she didn't know, only that he had been kind to her.

Would Miklos hate her for desertion? For the half lie she would tell in Rome, the ensuing scandal? He would perhaps despise her, but he surely could not miss her enough for hate. Her apparent ingratitude he would understand and not condemn. To him she had not needed to explain craving a life of her own; he had seen it in her face in the Pennines, in the sail-swelling wind off Como. He knew she would do anything to have it.

She had seen things in his face, too. She watched him idly strolling with Paolo and Guido, his head inclined toward the lake as he half listened to them. For him, the open water represented freedom he had lost, perhaps never had. How long could living creatures survive in cages? Eliza put down the tea, barely tasted. She would miss him terribly. She didn't know which she hated more: losing him or regretting his loss.

She noticed Enzo watching her from the boathouse garden. Suspecting he would follow, she walked toward the lake in the opposite direction from Miklos and his companions, who had paused to watch Bette, Paolo, and Marianna at croquet. As she reached the shoreline, Enzo's footsteps sounded on the grass. "Eliza, I want to talk with you." Jarring with the debonair nonchalance of his linen suit, his face was worried.

She said nothing, baiting him.

"I didn't know what was going to happen," he said urgently. "I never thought Miki would force himself on you. He and I have been friends since childhood."

"So you said in New York." She turned away.

"Miklos isn't what you think," he said harshly, "at

least, he wasn't. I ought to know him that well." He came close to her shoulder. *"I'm* not what you think."

"You're a procurer." She looked up at his smooth, perfect face. "Only in this case, the woman wasn't practiced, even paid. What were you paid, *Signor* Rossi?"

Anger, indignation, shame, swept his features. "Nothing! What do you take me for?"

"What does it matter? Can I hope for restitution from you?" Tensely, she stepped toward him. "I'm desperate for help. Will you give it?"

He was silent a moment. "What do you want of me?"

She darted a glance toward Miklos watching them from across the garden. Guido's spectacles glinted as he leaned against a pine. He muttered something to Paolo, who turned toward her and Enzo. "We can't talk safely here. Let's take out the pram."

Shortly, only the creak of oarlocks came over the water as the shore receded. The villa was pink-chalked among the palms and yellow roses that spilled over the lower terrace parapets.

"All right," Enzo said, resting the oars in the blue, glittering current. "Tell me."

Wishing she'd brought a hat for dignity's sake, Eliza brushed the wind-ruffled hair from her face. The braided loops her maid had concocted behind her ears were slipping, the peach rose beginning to tickle her bare shoulder. She gave the loops a resigned poke. Demure femininity had never been her forte. "I want you to take me to Rome to the pope. I have grounds for annulment, the proof, and witnesses to get it."

Enzo considered. He was perspiring, his linen jacket clinging damply to his shoulders. She could tell he was thinking of Miklos and his aunt's reaction, probably his family's as well. "I'll take you to Rome," he said at last, "but there's no need for scandal. Once you're out of reach, Miklos will let you go. Quietly, with an income. He will expect only that you say nothing, ever, to anyone about the cause of separation." He plucked uncomfortably at his sticking jacket. The sky was cloudless and heat shimmered mercilessly off the water. As the boat drifted farther into the lake, the shorelines faded in the white haze.

Enzo fought his cravat, finally got it loosened. "Your . . . nervousness about intimacy, Eliza, is known in Rome. You need only reiterate it. Miklos will be embarrassed, but free to remarry. The gossip will be trivial."

She frowned. "You're sure of all this?"

"I'm sure. You will stay with my sister in Rome until everything is settled. All will be very properly familial."

Guiltily, she shifted on the pram seat. With perspiration trickling between her breasts, she impatiently brushed damp hair from her forehead. A contract was a contract. Miklos hadn't precisely claimed her virginity with scrupulous fairness. He might be as unpredictable in a pontifical hearing. Besides, why should she feel guilty about being conniving if he didn't? She squinted at Enzo. "What if Miklos claims I'm lying?"

"He won't. He can't afford the noise." Then he added softly, "I wonder if you've really thought this out. Being a bride agrees with you. You're becoming lovely, you know, and it's more than laces and ribbons." He hesitated. "Eliza, many marriages are less than perfect . . . and Miklos offers several advantages."

"You're the one to play cupid," she scoffed.

"Miklos always has been a hero, almost a god, to me until yesterday." Enzo looked wistfully at the diminutive figures of the three men mounting the villa's terrace steps. "I suppose I haven't adjusted to thinking of him as less."

The shame edging about her mind bit hard. In his way, Miklos had been a god to her, too. This morning's presents had been nothing compared to the whole body, the new life he had given her, not to mention the fresh air inside her skull. To make him less than what he was, was shameful.

But to exchange her life for his pride? She couldn't. Too much of the world remained yet untasted, and he had brought its cup within reach.

After agreeing to take the dory at dawn to Bellagio,

where they would board a coach for Rome, Enzo unshipped the oars. "We'd better get back before Miklos grows suspicious."

Suspicious? Eliza trailed her fingers in the rushing water as Rossi hurriedly pulled at the oars. *Miklos can read your mind like a book, just as he can mine. The question is, will he rewrite, or tear out the pages?*

When Miklos met them ashore on the boathouse steps, she suspected the last. His craggy face was as forbidding as a bleak glacier on a stormy day. At his curt, "I want a word with you, cousin," Enzo paled to a sickly gray.

What sort of man is Miklos that everyone is so easily afraid of him? Eliza wondered as Miklos steered Enzo away along the shore path. Worriedly, she took the bricked walk to the villa. For all his bravado at dinner, Enzo *was* genuinely afraid of Miklos now.

So quick and quiet was Eliza in going to her suite, Bianca and Guido did not hear her pass their room. And its faint, acrid scent, Eliza slowed, frowning as she sniffed. What an odd odor, only . . . it smelled familiar. It reminded her of . . . now why should she think of tea? It smelled nothing like tea. Preoccupied with the prospect of escape, she hurried on to pack.

Minutes after she began to stuff a carpet bag in her suite, the king arrived.

Charles Albert, King of Piedmont-Sardinia, made an impressive show: outriders, a blinding gold, baroque coach, footmen, a regiment of Italian guards, baggage carts, and a wagonload of sweating servants streamed through the flame-tipped gates. Miklos, Guido, and Bianca didn't look surprised, but as everyone lined up to greet the king on the terrace, Bette, Paolo, and Marianna were dumbfounded and Enzo appeared horrified. Bellaria, Eliza noticed, wore the practiced smile of a tinware peddler.

Though passably handsome despite a lantern jaw, Charles Albert had rounded out by his late forties. He had large, wary eyes, a proud, fleshy nose, and a schoolmarm's mouth. Given a dress instead of his overly snug uniform

and lavish gilt braid, he might have been transformed into
a wealthy dowager. He greeted Miklos and Bette with
reserved cordiality and reviewed Eliza sharply from head to
toe. He waxed urbane with Bellaria, whom he studied in
an entirely different manner. The remaining houseguests
met with less approval. Though meticulously polite, he
recognized Enzo, Guido, and Bianca as liberal agitators;
Marianna and Paolo, he assumed, were from the same
hatchery. Eliza sensed displeasure. Enzo and his friends,
perceiving the same attitude, soon found excuses to return
to their amusements on the front lawn.

"I had not realized we were to be such a full party,"
Charles muttered as he walked between her and Miklos
into the house. When they passed the Rubens nudes in the
foyer, he turned his not altogether friendly attention to
Eliza. "Perhaps *Signor* Rossi and his companions are *your*
guests, *Principessa?*"

Eliza led the way into the drawing room. "Indeed not.
Signor Rossi, as Miki's cousin, needs no invitation, and as
for his friends"—Eliza caught Bette's uncomfortable
expression—"I met them upon their arrival day before
yesterday." Strolling to the piano, she gave Miklos a
wicked look. "You must ask Miki about *Contessa* Bellaria.
She belongs to him."

The king gave an unamused chortle at Miki's wry smile.
"The *contessa,* I know." He settled himself into a brocaded chair and glanced at Bette. "A singular young lady
you've selected for your nephew, *Principessa.* Equanimity
in marriage usually comes late, if at all."

"I'm glad you approve, Your Majesty," answered Bette.

"Do I?" he muttered vaguely, then sighed. "I suppose
I must. Better everything settled and one less thing to
bother about."

"A great relief, I'm sure, Your Majesty," returned
Bette with a mild touch of irony. "Are things so dreadful
in the capital?"

"Unsettled, as usual." Pulling out his snuffbox, he
looked dourly at Enzo and his friends furtively talking
beyond the terrace windows. "Always unsettled."

If Charles *was* supposed to be on the liberal side, as Enzo claimed, why, Eliza wondered, did he look so uneasy in their company?

Despite his guards studding the lawn, the king's discomfiture did not lessen as the afternoon at croquet and bocce on the lawn wore on. He weighed every word and when conversing with Enzo's friends, seemed to wonder if once the word was uttered, he should swallow it. "What sort of man is Charles Albert?" Eliza whispered to Bette as they waited their turns at bocce.

"History will probably say, 'he confused his enemies . . . and friends alike'," replied Bette, restabbing a crystal-headed pin through her chip hat. "He's politically fidgety. Which makes everyone else fidgety."

"One can't trust him."

"Can one? Nobody knows." Bette picked up her ball, then neatly bored a path to the jack.

Charles Albert, despite his reputation for vacillation, could be depended upon to notice women, Eliza observed. His peeks at her, considering her recent marriage, were as amusingly furtive as a schoolboy's, but his rapt interest each time Bellaria bent over the ball could not be missed. Bellaria, in danger of missing his attention, managed an arch wag of her rump when she swooped into her toss.

After bowling with Bette, Eliza drifted back to the villa. She was not only curious about the king, but the Sidoros and their mysteriously smelly room. Despite the king's antipathy, the group from Rome were determined to stay at Como during his visit. They hadn't uttered a peep about politics to him; possibly, they meant to keep peace, but then again, persuading him to cement an alliance no longer mattered . . .

Speculation was spun out of her mind when she reached the house to meet Marianna and Paolo coming down the stair with their luggage. Rushing down. And embarrassed to be surprised at it. Marianna's hat was askew, its ribbons flying loose. Paolo dropped his Gladstone bag on the stair, scrambled up a few steps to retrieve it, then practically fell down the rest of the flight. "Dearest *Principessa*," Marianna said quickly, "we are so sorry to have to leave unexpectedly. Paolo has just had a message of life or death from a client." She heaved a hatbox up on her hip.

"Life or death, is it?" Eliza repeated evenly. "Surely the servants can assist you with your baggage." She turned to the servant bell. "Meanwhile, I'll have Vincenzo bring Miklos to see you off."

"No, no!" Paolo begged as Marianna, a valise, and the hatbox hurried out the door. "There's no need . . . no time." He kissed her hand. "So serious. My apologies. Thank you so much." He bolted after his mistress.

"Oh, yes. Yes, yes," called Marianna over her shoulder. "Everything so nice. You're all very kind." They threw the baggage into the landau drawn up behind the house and clambered after it.

Bemusedly, Eliza waved them off.

As the landau raced about the fir-banked curve in a spray of gravel, she glanced at the pendulum clock. The others would be coming any minute to dress for dinner, as she must. Only her most fetching frock would do. She'd get Enzo to Rome if she had to drag him by her corset ribbons.

And yet, as the maid fastened her into an off the shoulder, topaz watered silk, then clipped an emerald and diamond pendant about her throat, Eliza's guilt returned. Though she had no intention of betraying him in the conjugal sense, she was using Miklos's generous gifts to deceive him with another man. She sighed glumly. She had no right to the dresses and jewelry; to leave them for his next wife would be only fair. As the maid arranged diamond-sprayed cream roses in her clustered ringlets, Eliza bit her lip. Miklos's new wife: what would she be like? Nothing like herself, for certain. He'd either pick a high-bred, raving beauty like Bellaria or an affable sow who would breed him heirs and mind her business. She hated her successor already. Miklos needed a companion, an equal; not a bauble or bovine breedstock!

Still muttering to herself, Eliza went down to dinner.

Sensibly, she didn't flirt with Enzo; Miklos might have

unstuffed him. Miklos was jealous, but he was angrier
with Enzo than with her. Miklos's gray eyes fixed Enzo
until that unfortunate grew restless in his chair. Enzo
might have been stretched across his plate; never had Eliza
seen veal severed with such precision, forked with such
cold accuracy. What *would* Miklos do to Enzo if crossed?
Surely he wouldn't call out his own cousin . . . yet, she
would not want to put Enzo's life at risk.

She was inclined to squirm herself. Although Enzo studiously ignored her, and Miklos's conversation was occupied with Bellaria, the two rivals' attention often wandered
to her shoulders and cleavage revealed by the topaz silk.
Even the king, his affability increasing with each glass of
wine he downed, stole a peek or two between bids for
Bellaria. Only Guido was oblivious, fixing attention on his
meal. Bianca, too, was strangely silent, her hawklike profile pensive. Eliza wondered if she and Guido were concerned about Marianna and Paolo's abrupt departure.

Two hours later, Eliza knew a good deal more about
dancing than when she first waltzed with Miklos after
dinner. He had little to say; she had less. They might have
been dragging lead weights about the floor. When their
waltz ended, he surrendered her to the king. After the
king, she endured Guido. Enzo, pleading a headache,
morosely mooned over the punch bowl for a time, then
retired. Eliza longed to retire herself, but feared it would
look suspicious. With only five hours until dawn, she took
a cup of tea from the maid to dilute the champagne and
steady her nerves.

Again, Eliza thought of the smell in the Sidoros' room.
She was beginning to realize why the odor suggested tea:
both came from China. Suddenly, her memory came back
fully; she was thirteen and following her father around one
of his warehouses filled with exotically scented tea bales
off a Singapore clipper. He had unlocked a storeroom
containing a small keg nestled in a much larger box of
sawdust. The keg exuded the same acrid smell as the
Sidoros' room. "There you are, Captain. Straight from the
Han himself," Wilson had informed the army officer with

them. "Be careful with transport. One of these fuses blew the hand off a careless sailor."

Were the Sidoros keeping similar fuses? No . . . she was jumping to conclusions . . . yet under the heavy scent of Bianca's gardenias tonight at dinner, she had caught that peculiar tea odor again. Both Sidoros seemed tense, expectant; she wondered why.

Guido, as a journalist, might know something of chemical printing processes. Bianca, Miklos said, was dangerous. Enzo was worried that the king had come. Paolo and Marianna had wanted to get hurriedly away . . . something was going to happen that Enzo and his friends feared: something possibly to do with Charles Albert. Eliza's brow furrowed. An explosive? That might involve chemicals, with a fuse to allow the perpetrators to escape.

She slipped out of the French doors and, picking her skirts up, sneaked through the palmettos past the army tents pitched on the rear lawn. A pair of sentries paced apathetically before the main gate and another sentry by the baggage carts. The smell and sound of horses almost stopped her at the stable door. She hesitated, then opened the door a crack and peeped. The villa grooms were off duty, but a pair of the king's hostlers were asleep in the straw. The stalls were full of Italian regimental horses. She sidled past them with her arms rigid at her sides.

Her nerve was rewarded. At the rear of the stable, the Sidoro carriage was hitched to matched sorrels with the baggage compartment loaded. Another life or death situation as urgent as Paolo's?

Eliza smelled a large rat. The king, perhaps the whole household, might be in danger. What if Miklos were killed? She'd be free, a rich widow . . . at a price she couldn't afford. She couldn't bear the idea.

Oh, God. Her heart sinking, she almost sagged in the stable mire. She was in love with him; not by half, but head over heels. She had never been so shaken and horrified in her life. Miklos had coaxed, poked, prodded, and beguiled her, rumpled her wits until they resembled an unmade bed, then had taken her to bed and made her never want to get out of it. Her heart had gone the way of her virginity: sneakily. Tempestuously. Permanently. The cocksure bastard had won. And she couldn't run with popinjay Enzo until she was sure Miklos was safe.

Chapter 8

Things that Go Bang
in the Night

Scratch, scratch. Dressed in the most demure of her new lingerie ensembles, Eliza pecked at Charles's bedroom door just after two in the morning. The house had been silent for the past half hour. Should Charles prove aggressive, hidden in the folds of her peignoir was a fireplace poker. With heart-stopping swiftness, the door opened and she was snatched into the room. The door thumped shut. She was enveloped in a suffocating embrace made more repellent by a faint, acrid scent. "Vanda, *carissima!*" Charles's moist lips found her throat, traveled lower. Subduing her resentment, Eliza delicately kneed the royal groin. "Aarrh!" Charles sat on the floor.

"I *am* sorry, Sire, but the *Contessa* di Bellaria has been detained." With the poker under her arm, she hurried to the armoire.

"*Principessa?*" he groaned. "Oh, *per Dio,* I am gelded!"

Eliza tossed the poker on the bed, then rifled the armoire's contents. Charles had an overwhelming capacity for clutter. Clothes lay scattered everywhere. His gluey shaving gear was in the armoire's top drawer instead of the dressing room. This nincompoop, who couldn't rule his own socks and servants, ruled Miklos's life. With mounting exasperation, she peered under a pile of linen. "Your Majesty, you're in danger."

He rocked miserably. "Mere danger is an understatement. My sympathies to your husband. You're a diabolical woman."

Deaf to his bleats, Eliza checked the chiffonier drawers. "Your Majesty, do you smell something strange?"

"Madame, I am hardly occupied with my nose." He gingerly peered at his crotch.

Eliza upended his jewel case. Charles had enough medals for a prima ballerina. Her heart was beginning to pound. "Sire, I believe a bomb may have been placed in this room."

His eyebrows raised. "Bomb? What sort of bomb?"

"I don't know." Uneasily, she looked about. The acrid scent was stronger at the center of the room. "A chemical bomb, I think."

"At the risk of being blunt, Madame, what do you know of chemistry?"

"Nothing." She crawled half under the bed.

Perhaps Charles heard the last, perhaps he didn't, as it was muffled by bedding. At any rate, the appealing presentation of her derriere proved more immediate than the dubious prospect of danger. He crawled across the floor and, grabbing her hips, buried his face in the folds of her nightgown. Eliza gave a startled yelp, her head rocketing painfully into the bedslats. She scrambled forward, the king scrambled after with a broad smile spread across his features. For once, Charles Albert had made up his mind.

Miklos moved restlessly around his bedroom. Was he to have another brandy and face a lonely bed again tonight? He wanted Eliza. Like a relentless pounding in his brain and loins, he wanted her. He wanted her slim body against his, to share her passion and laughter and discoveries. He wanted to fulfill her newborn desire so unforgettably, she would never leave him . . . and that was impossible.

Wearily, he threw himself on the bed. After Loise, the last thing in the world he needed was to fall in love again and for months, no matter how he fought, he'd felt it happening. These last days, he had acted like a jealous stag guarding a mate he hadn't claimed. Eliza awakened every emotion in him that was better dead. She was a clear, still flame in his brain, glowing there until he could think of nothing else. Like a gift, she had come into his life: a gift that for both their sakes, he was afraid to touch.

And given a breath of a chance, she'd be gone with Enzo. He reared up again, poured a double from the brandy decanter. If he went to her now, he could have her. For a night, perhaps more. He could make her senses flame . . . but he could not make her love him. He lifted the balloon to his lips. Love was their only shield against the inevitable future. If he had one proof she loved him, the buttons would fly, and he would fight for her to the last breath.

At Charles's door, Bellaria invitingly slipped her peignoir off her shoulder and rumpled her hair. If Eliza's wind-blown mop could intrigue men, Bellaria was not one to shun success. She tapped on Charles's door, softly opened it, froze. She backed away from Charles's bedroom, ran down the hall, and scratched frantically on Miklos's door. "Miki," she hissed, "come quickly! Your wife is with the king!"

His door flung open. Depressed, exasperated, and frustrated, Miklos twirled Bellaria around and gave her a push back the way she had come. "Enough's enough, Vanda! Amuse yourself with Enzo tonight if Charles is busy."

She stared at him incredulously. "Don't you hear me, you great brick?! Charles is busy, all right! With your bratty, bed-hopping wife!"

Miklos's eyes took on the hot glow of metal in a forge. He thrust her out of his way, ran to Charles's door, and threw it open. To see Charles gleefully toss the wriggling Eliza onto his bed, then land atop her.

Seconds later, Eliza uttered a muffled shriek as Charles was jerked by the scruff into the air like an erring mastiff pup. "Just what the hell is going on"—Miklos's metallic stare bored into Charles's fearful one—"Sire?!"

"Urgl," gurgled Charles, his breath cut off. Certain his last moment had come, he flailed at the embroidered bedclothes.

Winded from the exertion of wrestling with the king, Eliza panted, "Don't throttle him, Miki! It's not altogether his fault!" Thanks to Charles's pawing, one of her negligee straps had snapped and a strategic lace butterfly between her breasts had flown. She scrambled to her knees and looked under the bed.

"Noble of you to share the blame." Miklos ignored the king's thrashing.

The king gurgled agreement. With a sardonic laugh, Bellaria slung her trailing peignoir over her arm. This show was better than a cabaret.

"For God's sake, Miklos, he's turning purple," Eliza protested. "I came looking for Guido's bomb, not him!" She sniffed. "We must be practically on top of it! Can't you smell the stuff?"

Abruptly, Miklos dropped the king and heaved Eliza over his shoulder. "Vanda! See to Charles!" And then tore down the hall with Eliza dangling over his shoulder. Vanda towed the coughing Charles in their wake. Clamping his arm tighter across Eliza's thighs, Miklos pounded on Bette's door. "Get out, Bette! Anarchists!" He passed Enzo's door without stopping.

"What about Enzo?" Eliza pushed up on his shoulder as the bewildered Bette stumbled into the hall.

"He's probably halfway to Switzerland with that bitch Bianca and . . ."

A roaring blast knocked Miklos off his feet. He landed atop Eliza, covered her face with his hands as wood splinters and plaster chunks flew. Charles and Vanda pressed against a wall as blue smoke belching from the king's bedroom filled the hall. Bellaria let out several whimpering squeals that rose to a healthy shriek. Covering his ears, Charles shoved his face against her belly. Hoarse moans shook his shoulders. Finally, Bellaria, satisfied she was intact, wearied of her shrieking and Charles's snuffles ruining her negligee. She pried him off, sat up, and began to brush plaster out of her hair.

"Dio mio, I heard a terrible noise," came Enzo's worried voice through the coughs in the gloom. With his nightshirt stuffed in his breeches, he pawed through the rubble. "What's happened? Is anyone hurt?" Choked negatives came back from the smoke.

Eliza had nearly blacked out when she'd hit the floor with Miklos's weight atop her; now her head cleared as if splashed with cold water. Enzo didn't run off to Switzerland, she realized wonderingly. He waited for me. Then she caught sight of Miklos's tight expression as his face closed over hers. He'd had the same furious glint when he'd first seen her torn negligee. "Do you know how damned delighted you look to hear that bastard's voice?"

"Do you suggest I take acting lessons from Bellaria?" Eliza retorted, vastly relieved he was too mad to be hurt. As fire in Charles's bedroom rouged the murk, her eyes streamed from choking smoke.

"Eliza," called Enzo. "I hear you. Where are you?"

Only half listening, Eliza dazedly wondered whether she would have to run to Rome in her negligee. She would have a hard time getting to the rest of her clothes. She couldn't think. Miklos's tormented eyes weren't letting her think. She had won. Beaten him at his own game, saved his skin, and now owed him nothing. She was free . . . and empty inside. Hopelessly, she gazed up at his taut face. Was she going to be empty for the rest of her life?

"Why not answer him?" Miklos gritted, flipping the torn strap of her smudged gown. "Or is it too smoky to tell which man you're under now this busy night?" He pulled Eliza up. "I've got her, Enzo," then lower, "for the moment." He pushed her toward Enzo who was groping toward them. "Take Eliza and the others out into the air before they're overcome."

Her hair in curler rags, Bette appeared with towels dripping from her washbasin and slapped them over faces left and right. "Miki's right. Get along. Don't dawdle."

Enzo caught Eliza's hand, then motioned to Bellaria to

assist the still-quivering Charles. Bette took his other arm and they stumbled past Miklos down the hall toward the stair. As Enzo steered her away, Eliza saw Miklos head alone back into the smoke. With a sharp jab of panic, she threw Enzo's hand off and ran after Miklos. "Eliza!" cried Enzo.

In seconds Eliza was lost with Miklos in the smoke. Hearing the others' voices grow faint as they hurried down the main stair, she stumbled along the hall. Smoke wrapped her in a suffocating blanket. She began to cough. Then she stumbled into Miklos, felt his arms go hard around her, so hard her last breath was cut off.

"What the hell, you crazy little . . ." He sounded dumbfounded, then kissed her angrily, fiercely.

"You . . . the crazy . . ." Half suffocated, half exhilarated, she punched him weakly in the chest. "You think . . . Guido left another bomb," she choked, her eyes streaming.

"It's likely," he rasped, "considering my politics."

"Then, damnation . . . let it blow! Charles can afford the repairs!"

She thought she heard a faint laugh. "I can't. I've already had you fixed once." He pushed her away with a firm swat. "Run along."

She lurched, but held her ground. "Two can search faster than one. And don't think I'm sentimental about widowhood. If they're as stingy as you, your relatives would contest the estate!"

Miklos was silent. Unable to clearly see his face, Eliza wondered what he was thinking. Staring at her from a dim cave of smoke, his gray, wolf's eyes held a strange intensity, as if her following him had impelled some sort of decision. Behind them, the stair was a murky wall. Suddenly, he grabbed her wrist and hauled her after him. He shouldered open a door, then kicked it shut behind them. She felt a chill tremor of fear and anticipation.

"Your room?" The air was far easier to breathe.

"Yours." He squeezed her hand. "If Bianca got caught

planting anything, she could say she came for her borrowed dress.''

"Bianca?'' Not Guido. Eliza was stunned.

Miklos didn't reply as he felt his way across the room to open the windows. Stumbling against a chair, he let out a muffled oath.

Barely able to make out her furniture, Eliza groped the bookcase. Moonlight from the windows was paling the smoke. Eerie, thickening wisps and curls seeping under the door coiled about the room. Dim shouts on the far side of the house indicated Bette and Enzo were turning Charles's escort into a fire brigade. "I don't think a bomb's in here,'' she said after a few minutes. "I don't smell anything.''

Miklos rifled drawers. "You won't if Guido made the bomb. Paolo probably contrived the other one; the timing's sure as hell off.''

That gave her an idea. She threw off the coverlet to rifle the foot of the bed. "He and Marianna were nervous wrecks when they left . . .'' She found a lump. "Miklos, come here. A lump where I noticed the smell in Charles's bed. You can hardly feel it.''

Gingerly, he massaged the lump. "Bianca gambled on our being too occupied making love for that. A highly romantic woman.''

"How do you know her so well?'' she asked suspiciously as he felt under the mattress, then eased out a slim, black box from a stuffing slit.

"She painted my portrait once.'' He carried the bomb to a moonlit table.

She followed, nearly tripping over a footstool. "And you just intuitively deduced she knew as much about bombs as paintbrushes.''

Presuming Eliza wouldn't be calmed by hearing Bianca was an anarchist whose brothers had been hanged, Miklos didn't answer. Something in Bianca had snapped when her brothers' necks had snapped. She would kill for principle, for pay, for piddling amusement. He slid out a vial, let out a deep breath and dropped it.

Eliza jumped as it flashed virtually in his fingers. "That's it?" she whispered.

"About thirty seconds more and you wouldn't sound so disappointed." He examined the rest of the bomb. "Then again; no one expects raves from a cinder."

"I feel ill."

"Basin's over there."

"I *know*, dammit," she said weakly. "It's *my* room."

"At least it's not Enzo's."

She halted midway to the basin. "You're not starting that again!"

"Enzo's bomb." His voice sounded muffled.

"You thought Enzo might have made this bomb . . . is *that* why you risked your neck? To examine that thing before it blew?" Feeling small, she sat on the slippery satin bed. She hadn't considered Miklos might value a man as much as his life: a man she'd persuaded to turn on him. "He means that much to you."

"Have you no one that matters?"

His eyes were silver and disconcerting by moonlight. She stared at her bare, plaster-dusted toes. "Besides my father, my dog, Cory."

He went back to perusing the bomb. "Where is he?"

"Probably digging up elk bones in Montana with Papa and his new family."

"So Papa and his shotgun are miles away," he murmured.

"What?"

"Nothing." He put down the device. "So much for things that go bang in the night, hm?" He smiled at her oddly and she was even more uncomfortable. He held out his hand. "Come, you need a breath of fresh air." Avoiding his hand, she headed for the door. "Not that way," he murmured. "Out the window."

She turned wearily. "Don't joke. I've had enough excitement tonight."

"Have you? Picking apart bombs has exactly the opposite effect on me."

Eliza was surprised at how little argument she made. Perhaps she was too tired, perhaps the hallway was still too smoky, perhaps she had grown too used to following his lead, but minutes later she had her peignoir tethered about her hips and was halfway down the iron rose trellis after Miklos. Hearing her swear as a thorn raked her thigh, he chuckled from the base of the trellis. "Problems? Haven't you tried this route before?"

"I strongly considered it the night we came back from Courmayeur," she said dryly.

"Oh? Why?" She could almost feel his wicked grin in the dark.

"I was restless," she gritted.

"Ah, yes. Restlessness is contagious." He stroked her bare, descending instep.

She let out a little shriek, snatching away her foot. "Stop that! I might fall!"

"Into the arms of your adoring husband."

She didn't like the way he perused her bottom; he was evidently imagining it bare. He needed no imaginaton at all for her legs; his cheek was practically brushing the back of her thigh. "It's high time we ended this 'husband' farce."

His fingers waggled an inch below her descending heel. "I completely agree."

She stopped stock still. "You mean it? We can end it tonight?"

Miklos put his hands firmly around her waist. " 'Til death do us part." Plucking her off the trellis, he carried her across the front lawn to the sailboat. She yelled like a banshee, but the others were on the back lawn of the huge villa, servants and soldiers fighting the fire blocking the sound.

"Why so noisy?" asked Miklos impishly as he passed the ribald satyr by the boathouse steps. "You should be delighted that like the king, I've made up my mind."

"Miklos, this is rape, plain and simple," she gritted, pushing at his shoulder and jaw.

"Not rape, nothing about it plain, and as for simplicity, my anticipation of your seduction long ago developed florid variety." He appraised her bare, kicking legs and lengthened his stride.

"Well, you're carrying variety too far when you had my bed available," she protested in exasperation. "Why climb twenty feet down a wall through a thorn bush and go off on a clammy boat?!"

"Privacy"—he carried her out on the boathouse-shadowed jetty—"otherwise, ten minutes after the smoke cleared, we'd have your would-be lovers knocking on your door." He deftly stepped over the gunwale, then dumped her in a pile of sails on the moon-white foredeck. When she immediately tried to scramble up, he swiftly tied her. "You'll forgive me for not foreseeing a crowd. I hope to more than compensate for dawdling."

"Just pay me!" she squalled, feeling panic rise. He was going to do it *now*, when in a few short hours she might have been free. "Marriage is so permanent! You can't want to . . ."

"But I do, I do." He cupped a hand to his tilted ear. "Ah, the ring of those vows."

She bucked against the ropes. "You weren't even at our wedding! You let another man flinch through every 'do'!"

"How could I know what I was missing?" He stripped off his smoky robe and tossed it overboard into the summer night. In the cloud-reflected, pale light, he looked taller than ever; his muscles sleek, hard planes. The fur pelt on his chest was a silver blaze trailing to his groin.

Snapping her focus above his neck, Eliza glared up at him. "Marriage will hardly be all roses and the heavenly chorus after you've indulged your curiosity! We'll be stuck with each other!"

"Rump to rump for eternity." He gave her rounded hip a fond swat and cast off.

"You must be drunk," she accused sullenly, knowing he wasn't. Grinning, he happily capered in a sailor's hornpipe about the deck. In face of that carefree, primitive display, she became desperate. "You may as well know I don't intend to have babies."

He ran up the sail. "Oh, you may have your heavenly chorus. Cherubim have a way of taking care of themselves."

"Before that happens, I'll be gone with the first man who catches my fancy!"

"He'll have a damned long way to reach if I've anything to do with it," he muttered. The water glittered past the hull in a gathering rush past the jetty.

Eliza sensed she'd struck a spark. "You think you're that superior?"

He gave her a long look, then taking the wheel, said quietly, "I've made mistakes enough, but I don't think you're one."

Feeling suddenly ashamed without being sure why, Eliza subsided. If she tried to find out why, she might be lured into this craziness with him. When he untied her, she would jump overboard and swim for it. If she was quiet enough, he might not recover her at night. Morning either, if she sank. She had never swum farther than fifty feet. *Wünderbar*. She could either be his wife or wed the weeds.

Off the inlet where he first taught her to fish, Miklos cast anchor. Then untied her. She hopped to a crouch and they eyed each other like wary ferrets. Finally, he asked mildly, "Care for a swim?"

She measured the distance to the dark, tree-massed shore. The Italian operetta moon had lazed behind a cloud. With the graceful, deceptive shadows of the lindens overhanging the bank stretching well out into the lake, the real shoreline had to be farther than it looked. Still, with no wind, the water was still and flat as a mirror. She might make it to shore, but better not appear too eager. "I don't have my old bag of a middy."

"It's too dark for me to tell whether you're wearing a bag, a box, or a necklace of beans."

She still didn't move. The moon hadn't played coy while they'd sailed from the villa. She's been entirely too aware of the intent, lingering way Miklos had watched her in her flimsy peignoir; where it wasn't recklessly cut, it was lacily transparent, and worse, ripped to the hip by the scramble in the explosion and the trellis rose thorns. The mesmeric lure of those gold-fringed, pale eyes was forging an unbreakable, unseen chain about her. Perspiration dampened her spine.

"I'm not going to rape you. You know that."

Oh, she knew that, all right. She also knew she had better stay out of his reach or she'd be mush running through his fingers. She took a deep, unsteady breath. The boat deck was narrow, the water wide. She leaped into the water.

Unfortunately, she hadn't thought of how to deal with the entangling peignoir. Miklos had. As she struggled to keep her nose above water, she felt the water surge as he jumped in beside her. Silk ripped. The peignoir went one way, she went the other. And could not have told where she was headed to save her life. Like a bewildered bat, she went round and round.

Until she heard a murmur. "Shore's to starboard."

She hesitated. He was lying. He had to be lying. She headed to port, banged into the boat. Gasping from shock and fatigue, she flailed back, into his arms.

"Calm, calm," he whispered and kissed her.

Though she was tensely clutching his bare shoulders, his kiss was relaxed, unhurried, so much so that despite the stirring in her body, she realized something. "You're standing on the bottom! That's not fair!"

He laughed softly. "Is it fair for you to have hair and eyes of Nieblung gold, the body of one of its guardian nymphs? Fair, to be elusive while you beckon?" Lifting her higher until the sleek, wet silk of her hair curtained their faces, he kissed her again and a beginning, mysterious heat within her separated her from the chill current. She felt grand, powerful, as if she *were* a nymph seducing a man who seemed more god than mortal. They were both caught in the spell, one ensnaring the other, entwining, bewitching, each luring the other into reckless, irresistible folly. Her lips parted as his kiss deepened, teased her tongue into exploring, tantalizing him. Then he lifted her higher yet to find her breasts, feel their peaks swell against his searching, caressing mouth, hear her faint moan as her body arched back.

When Eliza wound about Miklos's lean hips, she felt a delicate, insistent pressure between her thighs, no more than a brushing of his sex against hers, an enticing, pleasurable tingle. He dipped his fingers into her, gently at first, then as his mouth grew intent, his exploration became more urgent until a spark flared, burst within her, seeming to ignite the swollen points of her breasts. Her hips thrust against his hand, seeking the source of that sweet, strange fire. His fingers fluttered, making her gasp with sensation; then suddenly, before she could recover, the flutter gave way to a warm probing. Dimly, she realized his sex was easing into her body. She stiffened as her sheathing resisted. She began to ache at the fullness of him, but when she would have pushed away, he held her fast, his sex slowly invading her. She whimpered, then shuddered as he began to delicately thrust, opening her, gentling her. Making her tentatively relax, accept, until she clasped his head to her with a little cry.

At her body's surrender, Miklos, his muscles taut with effort to control the unleashing of his desire, sheathed himself, then stilled, let her grow accustomed to him within her. Aching, uncertain, she clung to his neck, her body's weight voluptuously poised upon his sex. Her body seemed to protest, yet yearn for the ripe fullness of him. His lips teased hers as his body began an easy rhythm, almost rocking her like a baby, lulling her into lying against him, letting him ease away, fill her in a flow of movement that played with the glittering current, with her. Coaxed that spark within her into a fiery flower that spread a tracery of licking, lacy tendrils to her very fingertips in a blossoming of desire and need.

"Please, Miklos, I want . . ." she whispered, but . . . what did she want?

Only he seemed to know. With a soft, exulting cry, he surged into her, let her feel the pent power in him for the first time, gave her that mystery she wanted, craved until the blazing, scarlet roses burst and showered within her in a needling pollen of fire. With the sparks, she rose into a swirling night of stars: great suns of blinding light and heat that arched across the blackness until where there had been void was now filled by the silver, splendid constellation of her lover. Beloved, she whispered in silent jubilation. Oh, my beloved.

With a long sigh, like a soothing breeze along the shore, Miklos relaxed against her, the ache of him inside her easing until he seemed to melt away. He touched her face as if he feared she were some starlit illusion that might disappear in another breath. He enfolded her in his arms and for a long time, held her wordlessly close.

Finally, they went aboard ship and toweled dry in the warm, August moonlight. After flinging seat pillows into the narrow deck well, he laid her down, then settled himself beside her. She let out a teasing sigh as they squeezed almost nose to nose. When she squirmed to get comfortable, his manhood involuntarily roused again. "You're like going to sea with a rhino, you enormous fellow." When he laughed, she reached down to cushion the prod in her stomach, then caught her breath in shock. "It isn't possible. You couldn't . . . all that couldn't . . ."

"Fit? Even a rhinoceros is adaptable about some things." He kissed her fingers, then returned them to his groin. "I'm much less frightening than you think." Eliza curiously traced his magnificent virility from blond-clouded base to pale rose tip, heard him draw in his breath as his flat belly went rigid. She froze. "Did I hurt you?"

"Hardly. I'm not that delicate."

"You feel delicate," she murmured. A pearl of moisture glittered under the rising moon. She hesitated. "What's that?"

He grinned crookedly as with careful casualness, he folded his arms under his head. "The dew of life. Spring. Birds and bees. Tonight I'm fairly spilling over with it."

His eyes widened as Eliza touched her finger to the droplet, licked it. "Dew with a touch of salt. You taste

like a sailor." Peeping curiously, she gave him a slight
squeeze. "Is there any more?"

His voice sounded curiously tense, muted, "Taste me
again and see." But then as she lowered her head, he
caught her gently but firmly by the hair that spilled over
his belly. "Another night, *cara*. I shouldn't want to startle
you."

"I don't understand," she said uncertainly.

He touched her then, smiled as she shivered, and showed
her the glittering moisture on his fingers. "This is partly
from me, partly from you. This is how I know you're
ready for me, that you want me to come inside you." He
caressed her tiny bud, watched her lips quiver, her irises
dilate as he stroked. "What do you feel?"

She laughed unevenly. "That you're tickling me, only I
don't want you to stop."

"And?"

"Dew," she whispered, her lips near his. "I feel the
dew."

He stroked her hair with his free hand. "Then cover me,
mia cara . . . as if I were the earth and you its blessed
dawn. Take from me what you wish, only leave me not a
desert."

Unsure of what he wanted, Eliza tentatively kissed him,
felt his lips part in invitation to kiss him more deeply as he
eased her atop him. Then, knowing, she opened for him
like a cloud for a soaring mountain peak. This time,
Miklos entered swiftly, surely, making her gasp against his
mouth. Involuntarily she rose, seeking to escape, yet wanting his sudden invasion. Defiant, tempted to explore this
new terrain of passion, she thrust against him, moaned in
swelling pleasure. Like a gathering, windblown storm, she
moved quickly on him, too quickly, not comprehending
her direction, his raw desire. He aroused her so quickly
that she cried out in sweet rage when he spilled suddenly,
shuddered, and stilled beneath her.

Her body rained away into a colorless shadow. Where
had the wheeling stars, the mammoth suns gone so quickly?
Ashamed, thinking him disappointed as herself, she whis-

pered at last, "I'm sorry, I couldn't hold back. I was too quick for you."

Miklos heartily laughed until Eliza thought the tears must have come. Gradually, she became furious. "Damn it, then I'm not sorry!"

He tried to quell his mirth. "*I* am. If you only knew." Drawing her down against his hard, furry chest, he hugged her with a chuckle. "That was quite a race. I don't think you realize I lost."

Her brow puckered. "I don't understand anything tonight."

"Don't worry. I predict from sound experience, you'll be an amazingly quick study."

She punched him in the stomach. "*Roué!* If you know so much, my mother said it was supposed to hurt. My father can't be so . . ." She flushed. "Why didn't you hurt me?"

He laughed softly. "Perhaps the practice you reprove."

"So you've had a virgin before?" she asked as if she'd just found herself kissing a cannibal.

He sobered. "Only once."

"What was she like?"

"Would you like me to discuss you with my next virgin?"

She was aghast. "You're already planning the next one?"

He drew her down. "Um. The next. And the next, and the next. All with golden eyes and impossible dispositions."

She kissed him again. "So you think you're going to love all these difficult ladies into lambs?"

Lingeringly, he kissed her back. "Any doubts?"

"Baaaaa."

This time she got the full display of stars.

Before dawn, Miklos felt the weight of the boat shift. Cracking an eyelid open, he saw Eliza, wrapped in a bunk blanket, pull the dory within reach. Shivering, she crept into its bow as she tried to keep it from bumping the sailboat side. Every muscle tightened in him, but he didn't move. She pushed off, feathered the oars. Still stiff, he listened to the drip, drip, drip minutely flaw the silence, then fade.

Finding the villa at night took Eliza some time. The fire was out, leaving only a smoky haze darker than the mist against the skyline, but thanks to the lack of wind, the smoke stayed more or less put, allowing her to follow its scent. Shipping the oars, she crept along the villa's deserted jetty seawall. "Enzo," she whispered as she eased the dory into the looming cavern of the boathouse.

A dark shape bent down to catch the bow. *"Dio,* where have you been? I thought you'd never come. I've been going out of my mind with worry."

"I was with Miklos."

"Of course, I know . . ." he began, then hesitated as the odd note in her voice registered. "Willingly?"

"More or less."

"And rather more as the night passed," he said tightly, now making out the blanket and her bare shoulders.

He looked like a bereft, angry little boy. No wonder women spoil you, Eliza thought; you need it so. I do love you, Enzo; like this, in a dawn sort of way. Only I need the noon, its heat and light. Miklos, my Mykonos, my sun and center. "Enzo, I'm not going with you." She touched his arm. "Not after tonight. I'm not that much a liar."

"So you were lying before." The bowline snapped taut in his hand and water slapped the hull. "You can't imagine what life with him will be like." Then with a sigh, he dropped the bowline. "Never mind. I learned long ago never to try to convince a woman she's not in love. You'll find out soon enough about Miki." Reluctantly, he touched her hair. "Just remember, when you need me, I'll come."

"Thank you for being here now," she said softly. "I thought you'd be halfway to Turin."

"The king has had something to say about that. I'm to be on the road within the hour, but I'm lucky to get off with my skin. He has a few words for Miki, too, so you two had best be back by the time he disentangles himself from Vanda this morning.''

Gently, she blew him a kiss and pushed off.

The sailboat was wreathed in rising, dawn mist as the dory sidled up to it. Awkwardly Eliza balanced as she started to slip the bowline onto the sailboat's stern cleat, then froze as Miklos's towering shape formed out of the mist. ''Well''—his face was expressionless—''was he there? Waiting for you?''

''Yes,'' she replied quietly. ''He's off to Rome. Charles's orders. His Majesty is waiting for us.''

Miklos plucked her up onto the deck. ''Let him wait.'' His mouth came down, hard and forceful as the powerful hands that impatiently jerked off the blanket and moved over her body. He carried her down with him to the deck, came inside her with a swift thrust that made her cry out. There was no gentleness now, no giving her small body time to grow used to his big one. A kind of desperation seemed to drive him, then drive her as her body quickened to his. She felt she must be rent apart, yet the weapon that tormented tantalized, plunged her into a scarlet cocoon in the gray mist. A cocoon of raw passion that writhed, metamorphosed, scalded, until screaming against his mouth, she tore through its walls. Lay shivering.

Miklos was quite still, his heart thudding against her breast. Then slowly his head rose and he caught her head between his hands. ''You're my wife now,'' he grated huskily, ''if we stay here until I put a baby in your belly to prove it.''

''I came back,'' she murmured. ''What more do you want?''

His fingers knotted in her hair. ''More than a damned scrap of paper between us. I want blood of my blood, bone of my bone. Your hard little heart and your stubborn, scheming brain.''

She slid her hands around his wrists, locked them. ''I don't need to be conquered, Miklos. Why not just love me?''

He laughed shortly and rose from the rumpled blanket. "I can't even trust you."

She gathered the blanket around her. "If I wanted to run, sooner or later, I'd find a way. You know that. I think you knew when I left to go to Enzo this morning. You could have stopped me."

He leaned his head against the mast, the slope of his neck and back rigid; then, almost imperceptibly, it gave. "One animal to a cage, my love."

"Sorry, the door's shut. Besides, what about you and your pet panther, Bellaria?"

He eyed her thoughtfully. "Suppose we both behave long enough to give this mad marriage a chance?"

"I think I can manage if you can." She went to wrap her arms about his waist. "Hadn't we better begin by reporting dutifully to Charles before he begins to develop some mad ideas himself?"

"Where've you been?" snapped Charles as he paced the drawing room. "The servants and guards have been scouring the place."

Hooking his thumbs in cotton breeches pulled from a boat locker, Miklos smiled. "Decorum forbids, Your Majesty."

Eliza sat down, delicately arranging her blanket. As if it had been charcoaled, the villa smelled of smoke. Servants trotted up and down the stairs outside the door with cleaning supplies, armloads of sun-dried bedding, and damaged furniture. The lawns were covered by workmen and soldiers commandeered to repair the roof. "As you were occupied, Sire, we presumed our absence wouldn't matter."

"Matter?" floundered the king, then extended his scorched dressing gown. "For two hours, we thought you might have been burned!"

"Things did get rather warm, Sire," obliquely agreed Miklos.

The king grunted. "Things are getting rather warm, in general, Sztarai. You draw trouble like a magnet. You'll have to be off to Switzerland."

Miklos draws Bellaria like a magnet too, mused Eliza, comparing her husband's narrow middle to Charles's paunch. That's probably half the royal pother.

"I trust you'll inform the emperor, Sire?" inquired Miklos mildly.

"Naturally." Charles looked uncomfortable, then plopped down into a chair. "Mind you I'm not ungrateful. Your wife saved my life. I'll see Ferdinand hears of that." He edgily tapped the chair arm. "Your part, too."

"Perhaps if we remained here quietly, Your Majesty . . ." Eliza began.

"You haven't married a quiet man, Madame. You've married a noisy, troublesome man." He rose, waggling a finger. "That cousin of yours, Sir, ought to be hung. You'll never convince me he hadn't a notion of what was up."

"Nearly the whole house," Miklos suggested, "if Bianca'd had her way. She's no more fond of Hungarian royalty than Italian."

"Well, if Rossi puts a foot out of line again," affirmed the king, "I'll swing him off!"

"I take it Bianca and Guido are somewhat nearer in line for the noose," Miklos observed laconically, pausing before Charles.

With his audience stabilized, the king cheered up. "My troopers are chasing them like rabbits. They won't dare linger in the Piedmont."

"Not when they can go to ground in France."

"Those impertinent, traitorous . . ." Charles caught himself. "*Principessa*, forgive me, but you understand this is a matter between men. If you will excuse us."

"Certainly. At any rate, I must see to my goose bumps."

Both men wistfully eyed the goose bumps as Eliza redraped the blanket in geisha style and minced out.

In the foyer, she plucked a tiger lily from a vase, tucked it in her teeth, then waggled it at herself in the mirror. Making love was easier than learning to dance. I'm in love, she informed the mirror, and I see stars! I see Miklos in lights all over the sky! Humming, she danced across the foyer. With a flamenco kick, she removed the sagging blanket from the path of a passing workman, who bowed and grinned before discreetly leaving her the foyer stage.

She was still shuffling to her room when Bellaria, who had been searching the grounds for the past two hours, tore up the steps after her. "Whore! Adultress!"

Eliza began to laugh. Tears of mirth streaming from her eyes, she hiked up the blanket and kept going.

Bellaria's temper splattered off the walls. "Three men! One night! I saw Enzo slinking off to the boathouse after Charles told him to be gone. He went sniffing after you, you slut!"

"Why complain? Or was Charles huffy when you bounced into his bed? Wait. *Your* bed. His was in splinters." Eliza laughed until she choked.

Bellaria grabbed a fold of the blanket. "Miki doesn't want *you!* It's Loise he wants. Pretty little blond Loise!"

Eliza's amusement abruptly faded. Bellaria's face was twisted; perhaps in her jealousy, her mind was as much so. . . .

"Miki's still wild for her," Bellaria hissed, "the one woman he can't lie to, cheat; the one woman he can't have, can't fuck into needing him!" She flicked loose the blanket. "So, you're not laughing any more. You're beginning to see the joke's on you. You look like her. You could almost be sisters. His Eliza. Loise, Eliza." The names were a mocking singsong, a children's taunting ditty. "Loise, Loise, soiled, lovely dove. Will you die for pleasure or will you die for love? Either way, you cannot get away. Your mate will make you fly, only so you may fall . . . did you suppose Miklos fell like a ripe plum into your lax, inconsequential lap? A man like him? A prince, *per dio mio!* What thin story did he give you, eh? That he was a grieving widower?!"

Despite herself, Eliza went rigid and Bellaria's voice dropped low. "So you didn't even know he had a wife. *La Principessa* Loise Sztarai, former Baroness Nzetsy. Her ancestral line went back nearly as far as mine. Bette and

Enzo must have picked an ignorant bit of trash like you up off the streets. That's why Enzo kept sniffing after you . . ."

From the bottom of the stair, Miklos's voice cut sharply into her tirade. "You've overstayed your welcome, Countess. Be out of the house within twenty minutes or you and your baggage will be tossed out of the gate."

If Bellaria meant to screech, the idea immediately squelched itself when she caught the furious glint in Miklos's eyes as he swiftly mounted the stair. "I'll go," she snapped, "but you've only yourself to blame, Miki. You couldn't keep Loise in her coffin forever." Eliza saw the glint in Miklos's gray eyes turn savage. His hand snaked out, but Bellaria, thoroughly scared, prudently was already out of reach. Within seventeen minutes, she was out of the gate.

Without looking at Miklos, Eliza went to her room and closed the door. Huddled in the blanket, she sat on the bed and stared out at the distant lake. A soft knock came at the door. She didn't answer. It didn't come again.

Eliza stayed in her room two days. Without sleeping, without eating. Until the knock came again, this time not softly. When she didn't unlock the door, Miklos's boot came through it. In seconds, the inside key turned and he strode into the room. She was surprised to see how relieved he looked to see her simply reading. "You're going to eat," he said flatly.

"All right." She went back to the book.

He threw it into the empty fireplace; dead ashes clouded up. "We're going to talk."

"About Loise?"

Pain twisted his face, twisted her heart to see it. "Loise is three years dead. You're alive. It's as simple as that."

"And I look like her," she murmured. "Simpler yet. No wonder Bette took so long to find someone . . . suitable." Dazed from disinterest in eating, she played absently with the coverlet. "There's a name for what you want from me. I can't remember . . . something unspeakable."

He caught her drifting hand. "I should have told you,

but I couldn't. I still can't talk . . . think about Loise clearly.''

"She was with us that day you taught me to fish. She was in the breeze in the lindens. With us sailing on the lake and at Comacina." Her tone turned puzzled. "Why didn't I see her, too?"

Miklos eyed her pinched face and the circles under her eyes, then gave the servants' bell a yank. "Miss a few more meals and you may. You're addled enough from hunger.''

"What can one expect from an ignorant bit of trash picked up so easily.''

"That's right. Feel sorry for yourself. Self-pity put us both here . . .'' He broke off as a maid appeared. He snapped an order for dinner. After the maid left, he sat on the bed. "In two days we leave for Switzerland. A new start. I want you to come.''

"And if I don't want to come?'' she said listlessly.

"I'm not going to let you go anywhere else like this.''

Her head tilted to one side, she dispassionately examined him like an insect in amber. "Enzo said I'd find out about you. I didn't know what he meant.'' Her face took on a lost look. "Now . . .''

"Now, you eat. Tonight you sleep,'' he said tautly. "Day after tomorrow, we leave Italy. After that, we keep taking one step at a time.'' He stayed until she ate, then took away the tray himself and covered her.

But when he began to read her Gibbon's *Decline and Fall*, she laughed faintly. "Your Highness, you are indomitable.''

Chapter 9

Apollo's Appalling Shadow

Lugano, Switzerland: August 25, 1847

"Well, Aunt, this is where we leave you," Miklos said briskly. Max, the wolfhound, moaned as his master dismounted the coach, then handed a bemused Eliza down in a pouf of pink-scalloped silk onto the quay cobbles. As soon as he let her go, she mechanically retied her satin hat ribbon, then, like an indifferent, bandbox doll, she waited to see what new twist he meant to wind into her life. Wishing her heart were made of tin, she closed her eyes. She still couldn't reach the pain and pluck it out.

Bette was less sanguine. Clinging to a carriage strap, she stared at her nephew, then across the water. The inn was on the island that centered the turquoise jewel of Lake Lugano and its small, tile-roofed city. "But Saint Moritz is days away!"

"A very short trip. You've three lackeys and Vincenzo. You can send him ahead to open the chalet."

Bette shoved the dog away from the window. "And just where do you propose taking Eliza?"

"On a honeymoon." Miklos motioned the postilion to hand down their luggage. "The usual places"—then noting Bette's alarmed expression, added—"and a few unusual ones."

"Miklos," she muttered harshly, "you *cannot* do this."

"Not indefinitely, no." He grabbed the luggage, handed

153

a hatbox to the startled Eliza, waved away the rest of the bags. "We'll have better luck by traveling light."

"But you'll surely want at least a maid and valet . . ."

He patted Bette's powdered cheek. "Eliza and I can manage each other's buttons."

She grasped his hand. "Miki, Metternich will be furious! This is madness!" With gray ostrich feathers waving from her hat, Bette craned from the coach window. "Eliza, if this madcap expedition becomes too alarming, come to me at Moritz . . ." Miklos gave the horses' rumps a swat. "And for pity's sake, get a proper wrap in Paris or you'll freeze. Whoever heard of a tour in the rainy season . . ."

As his aunt's voice and Max's howl dwindled away with the coach, Miklos turned to Eliza. Her pink silk did look flimsy ruffling in the breeze off the lake. Her hat was slipping again, its veil flattening across her eyes to make them seem larger, smudged darker. Despite her finery, she looked again like the rich, withdrawn urchin who'd first come to Como. Now she was his wife so long as they both lived. "Alone at last. Frightened?"

"Should I be?"

He straightened her hat. "Probably. This proposes to be the most unpredictable honeymoon any couple ever had."

"I doubt it," was her calm reply. "The bride intends to sleep alone."

He picked up the baggage. "Fortunately, our income forbids such an exclusive arrangement."

"You may have bedded me with one lie, but a plea of poverty stresses even my credulity," she retorted skeptically.

"I pretend no such case, but my wealth is far from boundless, particularly as I temporarily lack access to it." He handed her another box.

"Switzerland," she said dryly, "is full of banks."

"One of which I propose to visit tomorrow. It will require a countersignature on my letters of credit from the Austrian diplomatic official in residence." He edged a valise higher on his hip. "If I request more money than he deems reasonable to complete our journey to Saint Moritz, he'll suspect a rat.'' He headed to the dock for transport out to the island inn.

"As well he might,'' muttered Eliza, trailing after him. "Royalty seems to breed little else.''

"Miki, why risk so much trouble by disobeying Charles's orders to go through the charade of a honeymoon?'' Eliza asked when they were settled in a comfortable, rag-rugged room overlooking Lake Lugano. "You had one with Loise, didn't you? You've got me under matrimonial lock and key now. You needn't parade the proof past muzzle bores.''

He took her cold hands. "But I do need to parade you. I want people to see the reigning Princess Sztarai. That's my privilege and your right. Better to face trouble and take freedom as it comes than hide and learn to hate each other like starving animals. You've always wanted to see the world. I can show it to you''—he stroked her cheek—"if you don't fight me over every marvelous inch of it.'' Reflecting the saffron light off the lake, his eyes were warm autumnal fires that made winter seem a lie at the same time they promised it.

"If I don't fight you . . . does that include in bed?'' she said slowly, her uneasy gaze flicking to the billowy four-poster.

"I want only what you wish to give.'' His fingers traced her mouth. "Lie to me with those pretty lips if you must, but not with their kisses.''

"Shall I expect the same from you?'' she murmured. "Lies, unless we lie . . . together?''

"I'll tell you truth as faith can bear and lie with you so long as that faith endures.'' His lips neared hers and she uneasily edged back in the chair.

She didn't dare let him touch her. If he did, she would lose everything: her dignity, her identity. Even now her face was fading, altering into a strange face she'd never seen, that only Miklos and everyone else saw in her. Part of her had been stolen by a ghost, leaving her bereft, angry, and uncertain. "At the moment,'' she said unevenly, "that faith is frayed to a thread, too poor to pillow a prince."

His eyes darkened as he perceived the extent of her distress. "You may be surprised to learn how lean a bed a prince might count himself lucky to find," he returned softly. "I may have found you by luck, but I'll not lose you to folly." He offered her a glass, then took up his own. "Kiss me when you will, Princess. If I turn a mottled green"—he swirled the silt in the glass—"blame it on the local water."

Her amusement mingled with relief that he would not force her to bed, she offered a doggerel toast, "Then a pair of frogs we'll be, sir, a' hopping from the emperor. A shrewd disguise . . . but to dine on flies would seem a bit extreme. Will the royal spy make outcry if I order veal tonight?"

With a boyish laugh, he clicked her glass. "Madame, you may have the whole calf . . . served on a lilypad."

The lilypad turned out to be a floating restaurant that cruised slowly about moonlit Lake Lugano. The veal the waiter braised on a portable grill by their table could not cloak the perfume of roses and gardenias drifting out from the palm-fringed shore with its pastel villas. Beyond the boat's gold and white striped awning, lights atop the island's black peak mingled with the stars, while city lights circled the shoreline as if some of the stars had fallen there in a necklace. Carriages rolled along the quay to stop at cafes whose patios spilled laughter over the black and gilt satin water.

"What a lovely sight," Eliza said dreamily, toying with her third glass of wine. "Lovely flowers, lovely meal." Languid in yellow chiffon, she wore baroque pearls with emerald leaves about her throat; a gardenia-clustered, seed-pearled snood gathered the heavy, honey mass of her hair. Through her wineglass, the view took on patterns of a Venetian glass paperweight: the surrounding, green-clothed tables with their pink-shaded lamps, their pink and amber people, their clear wines and silver forks. Peacefully, her attention turned back to the waiter pouring sauce on the veal. "What are those little green balls?"

"Capers." In his formal black, Miklos leaned back in his chair.

Cupping a hand to her cheek, Eliza shielded her words from the waiter, "Not frog eggs?" She gave him a conspiratorial grin. "I feel like a cannibal."

Miklos nodded at the white-jacketed waiter. With a flourish, the man spread lilypads on their plates and served the veal. Eliza's hand went over her mouth to stifle a shriek of laughter as Miklos hummed, "Froggy went a' courtin', um humm." Diners stared.

"This is what you meant by unpredictable?!"

"Only the first breath of it, Princess." He looked up at the huge, gypsy orange moon glimmering beyond the island. Their time had just begun. It would be mercilessly short. He prayed it would be enough.

Dazed with wine and moonlight, Eliza crooned "Froggy" as Miklos put her to bed and was nearly asleep as he eased in beside her. His mouth was soft on hers, his body warm and comforting in a strange bed. With a contented sigh, she burrowed into him, scarcely feeling his lips brush her temple as she wandered off with a dream.

Miklos lay wide awake with Eliza's sinuous body draped across his long one. When he'd undressed her, he'd roused with a sweet, warm ache. Now, as her breathing grazed his nipple, the stirring in his groin sharpened. He tried to think of something to wilt his interest; she needed reassurance she was more than the object of his lust, particularly lust for another woman. Unfortunately, his resolve was distracted by her rosebud breast tickling his armpit, and where her small belly sloped into the shadow of his groin, a fluff of honey teasing his sex. She stirred, burrowing closer against him. As if a baited serpent had risen to bite him, his body defiantly responded to provocation. Miklos eased the sham from his pillow. Not entirely noble, he imagined the sham was pink, passionate Eliza, and with a relieved sigh, firmly smothered the serpent.

Eliza awoke less pleasantly from cold, for in his sleep, Miklos had kicked off the yellow cotton comforter. His leg was across her hips, his arm across her breasts. Fortunately her head didn't ache, but she had goose bumps despite the early sun cutting across the bed. Fall had nipped a few trees and chilled the morning air off the lake. Though naked, Miklos was oblivious to the cold; he adored swimming in water that would have turned a duck blue. Shivering, she tried to ease from under him, but with a mutter, he wrapped her closer. Now, at least her front was warm . . . but once he must have held Loise just the same way.

She peered up at his tanned face. Serene, his highness looked; not so craggy as when awake, broken nose less irregular. His mouth was as flat and hard except for the corners; his brows as strongly marked, only the thickness of his gold lashes was much heavier than she had realized, giving him the deceptively lazy look he sometimes wore when most alert. Sleeping power, that was Miklos.

At a time like this, she liked best of all his warm, fuzzy spots. Even his sex was soft and warm against her stomach. With an ache of longing, she remembered him inside her, the way he moved and sought her. Those slim hips could drive against hers, pin her like a moth only to send her winging. Only now she didn't seem to have the heart to fly and she couldn't be certain if he had any heart at all. Nesting didn't have to mean she trusted him, did it?

And in her precarious nest, she slept.

When she awoke, Miklos, in a gold robe, was shaving. She was dimly disappointed he hadn't tried to seduce her, then had a surge of self-contempt. What *was* the point of making love, when he wanted someone else? If only he hadn't wrapped her in lace, made her know that ecstatic madness beyond the beginning of love . . . too soon, too soon for her to know her lover–enemy, too late to guard against his wiles. She caught his reflection mischievously smiling at her from the mirror; something about that smile reminded her of the boathouse satyr.

"Sleep well?"

"Hm." Had her face been still firmly flattened to his chest when he'd awakened? She pulled the comforter up to her neck. "What time is it?"

"Near ten. You'd best get dressed. We're expecting a caller in half an hour."

"Caller?" she asked a bit nervously.

"No one to worry about. *Signor* Pelli is an artist of sorts."

Also a crook, counterfeiter, thief, and pickpocket. Miklos knew the strangest people. Over *caffelatte*, Eliza watched with fascination while *Signor* Pelli scribbled several documents on fine sheepskin, signed them with several names, and stamped them with national seals from a collection in a neat leather case. He also fished out fat wads of German marks, French francs, and English pound notes. Miklos, after closely examining each document and bill, handed him a handsome sum in Swiss marks and saw him out the door.

"Nothing on this table is worth the paper it's printed on," Eliza protested, peering at a pound note by the window's bright light. "Miklos, we could rot in prison for furthering Pelli's 'artistry'."

"Rotting in Saint Moritz is only a slightly better fate." He thumbed through the marks. "But you needn't be concerned about the money; it's genuine. Pelli knows better than to give me anything else and he gives the best exchange rate in town."

"He's your private bank."

"With branches all over Europe."

"What about these traveling papers?" She prodded the sheaf. "I watched him forge them."

An unrepentant grin curved his lips. "I admit I'm less adverse to crime than a firing squad."

Exasperated, she put her hands on her hips. "If you'll forgive my advancing curiosity, just where are we likely to be welcomed with bullets?"

He waved a wax-blobbed paper tantalizingly. "Come,

leave a little mystery, a little excitement in life. They won't shoot *you*, after all . . ."

She threw the money at him.

Not that money mattered. They stayed at the cheapest inns on the Italian Riviera. The inns weren't dirty, but bedding a board's thickness from a goat made Eliza passionately wish for a cold and stopped up nose. Miklos was indifferent to whatever surroundings his penuriousness decreed. He might roar mightily at the innkeeper if Eliza's bedding was less than fresh, but slept himself without comment on the floor when circumstances demanded. "I'll show you the world, says he," teased Eliza one night while watching Miklos fold his considerable length into a tin bath little bigger than a bucket. "I must say it has a fascinating backside."

With an exaggerated leer, he squeezed into the water. "If you care to join me, I'd be delighted to extend the tour, ma'am."

"And just where would we fit me?"

He poured a can of water over his head, then dripping, grinned at her, curled up in a froth of Italian lace on the lumpy bed. "Oh, I imagine we could think of something."

"I'm quite content where I am, thank you," she fibbed. His wet, slippery nakedness made her edgy and sent her imagination into florid, cartwheeling flights.

Planting his foot against the tub rim, he inspected his toes as if they were wrinkled old ladies. "Ah, yes, dreary contentment. Safe but sorry, sane but senile."

Pricked by anger, she rose to her knees. "Don't patronize me. I wasn't the one who . . ."

"Lied," he supplied gently, then looked at her. "Not the least little bit?"

She let out her breath. "Very well, I did let you believe . . ." Slowly, she sagged before his level, gray eyes. "We're a disastrous pair. We'll never make a marriage on a mattress of lies."

"How do you know?" he queried lightly. "We've yet to try a mattress of any sort."

"Well, we're not starting with this one," she said quickly. "It's full of corn husks." Before she could change her mind, she dove under the blankets.

Santa Margharita: September 5, 1847

In Santa Margharita, Eliza had no such excuse as an inadequate mattress. Their floral-tiled rooms were charming, with a small balcony that overlooked the blue Mediterranean. When it *was* blue, which the innkeeper apologetically explained could not be much expected at this time of year. Aunt Bette had been correct in her verdict. The rainy season had arrived and nobody with any sense went out in it. The curving stony beach was cloaked with gray drizzle, the occasional, offshore fishing vessels fading into steaming mist. Except for a few wandering locals, the place was deserted.

Despite the weather, perhaps because of its poetic softness, Eliza loved Santa Margharita, with its pebbled beach and drowsing sea. Miklos, wandering like a boy along the shore, occasionally picked up odd, pretty black stones to bring her. In his canvas fisherman's breeches and worn, blue wool jacket, he was at ease here, too, his face relaxed as she'd seen it in sleep. He even teased her into walking imaginary tightropes along the jetties and skipping stones over the lazily lapping water. Finding a salmon canvas-covered skiff, they settled on its beached bow to watch the sunset burn through the sodden clouds. "Let's rent a boat and go fishing tomorrow," she proposed eagerly.

"Good idea," Miklos agreed. "We'll have a cafe pack lunch." He stretched out his long legs. "Just expect enough crockery and linen for ballast."

"Wonderful! We'll invite the clams to tea." With a delighted laugh, Eliza unthinkingly hooked her arm through his. "It's going to be wonderful fun."

Before she could shy back, he kissed her nose.

"Why did you do that?" she asked uncertainly.

He looked at her in her girlish, square-collared sailor

dress and big, floppy hat. "Because you're so easily pleased by so little."

Her attention fixed on her toes. "What sorts of things did Loise like?"

He was silent for a moment. "She liked gaiety, people, and parties. Pretty clothes." He gazed at the sinking sun, streaking the taupe sky with silver as if it were a curved, Cellini vase. "Sunshine and singing."

"And fishing," she finished softly. "You loved her very much." It was not a question.

"Yes." When her arm started to ease away, he firmly clamped it to his side. "Don't ever think you're her shadow, Eliza. You make your own shadows. She would have been a little bored today. Subtleties, while they didn't elude Loise, didn't interest her. She was very much a child of the sun. Clouds were for others." His voice had roughened as if something had torn it.

"I'm sorry," Eliza said unevenly. "I truly didn't mean to make you sad." The drizzle was beginning again, the mast tops of the anchored boats blurring into the horizon.

Miklos looked down at her mist-damp face with its dark-lashed, wide golden eyes. "You don't. Sometimes I think even you may bring forgiveness."

She was puzzled. "For what?"

He smiled faintly. "For blindness, most of all, I suppose."

"You're the most perceptive person I've ever met," Eliza said firmly, "when you choose."

"Ah, yes, when I choose," he echoed expressionlessly. "When I don't choose, I can be very dull indeed."

The drizzle was turning to wide-spaced rain slapping the beach stones, and she eyed his spare, irregular profile uneasily. Brooding, uncertainty, was unlike him. "Tomorrow won't be dull. The sun may even come out."

"Given time, all things are possible," he mused whimsically, "even clams at tea."

Gently, she tucked up his collar. "A man who serves up veal on lilypads should be able to easily marry clams to teacups."

"So you think I can do anything," he said quietly.

"Anything."

"Then I'll try not to disappoint you." Beneath her dripping hat, he kissed her softly, and this time it never occurred to her to try to dodge. He made their cocoon re-form in the rain; within it she felt the stubborn, fragile radiance of butterflies. Now, at last, as Miklos held her to his breast, Eliza knew she must risk change of all her being, lest radiance turn to dust, dry and dead, before it could emerge into brilliant life. Loise was dead; to follow her in fear was death, long and bitter. Miklos could do anything but yield her a place in his heart she was too timid to hold.

And so, after sunset, they made love. Unfolding, tremulous, Eliza lay in Miklos's arms, yielded more than her body to the searching, rich potency of his. Life joined life, quick and vibrant: in a spiraling glitter soared toward the hidden sun in all its blinding blaze of light, a sun once known that could not be eclipsed. Metamorphosis resumed for both, with all the irrevocable pain, exhilaration, and confusion of change. The barter of need, the generosity of a new spring.

France: September 9, 1847

And so it began. Palatial hotels in Monaco and Cannes, vineyard-surrounded chateaux and magnificent food in little inns in Auvergne. Beds in Bourges, Billancourt, and finally Paris.

Paris: September 18, 1847

Essential Paris. With a glory of autumnal leaves sifting into the jade Seine and a faint scent of woodsmoke in the air. Carriage rides on the broad avenues among brilliant chestnuts in the *bois*, pigeons kiting over the Place de la Concorde, the soaring, stone gargoyles of Nôtre-Dame.

They settled in Bette's svelte townhouse on Île Saint-Louis, where the perfume of blowsy, late roses in the tiny

garden drifted to the gilt and rose Louis XIV bedroom
under the eaves. Miklos took Eliza to Gagelin for ball
dresses, Falize and Fontenay for jewels. They went to the
Comédie-Française, L'Odèon, the Louvre, the *cafés
chantants*.

"*Ernani's* being done at the Théatre des Muses tonight."
Eliza tossed down the day's newspaper and with a sweep
of ecru satin, sat on Miklos's lap. "Shall we go? I've
never seen an opera. Mother only liked light plays."

Putting his arms about her waist, he grimaced. "*Ernani's*
hardly light. Verdi gives censorship and the Austrian influence in Italy a real flogging. Every revolutionary in the
city ought to be there."

"Then you think we oughtn't go?" With a finger curled
through the stud slit of his open silk shirt, she studied him
gravely. "Censorship is wrong, after all."

"Spoken like a true American democrat." His eyes took
on a wicked glint. "Metternich would have an apoplexy if
I turned up in a nest of radicals."

With mother of pearl opera glasses perched over her
nose, Eliza craned from their ornate box. The plush and
gold curve of the Théatre was a humming, swarming
beehive of irridescent lady bees and drone-coated males.
"Every Sorbonne student and Montmartre artist must be in
the upper stalls," Eliza exclaimed. "Look, that curly
haired mulatto has to be Victor Hugo, and that woman . . ."

With a grin, Miklos pulled her down by her gilt-
embroidered chocolate skirts. "Don't gawk, Princess.
Quizz." He nuzzled aside the dangling gold and diamond
earring on her porcelain ear. "The Ritters three boxes over
have already spotted me. If you like, stare at them."

"But that's . . ." She suddenly froze. "Bianca!"

He took the glasses. "Where?"

"Fifth row, right near the aisle. She's practically under
us." She watched him shift the glasses to the cerise-clad
brunette below them. The bold, aquiline profile crowned
by a Spanish comb and Alençon mantilla was unmistak-
able. "Up to something, do you think?"

"Perhaps. She usually is." He scanned the audience. "Guido doesn't seem to be around."

"I'd be a lot happier if he were. Where he is, one of his nasty bombs isn't."

"Don't worry. Bianca isn't hanging around to blow to Kingdom Come."

The gas houselights went down and *Ernani* began, but Eliza paid it scant attention, and though he seemed unruffled, Miklos trained the opera glasses more often upon the mezzanine audience and surrounding boxes than the stage. When the first intermission arrived without incident, they intently explored the crowd on the bronze-railed balconies in the lobbies, but to no avail. Then, when they returned to their box, Eliza spotted Bianca scanning the upper boxes while she reclaimed her seat. Unfortunately, Eliza's swift clasp of Miklos's arm caught Bianca's attention. She stood quite still. Eliza's fingers tightened. "Miki, she's going to bolt!"

Instead, Bianca sat down and began to languidly fan herself.

Eliza was stunned. "How can she be so cool? Whatever is she doing?"

"Bianca has a heart and brain of ice." Miklos sat down. "She's probably signaling someone with that fan."

"But aren't we going to notify the police?" His patient look made her flush. "I suppose not."

"Which Bianca can guess very well. Thanks to Enzo, she knows too much about me. We'll just have to wait her out."

Predictably, by the next intermission, Bianca's seat was empty.

As the audience streamed into the aisles, a dull scream from the lower foyer lapped over the crowd. A hushed silence fell. Another scream came, uneven in horror. Ripples of murmurs followed, then a shrieking woman rushed through the open foyer doors. "A man's been stabbed!" She turned frantically, distractedly in the aisle. "Oh, a doctor! Help him . . . he's bloody . . ."

Two men moved quickly to calm her as in fear and

curiosity, people rushed into the aisles. Miklos threw Eliza's gold lamé cape about her shoulders. "Quickly! The exits will be blocked by gendarmes in minutes!" Instead of following the crowd, he led her backstage to shoulder their way through the bewildered, distraught opera corps and stage crew to the rear stage entrance.

In moments, they were hurrying along Rue Auber to find their crested carriage, which the driver had parked several streets from the Théatre. Atop the Théatre's Corinthian-columned facade glowed a statue of Apollo, serene as if murder had not been performed in his shadow. Miklos and Eliza were about to give up searching for the carriage when it appeared through the press that issued from the Théatre before the doors were sealed. In erratic clusters, rattled men tried to soothe women shivering without their wraps. As they looked for their own vehicles, arguments flew. The wounded man was probably a libertine killed by a rival. Stabbed. No, shot. A politician. Claude du Monde, the publisher. No, he looked like Lamartine. The opera producer. Verdi himself.

With Eliza in his wake, Miklos pushed through the crowd and waved down their driver. When he stepped up on the coachbox to make their destination heard over the surrounding racket, he smelled liquor on the driver's breath. After a curt direction to the Place de la Concorde, Miklos dismounted and lifted Eliza into the carriage.

With a rustle of silk, Eliza turned to watch the brilliant Théatre lights recede. "Miki, you don't suppose Bianca and Guido had anything to do with that wounded man?"

"Possibly, but we'd best see tomorrow's papers before we jump to conclusions."

"Bianca's behavior was strange, though." She sank back into the green plush cushions as their carriage rattled into the narrow Rue Respail. "She almost seemed to be looking for us in the boxes that first intermission."

"She could have been looking for anyone." As the walls brushed by a hand's breadth from their windows, Miklos was silent a moment, then glanced out of the back carriage window. The street was empty.

"You think someone's following us?" Eliza asked uneasily.

"No, but I don't much like this route." His cane tapped on the driver's box. "To the Vendôme."

"That'll be bogged, sir. You said you wanted the Concorde as quick as possible."

"The Vendôme, if you please."

"Yes, sir," sighed the driver. He took the first left-hand street.

For a block or two after the turn, Miklos watched to see if they were being followed. Saw nothing. Shortly before the Vendôme, he tapped the coach box again. "Stop the carriage just beyond the street lamp. We'll walk home."

Relieved, the driver reined up. Making sure they were clear of the lamplight, Miklos handed Eliza down. The street was intermeshed with harsh gaslight shadows, its sooty walls a narrow corridor.

"Miki, weren't we safer in the carriage?" Eliza asked nervously as it moved ahead of them.

"No room to maneuver. We were like turtles in trap."

She hugged his arm. "Then you do think . . . ?"

He smiled. "Not really. Magyars just become restless in closed spaces . . ."

In that moment, the street lit with a dreadful roar. Their carriage ahead was a bonfire, obliterating all shadow. Its screaming, wounded horses bolted hopelessly, dropped in a few feet to kick and roll madly. The blazing driver was thrown backward over the carriage roof to drop to the street. His limbs jerking as he flailed up, he began to stagger toward them. Miklos ran to throw his cloak about him and roll him over the cobbles. As Miklos pounded bare-handed at the flames, the driver shrieked, whimpered as the fire died . . . and he died. Eliza caught a glimpse of bloodied, blackened, noseless features, a melted, glistening mass seeping from dark sockets. Black cinders smothered her.

Whimpering, Eliza woke in darkness, felt Miklos's arms go about her. She was in their tapesty-hung bed at Saint Louis. "It's over," Miklos whispered.

The pearl-shaded light burning near the bed reminded her of gaslights, roiling flames. "That driver—he looked as if he were in hell . . ."

"Don't waste your pity," Miklos murmured, clasping her tightly. "He paid for what he bought."

"What?" she asked dazedly. "How . . . ?"

"Sleep now. I'll explain in the morning."

Next morning, she awoke to find Miklos sitting on the bed while he read the morning papers. She sat up and peered over his shoulder. "Any news of the Théatre?" The room's light was hazy, as if a storm were coming. She laid her head in Miklos's lap and silently, his bandaged hands a trifle clumsy, he caressed her hair. With each stroke, she felt calmer, felt the knots of fear loosen.

"The stabbed man was Eugene Lavalle," he related finally, "his assailant unknown. As the most conservative of France's ruling council, Lavalle's removal makes Louis-Napoléon the logical royalist choice for candidacy in next year's election. Louis-Napoléon may be wailing condolences to the press, but he's likely dancing with delight in private."

"Bianca and Guido's work?"

"Considering Bianca's disappearance during Act 2 and our carriage explosion, I think it very likely." He tossed the paper onto the spread. "Guido must have spotted our carriage crest when we arrived at the Théatre. He would have been around to assure the attendance of Lavalle. Bianca came into the Théatre both to kill Lavalle and divert us while Guido located our carriage. He probably had an accomplice distract our driver with liquor while he placed the bomb."

"Bianca's a monster." Eliza sat up and clasped her satin-covered knees. "How did you ever get involved with her, let her stay at Como?"

"When she's not slipping in stilettos, she can be an intriguing woman. And she saved my life once." He rose and wandered to the window. "The payment she expected for that service, however, was too high. She acquired Guido two years ago. Some men are loathe to quibble with a beautiful woman over trivialities like assassinations." He seemed to feel her next question hanging in the air. "Loise was dead," he went on quietly. "I had no ties. No reason to quibble, but a pistol to my skull seemed cleaner than Bianca's messes."

"You were so unhappy after Loise died?" Eliza asked softly.

"I was a dead man," was the flat reply.

"She must have been wonderful," Eliza whispered miserably.

"Yes, a wonderful liar. A wonderful cheat."

She was startled, elated, guilty. "I lie and cheat, too."

He smiled. "So you do, but you go about it honestly. Also you have a serious talent for it. Loise could never be serious about anything. She lied and cheated with great imagination but no finesse." He paused, stepped quickly to the side of the window. A tall, thin man in a frockcoat and stovepipe hat was striding down the quay toward the house. A few steps away, he slowed, surveyed the house front, then made for the wrought iron gate. "We've a caller," murmured Miklos.

She turned pale. "Police?"

He flicked on a cravat and morning coat. "Probably a lower rung, diplomatic flunky. Breathe easy, but be ready to pack."

Miklos was upstairs again in half an hour; their visitor was gone. "An Austrian legation secretary," he explained briefly, "courtesy of the Ritters and several other buzzards who spotted us, particularly when we were leaving the Théatre before the security cordon closed. I've put him off for the moment, but he'll be back with a couple of armed legation guards. Pack."

Chapter 10

Stage Actors and Stilettos

London, the Thames: October 17, 1847

The maples above Eliza's slowly twirling, yellow parasol were a filigree of scarlet orange and filtered, copper
sunlight as the slim gray punt slid along the Thames.
Between London and Oxford was a sweep of saffron and
cream meadowland ruffled with medieval shades of autumn
in the trees along the banks of the deserted river. At
the water rim, geese and waterfowl searched for harvest
seeds and sleepy frogs. Eliza, looking like a daisy in
yellow, floral silk and green grosgrain basque, had Miklos's
head in her lap as he stretched his twill-suited length along
the boat. She idly caught at a lilypad tendril, dripped it
across Miklos's dozing face. The boat lurched dangerously
as he snapped awake and turned on her. His hands shot to
her throat. "Don't!" she yelped. "Oh, please, I'll be
good."

His face an inch from hers, he stroked her throat. "How
good?"

"Delectable," she growled through the veil of her feathered hat. "Delicious. Deliriously, diaphanously . . .
difficult."

His fingers tightened slightly. "Still bargaining?"

Their lashes fanning up against the net, her eyes widened, grave and a trifle uncertain. "Until I get what I
want."

"What's that?"

"I don't know," she said softly, lying back on the lavender boat pillows. "You've made me feel so close to it. As though any moment I could touch it and yet . . . I don't know where to reach."

His blond hair sun-dappled, he kissed her lingeringly. "This give you any ideas?"

Her arms wrapped about his neck. "Several that might scandalize the swans."

He laughed. "Speaking of scandals, *The Marriage of Figaro* is playing at Covent Garden. Shall we go to the theatre this week and watch Mozart take swats at our overbearing class?"

"You gorgeous, insensitive lump"—she shook him slightly—"I don't care if I never see a footlight again."

"Then perhaps we should catch a few swans for the bathtub and boggle their eyes."

She lowered the umbrella over their heads as the jade river slid by. "Boggle the bathtub. Who wants to wait?"

Two afternoons later, while Miklos was off to his "private bank," Eliza went shopping for a carriage robe in the Strand off St. James' Park. Because the day was pleasant, she was in no hurry to make a selection and her driver soon became resigned to dozing outside luxury emporiums while she browsed, eventually emerging with leather riding gloves, cravat pins, and studs for Miklos. She also bought a practical pair of woolly bedroom slippers for herself due to the English aversion to heated rooms. She would have included a flannel nightgown to warm the rest of her had Miklos not asserted he could deal with that problem and directly proven his point. She was about to remount the carriage for the third time when a familiar voice drifted toward her. With a choked gasp, she ducked behind the open carriage door.

The foreign woman and her blond companion entered the Golden Apples Tearoom down the street. Eliza had been hideously right about the voice she heard; it belonged to Bianca. Impossible! she thought, her hands going clammy.

My God, that evil creature is like a pursuing nightmare! Wherever Miklos and I go . . . Eliza quickly climbed into the carriage to wait. Why *is* Bianca here? she wondered tensely. Is she following us? Logic fended off panic. She and Miklos had not been followed from Paris. Bianca must be after bigger fish, but if she and Miklos were to interfere again, as willy-nilly they seemed to persistently do . . . Eliza recalled too well the Paris driver's seared face.

In less than an hour, Bianca emerged alone from the restaurant and took a cab. Eliza's driver, upon being told to follow her, did so with alacrity, but promptly lost her near the warren of crowded streets near Charing Cross.

"Miki, do you know this woman?" Sitting on the edge of the copper tub in their hotel suite, Eliza showed Miklos a sketch of Bianca's blond companion.

"No." Scrubbing his neck, he grinned wickedly as he sank deeper into the sudsy water. "But I'd like to. She looks like she couldn't say no to a troll."

Eliza grimaced. "She may even seek them out. She was lunching with Bianca."

Abruptly, he sat up. "Where?"

After she told him, his face went so stern she was almost frightened. "You *followed* her? Why not grab an adder by the tail?" He heaved himself out of the tub. "I'll see to her."

"No!" Trying to push him back down again was like trying to shift a house. "She's nearly blown you up twice. Three may be her lucky charm."

With maddening patience, he smiled quizzically down at her, bright pink with strain from hauling at him. "Then what do you suggest?"

Her hands kept sliding on his wet skin, so she gave up tugging and exasperatedly threw him a hand towel. As he flicked the scrap under his armpits, she flung herself into the damask chair by the tub. "Why not send an anonymous note to the police?"

Miklos pensively sawed the towel back and forth across his bottom. "As far as we know, Bianca and Guido have done nothing in England. Their dispatch of Monsieur Lavalle is likely to elicit a response as languid as . . .''

"Molasses in January," she finished grimly. She kicked off her shoes to pad about the rug, then squirmed out of her hampering crinolines.

"The English reaction may prove considerably livelier than molasses if the Sidoros' strings lead to Louis-Napoléon. To them, he wears the horns of his greedy great-uncle. But until I can prove that link . . ."—Miklos crooked a finger under her chin in mid squirm—"would you care to join me for a bath?"

Swirling the vacant crinolines, she teasingly danced out of reach. "Haven't we spent enough time in the tub the last two days? I'm developing wrinkles."

He caught her by the waist, spun her around, and began to unhook her bodice. "Before we've had enough time, the wrinkles will be permanent." His hands slid tantalizingly to her breasts and she caught her breath at the entrapment. With deliberate slowness, he eased the bodice away to savor the softness that filled his palms, the bare rosy peaks that teased his fingertips. He buried his face against her neck as she eagerly pressed against him, lifting her breasts for his caress. "Eliza," he whispered breathlessly, his own hunger overtaking him. "Eliza, the tub is too far . . .'' A moment later, they were lying in a cloud of wildly wafting crinolines.

Eventually, the bath was accomplished, but as she left the tub, Eliza yelped at her wet footprints on the scattered newspapers. Twisting, she tried to avoid setting her foot on a lithographed face garlanded by flowers. "Miki! It's her! The woman I saw with Bianca." Quickly, she tore out the picture and accompanying article. "She's opening this week as Ophelia in *Hamlet*. Mary Hamilton's her name." She peered at the last water-splashed lines. "Czar Nicholas, suggested to be her fervent admirer, means to show up opening night, so she'll be guaranteed some success even if she murders every line."

Frowning, Miklos examined the picture. "So long as that's all she murders."

The Drury Lane Theatre, London: October 20, 1847

"Another deadly evening at the theatre." Lush as a rose
in cinnamon panne and gold, Eliza fidgeted as the orchestra broke into the traditional fanfare for Czar Nicholas.
"I'd really like to throw a rotten cabbage at Bianca; she's
altogether too hammy. *Hamlet*, the killing of a king, the
czar of Russia, God save us!" She peered for the thou-
sandth time over their box rail about the Victorian theatre,
then up at the royal box where the czar stood to acknowl-
edge the salute. "Where *is* she? This is worse than Paris!"

"Nicholas is safe for the moment," Miklos soothed her.
"His bodyguards know their business. No one can get at
him while he's in the royal box and a pistol won't carry
that far with any accuracy."

Unconvinced, Eliza picked nervously at her ostrich fan
as the audience settled and the maroon velvet curtain went
up. Several minutes into the ghostly visitation of Hamlet's
royal father at Elsinore and his description of betrayal,
Eliza bounced up. "I can't bear it! We've got to find
Bianca or warn the czar!"

Firmly, Miklos drew her down. "Don't attract attention.
Bianca and Guido could easily be in the theatre without
our recognizing them. Bianca's clever. A bit of paint and
putty at masquerades and you'd not know her." He squeezed
her hand. "As for warning the czar, we've no real evidence other than our suspicions. And despite court gossip
of his affair with Hamilton, we can't just whisper in his
ear that his latest primrose means to put a terminal thorn in
his pecker."

"But what are we . . . ?"

"Quiet, chatterbox; I'm thinking."

Miklos thought through both acts 1 and 2. By Act 3
Eliza was beside herself. From his pensive face, she strongly
suspected he had set aside the czar's possible fate and
become absorbed in the play and Charles John Kean's
magnificent performance as Hamlet. Miklos was as moody
as Hamlet through the famous soliloquy. She could not

realize how deeply he was drawn into the play, how like needles its words pried into his heart.

> For who would bear the whips and scorns of time,
> The oppressor's wrong, the proud man's contumely,
> The pangs of déspised love, the law's delay . . .
> When he himself might his quietus make
> With a bare bodkin?

Restlessly, Miklos watched the transparent dissimulation of Mary Hamilton as the inept Ophelia. His mouth twisted wryly as she attempted to feint with Hamlet.

Aye, Loise, thou pretty liar, he reflected grimly, I did love you once. He could scarce wait for Miss Hamilton to hie her doubly scheming self from the stage. Lies begot lies like deepening mold upon a bread crust, the taint immediate to the taste. He knew Eliza sensed Loise's presence tonight, although she could not yet name it. She wanted to protect the czar's life, yes; but more, she wanted Loise made less powerful by asking him to put aside her secrets. Ah, the wiles a woman could put upon a man.

As Act 2 with its mummer's play began, Miklos watched the handsome serpent, Hamlet, choose where to coil and unnerve his victims, then with ironic lechery settle on Ophelia.

"That's a fair thought to lie between maids' legs."

Czar Nicholas was smiling at the line with much the same expression as Kean. Does lust not make us more the fools, to know what we amble after, yet pursue it to the grave? Unnoticed, Miklos shifted his gaze to Eliza. In her lay both courage and cowardice, passion and coldness, honesty and deceit; fortunately, thus far virtue had the edge. In the past few months, they had learned to tentatively trust one another, yet their bond would bear no strain attached to Loise.

Miklos's eyes narrowed. Victoria, with Albert faithfully dogging her tracks, had just unobtrusively entered the

czar's box. Nicholas looked taken aback. Clearly he'd not
expected a familial turnout for his dalliance with Miss
Hamilton. Aides efficiently settled the newcomers and
their small entourage without attracting much notice in the
semidarkness. Eliza, however, spotted them as quickly as
if she'd been a bat. Her fingers knotted painfully hard on
his.

"Well, there's no getting out of it now," Miklos muttered, then kissed her hand. "Stay here. If I'm not back in
half an hour, go back to the hotel. Have the concierge hire
a driver to take you directly to Eagle Schloss at Saint
Moritz."

"But what about you?"

"I may be bound in political complications for a time,
but I'll join you directly."

She looked dubious. "Miki . . ."

"We've not time to argue. Trust me."

She bit her lip. "Kiss more than my fingers. I'd sooner
believe a snakeoil salesman."

He readily obliged.

After Miklos left, Eliza fixed her tense attention on the
royal box. Miklos and a sandy-haired man shortly appeared
at the door of the royal box. After several minutes of
whispered argument with Albert's aide and the chief of
Russian guards, they gained entrance to the box. Victoria
and Nicholas were impatient at the intrusion; only Albert
was inclined to hear out Miklos and his companion, whom
she supposed to be a diplomat. The aide appeared to be
insisting that the royal box had been searched before their
majesties' arrivals.

Miklos pointed to a chair. The queen was perturbed,
particularly when the aide apologetically suggested everyone move to another box for safety's sake. At her refusal,
Albert suggested that a reinspection might at least be in
order. The queen abruptly waved for the aide to proceed.

While Victoria stolidly viewed the performance, the
royal gentlemen rose to have their chairs quickly upended,
split open for a bomb search, and replaced. Feathers wafted
about Victoria's pug face. When her turn came, her maj-

esty, deeming her point proven, refused to budge from her chair. Victoria brusquely waved aside Miklos's urging for further investigation and presumably a search for the Sidoros. Nicholas, impatient to watch his mistress, added his demurral. Miklos and the diplomat retired from the box.

When Miklos did not return immediately, Eliza surmised he was seeking the Sidoros; he could as easily trace a needle in a haystack, for their only lead was Mary Hamilton. Nicholas's attention was more fixed on Ophelia than the mummers croaking onstage.

A short while later, Eliza crept among the flat stacks backstage, her gilt mantilla draped high about her head and shoulders. The disguise was useless for she was corralled almost immediately by the stage manager. As his firm hand locked under her elbow to escort her out, she blurted, "I've a message for Miss Hamilton," then as he raised a dubious brow, whispered, "from the czar."

His hand promptly shifted direction and steered her to a dresser who steered her to a dressing room. He knocked. "Miss Hamilton. A lady visitor to see you."

There was a sharp silence, then Mary Hamilton's voice, nervous and higher pitched than on stage. "For God's sake, send her away. I've the mad scene coming up!"

As the dresser indicated the way out, Eliza leaned closer to the door. "Pity. Nicky regrets."

The door snapped open. "Regrets what?" Hamilton's white face told Eliza more than words.

"More than I can discuss publicly." With a regal shrug and swirl of cinnamon panne velvet, she strolled into the room and quickly scanned her surroundings. The door closed behind her.

"Now, tell me," Hamilton said urgently, "what message did the czar give you?"

Eliza prowled the cluttered dust- and talc-dulled room with its hanging costumes, its scent of stale perfume, and faded Yorkshire rose wallpaper. "Very much the same as he indicated to you, Miss Hamilton." She eyed the brocaded dressing screen. "May I congratulate you on your performance. As a woman, I appreciate how much experience a pretense of inexperience requires.''

"Thank you," Hamilton replied warily, "but you must appreciate how little time . . .''

"Before your mad scene . . . yes.'' Eliza drifted to the screen. "That's your last scene, isn't it? And then . . . let me see if I have it right . . . Nicky pays you a visit.''

Hamilton gripped the back of her dressing chair. "Has anything changed his plans?''

"Um.'' There it was; a distinct odor of gardenias overlying the other perfumes. "Vicky and Albert. A dull, disapproving couple that. Nicky might be wedged between a pair of bookends.''

"He's not coming?'' stammered Hamilton.

"You can see it might be awkward.'' Intent on summoning the royal bodyguards, Eliza edged toward the door. "Better hunting another time. So sorry . . .''

"And shortly sorrier, indeed, to be so persistently meddlesome; my not-so-dull-witted friend,'' came a familiar, ironic voice behind the screen. A white, beringed hand appeared. The screen moved aside and revealed a queen. Rather, twice the travesty of a queen. Hideously lovely twins of Queen Gertrude, Hamlet's mother: the one, standing, a white-painted, kohl-eyed Gertrude with red smile painted wider than a mocking mouth; the other, sprawled among her mock royal robes, with her carmine mouth smeared into her hairline. She was dead, her skull and paste crown crushed by a lead gilt jewel box. Scattered glass jewels were repasting themselves in blood to the carpet. Minutely reflected in their fragments was the dismembered image of a smiling monster who carried the heavy scent of gardenias. "Lock the door, Ophelia dear,'' murmured Bianca. "Our visitor will not be leaving.''

Exasperated by further argument with Pomeroy, the British diplomat, Miklos returned to his own box for Eliza. Their luck had to run out; the faster they left London now, the better. He found the box empty, except for her note tucked into his chair seat. "Off to crack Ophelia's nut.

Wish me luck!'' With a muffled oath, he crumpled the note and half wished it were Eliza's neck.

In the midst of his frustration and anxiety for Eliza, Miklos was annoyed by yet another grating note; a rabbity note that quavered, scrambled about the vocal scale as if pursued by an angry mink.

The rabbit was Mavis Holcomb, the apprenticing stand-in for the missing actress in the role of Queen Gertrude; the mink was Charles John Kean. An Italian stagehand had come for Mavis in the supporting cast dressing room and nearly broken her arm rushing her to the stage. She'd damned well better manage the part, he threatened, or he'd slice off her silly nose.

Mavis, literally thrown head foremost beyond her wildest dreams and experience into the most demanding scene in the queen's role, faced Kean, who met her with his eyes nailing into the offstage manager's, his voice a welcoming bore drill. ''Now, mother, what's the matter?''

Queen Mavis, not eighteen, frantically babbled her first line. Behind the manager stood the stagehand, his bespectacled, black eyes threatening pure murder. Desperately, Mavis speeded up, and turning his back to the audience, Kean hissed to the manager, ''Get this mewling babe off! She sounds about to puke!''

The manager firmly shook his head, extending his hands to display his helplessness. Behind him, the stagehand glared furiously at Mavis, then disappeared, no doubt to find a knife. The girl's courage failed completely. She bolted from her chair.

Like a badgered but resigned bulldog, Kean blocked her attempt to flee the arena. ''Come''—he snagged her— ''come, and sit you down.'' She bounced up, his hands slammed against her shoulders. *''You shall not budge!''* he thundered.

''What wilt thou do?'' she returned feebly as the audience began to squirm, puzzled at the extraordinary erraticism and inexplicable twist of the scene. ''Thou wilt not murder me?'' she blurted. His stony glare inspired a suddenly remembered, ''Help, help, ho!''

Behind his canvas arras, Polonius, eager to restore proper feeling to the tale, howled, "What, ho! Help, help, help!" as if his tail had been caught in a door.

"How now! A rat? Dead, for a ducat, dead!" snarled the disgusted Kean, and as the audience gave way to titters, jabbed the arras vengefully with his blunted foil.

Polonius yelped in pain as his kidneys were prodded, and the audience howled.

Miklos, no more amused than the actors in the play's having gone afoul, but profiting by their confusion, immediately went to the dressing room section under the stage. He collared the dresser who, still trying to ferret out the missing queen, was pawing through the gloomy, underlit wardrobe room. "Miss Hamilton's dressing room, if you please, sir."

"You can't see her now," defied the dresser valiantly. "She says no more callers before the mad scene." The cravat tightened and the man stubbornly pushed away. "Good God, man, she's had one visitor in the past quarter hour. Have the courtesy to push off until the poor bitch's done with her pansies and rue!"

Miklos frowned. "A visitor?"

"A lady." The dresser's chin bunched. "Now off with you or I'll call the manager."

"Show me to Miss Hamilton's dressing room or I'll turn those pearly teeth of yours into shirt studs," rebutted Miklos mildly.

The dresser swiftly pointed. Then to Miklos's surprise, his eyes rolled back in his head and he fainted. The abrupt drop of weight momentarily cost Miklos his balance, but saved his life as a swiping battle-ax from behind shaved his cheek and clipped off the rim of the dresser's ear to land against a costume rack. Though a blunt prop, the weapon had enough edge and heft to be lethal. In an avalanche of costumes, Miklos whirled to find the battle-ax sideswiping at his neck and Guido's inky eyes a fixed scorpion stare. Miklos ducked, shoving over a tin suit of armor as Guido whipped out a stiletto. The grate and din of crashing metal carried up onto the stage.

In the royal box, the diplomat, Pomeroy, had his own problems. Czar Nicholas, his imagination warmed by Kean's vivid conjuration of "an enseaméd bed, stew'd in corruption, honeying and making love," was eager for Mary Hamilton's dressing room couch. Pomeroy, mulling over Miklos's warning, was loathe to let him go anywhere, and when Nicholas rose, ostensibly for a breath of air, Pomeroy hastily suggested he could do with a bit of the same. Unwilling to unduly draw Victoria and Albert's notice to his proposed absence, Nicholas hesitated to scotch his presumption.

While Nicholas considered how to deal with Pomeroy, Bianca was dealing with Eliza. "Nicholas will come as planned," she calmly informed the panic-stricken Mary Hamilton. With a weird smile through her paint, she gestured languidly at the dead actress at her feet. "And when he slips away to see you, our Bea Fox here, envious, aging actress and sometime hysteric, slips him . . . this." Moving closer to Eliza, she eased out a carnelian-hilted stiletto. "In Bea's dressing room will be found newspaper clippings of Nicholas; across one will be scrawled 'down with oligarchy.' Simple, to create an assassin." Her Medusa's gaze shifted to Eliza. "You, Princess, will be an unfortunate bystander, stabbed with the czar before Miss Hamilton could club the assassin with her jewel box."

Eliza debated screaming, but she'd likely be dead in mid shriek; if anyone inquired, Hamilton could pass the racket off as one of her own nervous tantrums. Bianca was again moving closer. "And how do you propose to dispatch Miss Hamilton?" Eliza said hurriedly.

Bianca's eyes narrowed and Hamilton's shot wide. "What?" the actress croaked.

Eliza sidled away. "She can hardly let you live. Bianca doesn't like to watch her back."

"*Four* bodies? That's a bit much, even for me," scoffed Bianca. "Don't listen to her, Mary. She's only trying to confuse you."

"That's just why Bianca means to be rid of you, Miss Hamilton. You're easy to confuse, to persuade; that's how

she talked you into this . . .'' Eliza dodged back as Bianca
sliced at her and Hamilton stifled a shriek. ''You're
already nervous. Would *you* leave a nervous accomplice,
Miss Hamilton?''

A crash thundered on the stage above and Hamilton
grabbed at her neckline. ''What's going on up there?''

In fact, Hamlet's ghost was walking, but his ramparts
were overcrowded with a pair of flitting figures pursuing
each other through the suspended drops and pulleys. A
second crash occurred as Miklos pulled down another back
stage set to barely interrupt a lethal thrust of Guido's
stiletto. Grabbing a belaying pin from a drop support,
Miklos tried to beat off another attack. With Kean
hammerlocked about her neck, the neophyte queen sat
rapt, staring at the hot-hearted pair offstage beyond the
uncertain Ghost, who feared as much their bizarre gam-
boling as her forgetting the whole scene. ''But look, amaze-
ment on thy mother sits,'' the Ghost groaned to Hamlet.
''O, *step* between her and her fighting soul!''

Kean, startled, but no dullard, took the cue and blocked
Mavis's view of the strange men hacking and slashing at
each other on the ramparts just offstage. He need not have
bothered for at last, spent with frantic fear and distraction,
Mavis resolved to bear no more. She would ignore the
men chopping at one another in the wings. They could not
be real. She also ignored all mention of the Ghost in her
next line, and Kean was obliged to supply his presence.
''Do you see nothing there?'' he coaxed her.

''Nothing at all, yet all that is I see,'' Mavis replied
peacefully.

But by now, even the wing audience had fleeting glimpses
of the dueling assailants and began to mutter.

''This seems less a play than a bad rehearsal,'' stated the
czar impatiently. ''If you will excuse me, Your Majesties
. . . Mr. Pomeroy, please do me the honor of attending
Their Majesties, I shall return directly.''

Though Pomeroy could not tell exactly what was happening backstage, he was now convinced Denmark was
displaying far more disturbance than its moody prince

customarily commanded. Before Nicholas reached the door,
Pomeroy confided as much to Albert. Albert, aware of the
Nicholas–Hamilton affair, promptly joined Nicholas. "I'll
join you for a smoke, Nicky. I've been wanting to discuss
a sensitive matter with you." Firmly, he hooked his arm in
the czar's.

In those minutes, Miklos lost Guido in the labyrinth of
painted sets stacked backstage and exchanged his belaying
pin for a sword. His new weapon was a dull, unbalanced
prop, but steel more sure than wood. Pursuing a killer with
a toy sword was little to his liking; following him through
dark, narrow tunnels of canvas where only a rat had room
to fight was less so. As he stole uneasily along the creaking boards behind the central set, a muffled cry and thud
came from the arras where Polonius supposedly mouldered.
Like a swift, savage kiss, Guido's stiletto blade thrust
through the canvas drop and slid past Miklos's face. Miklos's
responding sword rent a bigger slit with a rasp of canvas, a
sickening grate of steel on bone. A body slumped onto
Polonius's limp form as black blood seeped down the canvas.

Eliza held out Mary Hamilton's dressing chair like a
cornered trainer against a panther. The stiletto nicked a
chair rung and splinters flew. "Grab her!" Bianca ordered
Hamilton.

Instead, Hamilton began to feverishly weave artificial
flowers into her hair. "You grab her! I want no more of
this. I'm going to do my scene now. Then I'm going
home. I want you all out of here. Right now!"

"You're not going anywhere," snarled Bianca, "until
we're finished with Nicholas!"

"I *am* finished with Nicholas. I did my part. He's
coming." Mary Hamilton's fingers flew. "Do whatever
you like with him. You promised me notoriety, not
witnesses." She circled for the door.

Eliza circled with her. She had to get out of the room
with Hamilton. She'd last less than a minute alone with
Bianca. Almost witless with panic, Hamilton fumbled with
the door lock.

"If you leave now," warned Bianca, "you'll be linked with the assassination, not as a romantic heroine, but an accomplice. Everyone knows you've been in here since Bea Fox disappeared. They won't believe she hid behind your dressing screen all this time!"

Not the quickest of wits, Hamilton hesitated.

"They won't believe it, anyway," Eliza bewildered her further. "Bea Fox wouldn't dare miss a whole act to waylay the czar. Don't you see, Bianca *has* to kill you!"

Hamilton wrenched at the door. She was halfway through, Eliza guarding her rear with the chair, when suddenly Bianca made a jab. It glanced off the chair, buried in Hamilton's buttock. The actress screamed with all the power of her practiced lungs and fell into the hallway. At Bianca's next swipe, Eliza dodged back, tripped over the prostrate, howling Hamilton. She scrambled to her knees as Bianca lunged. Bianca's eyes abruptly widened in a catlike glare; she grabbed the chairlegs, thrust Eliza powerfully backward. Eliza felt strong hands catch her as she hurtled to the floor.

"Tonight, Bluebird, you are going to get the spanking you have long deserved."

She wriggled free to see Bianca running down the hall. "Miki! Stop her! That's Bianca! She's after the czar!"

Miklos headed after Bianca, but was shortly back, his face tight with frustration. "She got to a rear exit and a waiting carriage."

"Yaahh!" shrieked Hamilton. "I'm dying!"

"That"—Eliza pointed at Hamilton's quivering, blood-stained rump—"was Bianca's bait."

Wearily, wondering if this nightmare performance would never be done, Kean swept aside the arras curtain to "lug the guts" of Polonius offstage and finish with the scene. He sighed philosophically as the audience gasped; two bodies were in the arras, with the wrong one dead in a pool of real blood. Pinned beneath the corpse of Guido, Polonius whined pitifully.

Brussels, Belgium: October 26, 1847

Eliza never got her spanking. Leaving the English to sort out the Sidoro plot, Miklos had her on a steamer to Brussels by sunrise. "I'll write Pomeroy when we're safely out of reach." That was not easily done. The British ambassador and an aide to the Spanish Netherlands were at their Brussels hotel door scarcely a day after their arrival. Miklos flashed his forged papers, told them all they wished to know about the Sidoros, but flatly refused to return to London to give evidence. "You'll have to tidy your own mess, gentlemen."

The ambassador steadily argued for another half hour, but as Miklos was not an English national, had to give up.

"We'll take only what traveling clothes we can easily carry and catch the afternoon train for Stuttgart; from there, another to Ravensburg. If necessary, we'll get across the Swiss border by donkey cart," Miklos said quietly when he and Eliza were alone again. "If that unimaginative paperstamper found us in less than a day, he'll have enough sense to send an inquiry about my diplomatic status to Metternich."

Metternich was the powerful chancellor of Austria. Miklos had described him as the man to whom he must answer for breaking his terms of exile. "Why were you exiled, Miki?" Eliza murmured. "I've been hoping you'd tell me without my asking."

He caressed her cheek. "Then don't ask now, sweeting. Not yet." His eyes shadowed. "I did a shameful thing once. I didn't plan what happened, but exile was my punishment, a punishment I once thought too light. It became a living hell. I will not take you with me further into that hell than I must."

Her eyes searched his. "What will Metternich do if he finds you?"

"I'm not particularly important, so I doubt if he'll give me much thought."

Eliza wasn't sure she believed him. How much thought

must Metternich take to destroy a man? Exile was a single thought; a single, lonely howl against the heedless wind.

"Time's running out, isn't it, Miki?" she said quietly. When he didn't answer, she put her arms around his waist. "If the honeymoon's done now, I've had a wonderful time. Even Bianca couldn't ruin it." She squeezed. "I don't need to be spoiled."

"Oh, yes, you do," Miklos replied softly. "Sometimes I wonder if I've world enough and time to smooth away all your old scars. At the least, we need years together, not weeks."

"Why do you sound as if our marriage were coming to an end?" She studied him uneasily. "Isn't it just beginning?"

"The marriage is beginning"—he smiled crookedly— "but the honeymoon is almost over."

"Does that matter so much," she murmured, "if now we will have our years?"

He looked down at her for a long moment, his eyes filled with sadness and uncertainty. The haunting, passionate songs he'd sung with his *balalaika* at Como drifted into Eliza's mind. Then his mouth came down on hers, hard with unguarded urgency as if he wanted something from her he didn't know how to get, even with his body. And moments later, when he took her to bed, he forged to her as if fearing at any moment he might be wrenched away.

Friedrichshafen, Württemberg: November 5, 1847

The honeymoon was ended less than two weeks later by an Austrian military attaché accompanied by six dragoons. Miklos and Eliza were driving an unsprung cart through a forest near the Swiss–Austrian border when they heard horsemen. To elude possible pursuit and avoid being trampled on the snow-patched path, they pulled off unseen into a sere thicket of bushes among the firs. Melting snow dropped solemnly from sagging branches, hooves stirred the wet, rotting leaves as the horsemen passed. Due to ground soft from early snowmelt, they soon returned and fanned through the wood. Hearing the nearing jingle of bridle bits, Eliza whispered, "They must be looking for us! Run! I'll tell them I'm lost and looking for help. I can keep them busy until you can reach a farm with a horse or get to Bregenz across the border."

He shook his head. "We don't separate, *cara*. Can you ride?"

"If I could, do you think I'd volunteer to play decoy?" Eliza gave him an unhappy little shove. "Go on! They'll just send me to Bette sooner or later."

"Until then, Metternich would just use you as *his* decoy." He kissed her nose. "And you're not one this sitting duck could ignore."

"So what do we quack? 'Liberty or Death' or 'Long Live the King'?" She slipped her hand into his.

He could feel that hand shaking.

Chapter 11

The Phoenix in Winter

Saint Moritz, Switzerland: November 11, 1847

In the Eagle *Schloss* courtyard, dragoons sent stableboys stepping to stable their horses. Their commander quickly ordered four men to take up posts about the house; another two, spurs jingling on the stone veranda, to guard the main door. He escorted Miklos and Eliza from the coach, then waited with them after summoning the butler. Bette, a few steps behind the butler, gave him a chilly glance, and after throwing wide the door to the Sztarais, abruptly left him in the cold.

"Good heavens, what are you doing here?" she demanded as servants brushed snow off the royal newlyweds. Wriggling with joy, Max bounded about Miklos's feet as Miklos wooled his fur. "I should have thought Metternich would have carted you off to Vienna."

"Metternich has his hands full enough with threat of rebellion," grimly replied Miklos, shrugging out of his cloak. He gave it to one of the Tyrol-coated lackeys, then helped Eliza out of her fox furs. "For now, he's just leaving one of his pet armies at our door."

"Your little 'banks' give you deuced quick information," Bette observed, giving Eliza an absentminded hug.

"Also reliable. That's how they stay in business." Putting his arms around both women's shoulders, Miklos escorted them into the library. Max, his tail wagging, delightedly trotted after them.

Eliza observed that the *schloss* rooms were smaller than those of the Como villa, though no less luxurious with their handsome, walnut furnishings, great Turkish rugs, fur throws and Flemish Renaissance paintings. The ornaments that appeared to be brass were gold, the priceless Chinese T'ang dynasty vases mixed with charming delftware. While Eliza preferred Como's sunny villa, she was as much at home in the *schloss*, with its heavy oak beams, huge fireplaces, and mullioned windows. After the long, military-escorted train ride from Germany, anything that didn't rattle or hiss with every icy draft would have appeared cozy. She was numb to the teeth and her legs and back ached as they had not in months.

Miklos seated her in a bargelloed wing chair near the fire, then wrapped her in a fox throw. Bette smiled as he poured Eliza mulled *gluwein*. "I gather you enjoyed your honeymoon."

Miklos and Eliza exchanged glances. "Getting away was exactly what we needed," Eliza replied.

"Unfortunately, the only dull spot was Metternich's prevention of our getting away altogether," lightly added Miklos as he sipped his wine. "So now here we are and must make the best of it."

And in the three weeks that followed, he did. Like a hawk forced back to its cage after a taste of freedom, Miklos threw himself into every diversion the remote mountain spa had to offer. Aware of his desperation, Eliza accompanied him. In the velvets, jewels, and furs he had bought her in London and Paris as if their wealth were endless, she caroused and danced with him both in the mountain mansions of the wealthy and the countryside's inns, drank wine until dawn. Doggedly, with false brightness, she stayed by him. He had never needed her before, but he needed her now in a way she knew he scarcely realized. What could he have done that haunted him so? Surely, the crime had become exaggerated in his mind. She was sure Miklos, while he could be dangerous, was incapable of dishonor. Though he laughed and teased her much the same as he always had, he was burning away inside, with strange, dark moods coming upon him. With each day, she grew more afraid for him, more protective of him.

On surface, life went on. In clear weather, they donned Norwegian skis to cross the sunny summits of the surrounding mountains, where he tempted her down relatively simple runs that terrified and exhilarated her. Finally, she took the entire length of the Piste Noire stubbornly, but wisely, on her bottom.

With Max tagging along and skis strapped to their backs, they climbed much of the lower range, but unable to manage telemark turns, Eliza ran into trees, careened uncontrollably off hummocks. Their guards, after doggedly trailing up the mountain sides for a week and observing her progress, decided she was highly unlikely to escape with Miklos on skis. Now, they wiled away afternoons in the town cafes.

At length, Miklos came to the same conclusion as the guards. With a sigh, he finally toppled Eliza into a snow bank and kicked off his skis. He'd hoped to leave the ski-less guards and cross into Italy, but Eliza would never manage the passes. With a wry smile, he looked down at her, adorable and disheveled, as she tried to scramble out of the drift. Bouncing into the flying snow, Max licked her face and she squealed. "Such exquisite form merits only one reward," murmured Miklos. And there under a cobalt sky, with his body blocking the cold, he unbuttoned and made love to her, quickly, deeply, and deliciously. Her first laughing protests, he scotched. "No one's out here but Max. Besides, Swiss wildlife is never so unSwiss as to appear shocked by anything."

Afterward, when he lay wrapped about her in the sun-glinted crystal, she burrowed her nose against his neck. The village was far below, all about them the lovely wizardry of winter. Max wallowed on his back, then with tongue lolling and snow frosting his muzzle, flopped over to grin at them. "This is nice," Eliza softly growled.

"Um," Miklos agreed sleepily.

"But not nice enough."

"How do you mean?" Now he was completely awake.

"Fun isn't fun anymore, is it?" she replied quietly. "You're wearing your wings out, beating them to tatters, trying to reduce yourself to being a flightless chicken."

Slowly, he rose to his knees. "Running you ragged, am I?"

"I don't mind. I did a lot of sitting for a decade, remember. Besides"—Eliza propped her head up on her elbow, her voice dropping shyly—"I'd much rather be with you than not."

She was startled by the surprise in his eyes, then they filled with a shyness like her own, a sweetness like a boy's. Without a word, he made love to her again, slowly, his mouth warm on hers, his sex warm, probing within her to discover a virginity in them both, a blinding sunflare of joyous revelation and delight.

That sunflare was dimmed, nearly obliterated, by a message waiting at the *schloss*. Eliza watched Miklos's face as he read it in the study. "Bad news?"

"That depends on how you look at it," he said expressionlessly. "We're summoned to Christmas court in Vienna." Where, as befits my exalted rank and Metternich's pressed agenda, I shall no doubt be invited to discreetly blow my brains out to the tune of Yuletide bells, he thought grimly. Thank God, Eliza's unaccustomed to European methods of erasing aristocratic embarrassments connected with their military. Aloud, he merely commented, "You'll have a chance to show off your furs."

"I'd sooner wear gray woolies in Lapland." Eliza began to pace uneasily in front of the fireplace with its brass eagle andirons. With the firelight sculpting their flaring, brass pinions, the eagles appeared to be indestructible phoenixes. Uneasy at the tension in the room, Max sniffed at Eliza's skirts. She turned to Miklos. "Isn't there any way out?"

"Of course." He nodded at the carved oak door and Metternich's detachment beyond. "Through them."

Eliza sensed he was holding something back. "If I had known how to ride a horse," she said slowly, "we might have escaped in Germany."

He shrugged and tossed the letter in the fire. "Possibly." Then added offhandedly as the wax seal of Austria spattered, melted like a bloody stream into the coals, "You never went near the stables at Como. I assumed you disliked horses."

She looked at him sidelong. "A pony not a great deal bigger than a mastiff broke my back."

"*You* broke your back. Unless he turned and sat on you, the pony had little more to do with it than a log."

"He shied . . ."

"You shouldn't have." He poured wine for them both, stirred it with a cinnamon stick. "A horse may be sly, but it's not clever. You're smarter by far."

"Thank you," she said dryly.

He smiled, handing her one of the glasses. "If you want to ride again, I'll try to see you don't break anything else."

She set the wine on the Biedermeier table. "I *don't* want to ride again. I'd rather have my head bitten off. Only . . ."

"Only what?"

She threw up her hands. "I'm not good enough to *ski* out of here. With only two roads out of town, a carriage is too slow. The dragoons would divide and catch us before we got ten miles. And there's no getting them drunk. You must be quite a boy in Vienna. They don't trust you a lick." She began to pace again. "So how do I learn to ride within a week, if we have that long?"

"We have four days and you don't have to learn to *ride*. You simply decide not to fall off. You can do that in twenty minutes." He smiled. "Besides, you want to learn to ride."

"Ugh." She flopped onto the tufted, plush couch and

stuck her head under a pillow. When Max shoved his cold nose under the pillow, she hugged him so tightly he squirmed away.

The next morning, under the wide, snow-blanketed eaves of the *schloss*, Miklos had to bodily place Eliza on the mare and clamp her hands on the reins, so stiff with fear was she. "Heels down." He jammed her heel down in the stirrup. "Knees tight." He clamped her pant-clad knees. No ladylike, lady-killing, accident prone skirts and side-saddles in Miklos's class. He led her up the snow-covered rise behind the stable with its spruce- and aspen-clustered windbreak.

Her muffler wrapped up to her nose, Eliza hunched miserably in the saddle. "Oh, Lord, why not just put skates on this nag? Why doesn't Metternich have us for Easter court and bunnies and sane weather?" She complained for some time to distract herself from the mare's occasional lurches in the track grown slippery from repeated circuits.

At length, Miklos cut her short. "Concentrate on riding instead of yelping or you'll be on your backside under the mare's feet." Eliza shut up, but her hands inched over the pommel. "Depending on a handle with a girth loose will leave your brains on a tree trunk." Her hands inched away.

With Max trailing them, he led the mare a few rounds, then let her out on a training leader. Driven by his private turmoil, never before had he been such a disciplinarian. She might as well be in the army. At the end of an hour, he had her make a circuit on her own. Halfway through it, she froze up when Max cut in front of the horse after a chipmunk on the *schloss* woodpile. Miklos had to unlock her hands from the reins. "Fine," he murmured. "You've reached your limit for today. Tomorrow we'll have another go. Unless . . . you'd rather not."

"I'd rather not."

But next morning, she was stonily waiting by the paddock fence.

Near week's end, Eliza, though board stiff, had recovered her childhood ability to put the mare into the correct lead for a canter. When Miklos caused the mare to shy and crowhop by clapping his hands and switching its fetlocks, Eliza, white-faced, stayed in the saddle. Finally, he hauled her off the horse with a hug. "Well done, Gluebottom. Now we're off to the races!"

He meant literally, not off in a plunge across Europe, Eliza found shortly; the real thing was worse. In her opinion, to run a horse on ice was demented, but as she sat bundled with Bette in their sleigh alongside the befurred, aristocratic crowd lining Saint Moritz's snowbound racecourse, she saw such dementia was considered sporting. Miklos, in wolf fur shako and ankle length coat, was mounted in a capering, cavorting pack of riders warming up their entries before the starting line. Fat snowflakes powdered down, blotting visibility to dimly colored shapes. When the gun went off, Miklos, in a cloud of snow, seized the lead. To show her a horse stood no chance against human will, he drove his stallion as if he, not the animal, suspended his weight; that if the horse fell, he would go on just the same. In his wake, the riders floated chest deep in flying powder snow.

What an amazing, misleading illusion, she thought. What folly, as well as force and intelligence, Miklos's determination could screen. Her hands clenched in her muff, she slowly stood as the crowd cheered. A rider went down, disappeared like a crumpled potato sack under pounding hooves. Two more riders carommed together, crazily ricocheted on the ice against a cluster at their heels, went down with horses screaming as bones snapped. Men ran to carry them off the field. She'd lost a glove in the sleigh furs; her nails dug her palm under the muff as Miklos's stallion lost footing on the curve, scrambled. Regained. Putting his paws up on the sleigh rim, Max barked, and the driver, with a muffled oath, checked the startled horses.

"Win!" Eliza screamed without hearing herself. "You'd better win, you lunatic!"

Crossing the line first was the last thing on Miklos's mind. He had not claimed the lead to win, but to die. The decision was not premeditated; he'd coldly made it just before the race as he'd driven Bette and Eliza from the *schloss* and watched a sleigh mow across the flat ice below the town. The cutting blades of the sleigh's runners, the galloping hoofs of the team, suddenly promised an end to his being a "flightless chicken," as Eliza put it, of having his spirit gnawed away so much farther than she could guess, farther than liquor could make him forget, leaving him other memories, horrors. *Eli, Eli, lama sabachthani.* For his crimes, there was no escape, no forgiveness.

If the only unforgivable sin was despair, he was damned, for he knew only icy cold despair. In Vienna awaited more humiliation and, if Metternich had his way this time, a disgusting death. Miklos pictured putting a revolver in his ear, in his mouth. He could do it. With no emotion other than repugnance. He'd considered it often enough, particularly in the days after Loise had died. She died because he'd lost control. Afterward, he'd never completely gotten it back. He'd also lost his freedom and all hope of getting *it* back short of fleeing civilization. Now Metternich meant to wring his neck and be done.

Unless he arranged an accident for himself. Then, Metternich would never know whether he had won or not. Not that it would matter to Metternich; he'd have what he wanted even if unsure how he'd gotten it.

But it will matter to me, Miklos reflected. In that last second, I'll be flying free again. Choice screamed in his brain. Free. Free. Free.

He'd climbed quickly down from Bette's sleigh, then spoken to her only briefly, a quick kiss, but none for Eliza, just a squeeze of her hand and a glimpse of her eyes: uneasy, uncertain. That look stabbed at his resolve, at his heart; if he had stayed to take it away, he either would have left her with a lie or not at all.

Now he just had to stay in front of the race, pick his

moment. A horse cannoned against his leg, his mount skittered. Now! Now! Then in the blinding snow, he glimpsed Eliza's small figure in red fox standing, yelling, shaking her muff as if she were swearing at him, as if he'd stolen something from her.

He wanted to laugh. A Sztarai toppled in a horse race. Some would never believe it. Eliza would never believe it. She might eventually know why, but she would never forgive him. He'd played god too long, become her new crutch; now he was going to jerk it away without warning. She wasn't ready, not even with his wealth to shore her up. All those lessons, even riding lessons when he knew the guards weren't imbeciles and she'd never be competent in time to risk an escape; the lessons had been his way of pacing his cell: learning for her, methodical distraction for him. Control of a sort.

But he'd manipulated her life, reshaped it, and had no right to leave it half done. How fragile Eliza had been under the old bluff and bluster, still was, under her new, deceptive assurance. He'd taught her how to use freedom she would never have, tied to him. But could he give her to another man?

Thief, she seemed to cry. And was right. Whether he died or not, she would one day learn just how much he'd lied, and he had to be there to keep her from cracking; shield her from all the paradoxes as she pranced on her new legs. Then, his neat accident became brutal, like a bludgeon, poised not just over his head but hers.

So he won.

"Why, Eliza, your hand is bleeding!" commented Bette, startled.

"Is it?" Eliza said dazedly. "Did you see?! Miklos won!"

"He usually does." Bette dug for her chambray handkerchief to wrap about the ignored hand. "Losing comes so much less easily to him than winning; I think it's the only thing he doesn't know how to manage. When he loses, he's an overly polite gorilla. Be glad he won today. There won't be much winning in Vienna.''

When Miklos suggested a sleigh ride that night, their last in Saint Moritz, Eliza hurriedly began to pack traveling essentials in hidden pockets she'd sewn into a warm, velveteen dress and lining of her sables. The sale of the furs alone would see them across the world. Miklos, watching her collection pile up on their big, canopied bed, smiled slightly, but said nothing.

In a gay jingle of harness bells, the cavalry-escorted, scarlet and gold sleigh drew up to the cut glass paneled door. The driver jumped out in lightly falling snow to hand the reins to Miklos after a servant settled them under fur throws and held out a silver tray with tiny glasses of kirsch. Tears came to Eliza's eyes as she swallowed a mouthful of the watery-looking liquor. Gingerly, she exhaled. ''A dragon could wean on this. Am I breathing fire?''

Miklos kissed her. ''Saint Michael would be cinders.''

Leaning forward, the servant bearing the tray murmured something to Miklos in German. Miklos shook his head, produced a silver, stag-headed flask for the man to fill with kirsch.

''What did he say?'' asked Eliza, still trying to cope with the ever changing languages of their travels.

''He wanted to know if we needed him on the ride to pour the kirsch.''

''Silly man,'' she muttered as Miklos directed the sleigh away from the *schloss* through the snow-laden, black pine forest. ''What would newlyweds want with a live pitcher?''

Miklos laughed. ''That's an American problem. Many Europeans don't see servants, much less contemplate their degree of animation; unless it's inefficient.''

''You mean you could sit here, kissing me in front of that man?'' she asked incredulously.

''I just did.'' Miklos grinned. ''If you didn't notice, I must do it again.'' He did. Noticeably.

''But Miklos,'' Eliza protested breathlessly, ''that's ter-

rible . . . oh, not the kiss, the behaving as if people didn't
exist. He must have a wife, children . . .''

"A half dozen, if I know the practical Swiss. They
recognize the benefits of cheap labor." Miklos flicked the
reins over the matched Percherons. "Besides, he has a
right to privacy as much as I. He's just doing his job. Not
staring at each other makes things more comfortable all
round. For instance, those six fellows behind us saw me
kiss you. Don't you think they'd rather be in my place
than freezing their rumps off as chaperones?"

She slid him a look under her snow-dusted lashes.
"And of course you wouldn't be out to tantalize them
rather than your wife."

He studied her flushed rose cheeks and lips, her porcelain face in her dark, glossy furs. "I just forgot myself."

She snuggled closer. "Forget yourself again. They *are*
nuisances."

After some time and much forgetfulness, the horses
nearly wandered off the side of the mountain. "Where are
we going, anyway?" Eliza whispered at last. "Shouldn't
we be either heading back or luring our nuisances into a
crevasse?" While she wasn't altogether serious about dispatching their escort, she was growing desperate under the
relaxed mood she'd projected to keep their spirits up.
Heady and sweet as they were, Miklos's kisses were evasive lies. Some terrible fate awaited him in Vienna.

"I'm afraid crevasses are out," Miklos replied quietly.
"I couldn't find a guide worth his salt who would lead us
at night, so dumping our escort into one would merely
leave us to end up the same way." He put an arm about
her. "We're going to an inn tonight and Vienna in the
morning."

"Then why did I learn to ride?" she hissed in his ear.

"For fun"—then, when she started to squeak—"and
just in case."

The small inn topped a high bluff overlooking the valley
where a few lights winked around the town church spire.
Against the stars blazing the inky sky, the Milky Way
hazed a glittering trail that seemed to spill across the inn

roof; its icicles daggered drifts against edelweiss-painted walls.

As Miklos and Eliza went into the inn, their escorts took up their stations. "We'll have some nice, warm soup sent out to you and your men, Ensign," Eliza told their commander sweetly just before the door closed.

While the inn was tiny, its rose mahled furnishings and copperware were charming, the service of the innkeeper and his staff as suave as a Zurich hotelier's. Their cheerful blue, yellow, and white wallpapered room, with its curtained cupboard bed and Tyrolean balcony, overlooked the valley. The linens were lace-trimmed, the crystal vase of dried wildflowers and candleholders German. Hot soup, pastries, and a samovar of tea waited on a prettily set table. "Is it all right?" Miklos quietly asked Eliza when they were alone.

She was slightly startled; never once in their travels had he asked an opinion of their accommodations, whether fit for pigs or kings. She knelt on the window seat to look out of the ice-etched window at the lovely, silent valley sleeping under moonlit snow. "Everything is charming. So quiet and private."

"It ought to be. I reserved the whole inn."

"But why?" She turned eagerly. "Are you planning something?"

"Yes." He took her in his arms and kissed her lingeringly. "A long, winter night of lovemaking."

She rested her head back on his arm. "And a dawn escape."

He shook his head. "Vienna."

She sighed in frustration. "But why?"

Because if we try to escape, he thought, that icy, hostile ensign has orders to shoot to kill with an "accidental" bullet for you, my little Hottentot. "Impractical," he said simply.

"I don't ride well enough," she said mournfully.

"A horse crashing through rotten ice doesn't give a damn what's on top of him." He nuzzled her throat, eased open her bodice and kissed between her breasts. "You've the heart of a lioness, Eliza, and I'm proud of you."

"Really?" She gave a pleased sigh.

"But tonight, all I want is a soft, tawny pelt, not teeth and claws."

"Maybe you'll get both." She nipped his underlip.

That winter night was not long enough; no night could have been for the lovers who sensed it might be their last, and there was little softness about it until fatigue lulled them both from their impatience, their fevered ravaging of one another. Their clothing scattered to the floor. When Eliza lay naked beneath him, Miklos parted her thighs to take her with his mouth to tantalize himself, intoxicate her until she surged upward to receive his first hard, almost uncontrolled thrust when swiftly rising desire drove him to mount. His was a brute, instinctive act of possession, hers as strong in taking, molding his powerful surge. As if they meant to mark each other and leave indelible scars that would live beyond the night, they mated wildly, wordlessly, heedless of pain, taking pleasure as if they hunted it, plummeting upon it only to seek their prey again.

Then the sun cut through the mullioned window in wells of light, marking dazed fatigue and still restless hunger. Miklos made love to her softly, almost wistfully, as if she were down in which he could hide in peace and secrecy, yet even with that last ecstasy came loss.

And certainty to Eliza. Miklos had once brought Loise here: his shadow mate.

When they left the inn, they were pale, their eyes smudged with sleeplessness. Melting icicles on the trees and inn roof dripped, and in the pine forest, snow thudded from the weighted branches into the deep, shadowed drifts. The dragoons were silent, irritable, their faces pinched with cold. Why is it, Eliza wondered, blue as these men are, they were the lucky ones last night? Better to lie with ice than a lover one must lose. Whether we face the slow rot of exile or prospect of prison, Miklos smiles and smiles, and in facing death, would smile so. Just so. With lying calm as if life were small matter. Life with me, small matter. She settled silently into the furs piled into the sleigh. I'm still no more than the selfish child you found me, Miki. I'm not ready to give you up. With grace or any other way.

Chapter 12

Christmas Court

Baden, Austria: December 15, 1847

As they crossed Austria, Eliza saw Miklos had been right. In Metternich's hierarchy of irritations, Miklos must be a mere blister, for Austria itself was a festering boil. Despite spectacular mountains and rolling hills that might have been shaped by music, in the muddy-roaded villages she sensed unrest like a sickness, as if Austria were an invalid maddened by infirmities and weary confinement. Everywhere, the peasants were sullen at the sight of their military escort and carriage with Hapsburg eagles in its crest. After three men were detached from the escort, the muttering peasants' angry abuse was made bold by the escort's small number.

"Detached." Bette sniffed. "Metternich wants to provoke an attack and be rid of you, Miki. He knows some of these surly oafs may recognize you once we're close to Vienna."

"Miki?" Eliza was puzzled. "Why should any of these wretched people know Miki?"

Miklos gave her an oddly hesitant look, but when he started to answer, Bette quickly cut him off. "As an army officer, Miklos was based in Vienna. Large numbers of peasants served under him. Just now they resent any reminder of authority."

Peasantry beyond Baden certainly knew him. The name

Sztarai was hurled amid blistering German at the coach as
it hurried through a dawn-drowsy village. The nervous
ensign took a shortcut across a desolate, windswept field a
mile beyond the village. A peasant watched them from the
hillside, then disappeared. When Miklos gravely advised
against leaving the road, the ensign briefly thanked, then
ignored him. Shortly, the heavy carriage was bogged in
mire from snowmelt. The complaining soldiers dismounted
to cut a tree to pry the carriage out. No sooner were two
escort mounts hitched to the carriage team than peasants
loped over the rise. Scythes, bows, axes, and homemade
spears silhouetted against the sky as a mob of thirty men,
women, and children howled across the fields toward them.
"Have you got your pistol?" muttered Miklos to Bette.

When Bette, pale but stern-faced, jerked it out of her
sable muff, he called to the escort commander, "Toss me
a sword, Ensign! I'm at your service!" Readily, the ensign
did so while deploying his men to fan. He dismounted to
shelter behind the carriage. "Lie down," Miklos ordered
the women as he swung down from the carriage.

"Am I the only one without a weapon?" protested the
ashen Eliza.

"Do you know how to use a gun?" rebutted Miklos.

She grasped her green velvet bonnet. "Don't you think I
shall be directly presented with sufficient practice?"

His gray eyes burning into hers, he hauled her head
down, gave her a hard kiss, then handed her a tiny gun
secreted in his cloak. "Two shots, love. Merry Christmas."

The peasant leader, a burly man yelling in the forefront,
suddenly slowed, not due to two charging dragoons, one
of whom was immediately picked off by the bowmen, but
at the sight of Miklos behind the coach awaiting their
onslaught. "Sztarai!" he shouted. "Fuck my mother, it's
the big Magyar wolf!"

"Sztarai?!" took up another, hesitating. "The colonel?"

"Kill him!" shrieked a woman. "Get the butcher!"
Capering, she screamed taunts and obscenities.

Had the woman been within range, Eliza would have
been strongly tempted to put a bullet through her mouth.

A spear fell short, but another arrow thumped into the carriage a hand's breadth from Eliza's face. She plummeted into the coach bottom. Miklos and the soldiers knew better than to waste pistol ball until the range closed.

She surged up again as one peasant voice soared over the others. "I'm not going after Sztarai," abruptly announced the leader, halting and folding his brawny arms across his chest.

"Come on. He shot Petrus!" The other man who knew of Miklos shoved the big one on the shoulder. The big one turned on him, tripping two others dogging his heels into the snow. Eliza gathered the look in his eye was fearsome, for the other man awkwardly backed, blockading another peasant. Momentarily leaderless, the rest hesitated, waiting to see what would happen.

"Petrus was a horse's prick," flatly stated the big one, "too stupid to steal from his brothers' kits without getting caught and having to shoot an officer in the back. You want Petrus's kind back in the village so bad . . . here!" He threw a clod of frozen horse dung at the man. "Wear this for brains!" He clodded the others. "You and you, too, dungheads!"

Oh, Lord! Eliza steadied her shaking pistol. This peasant Spartacus was going to get himself and Miklos torn to shreds.

"Sztarai's a murderer," screeched the woman, ducking. "His own kind! Rotten, mucking aristos! Down with them and their lying laws, I say! Take their heads like the French did!"

The big man's jaw jutted into hers. "Maybe Sztarai had reason. Cross your legs lately, eh, frogface?"

She spat at him and he slammed a fist into her face, flattening her into the clodded snow. She didn't get up.

He stared down the others, then slowly turned toward the coach. "Colonel? You in charge of these blue-coated nits?"

The dragoon ensign tensely eyed Miklos. Would he protect his escort? "I'm the ranking officer," Miklos returned easily. "Sorry, I don't recognize you with the beard. Were you in my corps?"

"Hans Krafft, Colonel. From the Seventy-third Artillery."

Eliza's throat went dry as Miklos handed his gun to the captain. "Ah, yes, sergeant of gunnery." With a smile, he strolled out to meet Krafft. He gave a casual salute, which Krafft awkwardly returned. "I saw you at the Innsbruck maneuvers when I was aide to the inspector general. You took over your gun team after your sergeant fell off the caisson and broke his knee. I was so impressed by the team's improvement, I got drunk with your captain that night and recommended you for promotion."

"I heard, sir."

"You've retired from the army?"

Krafft held up a hand missing all its digits. "Discharged. A twelve-pounder blew up."

"Hard to work the land now."

The man shrugged. "Three bad years all round. Count von Werdenberg wants his cut just the same." He glanced at his gaunt, hostile companions. "They're as bad off. Typhus, wormy flux. The best men taken for the army. Winters are getting worse and Werdenberg's sold off the timber to keep his city whores. He parcels off the property to squeeze out easy rents; that squeezes what's left of us tighter on tired-out land. Same all over." He leaned on his scythe. "But all this is no matter to you."

Miklos looked at a hollow-eyed girl of eight. Her lips drawing back, she gave him a feral snarl. "Is Count von Werdenberg now in Vienna, Sergeant?"

Krafft snorted. "These past three months. He doesn't winter here, I can tell you. Flies out when the ducks are shot off."

"If I have opportunity, I'll speak to him."

"Of what?" demanded the thin serf at Krafft's side. He poked at the eight-year-old. "Of what he's missin' in the country? What he amuses himself with when he's bored enough?"

Eliza wanted to be ill.

"The count may see reason," said Miklos tightly, "given appropriate persuasion."

"Only thing you can do is beat him to death or buy us." Krafft smiled crookedly. "Beating him isn't practical and as for buying, this place is cold enough; we got no itch to freeze in Hungary."

"Unfortunately, I can't afford all of you." Miklos lowered his voice, "But some other arrangement might be reached with Werdenberg. Would you like to be free?"

The thin one laughed shortly. "Free to starve. No law, even what little shit we got, to protect us. They're scared of us now, don't want us roaming around." He grinned skeletally. "Just mind your business, foreigner, and leave us to take what we've paid with our hides for. Go mind your own chickens." He leered at the women in the carriage.

Miklos's face went cold. "Turn to brigandage and murder, and you'll hang." He looked at Krafft. "You deserve better, Sergeant."

"If you run with wolves, learn to howl . . ." The former sergeant didn't finish the quote. "Each to his own pack, sir." He skeptically eyed the dragoons. "Watch your ass in Vienna, Colonel. Metternich might try to make a sop of it." He smiled mirthlessly at his little band. "You see how it is. To look at us, you'd think we'd settle for anything."

"All the same, Sergeant," Miklos said softly, "there are worse things than freezing one's ass off in Hungary." Briefly, he thought of dispensing the gold in his pocket, then dismissed the notion as dangerously provocative. The peasants couldn't miss the idea of the soldiers having pockets as well. "God go with you all," he said quietly and left them. In minutes, he, the ensign, and the three remaining, sweating soldiers had the carriage pried from the mire under the peasants' hard eyes, and the thing lurched off the way it had come.

No one in the carriage said anything. Eliza was numbly detached, cut off from Miklos and Bette. She had been thrust back a thousand years with all their injustice a

sucking black mire about her. Two brave men had briefly
reached to each other across the breach of birth and foul,
ironclad habit. As a result, she was alive with a handful of
others who might now be justly hacked to bits in the
muck, not because they were evil, but because they had
not destroyed evil.

Vienna: December 15, 1847

Late that night, Eliza, Miklos, and Bette were installed
in a coldly barren, guarded suite of rooms in an inn off the
Ringstrasse. When the dragoon ensign had escorted them
to the inn, Bette put up a deliberate fuss, demanding that
they be taken to her palace near the Belvedere. The ensign
refused; her palace was too difficult to guard. She and
Eliza might go there if they liked; Miklos was to remain at
the inn. The women flatly refused, so all three were
wedged into the suite's tiny, top-floor rooms that smelled
of rancid grease from the restaurant on the ground floor.

When they were finally alone, Eliza brought up the
question that had haunted her mind since the morning
attack. "Those peasants called you a murderer, Miklos.
Why?"

When Bette started to answer, Miklos cut her off. "She
has to know, Bette." His voice turned grave. "After all,
they have reason for the accusation."

"Without proof, without witnesses," Bette objected.

Eliza was confused. Was it something they had done in
the army? "They think he killed serfs?"

"No, one of our class; otherwise, they would have
killed him." In her fur-lined cape, Bette looked incongruous against the gaslight-blackened wallpaper and discol-
ored mirrors. "What do you think?"

Eliza's nerves steadied. She might have guessed. Miklos
had fought a duel with another aristocrat. Duels were
illegal and nasty, but they still happened. She didn't hesi-
tate. "Miklos is no murderer."

"Unfortunately, Metternich and a great many other people think I am," Miklos replied flatly.

208   **Christine Monson**

"Now it appears they mean to execute him," added Bette.

Not having meant Eliza to know *that*, Miklos angrily turned on Bette, but too late.

Eliza had gone white. "What of a trial?"

"The supposed crime took place three years ago," Bette said flatly. "Given his royal attachments, Miki was not tried then. He will not be tried now."

That's why he was in exile, thought Eliza. Why he was so eligible, especially to an ignorant foreigner. Why we hid and ran all over Europe. "But assumption that he's guilty is as atrocious as exempting him from trial!" She looked hard into Bette's cool, blue eyes. "Why execute him *now*? Why the wait?!"

"Your romantic bolt across Europe was not viewed with indulgence in several quarters. As Sergeant Krafft suggested, a sop to the gutter populace may be in order." Bette went on dryly, "I say they'll regard it as a sign of weakness. But undoubtedly Metternich will hedge his wagers. The punishment will be exacted, but so discreetly it can be interpreted to suit everybody."

Eliza felt rising panic. "What do you mean?"

"Miklos will probably be ordered to commit suicide."

For the first time in her life, Eliza fainted.

She awoke to hear Bette and Miklos arguing. Familiar. Like her first night at Como a million years before. Only this time she was lying in Miklos's bed. She was his wife . . . but would she ever know what he was?

Bette was protesting, "You can't protect her forever, Miki! Not at the price of your life! You *need* her help! Besides, she was bound to ask, after those peasants yelling for your blood this morning."

"I would have told her when she came to Como, but she had troubles enough!" Miklos said furiously. "She's my responsibility; you should have let *me* explain to her . . ."

"She believes you're innocent. That's all that matters, isn't it?"

"All that matters," echoed Eliza faintly.

Curtly waving Bette out of their bedroom, Miklos was instantly at Eliza's side. His eyes went sick, almost colorless, as he saw the misery in her face, and he hadn't the heart to tell her the rest. His long hands went impulsively to her cheeks as if he would fend off all the unhappiness in the world from her. "I'm sorry you found out this way," he whispered.

"Once I would have run," she murmured, then focused on him clearly. "I won't run now."

Miklos let out his breath. Now he could do whatever he had to do. She was strong enough.

Stronger than he realized. With Bette, Eliza worked out every possibility of thwarting Metternich. "The three counselors under Emperor Ferdinand agree only to disagree," Bette told her. "Whatever Metternich wants, the other two—Graf Franz Anton Kolowrat and Archduke Louis,—will try to block, simply to contain his power. That's part of the reason this country is at the point of rebellion. To provoke Louis and Kolowrat's interest, you must see Louis's duchess and Kolowrat's wife. I'll arrange the meetings. Plead romance to the duchess, Teutonic virtue to Mme. Kolowrat. She's like her husband, that tally book."

"What of Ferdinand himself?"

"Useless. An ineffectual child everybody ignores."

"Charles Albert?"

"I wrote him the moment you and Miklos ran off on that idiot honeymoon." Bette sighed. "No reply."

"What of your royal relatives?"

"That's what kept Miklos from the vultures the first time. Now they're concerned about their own necks with the peasants making a fuss." She patted Eliza's hand. "I took the precaution of writing Prince Albert in England after your note about encountering that witch Bianca, but no one ever knows what tack Victoria will take. While Albert would be quick enough to help, she likes to keep him under her thumb. Whatever else we do, we must arrange a presentation at Christmas court, the most public display possible. That way, Metternich can't just shuffle us off quietly. Rave about your honeymoon to the rafters. The world loves a lover, *et cetera, ad dreariam.*"

So, while Miklos gritted his teeth under house arrest with all requests for an interview with Metternich refused, Bette and Eliza, past antagonisms shoved aside, began their campaign in the brilliant, palatial city of Vienna. They ceaselessly went to teas, the Court Theatre and opera, dinner parties and balls where Eliza rhapsodized about Miklos until her throat was raw. The Viennese aristocracy were charming, warm-hearted and hospitable, and despite Miklos's ill favor with the emperor, Bette and Eliza never lacked for invitations to their grand apartments.

The whole city was vivacious, its Christmas throngs hurrying through the broad streets with Christmas packages and great sausages and game birds for feasting. About the Gothic spire of Saint Stephen's rose singing and a soaring of pigeons, and in the city park, baby carriages with bundled occupants rolled under statues of the city's splendid wealth of musical immortals. Children balanced on the curved balustrades of the orchestral platform to throw snowballs. The tranquil, white grounds of the lovely Belvedere Palace were scattered with visitors at every hour, for the Viennese loved to stroll out of doors.

Yet everywhere, from the palaces to the coffeehouses, was unease about the possibility of rebellion coupled by determination to carry on life as usual.

And in that vein, the interviews Bette arranged with the counselors' wives went like butter. Bette had been right. The Viennese, even more than the French, were susceptible to romance.

"You *do* adore that handsome fellow," warbled Louis's archduchess.

"The Roman ideals of loyalty and fortitude will see us through these terrible days," intoned Mme Kolowrat.

Both women were as oblivious as the rest of the aristocracy, judged Eliza, her gratitude modified by the shallow, capricious motives of her new allies. Where were the common virtues of justice and compassion in their talcumed lexicons? No one cared if the peasants were starving, if

Miklos was guilty: their only concern was the face put on those situations before the uncertain world. Painting a rosebud glow about her and Miklos reassured them all was safe and sane about themselves.

In Italy, Charles Albert stared glumly at Bette's letter. Bad of her to bother him with more trouble when he was trying to decide whether to oust her Austrian crowd out of Piedmont. Still, Sztarai's bride was a pretty little thing. Pity. Should he bother to dictate yet another letter before lunch? His stomach growled and he eased the letter further back in the pile.

Despite Bette's advice, Eliza obtained permission through Mme. Kolowrat to see the king. The Winter Palace, eight blocks away on the Ringstrasse, was a handsome block affair, its entrance guarded by statues of Hercules, its arched, inner gate flanked by statues of men fighting a bull and a lion. As an imperial aide in a mink-collared frock coat marched into the courtyard to meet her, Eliza almost felt she needed a boar spear rather than a muff. Keeping well away from the busy central corridors, the aide took her up a rear stair to an empty anteroom adjoining the audience chamber. There she waited alone for over an hour. No tea was offered, no fire lit in the Meissen tile corner stove. Only two straight-backed chairs were in the carpetless room. The curtains were drawn and she gathered she was not to open them. This was the place where the unwelcome were made to feel their disfavor. Finally, the door to the audience chamber opened and the gimlet-eyed court chamberlain brusquely summoned her into the imperial presence.

When Ferdinand rose awkwardly from his chair to greet her, Eliza instantly saw her mistake in coming. For one thing, Ferdinand, no child, was at least in his fifties. As she curtsied, Ferdinand, at first not seeing his chamberlain's frown, made a shy, vague gesture toward a chair. Then he registered from the frown that to encourage Princess Sztarai might be time-consuming and unpolitic. He stood puzzled, wondering what to do about the chair. As the court chamberlain started to intervene, Eliza helped the emperor out. "Thank you, Your Imperial Majesty, but given the circumstances of my visit, I fear I am somewhat restless. May I stand?"

Ferdinand nodded gratefully, clearly having forgotten his briefing on why she had come. The chamberlain sighed, muttered a reminder in his ear. The princess was not to be encouraged. He was to say nothing definite. The council would decide the problem. Like a loose-headed doll, Ferdinand nodded for Eliza to state her case. After she had done so as persuasively as possible, despite his alternately staring at her with his pale eyes, then letting his attention drift out of the windows, he nodded again. "Would you care to see my soldiers?"

As if in some bizarre dream, she walked about his collection. He knelt down to straighten ranks of lead hussars, pointing out his favorite squadrons. "The finest, of course, are the uhlans."

"My husband was a colonel in the uhlans," she said quietly.

Ferdinand looked up, eyes shining. "Splendid! All the uhlans are heroes. They led the field against Napoleon."

She slipped a small cannon from her muff. "This is a model of a cannon that supported my husband's corps on maneuvers. Miki wondered if you might like it." Miki wondered nothing of the sort; he'd never seen the cannon, for she'd bought it in a city toy shop.

"How kind of the colonel."

Ferdinand was so pleased Eliza was ashamed. She watched him pump the caisson up and down. "They won't let Miklos be a soldier any more. He hates that."

"I'm sorry. Soldiering is a fine profession." Giving her another pang of guilt, all Ferdinand's doomed dreams came into his eyes. "I'm commander of the army. Sometimes the army parades for me"—he hesitated—"but my nephew, Franz, relays most of my orders."

"Perhaps, as Your Imperial Majesty is so taken with duties, your nephew might relay another order for you,"

Eliza murmured, her back to the prowling chamberlain. "When a soldier's duty is done, he's allowed to go home. My Miki asks only to go home."

Ferdinand looked at her sadly. "Franz is *Graf* von Metternich's friend."

And the emperor of Austria and Hungary, the ruler of millions, is not merely ineffectual, she thought wistfully moments later as the chamberlain briskly escorted her from the chamber; the poor man's an idiot.

As she walked through the guard-lined hall toward the front entrance stair, a door opened. A tall, muttonchopped man in uniform emerged with a dark-haired, smaller man. Seeing her and the direction from which she had come, the small man hurriedly whispered to the larger one. Muttonchops's eyes narrowed. He surged forward. "Princess Sztarai, I presume?"

With a plummet of her stomach, she halted.

"May I introduce myself? I am Chancellor Metternich." A bludgeon was more self-effacing.

"How do you do, sir?" she replied timidly. Let him presume her a gauche, harmless American.

"You are enjoying Vienna?" Blam, blam, blam.

"Ever so much, sir." Her eyes wide, she dropped a parlor maid curtsy that clashed with her ermine shako and cape.

"Try the Arboreum Garden," he commanded coldly. "So much more suited to ladies than His Imperial Majesty's tin hussars."

"Thank you, sir!" She scurried out of the palace. The fat's in the fire now, Miss, she told herself as she hurried into her carriage. Metternich knows I had an interview and can guess how I got it.

Bette threw up her hands when she found out about the palace visit. "I tried to tell you that inbred Ferdinand was useless! Metternich won't like being upstaged; our tampering through his rivals may trigger a very quick, nasty decision." She flung on her cloak. "Stay here. If a message comes from the palace, see it doesn't get to Miki. Eat it, burn it, throw it out the window, but get rid of it!''

No need to ask what instructions the message would contain, Eliza reflected tensely as she watched the street after Bette had left. Metternich would try to circumvent his rivals' possible objections to Miklos's destruction by ordering his death before they demanded a part in the decision. She eased into the bedroom. Miklos was fitfully asleep after another night staring into the fire. What did he think of, remember, behind those flame-glinted, gray eyes? Another world beyond this limbo. A future with hope of children and Christmases and white hair.

Eliza smoothed his hair, lay down beside him on the worn comforter across the iron-framed bed. His arm eased around her, his mouth over hers. She wanted to tell him her secret, but he gave her little chance. Strange to make love with her clothes on, merely opening them where his flesh sought to enter hers. She felt the chill, his warm hands on her breasts under the parted bodice, his warmer sex slowly sliding into her. Drowsy snowflakes seared her skin, began to burn and melt in her belly, build like an avalanche to hurtle her into a place of blazing ice. She heard a falling cry; Miklos's, her own, she did not know.

For a long time, she clung to him. His golden hair was against her mouth and she closed her eyes, wanting his sleepy weight. He smelled of sandalwood and the pipesmoke of his funny, old meerschaum. He'd ruffled her hair when he found her minutely examining its carved face one day at the *schloss* in Moritz. "My father's pipe. As a child, I thought it had the face of Santa Claus and I used to ask it for things.''

"Any luck?''

"Wonderful luck. Because I repeated most of the pipe discussions to Papa, I never had a disappointing Christmas.''

She laughed softly, remembering, then her distraught mind tugged her into sleep.

Dusk had fallen when a sharp rapping at the door jerked her awake. The city lights were a dull glow through falling snow, Miklos's alert face on the pillow white-carved against the window. "Go back to sleep, darling," she advised calmly, hoping he wouldn't notice her fingers shaking as she fumbled at her bodice in the dim light. "It's the delivery boy with dinner from The White Angel down the street. As you missed lunch and the food here is so taste-less, I told them to send him at five o'clock. He's late."

As she rose, Miklos eased back on the pillows. "No matter," he murmured. "Nothing is on time when it snows."

The imperative rap sounded again as Eliza closed the bedroom door behind her. She answered the summons to find a dragoon colonel standing between the guards in the hall. "Princess Sztarai?"

"Yes."

"I am Colonel von Weitten. I have a dispatch for your husband from the palace."

"My husband is asleep"—she extended her palm—"but you may be sure I will see he receives the note the moment he awakens."

"I'm sorry, Your Highness. My orders are to personally see the prince receives the message."

Gracefully, she retreated with a billow of green velvet skirts. "Won't you come in, Colonel?" When he stalked inside, she stood for some moments, both playing for time and scrutinizing him. Ruddy-faced, average looking, he was a little younger than Miklos, but stiffer and without expression; perhaps he knew his business. She went to the decanter, filled a glass. "The ride from the palace must have been chilly. May I offer you a glass of port, Colonel?"

Too quickly, he declined. So he did understand his errand.

"The ride was a short one, Your Highness, and I am expected back within the hour." His lips tightening, he looked about at the little tree she'd bought, the stubbornly cheerful decorations, the big, watchful dog.

"What a pity. I'm sure the prince would have enjoyed a chat with you." She sipped the port to bolster her cour-age. "Unfortunately, he was taken with a chill on our journey to your beautiful country, and I fear he's much too ill to see anyone.''

"I regret, Your Highness." The colonel purposefully headed toward Miklos's door. Max, snarling, stalked forward. The colonel drew his sword and stood his ground.

Eliza closed the dog in Bette's bedroom lest he be skewered, then grimly blocked the colonel's path. "If you insist, I shall disturb the prince; however, I should not wish to do so without proof of your mission. My husband has enemies." Her head came up. "You have not come to assassinate him, I hope."

The colonel, coloring, put up his sword. "Indeed not, Madame."

"Good," she replied dryly. "It is, after all, Christmas."

Hastily he produced the heavily wax-sealed missive.

In a breath, it was soaked in port and sailing into the fire. With a muttered curse, the colonel went after it, only to find Eliza, like a snapping foxhound pup, dancing maddeningly in his path. By the time he forcibly put her and her crinolines aside, the waxed, alcohol-soaked letter was flaming gaily. "This was not well done, Madame," he growled.

"I am protecting my husband," retorted Eliza. "Would I have done better to have shot you?" She opened a round-top table drawer, waved her tiny pistol. "Go home and kiss your children, Colonel, if you have any. Then pray they never learn what foul garbage you carried."

The man went white. "I merely follow orders, Your Highness."

"Then you're a stick, not a man!"

"Do you think you make me more of one by cindering my mail?" drawled Miklos from the bedroom door. "Colonel, you may relate your message."

The colonel stared at him, then at Eliza's desperate face. "I . . . I confess I don't know what was in the note." He smiled lamely into her astonished, grateful eyes. "The excitement of Christmas, I suppose. My superiors forgot to tell me."

"I suspect next time they'll remember," observed Miklos dryly.

"Would you care for another port, Colonel?" inquired Eliza, demurely sliding the gun back into the drawer. "I apologize for being so clumsy with that first glass."

"My fault entirely, Your Highness," said the colonel. "Perhaps another time when I'm not expected . . . elsewhere."

When Colonel von Weitten had gone, Eliza sagged against the drum top. "Why didn't he relay the message? I'm sure he knew what it was."

"Perhaps because you reminded him of one of those children he probably hasn't got," Miklos said softly. "You shouldn't have put him . . . and me into such a position, Bluebird. Metternich is likely to trot him off to winter on the Russian border because he failed in his duty and I hid behind your skirts."

"Weitten ought to think the winter well spent," she replied unrepentantly. "I'd have shot him if necessary."

"And no doubt, splintered a vase instead."

"At arm's length, I could have blown his head off as well as yours!" she bridled, then abruptly burst into tears. "Oh, you honor-loving asses!"

"There, there. Women have their soft spots, too." He took her into his arms, then back to bed. Besides other things, to wait.

Near midnight, a tap sounded on their bedroom door. Firmly, Miklos motioned Eliza to stay put. Bette's tired face appeared in the door crack. "I've just come from Kolowrat. With a bit of urging, he and Louis pounced on Metternich just before dinner and demanded a council with three days to review the evidence. You'll receive the verdict sometime Christmas week . . . what's that horrible noise?"

"Eliza throwing up in the basin," replied Miklos laconically. "I can't imagine why. We skipped supper."

Three days passed without word and Eliza's relief began to dissolve into panic. An invitation for Bette to the Christmas Eve Ball at the Winter Palace arrived. Christmas Eve

day arrived. "We wait no longer," Bette declared. "Eliza,
put on your prettiest ball dress, your best jewels! Throw on
the ermine cape! Miki, your uhlan dress uniform with all
the decorations. We're going to waltz with that old walrus,
Metternich, tonight!"

"Miki and I aren't invited," Eliza protested feebly.
Miklos merely shrugged, and she didn't trust the look in
his eye.

"Pish!" was Bette's last word on the subject.

The snow-covered Ringstrasse outside the Winter Palace
was choked with the carriages of diplomats, Austrian,
Hungarian, Russian, and French nobility. Bejeweled women
in glistening silks, satins, and furs were escorted over
plush carpets laid across the snow into the chandelier-
glazed Palace. The heavy lines of the place were snow-
softened so that it looked less like a Milanese bank.

Bette swept by the majordomo. "The Princess von
Schmerling; my nephew, Prince Sztarai, and his wife, the
Princess Elizabeth."

The majordomo hastily scanned the list, found Bette's
name, but not the Sztarai's. By the time he looked up, the
whole royal group was gone into the crowd. He sighed.
Quibbling with royalty only led to quibbling with more
royalty. They all had long, vindictive memories and the
leisure to get even, particularly that old horse, Elizabeth
von Schmerling.

And when the time came to enter the ballroom, the
diamond- and ruby-weighted old horse had herself announced
with Eliza and Miklos on either side. Like inflexible
parade ground cadets, they marched forward. Miklos,
unsmiling in his white and gold uniform with a leopard cape
and jacket rakishly slung over his left shoulder, was more
splendidly Austrian than the Austrians. Eliza, in pearl-
embroidered cream satin with gold lamé roses and pearls
in her gilt-snooded hair, calculatedly looked like a bride.
Miklos's Christmas present, an Italian Renaissance necklace of pearls and diamonds set in gold, circled her throat.
Her bright smile set in lead, she felt sick at her stomach
again. Blinded by the gleaming marble, vast chandeliers,

and jewels, she hardly saw the shocked faces, heard the whispers. She didn't even notice Metternich's beet red face until she, Miklos, and Bette halted before Ferdinand. Numbly, she dropped into a curtsy with a spill of pearl-studded satin as if she were strung to Bette's perfunctory dip. She rose to see Ferdinand smiling at her and her confidence edged back. Bless the poor, lonely man; he remembered her.

His sister-in-law, the Archduchess Sophia, despite the imperial diamond order across her silver-embroidered blue brocade, was a prim, resigned-looking woman rather like a nanny minding her charge. She looked neither pleased nor displeased at their intrusion; probably she knew nothing of it and cared less. She appeared to merely want to be done with greeting eight hundred people.

Franz, Ferdinand's nephew, was handsome and, despite his adolescence, unbending, but reasonably bright.

"We are pleased to see you this evening, Princess." Ferdinand nodded to Bette, then held out his hand to Miklos. "Thank you so much for the splendid cannon, Your Highness."

Miklos, shielding his bewilderment, shook his hand. Then he realized what the emperor meant and shot Eliza a hard look. "My wife is developing a fondness for artillery as well."

As Sophia sighed her impatience, Eliza chirped faintly, "Toy guns, Your Imperial Majesty. Miki and I are about to have a child, you see."

Miki *hadn't* seen; the rapt, startled gape of delight he gave her won the hearts of every woman within earshot.

Bette grinned from ear to ear and even the archduchess smiled. "You did not know, Your Highness? What a wonderful Christmas present for you both."

Ferdinand fairly bounced. "May I announce the event? I should be delighted . . ."

Miklos hesitated, but Ferdinand was focused on Eliza's vigorously nodding head. "Ladies and gentlemen," he crowed, "a child is to be born to their Highnesses Sztarai!" As Ferdinand burbled on through pockets of silence, malicious gossip, speculation, and benevolence, Metternich looked mad enough to spit. The rest of the guest list was rattled through, then the first of a set of Tauberwalzer was struck by the orchestra. Ferdinand plowed happily through the first gay bars with Sophia, to be followed by Franz and a German princess. More couples fell in, minus Metternich, who sourly pleaded gout. In a round of felicitations, Miklos and Eliza joined the rest of the glittering crowd moving onto the floor.

"Why didn't you tell me?" Miklos asked Eliza softly as he swept her into the intricate pattern circling about the ballroom.

"You had enough on your mind and I wanted to give you a stupendous Christmas present!" she said brightly. "Besides, if you hadn't *really* looked surprised tonight, everyone would have suspected you were manipulating their goodwill."

"As it is, you're managing that well enough by yourself," he retorted in mock reproof. Their hands on their hips, they executed the traditional, heel-clicking folk step up the center of ranks of dancers. "You give Ferdinand a toy cannon and me a baby; why shouldn't we dance to your tune?"

She gave him a sultry look under her lashes. "Widows have little opportunity to dance. I don't relish black pantalets."

He bit her ear. "I do."

"Fat lot of good that would do you demised."

He grinned. "For you, I could rise from the dead."

She shot a look downward and went pink. "Miki! Lazarus wore a shroud, not tight breeches!"

Laughing, he clasped her waist and they pranced into the outer ring of dancers. Eliza's skirts bloomed like one of the creamy, gleaming roses in her hair. Her pale shoulders, her gilt-bound hair, intoxicated him. Where could he take her? he wondered impatiently. Where, so that he could spill that hair about her bare breasts, be rid of corsets and crinolines and people. He was bursting with pride and desire. Firmly, he steered her through a portal and tugged her up the stairs. Breathless, she gasped as he caught her against him in the empty hallway. Then her arms went hard around his neck as his lips hungrily covered her own.

"Come," he whispered, and she followed him hand-in-hand down the corridor. He knew the palace, and on the third floor they reached a dark, deserted waiting room much like the one where she'd awaited her audience with Ferdinand. There he quickly found a brocaded couch, her eager body in the darkness. The room was chilly, their desire quick and hot. In moments her crinolines and satin spilled onto the floor. With trembling fingers, she unfastened his tunic, then his breeches. Miklos groaned softly, his hands burying in her hair, tugging away the snood to clasp her against him. Her mouth was silky, eager; her caress as she freed his sex delicious torture. His lips left hers to roam feverishly to her throat, to the peaks of her pale, ripening breasts.

Eliza gave herself utterly to the searing, scorching demand of his kisses, the intoxication of her own frantic longing. "Ah, come, darling, come to me now," she whispered raggedly. With a choked cry Miklos bore her down upon the sofa. Their bodies arched, strained together in delight and fear of discovery that goaded their passion. In a heartbeat, his hardness plunged into her liquid warmth, found her wanting him, welcoming him so completely that he moaned against her parted lips. Her tongue teased, probed until his mouth slanted across hers and he drove into her with a fluid, hungering rhythm. With fierce abandon, she responded to the intoxicating, shimmering urgency of his loving. Their hearts pounding, breath quickening, they were wild, running creatures of the night wind streaking before flames that shot through the moon-bright clouds. They celebrated the new life they had created, the fresh passion that welded them together. Their desire flared, its flame racing uncontrollably to explode like a single, high, blinding star in the blue darkness.

Finally, reluctantly, they dressed. His fingers lingering in her hair, Miklos caught its gold into the snood and

kissed her nape. She turned to caress his cheek and he
caught her in his arms in a last, lingering, consuming kiss.
Quietly, they returned to the ballroom. They had been
missed, but Eliza's bright eyes and flushed cheeks, her
hair touseled beneath the snood, roused amused suspicions
among some of the guests, particularly when Miklos could
scarcely take his eyes off her.

Shortly, Archduke Louis, well Christmas-punched, wandered up to them. "Good evening. May I congratulate the
fortunate parents?"

"You may indeed," replied Miklos with a grin.

"Brace yourselves. The first baby's always more trouble than the others." He eyed them puckishly. "Stay here
until the happy event, will you?"

"Have we any choice?" Her heart quickening, Eliza
tried not to sound tense.

"On, I should think so," Louis drawled. "Your heir
might prefer ancestral snow. That igloo that old walrus,
Metternich, has you in must reek of schnitzel and sau-
sage." He smiled blandly at Miklos as he flagged down a
red-coated flunkey with a silver tray of champagne. "Surely
you must dream of chicken paprikash and goulash?" He
handed champagne all around.

"Actually, I dream of schnitzel." Miklos gave him a
matching smile as he accepted a glass.

Louis laughed. "Do you?"

"Stop teasing them, Louis," quietly admonished Kolowrat, who appeared at his elbow. He motioned away the
flunkey. "Hasn't tweaking Metternich been enough for
you?"

"I can hardly be blamed for that!" protested the archduke. "Princess Sztarai counted quite a coup tonight." He
grinned widely over his champagne glass at Metternich,
who, surrounded by his relatives and aides, was slouched
sulkily on a settee across the ballroom. "All one need do
to give the walrus an apoplexy would be to shake a baby's
rattle at him."

"A Sztarai heir was rubbing it in a bit." Kolowrat
owlishly eyed Miklos and Eliza. "You've won, you know.

You can go home to Balaton. You were to find out in the morning as a Christmas present.''

Miklos looked so suddenly drained that Eliza, stunned herself, involuntarily took his arm. "Are you all right?"

"Yes," he murmured. "You must forgive me, gentlemen. I cannot thank you enough for what you've done, but I'm at a loss . . ."

"Oh, you'll pay," Louis assured him. "Metternich expects you to expend every effort to cool the stew in Budapest. Any hint of encouraging Kossuth's crew and you'll see Balaton snapped from under your nose."

"Even the walrus doesn't like anarchists," said Kolowrat briefly. "All in all, you were owed something. The king of Piedmont-Sardinia and the Queen of England say so. Most importantly, Nicholas of Russia says so, and we may shortly depend on his good will."

He flinched slightly as Louis chirped in, "Charles Albert ought to be groveling with relief. Rumor has it he was boffing on a bomb."

Fancy that, Eliza recalled weakly. I heard the bomb was on top.

A passing polka dancer brushed her skirt and with a startling yell, Miklos lifted her high into the air. "Excuse me, gentlemen, but I have the honor of this dance with the mother of my child!"

Chapter 13

The Return of Cain

Vienna: December 25, 1847

Miklos had everyone up at dawn. "We'll celebrate Christmas at Stagshorn, in Hungary!" he vowed, and both women laughed as he bounded about like a boy. Not waiting for the lackeys, he threw most of the luggage in the carriage himself, then fretted, throwing snowballs with Max and the hostler boy in the street, while the women finished their morning chocolate. Ten miles out of Vienna, his stomach began to growl and Eliza, with a laughing shake of her head, fed him strudel from a napkin. Grinning as Max drooled, he wolfed them. *"Wünderbar!"* Then he growled in her ear, "Tonight, I shall devour you!"

She swatted him. "I may be frozen by then. Where is this Stagshorn?"

"Stagshorn belongs to Count István Széchenyi, one of Hungary's greatest statesmen. It's a hunting preserve with a magnificent lodge a few miles over the border. We should be there by midafternoon."

All of them were dizzy with relief at leaving Austria and Metternich behind, and the ride was a merry one, with stories and jokes and exchanges of riddles for small Christmas trinkets. With each passing mile, their spirits grew lighter.

Though snowbound Hungary looked no different from
Austria, Miklos had no difficulty discerning the instant
they crossed the border. "Kiss the earth!" he cried, leap-
ing from the coach. *"This* is Hungary!" With a shriek of
laughter, Eliza followed him to throw herself into the
snow. Waggling her arms and legs, she made an angel.
With Max excitedly barking, Miklos landed beside her to
make a great archangel, then messed up both angels by
rolling over and kissing her in the snow until she was pink
and kicking.

They reached Stagshorn, not in the afternoon, but
at midnight. Deep in snow, sprawling Stagshorn, with
its cupolas and lead crystal windows, was undoubtedly magnificent, but deserted. "Does Count Széchenyi live here?"
Eliza asked as their boots tracked through virgin snow
drifted on the broad veranda.

"Only a few months a year. He's probably in Budapest
now." To Eliza's surprise, the door was unlocked. Aunt
and nephew, appearing to take the case for granted, strode
into the house with the lackey and maid scurrying to light
candles and tripping over unfamiliar furniture in the dark.
Eliza stumbled into Miklos, then, wondering why he had
stopped short, noticed him looking at a dim glow down
one of the halls. Max whined and stiffened. "Miki," she
whispered, "someone's here. Perhaps we should announce
ourselves."

"No need, I assure you," grated a soft voice. In the
darkness, she was reminded of some creeping leviathan.
"Everyone in Hungary will soon know your luck is still
holding, Miklos. Welcome home."

She felt Miklos tense, then relax. "Thanks, Vlad. I
should have expected you'd be here. Still keeping an ear to
the palace floors?"

Vlad, a small figure she now perceived dimly silhouetted in the hall doorway, laughed humorlessly. "Tricky to
hear much over the scuttle of vermin; however . . ." The
shadow in the door shifted slightly. "How is Victoria,
Miklos? Still blandly breeding?"

"Her Majesty seems content." Miklos's voice held an

edge. As if sensing Eliza's sensitivity about her own pregnancy, Miklos put an arm about her. "Eliza, I should like you to meet Prince Vlad Rakoczy, misogynist and patriot. Vlad, my wife."

"Am I to have no sobriquet?" she teased, attempting to lighten the mood of the encounter.

When Rakoczy moved forward, she almost involuntarily took a step back. Perhaps in his early forties, he was a tiny man, almost a dwarf, with an outsized head made more disproportionate by a thick shock of black hair and drooping mustache. Very pale, his face, with a high, intelligent forehead, thin mouth, and jutting cheekbones, might have been distinguished but for pendant, outsized ears. His huge, dark eyes were the most striking of his physical paradoxes. Both cold and sad, liquid and calculating, bright and dull, they fixed one with a spider's intensity; nothing could be reconciled in them, nothing forgiven. Those haunted eyes studied her for a long moment, accepting, then brushing aside her instinctive revulsion. "You need no evaluation, Eliza. I know you. You will have little patience with shadows and Hungary is full of them. And for you, Hungary is now home as it is for Miklos and me." He smiled faintly. "The Princess von Schmerling is an Austrian at heart. I wonder how long you will be able to stay an American."

"Don't tell me what I am, Vlad," snapped Bette, "and don't waste your witch-doctoring on Eliza. You're a quack; you always were. Run outside and practice spooking the grouse if you're bored."

Though Rakoczy's expression did not alter, Eliza sensed he was deeply offended. "The princess is an advocate of teapot rule," he murmured. "She demands a precise place for every napkin. Napkins and precision can be unbearably tiresome, don't you think?"

Eliza was surprised to find that though she resented his familiarity, she agreed with his attitude toward napkin policy and felt increasing sympathy for the little man. She remembered too painfully the loneliness that could come with a distorted body, the curious turns the mind could take to make up for that body's differences. "Perhaps tomorrow morning, Your Highness, you and I can go together to persuade the grouse to present themselves for dinner."

For a moment, she wondered if Rakoczy was offended again. He shot a look at Miklos and following it, she was startled to see disapproval plain on Miklos's face. To ask his permission had never entered her head. Miklos shrugged. "Why not? Only don't make it dawn."

"Ah, yes, I had forgotten," murmured Rakoczy. "You are still enjoying your honeymoon. After breakfast perhaps, Princess?"

"Perfect."

As Eliza and Bette mounted the animal-carved stair with Miklos, Rakoczy faded into the dark. In a moment, low voices came from the lighted room down the hall. "He's an eerie sort," she muttered. "Do you suppose he's talking to dead ancestors?"

Bette snorted. "That's likely. Vlad was cradled in a coffin."

"Actually," Miklos explained briefly, "his gang is probably with him. He dislikes being alone."

"Gang?"

"A few cronies. All from respectable families. Vlad is nothing if not respectable," he added dryly.

"A stew of malcontents," muttered Bette, "with him the bloodless marrow bone." Her candlestick held high, she impatiently motioned her maid to open a bedroom door in the upper hall. Light glowed off cream plaster walls lined with paintings of hunt scenes and landscapes. "Rakoczy probably has his cobwebs spread all over Széchenyi's room, so I'll take the second suite. An old woman needs a big bed; lovers don't."

"You're angry about my meeting Rakoczy," Eliza told Miklos after his valet had flipped the covers off the heavy furniture in their room and turned down the huge, feather bed. "Surely, Miklos, you can't be jealous of that ugly little man." She opened the oak armoire, then took a dressing gown from her trunk.

As she hung up her furs, he laughed shortly. "I very much doubt if Rakoczy has any carnal interest in you, any more than the Almighty lusted after Eve. Vlad sees you merely as a possibility of either annoyance or persuasion."

"Of you? To what end . . . falling into his stew of malcontents?" She unfastened her traveling dress.

"More or less." He flung himself onto the bed to watch her undress.

"But you dislike him." Her body outlined against the fireplace, she stepped out of a puddle of velvet and crinolines, then shivering in the chilly room, caught up her silver-fox-trimmed dressing gown from the bed and moved toward the fire the valet had lit.

"No one likes Vlad, but stepping on him would make quite a mess." His eyes darkened a fraction, distracted as she slid on the dressing gown.

"Why?"

"I'm sure he'll be glad to tell you while you flirt with the grouse." He reached out, caught the end of the sash as she started to tie it. He reeled her in, pulled her down and threw a leg over her. "But for now, little *mamuska*, I want your undivided attention."

He got it.

Eliza paid considerably less attention to Rakoczy next morning as he walked her across the flat, snow-covered grounds to the north of the house. His pleasantries were perfunctory, dusty with his own disinterest, exactly as if he were leading a cortege for a relative he'd never met. The sky was gray, filled with promise of snow above the black-spiked oaks and heavy firs. Rakoczy's voice was also gray. Not a bird disputed his monotone; not a grouse disturbed the preserves about the icy pond. Two horsemen, probably part of his "gang," rode across the distant fields.

Eliza wished she'd been less impetuous. She had only suggested the meeting because she felt sorry for Rakoczy. He'd been somewhat irritating the night before, but clearly Bette's blunt antipathy for him had been longstanding.

Life could not be easy for a man so ugly. And as she had once, he had all the hypersensitivity of a cripple.

As if he guessed by her polite restlessness that she was merely enduring him, he began to lecture her with dry pomp about his lineage. While it was impressive, she knew Miklos, aware of what she had invited, must be silently laughing at her. Certainly he was right about "stepping" on Rakoczy. The fame of the man's family was woven warp and woof into Hungary's history.

Vlad was the umpteenth Rakoczy of the Transylvanian Rakoczys, and he detailed every inch of their progress through time. Not that his forebears were bores; extremes of good and evil were mixed in Vlad's lineage as they were in his face. During Hungary's cradle years, Vlad the Impaler derived his name from skewering live enemies on spikes. On the other hand, Ferenc Rakoczy, Vlad's great, great grandfather, who valiantly tried to free his nation from Austria and ended in lonely, Turkish exile, was one of Hungary's most honored heroes. "The Austrians took his lands from him for that," Rakoczy rasped. "*My* hereditary lands. All Transylvania. But Hungary has never forgotten the greatest of her heroes.

"Miklos Sztarai is a hero," he finished flatly. "Even when he was a boy, everyone expected outstanding performance from him. He always gave it." He acidly studied the sullen horizon. "Even as a criminal, he was outstanding."

"How dare you!" Startled and furious at his unprovoked attack, she spun away. Bette was right. He was rancid!

He snapped her around so powerfully her head rocked. "You may have wheedled Vienna into disregarding Miklos's crime; surely you've not fooled yourself in the bargain. A holocaust, his retribution, is coming soon. Do you think you will evade it with lies?" Suddenly, seeing the total disbelief and anger in her eyes, his own narrowed. "You don't know, do you? Or has Miklos so besotted you, that you've not dared to question him? Ask him. Ask him who he killed." And when she began to run, he howled after her, "Ask him why he destroyed what he loved most. Why he was driven like Cain from his homeland!"

Miklos must have been watching from the firs for he caught her when she raced through the tall, dark trees to the house. Snow spilled from fir branches as she stumbled against them. Icy powder clouded her green velvet skirts and hooded cape, making her choke, her lungs ache. "What did he say to you?" Miklos's hands were so tight on her arms that she gasped at the pressure.

"Does it matter?" she cried. "He's full of lies and malice!"

"You think because he's ugly, he's a liar?" Miklos asked slowly, his bare head sifted with the snow that had fallen. His face white and drawn as if he'd aged years, he might have been a statue of ice.

"You're my husband." She faltered. "I didn't marry a murderer!"

"Be honest, Eliza," he said tiredly. "You didn't much care who you married."

"I care now," was the muffled reply.

"Would you leave a murderer?" he asked softly.

Had she been mistaken? Hadn't he fought a fair duel? "You didn't murder anyone." She gazed wildly into his bleak, gray eyes. "Tell me you didn't!"

"Three years ago, I found my wife and brother together." His voice sounded dead. "I killed them both."

Eliza retched. Stumbled about until she was cold and empty, her stomach tightened into a rock. Yet when Miklos steadied her, she did not turn away. If he had put a pistol to her head, she could not have turned away.

She was not sure what was expected of her. A biblical denunciation of wickedness? That required virtue that she had not. Forgiveness? Go thou and sin no more? How many times did a man murder his own blood unless he was mad? Retribution? None was sufficient. Death could not replace life. A token, then. Take his child. Yet after seeing his face at learning of that child, she could not. She had mixed her life and her child's life with a murderer's. A man who had not given her death, but life and freedom when he had not known from day to day if his own might be taken from him.

Miklos knelt beside her in the snow, then his fingers hesitantly touched, stroked her nape, as if trying to comfort a child. Without thinking, she flung herself into his arms. "I don't believe it, Miki! I don't care what *you* say, what anyone else says!" She tried to gulp back the sobs. "I've never seen you do anything mean or small . . ."

"Sweeting, you've not known me a year," he said roughly. Something seemed to catch in his throat and his arms tightened about her, his cloak falling about them both. "When does it end, the pain that had so small a beginning?" he muttered despairingly. "A punishment that seeks every turn in hell, each one sinking lower, dragging down the innocent to deceive the guilty into hope, tempt him to twist his crime into something less, only to blacken it." He grasped her head and forced her to look at him. "The guilt must be mine alone. Lie for me, *to* me, and you become my accessory, Eliza."

His hands dropped and he sighed. "I've been lying to myself longer than to you. Perhaps in you, I see a chance to undo what I did to her. When you first walked into the study at Como, I knew you were no accident, not just Bette's obvious ploy. I knew keeping you could go either way: to clear the air or that next turn in hell."

"You never wanted another wife," she said tonelessly. "That was Bette's idea."

He sat back on his heels. "Yes."

"She wanted to make you look respectable again . . . so you could come back to Hungary."

"Bette's not that much of a sentimentalist," he replied dryly. "The lands of a felon can be confiscated by the crown. Had I died suspect, Metternich would have traded Balaton to another nobleman for political favor. She meant to make sure Balaton stayed in the family."

"And what did you want? Your Loise doll aside?" She couldn't hide the wave of bitterness beginning to blacken about her.

He started to touch her, stopped when he saw what was

coming into her eyes. She had been used. She had blindly
fought for him in Vienna and now she was realizing just
how much of a pawn she had been. "Would you care if
you never saw America again?"

"No."

"For me, living outside Hungary is living without
arteries. My heart beats . . . pointlessly." He stared out over
the sere land. Snow was beginning to fall, clouding the
black trees, swirling in dervish gusts over its white world.
"I wanted to come home."

"That's why you wanted the honeymoon away from
everyone," she said neutrally. "Because sooner or later I
had to find out."

"And because once you knew, I wanted you to be able
to choose whether you wanted to stay with me. For that,
you had to have a taste of freedom; you couldn't realize
what you would give up if you'd never had it. For one
who cannot bear confinement, death can seem a joy."

"But Balaton won't be prison; it'll be home for you."
Seizing a tree limb, she pulled herself up. "What can it be
for me?"

"Don't you think I'm unsure, too, about going back to
face my ghosts? That I won't hear vengeful, jibing voices
in the night? If I could undo what I did, Eliza . . ." He
rose to his feet with a low, tearing cry muffled by snow
before it skimmed the icy pond. "Penance, death, nothing
will bring them back! A moment's madness . . . and of
two young, living, laughing beings remained nothing." He
scooped up a handful of snow and scattered it through his
fingers. "Dust!" He spun. "If I have any chance of
redemption, it lies in your heart and your womb. A life
given for what I've taken."

"Two lives," she corrected softly. "I wonder if you
were kind, or clever, to place me so in your debt." She
began to walk out of the fir stand toward the meadow
where she'd seen the horsemen. "If I asked Rakoczy to
take me back to Vienna, would you try to stop me?"

As he followed her, he was silent a moment, then said
flatly, "I'd never trust you to Vlad."

She laughed shortly. "So I have no choice, after all."
The trees passed like a black cage they were pacing.

Halting at the edge of the fir stand, she looked out over
the hoof prints in the snow. "Rakoczy must have several
men with him."

His eyes narrowed as his gaze traced hers to the tracks.
"He'll have several less if you involve him."

"Do you know what I noticed first about you, aside
from your size?" she murmured. "The choices you offered were never choices." Her hands knotted to keep
them from shaking, she said calmly, "All right, I'll go to
Balaton. I'll have the baby. But I won't bed you. I won't
be your 'accessory.' I won't let you rob our child of its
choices."

"Eliza, I don't want you like this."

"You never wanted me at all, remember? And now it's
really the child you'd fight Rakoczy for. Hungary has your
heart. I'm only your penance, and penance is supposed to
be unpleasant." She headed for the hunting lodge.

When Eliza reached the lodge, Bette was embroidering
in the huge, oak-raftered drawing room. She sat in a
burgundy plush chair beneath a Flemish tapestry of boar
hunters. Having never seen Bette embroider, Eliza suspected she merely wanted a vantage point from the drawing room windows to watch the drama near the pond. As if
she were sleepwalking, her hands tight fists, she moved
toward Bette. Dimly, she noticed that the folk design in
white cotton thread on white lawn was utterly unlike Bette's taste for elaborate French silks. "A christening gown,"
Bette explained without being asked, then looked up. She
seemed to age as she studied Eliza's face. "So it's
happened. Rakoczy?"

Longing to claw her face, Eliza felt her fingers curve.
"Yes."

"I wondered why he was here. He would have guessed
Miklos might come first to Stagshorn. He must have enjoyed it, the little spider." She glanced at Eliza's hands,
then erecting a calm, impassive shield, went back to her
stitching. "What will you do?"

I owe you no explanations, Eliza thought; Rakoczy isn't
the only one fond of webs! "Ask Miklos . . . and you may
as well forget planning a baptism. My child will choose
his own religion."

Vlad Rakoczy's laugh sounded behind her as he sauntered through the trophy-hung doorway. "Good for you;
but I wonder if you'll show so much spirit after the child is
born. Difficult wives can be sent away, put in convents . . ."
He pulled off his coat, and like a mocking, malevolent ape, hooked his arms over a chair. "Miklos isn't one
to limit possibilities when he wishes to be rid of a wife."

"Would you like your throat cut on Széchenyi's carpet
or neatly, out in the snow, Vlad?" curtly invited Miklos,
who'd silently come into the room. Without looking at
Eliza, he stepped between her and Vlad. Eliza glimpsed a
hunting knife at his belt beneath his open fur coat.

"I shouldn't think Szechenyi would mind either way,"
rasped Rakoczy, but he didn't move. "I doubt he'll ever
see this place again unless he's buried here."

Miklos frowned. "Why not?"

Rakoczy's voice lost its mockery. "You've been gone
too long. I think I should like a glass of wine. Anyone
else? No." He went to the sideboard. Eliza gave him
credit; he had nerve. Miklos had carried that knife when
he'd followed them out to the pond, whether to protect her
or silence Rakoczy she couldn't be sure, but just now, in
his snow-dusted furs, Miklos looked like a great, cold-
eyed wolf, hoping for his quarry to make a wrong move.
But Rakoczy, as if he hadn't spitefully wrecked her and
Miklos's lives that morning, was now as calm and detached as if he were two different people. Still, he had
prudently put as much distance between Miklos and himself as possible.

"I don't altogether agree with Széchenyi, mind you,"
Rakoczy said as he poured a glass of pale Tokay. "Taxing
his own class, freeing the serfs, tearing up the constitution;
no one who owns a *selo* of property can take all that
seriously." He leaned against the massive mahogany sideboard. "But he has tried to talk your Magyars out of trying

to shove everyone else—Croats, Serbs—into becoming
Magyars." He admired the Tokay's color. "He's right.
My Transylvanian Rumanians won't have it; the Croats
and Serbs won't have it. Only Kossuth and his crowd
don't listen to him now they've the bit in their teeth.
Austria is well aware we'll have to watch our backs in a
fight."

He sipped his Tokay, then poured another glass. "But
Széchenyi won't cut the Austrian leash. His willingness to
leave Hungary tied up like a pet hound has finished him.
He's not the man he was, Miklos. Kossuth has totally
eclipsed him. Hungary is a juggernaut headed for revolution and Széchenyi has lost all control of it. His mind is
being eaten away by failure . . ."

"I don't believe it," Miklos said curtly. "You've spread
enough manure today."

Rakoczy's dark eyes narrowed. "I welcome Széchenyi's
ruin no more than you. He's devoted his life to Hungary,
but times change." He held out the fresh glass to Miklos.
"If you refuse to mount the juggernaut, it may crush
you."

Miklos strode to him and seized the wine. "Your juggernaut's manned by crackpots, students, and fools. I'll
sooner make way for a farm wagon. To Széchenyi and
Austria." He emptied the glass, tossed it in the stone
fireplace. "Ladies, we leave for Balaton by lunchtime."

As Miklos left the room, Eliza noted Rakoczy's eyes;
they held a gleam of genuine amusement.

Chapter 14

Balaton

Lake Balaton, Hungary: January 23, 1848

Miklos's estate at Balaton was lovely, particularly in winter, though any destination that ended their hellish trip across Hungary would have been heaven. A white drift of birches swept the shoreline of the vast, hill-bounded lake. Even on a clear day, Balaton's far side could not be seen, giving an illusion of an endless, frozen sea.

Hungary, fortunately, had not been endless, though Bette's relentless efforts to teach her rudimentary Hungarian and the inhospitable terrain of the flat, mysterious steppes made it seem so. As the coach was too confining, particularly considering their tension, they kept the leather window flaps open except at night and in foul weather. Their coach careened and inched over roads that were little more than shifting ruts that often swallowed the wheels to the axles. Though drifting snow that concealed the ruts made them more treacherous, Bette complained of insufficient snow to support a sleigh, which would have made travel easier.

When Eliza wondered at the total absence of railroads across the vast steppes, Bette gave her a tolerant smile. "That's Ferdinand's father's doing. He was afraid railroads would encourage rebellion. Not a railroad was built in Austria and Hungary until after his death in '35. He was a shortsighted, suspicious man. Even his own class doesn't miss him much.''

''But surely people have to get from place to place to carry on trade,'' Eliza countered. ''Do they use the rivers?''

''Half the year the rivers are deathtraps due to floods and ice,'' Miklos said tonelessly. Remote and preoccupied, he sat opposite her. His joy at being home had faded. As they crossed Hungary, he stared unseeingly at the landscape, then after several days asked Eliza for her journal. Mile after mile, he made endless lists of farm equipment, stock, and seed varieties, as if he were trying to stay sane. Two days ago he'd run out of lists.

''What about bridges?'' she asked. She had exchanged less than ten sentences with him since leaving Stagshorn.

''We still barge across the Danube River in the heart of Budapest.''

She subsided, to stare out at monotonous, wind-blasted steppes where gray, longhorned cattle and farm beasts left to forage for the scant harvest stubble often staggered from hunger. At bundle-burdened peasants thronging the roads in search of places to resettle that could be little more hospitable than the old.

''Likely runaway serfs: kulaks, we call them,'' Bette observed as she took out her embroidery and sharply chafed her hands. She had clipped the fingertips off her gloves to use a needle, so her hands stayed stiff and cold. ''These last years, more kulaks have taken to the roads. The idea they may soon be set free makes them more restless and dissatisfied. They'll probably be run down and returned to their masters in the spring.'' She caught Eliza's expression. ''They're just as well off. This is a hard land. With merciless weather, wars, natural disasters, and disease, they can't survive on their own, and a change of master will probably make little difference in their lot.''

At Eliza's skeptical look, Miklos explained flatly, ''The crops fail completely one year out of ten, and partly fail another two. That ruins a peasant. So does illness and injury. A landlord can get by.''

''New England has miserable weather, but it doesn't

have serfs! Half-frozen children are struggling along out there!''

''New England never had centuries of plague and Turks.''

''We had diphtheria, pneumonia, and Indians,'' she argued. *''And* a revolutionary war!''

''Which boils down to piddling little. Those kulaks play their part in the system. They'd rather starve than plant potatoes.'' He mockingly touched his temple. ''A potato is a new idea, you see.''

''I've read about serfdom in Russia,'' she countered. ''Every so-called 'benefit' of protection offered the free peasantry was poisoned! Do you wonder they don't want your 'new' potatoes?''

To her surprise, he smiled slightly. ''No, I don't wonder. They occupy an untenable position in an obsolescent system. It's not serfdom that keeps this part of the world in the fourteenth century, but our missing bridges and education and railroads. Besides, when they stay put, our peasantry usually eat better than *les miserables libertés* of France and England.''

''Yes, I heard how well Count von Werdenberg's peasants manage.''

''He isn't typical. Werdenberg doesn't care about his own wife, far less his peasants,'' put in Bette.

''How fortunate''—Eliza coolly regarded Miklos—''that your nephew is more considerate.''

That barb got no rise from Miklos. Nothing she said affected his determination to keep her. He neither pleaded nor argued, and though relieved he never tried to make love to her, Eliza was also troubled to find she still loved and desired him. Just as she missed his lovemaking, she missed his banter and companionship. While pleasant, he was preoccupied. A door had closed between them; but for him, the first weeks at Balaton held much less emptiness than for her.

When they arrived at Balaton, they found the estate, after three years without Miklos's supervision, near ruin. The kulaks disliked and mistrusted the manager, Malcolm MacGregor, a practical Scot Miklos had appointed in his absence. All improvements, even repairs, the man had tried to implement had been either ignored or neglected. Not one to forfeit a comfortable income, MacGregor had stayed on to keep a nominal, if ineffectual, eye on the place. The worn out fields were run to brush with only sheep surviving to forage the barrens. The farm tools had dwindled to those used to tend tiny plots kept by the peasants to glean a bare subsistence. The estate's timber had been sold off to maintain Miklos's income in exile.

The huge, wood-beamed house, more in the style of a sprawling dacha than the mansion Eliza expected, had wind blowing through every crack. All the family memorabilia, personal possessions, and art had been packed away when Miklos had been exiled to Como. The French furniture was rat-eaten beneath its covers.

MacGregor, a competent manager under normal circumstances, altered the accounts sent to Miklos to conceal his major, dwindling source of revenue. He had planned to be gone before Miklos returned or the money ran out, whichever came first. Eliza expected Miklos to roar when he saw the place; Bette certainly did. As they ended their depressing estate tour in the main barn, Bette went after the Scot with a pitchfork. Denouncing him as a thief and idiot, she pursued the white-faced man with lethal adroitness through the empty stalls. But to Eliza's surprise, Miklos said nothing, and did nothing to the manager besides allow his aunt to give him a good scare. Firmly placing a large hand on the man's shoulder, Miklos escorted him to the house study, where they went over all the Scot's private accounts and inventories into the night. Eliza waited for Miklos to come to bed. "Are we ruined?"

"Oh, yes," he answered calmly. "Mr. MacGregor kept track of every jot and jittle of what we no longer have." Sitting on the bed, he pulled off his boots. "A Hungarian manager might have made no improvements, but at least he would have held the place together. I intended MacGregor to modernize the estate, but I should have known no foreigner could handle the peasants. The mismanagement was more mine than his." He tossed his shirt after the boots.

"What are we going to do?"

He slid under the covers. "Go to sleep. For all purposes, you are now a farmer's wife, and farmers get up at four in the morning."

"Miklos"—she poked him—"I don't know anything about farming."

"You didn't know anything about fishing," he answered softly.

She subsided. Remembering that day made her want to cry. Miklos had rarely been anything but patient and kind. How could he, who could so gently treat a wife he had neither chosen nor wanted, as well as forgive a man who had ruined him, kill Loise and his brother out of hand? She was cold. She wanted his arms about her and the warmth they'd shared for so many happy, hair-raising months of their honeymoon. But she couldn't reach for that warmth. Never again. She could only endure.

Four in the morning came early to a young woman who loved to linger abed, but Eliza was determined to prove a match for Miklos. That proved hard. In the weeks that followed, when she wasn't shivering, she was either vomiting or contemplating it. While Miklos was active, she was forced to drift and brood. She knew she was much of the reason he threw himself so completely into work. To lie so near in the same bed was a nightly torment. He rarely came to bed until he was stupefied with fatigue from supervising repairs and revitalizing the estate. Work was his only escape from their terrible estrangement, and she needed that escape, too. Work might keep her sane, keep her placing one foot in front of the other as, like automatons, she and Miklos went through their daily lives. Keep them speaking to one another though their eyes were averted and dull. Once as an invalid child, she had come to ignore the activities of her family and household; now, nearly incapacitated by nausea, she watched everything in her new surroundings with a stark intensity like a racer poised on the mark.

Finally nausea waned and she threw herself into helping
Bette clean house. The five women servants politely
ignored her hesitant, pantomimed orders, but they scurried
quickly enough for Bette's field marshal snap. All Eliza's
kindness, patience, and repetition had no effect, and she
invariably ended by attempting the task herself. "How do
you do it?" she muttered to Bette one afternoon in the
antiquated kitchen after she'd failed to increase a balky,
broad-beamed scullery maid's tepid efforts to decrease a
week's pile of food-encrusted dishes; the ones washed
were scarcely clean.

"They know I'll beat them," said Bette crisply. "They
don't know what you'll do, and they're waiting to find
out."

"Well, I certainly don't intend to beat them," Eliza
declared loudly enough in her toddler Hungarian for the
scullery maid to hear. "That isn't the American way." So
saying, she picked up the kettle of boiling water and ignoring the maid's startled yelp of pain, doused the dishes
drowsing in the washpan. "Ask her if that's hot enough to
clean them properly," she directed Bette, "or whether
she'd like her dishwater to hiss."

The dishes were cleaned. Another maid, reluctant to
scrub the kitchen tiles, was abruptly doused by a scrub pail
spilling over the floor. "Now, ask her if she would prefer
to scrub the kitchen or the snow off the veranda while
she's soaking wet." Clotheslines somehow got tangled
about feet, drawers pinched on fingers, and laggards
given extra days to squirm on household duty. If nothing
else, having to keep a sharp ear out for Eliza's catlike step
and avoid unpredictable traps made the women eager to be
done with their house service and back to their own huts,
out of her reach.

Shortly, Eliza learned enough household terms in
Hungarian to point and snap nearly as well as Bette.
Things quickly improved as the servants found Eliza was
the most generous, patient of mistresses when they were
reasonably cooperative; any less and she made life hell.

At the same time, when food was bought to replenish

the manor supplies, Eliza saw that each family received a share. "Send your children to their commune elder each day for soup," she had the reluctant Bette tell them in the drawing room. "Saturday next, the women may come back to the manor to receive woolen cloth. We will cut new clothing and repair the old."

When Bette balked at the unprecedented largesse, particularly in view of their financial straits, Eliza fumbled through the announcement herself. "You have taken care of the Sztarais; we will take care of you. We shall eat or starve together." The peasants stared at her, shuffled off.

Bette was quick to inform Miklos his wife was completing his pauperdom single-handed, but he refused to interfere. "Eliza's my wife; she speaks in my name. Besides, she's right. Cold and starving and left to MacGregor for three years, the kulaks are nearly useless."

Miklos had his own problems. He didn't dismiss MacGregor; he used him to do the job for which he was first appointed. Letters were written to England for breedstock in horses, cattle, swine, and poultry. The fields were resurveyed and divided into wider strips that could be crossplowed, and every two out of three *seloes* appointed to be planted with timothy and red clover in spring to improve the exhausted soil. Forage was to be planted in the far meadows to sustain the new farm beasts. He reset the peasants to constructing plows and farm implements from the Scot's previously ignored designs.

Few kulaks dared to argue with Miklos, particularly after he built a heavy plow himself and demonstrated its vast improvement over the customary light, damageable plows for cutting the heavy soil. As he had no draft horses, he used his Lippezan army charger to pull the plow across the ground's frozen surface. "Your nags can't manage a big enough plow," he explained to them. "We need to breed Percherons and Clydesdales."

That night, watching Miklos go over the account books, Eliza commented, "Do landowners here really have to be tricked into the nineteenth century? Surely you're not the only one who sees you must join the commerce and pace of the rest of the world."

"Must we?" He sat back in his chair. He looked exhausted. "For the most part, our educations were received from foreign tutors, some of whom have as much vested interest as landowners in keeping things as they are. In Eastern Europe, property is divided among all the heirs. As we're overflowing with princes and minced up inheritances, only a few of us are really wealthy." He waved at the mouse-eaten, worn upholstery on the furniture, the rationed wood supply by the fire. "A good many nobles live like peasants. Some become serfs themselves. Because the land can rarely support us, we're virtually all in debt." He tossed down his pen and came to warm his hands at the fireplace where she was burrowed in her chair. "Here, debt is acceptable, a poor show is not. Many do not even attempt to pay. Change requires money, effort, and great risk. Serfs are the sole support of a ruling class that has for six hundred years counted wealth not in acreage but in male serfs, so you can see why property owners are cautious."

Rubbing his hands, he wandered to the window to look out over the snowbound hills. "We desperately need money at Balaton, but to borrow, I cannot use its land as collateral because it is inviolate. Unless I commit treason, the government cannot seize it, far less can a bank take it for my failure to repay my debt. I must apply to a special bank or fellow landowner at a usurious rate, which I cannot begin to repay for years, even if I'm lucky. As the nearest town is Sárbogárd, sixty miles away, I can't grow bulk and garden crops for sale. You've seen our winter roads; in spring and summer they become mires of mud." He leaned tiredly against the window frame. "The peasants have little interest in what they *do* grow. Why should one improve his strip of land if it's reapportioned to another serf the following year? MacGregor was to end the reapportionment, but because the serfs didn't trust him, nothing improved. And if I sell serfs, I can't afford to replace them with hired labor."

Eliza listened, curled up in her nightgown and sables. Miklos wondered if she had any idea how small, warm, and adorable she looked. Her sharp mind was so incongruous with her rounded softness, the sables and lace that caressed her body as he longed to do. Now that her morning sickness was past, pregnancy agreed with her. In the shifting firelight, her skin had the glow of a rosy peach, her eyes were shadowed amber. Behind those long-lashed eyes, was she thinking only of business?

She sat silently for some time, then said simply, "Suppose we grow only crops to feed ourselves and our dependents? Any extra grain might be turned into liquor; that wouldn't be so hard to move, would it?

"And as for stock, sheep can manage upon very little. Temporarily turn the unused land to forage, then spring seed it to feed the new, improved stock from England. Animals can transport themselves; they might be sold to other estates. Perhaps if we borrowed just enough to pay for them, we might not go too far in debt."

He smiled approvingly. "You've a sensible head for management."

"I'm a shopkeeper's daughter; Mother was devoted to business. In our predicament, she'd probably start some sort of cottage industry, even a factory. Northern New England has less of a growing season than Hungary. Why sit idle all winter and struggle all summer for mere sustenance?"

"Kulaks don't take to factory work; being bound to a factory is usually worse than being bound to the land. Still . . ." He pondered. "I might put our blacksmith to turning out a few things, give him an assistant or two and see how it goes."

Eliza was only half interested in what he was saying. Part of her was simply listening to the sound of his voice as if it were a long-loved lullaby she missed. He was so weary and alone. How she wanted to take his tired head in her lap and stroke his brow that he might rest for a brief, precious while . . . She closed her eyes and forced her mind away from him to his dry report of their economic problems.

He leaned against the sill. "I'm a little surprised at your interest in management. Few Hungarian men I know care much for it. They leave such matters to the stewards and commune elders."

"Our child's future depends on what we accomplish. To that end, I will help you in any way I can," she said coolly, "but no child of mine will own other men. Whatever your customs and reasoning, it's a filthy habit."

His head came up. "But one to which you've adjusted quickly enough. Your crude method of bringing the house servants to heel would never have worked with freemen. You relied on their helplessness, not their loyalty, to keep them coming back to work every day."

Eliza flushed scarlet. "Perhaps I didn't manage things well, but then I've never had servants to manage, particularly a lot made surly and uncooperative by centuries of someone else's mishandling. Do you suppose they love you, who drained their livelihood amusing yourself in Italy?"

"No, *cara*," he murmured. "I don't rely on their love and loyalty any more than I rely on yours." As her flush deepened, he resumed his desk. "Tomorrow you will begin your experience at managing servants," he said quietly. "I must go to Budapest on business, and as she has never been fond of country life, Bette will go with me. Concerning matters outside the household, MacGregor has my orders. I should be back in six or seven weeks."

Eliza was stunned. The strain of the Moritz and Vienna ordeals, the long, wretched trip to Balaton closed in, along with the final trap of pregnancy. She was to be left, *left* on this godforsaken icy plain! Rakoczy had said Miklos could be easily rid of her. What could be easier than riding away for weeks, months, even years at a time? Not only had she no money, she had no way out alone in winter, no one to turn to . . .

He was watching her. "I've no wish to leave you here, Eliza, but your condition forbids more travel, especially in winter." His face was gentle, his voice soft, as if he were speaking to the seven-year-old who'd fallen from her horse. "We've never had trouble with serf risings at Balaton, but I have no way of knowing what awaits on the road to the north. You have certain food and shelter here, also women experienced with pregnancy. I trust you will be comfortable."

Thinking, thinking, she tried to fight panic. Then thought of a way to escape. No! her heart and common sense argued. Give him a chance. He does have crucial business as he says. The loan arrangements mustn't wait; too many people depend on it. And any doctor would agree travel now is a bad idea.

"Yes," she answered hurriedly. "Go. By all means." She rose, unaware of the shadow that crossed his face at her blunt answer, her apparent eagerness to see him gone. "If you don't mind, I shall sleep in the corner room tonight. I've not rested well lately and as I presume you mean an early departure . . ." She was rattling to hide her dismay at being left, but if she slept with him tonight, she might weaken and surrender to him in trying to reassure herself he would return. Without looking at him, she hurried out of the room.

Despite the window draft chill against his shoulders, Miklos turned back to watch the snow. Eliza was like one of those snowflakes. To know her required minute inspection. She could be cold, seemingly frail, yet able to endure the worst blasts of winter. Then again, she could melt so easily and suddenly in his arms; now she was so far outside them, he could not imagine how to reach her. In a few hours, he must leave her among strangers and knew not what he would find upon his return.

He wanted to strangle Bette. He had relied upon her staying with Eliza, but instantly upon finding he had to go to Budapest, she'd insisted upon accompanying him. All his persuasion and angry argument had failed to dissuade her. "You know perfectly well I'm no nursemaid, Miki, and with Eliza turned so serious of late, Balaton's just too boring." He'd known Bette was self-centered, but under the circumstances, her desertion of Eliza was inexplicable. To Bette, family was all.

When Miklos reached his room long after midnight, he found a chamois pouch with a note on the dresser. "Collateral. I assume it's paid for. Good luck." In the bag were all the jewels he'd given Eliza. Her furs were heaped on the bed.

Eliza, shortly hearing her door whisper open, lay breathlessly still. She knew Miklos's movements well enough in the dark. He stood by the bed so long she thought he must know she was only pretending to be asleep. She longed to give him some sign she wanted him to stay and hold her, not like a woman but a child, like the child whose existence she could not quite comprehend in her womb. How could she tell Miklos she had that child's blind, selfish, consuming need for succor? *Don't leave me alone.*

Suddenly, Eliza realized she'd never been alone; often lonely, but never far from familiar faces, not even at Como, for she had been still so immersed in memories of her old life and herself that she hadn't felt the distance from New York. Now she was trapped on some other frozen planet that spun silently in its own ancient, unvarying orbit. New York and the old Elizabeth Hilliard were gone. Princess Sztarai was a stranger wed to a stranger with another stranger inside her, and all of them stuck to a mammoth block of ice spinning in a gray, terrible sky. With a low cry, she flung her hand out to Miklos, but found nothing. He had gone.

In the morning, Eliza found Miklos had taken only the most valuable family jewels. The pieces he'd bought her in Paris and at Christmas, the childlike trinkets he'd given her at Como, were still there; so were all the furs. She put on the tiny pearl and diamond locket. Laughingly, she'd snipped a lock of Miklos's hair in England to put into it. The locket and all the small pieces must once have belonged to Loise, but they were the ones she loved best to wear; particularly now, as her sympathy stirred for her predecessor. Had Loise, too, been left at Balaton alone

. . . until loneliness had been unbearable? Until she'd taken a lover? And died for it.

By the winter dawn's dim light, Eliza, with Max forlornly trailing her, wandered about the house. Most of the Sztarai memorabilia had been unpacked and replaced in the big, drafty rooms. The walls were dark green and gold like a deep forest, the Oriental rugs luminous by day as a forest floor. Had the murders happened here? Or as the lovers fled across some snowy, faceless field? She went into the study where the walls were covered with portraits: dead Sztarais, beginning over the fireplace with a romantically imagined image of the Magyar chieftain, Lazlo Sztarai, who looked like a Tartar with his *turul* hawk standard, and was probably no better than a clever thug. The collection ended with Petyr, Miklos's brother; and Loise.

The two small portraits, probably painted after the lovers' deaths, hung directly across from Miklos's desk chair. Only Miklos would have the audacity to place them there as a constant reminder of his "moment's madness." They were young: dark haired Petyr with his downy moustache reminded her of a baby goat. The mouth looked odd, as if its expression had been altered in the course of being painted from a sober expression to a smile more usual to its subject; the result was neither serious nor happy, only hesitant. Petyr's face was more open and appealing than handsome, the typically dark, craggy Sztarai features softer than Miklos's. Petyr's eyes were a trifle startled, as if he were being accosted by a stranger and meant to be polite, but not taken advantage of. Loise was smiling as if she would smile more widely, had the painter been more sure of the shape of her teeth. Pretty did not describe her; she was lovely, a happy sprite among sober in-laws.

Miklos was right, Eliza realized. I look nothing like her. My hair's lighter and I'm probably taller, but she eclipses me as if she were a sun. Like a grim cat, Eliza stared for a moment. "I think had you lived, you would have grown plump, Loise," she muttered under her breath.

The portraits must have been painted from description: Miklos's, she guessed instinctively, but was he remember-

ing Loise and Petyr as they'd been just before the end or
before they'd cast aside their loyalty to him and turned to
each other? "Loise couldn't face the reality of anything,"
Bette had once commented. "Butterflies never outlast foul
weather." At the time, Eliza had ignored the bait, but now
she wondered what storm had crushed Loise and Petyr. A
brief brush of wings and their summer's day was gone.
She touched the portraits as if they might be warm, but
they were cold and dust-filmed: two flat planes of paint.

As she started to leave the study, she noticed a sealed
letter on the desk. It bore her name and for a moment, she
thought it was from Miklos, but the writing was Bette's
hasty scrawl.

> Don't worry too much. The commune has three prac-
> ticed midwives if anything should happen. Miklos has
> left orders with the elders that you are to be well cared
> for. Anna, the best of the maids, will act as chief
> housekeeper. Her husband, Paul, is a tolerable steward
> if you lock up the brandy. Sorry to desert you, but
> endless tundra doesn't amuse me. Write me in Budapest
> or Enzo at the Palazzo Negri in Rome if you've any
> problems. *Auf wiedershöen*, my pet.

Write Enzo Rossi? Eliza refolded the letter. She'd thought
of it last night, but why would Bette? Had she thrown
Loise and Petyr together in just such a way, at just such a
time? Bette had shown more than once she could not be
trusted. She was always trying to make everyone dance to
some tune only she could hear.

Eliza tossed the letter into the grate. So the tundra is
dull, is it, Auntie Bette? Time it was livened up a bit?
Eliza's eyes took on a tawny gleam.

From that day, Anna and Paul spent less time in managing the household than teaching its mistress Hungarian and
Eliza most of her time stockpiling supplies, reviewing
accounts, and luring the commune children to school; the
last was far from easy.

After a month, matters peaked, when with her old talent

of eavesdropping, Eliza derived from household gossip that many of the serfs, fearing Miklos meant to cut his losses and leave them to fend for themselves, were on the verge of bolting for Kaposvár in the south. To begin, she called an assembly not only of commune elders but of general peasantry. In halting, horrible Hungarian she'd had MacGregor outline for her, she told them flatly, "We're in trouble, without time to lose. My husband has gone to buy strong animals that can work the land and last the winters. While he's gone, we'll make a beginning. With the cut lumber that still lies in the remainder of the woods, we'll repair your houses before the spring rains . . ."

She could read their faces. Our houses? Not the manor first? And in winter?

"In spring, we'll be planting with no time for repairs. If you need tools, shutter hinges, and so forth, present your list to the commune elders, then see our blacksmith. There will be no charge for personal items, but anyone who requests more than his immediate needs will be denied them. This winter we will be busy making beehives and stills for brandy."

Pleased murmurs went up, then settled as she went on. "As my husband and I will provide for the raw materials from Balaton's coal mines, iron from Dunáujváros, and other expenses; you, the labor. The profits will be split two thirds/one third." She had early learned the peasants dealt in simple fractions, not percentages. They appeared even more pleased and she took a deep breath. "Taxes will also be split two thirds/one third." They were aghast, and she dreaded to think what Miklos would say. MacGregor was staring at her as if she'd lost her mind. Peasants paid *all* the taxes. "Any other projects we devise for self-support and profit will be likewise shared . . . as will the losses." Now their eyes were narrowed, first in disbelief of all she'd said, then in suspicion. Losses, like taxes, had always been carried by them, not the landlord. Despite her rosy words, they were going to be cheated somehow.

She held up a French sapphire necklace, then with MacGregor's knife, pried out a large stone and gave it to the commune elder. "As long as these stones last, materials and wages will be paid for monthly. Your elders will take the necklace to the local Benedictine monastery, where the abbot is willing to convert the stones into cash. All business agreements between you and the Sztarai family will be signed before the abbot and the sheriff of Sárbogárd." The serfs still looked uncertain; they considered both the serf-owning monks and the sheriff unreliable guarantors. "I can offer no more assurance than the Sztarai word for the lifetime of my husband and myself, so long as we own this land," Eliza said. "The choice is yours."

Knowing full well the serfs would not speak openly in front of her, she left the commune with MacGregor and took the elders with her, as they often waved the *seigneur's* banner too determinedly. The arguments went on until dawn. Eliza did not hold her breath. What she offered seemed so simple, logical, and fair, yet for them it was unheard of, either lunatic largesse or a new scheme to deceive them into worse straits than they now endured.

Finally, lunatic largesse won out versus foul weather. The sapphires went to the monastery.

But Miklos stayed in Budapest. Along with wheedling loans and making stock orders, he visited Count Széchenyi to plumb the city's political currents. He found Széchenyi haggard and depressed, his assessment of the nation's position grim. He considered revolution imminent and unpreventable, Hungary become a hydra with each head biting at the others. The Rumanians, Croats, Serbs, Magyars, all wanted their own separate states, and Metternich was playing them against one another. Even if Hungary won her freedom, he predicted her dismemberment by Russia, Turkey, whoever wanted to gobble her up.

Sadly, Miklos watched his once graceful, charming friend rant on in bitterness and self-blame. Rakoczy, with his bizarre balance of ambition and nationalism, his hatred and love of power, was scarcely sensitive to lunacy, yet after a time, Miklos could not help wondering if Rakoczy was right in thinking Széchenyi's mind was becoming unstable.

Long after midnight, he left Széchenyi to roam the silent Budapest streets. He'd had little time to retrace his memories of the ancient, lovely city. Here he had met Loise and married her. Here Petyr had gone to university. Centuries before, the Romans, Huns, and Turks had come and many armies after them, until parts of the old city still slept in weed-grown rubble. All periods and blends of architecture molded the city profile into a gentle sweep that little disturbed the horizon.

He wandered along the silvered Danube, wound past Saint Margaret's Isle below Saint Mattias' church, and looked up at the lights of the Gothic government houses and Taralyi Palace gleaming on Gellert Hill. *Mamuska*, more than my mother you are, he thought, you seem unchanged, yet even now, asleep, you are restless, as if disturbed by an ending dream. An uncertain, fiery dawn breathes under your paling stars and the latest of your children is impatient for life. He kicks in your belly, *Mamuska*. Soon, hurting, you must spill him forth, and swaddled in that red, waiting dawn, he will utter his first, great howl of battle. Into that dawn, my child, too, will be born. Will he look to a human breast for nurture, *Mamuska*, or to yours as I did? Will he leave a girl alone and lonely, as I did? A girl too young to be a mother, who wants no child from me. Her eyes have turned cold and I am shivering, *Mamuska*, even against your breast.

Drawn toward the old Rose Hill ruins, he walked through the rubble. So little was left of it, like his marriage. He turned toward the southern plain stretching away into the darkness beyond the city lights. Eliza, Eliza, if only you were not so far away. These very stars are your eyes, everywhere following me, accusing me, luring me to fly home to you and be done with fruitless duty. Together we may steal some breath of hope; apart, none.

He wandered the hill until the cold gnawed his bones, then headed to his hotel rooms. A gaslight he had not lit was burning low in the window. Silently, he mounted the stair, then after easing out his pistol, slid his key in the doorlock of his room. The door opened even as he turned it. *"Ciao,* darling." Vanda Bellaria draped a fold of her black lace peignoir over the muzzle of his gun.

"Just passing through?" he murmured sardonically.

"No one just passes through Budapest. I came to look for you." She studied his face. "I can see I was right. Marriage never agrees with you."

He flipped the peignoir off his gun and threw his hat on a chair. "Your record is better, I suppose."

She relieved him of the gun, then helped him off with his cloak. "Even I learned when to stop. Both you and I know you're never going to marry me, so we understand each other." Insinuating herself into his arms, she smiled invitingly up at him. "The bed's that way, darling; remember?"

He smoothly disengaged. "My honeymoon is scarcely over, darling; remember?"

"I hear it's very much over," she purred, "and the bride disagreeably pregnant. But not to worry. After a year of watching turnip eyes sprout at Balaton, she'll agree to a separation quickly enough."

"Bette's had you to tea, I see," he said dryly. "You should know by now her gossip is not altogether reliable." He tossed Vanda her black fox cloak. "My coachman will see you home. You might catch cold walking the streets."

With a shrug of her pale shoulders, she smiled without warmth. "Don't be peevish, just because you can't afford the price, darling." She slid into the fur cloak. "It never gets lower and you just get hornier."

Grinning, he opened the door. "I'll bear up."

"You always do"—she patted the front of his breeches on the way out—"but I'll call again soon . . . just to test the suspension."

Balaton: February 29, 1848

Still awake in the middle of the night, Eliza fingered the blond lock of Miklos's hair from her locket. What was he doing now in Budapest? Sensibly sleeping, no doubt, when she could not. Sensibly sleeping with a woman. She stared down at her swelling belly. She didn't look fruitful; she looked fat. Nothing fit any more except her nightgowns. She'd have to send Paul to the monastery to buy cloth for—what should he tell the abbot—tents?

Thank you very much, Miklos Sztarai. No wonder Cinderella's fairy godmother warned her to leave the palace by twelve. The prince turns silly girls into pumpkins!

Chapter 15

Turnip Eyes

Budapest: March 2, 1848

Both to avoid Vanda and cull political gossip, Miklos began to spend his evenings at the Casino. His reappearance in Budapest society attracted attention, mostly unfavorable. Many Hungarians, assuming he had bought his way back to Hungary by becoming an Austrian collaborator, avoided him. He had little liking for the ones attracted to him because he was scandalous, particularly the women. Usually, he either ranged alone or with a handful of men he'd served with in the Austro–Hungarian army.

One evening, as he was playing cards with a captain from Miskolc, he overheard a drunken man loudly demand a bottle of wine from the steward. The drunkard was Count von Werdenberg. Belligerent and short of money as usual, he could find no one to give him a card game. Miklos watched him a moment. Then, winding up play with the captain, he excused himself and walked over to the count's table. "Count, may I offer you a drink? I'm Miklos Sztarai. I've hoped for some time to make your acquaintance in Vienna."

"Sztarai?" The count's bluff, pouchy face registered neither recognition nor interest, yet Miklos's clothing indicated he was a gentleman: a gentleman offering a free drink. "At your service, sir," the count muttered. "Make mine a Bull's Blood. This Tokay's woman's stuff."

Miklos seated himself, nodded to a waiter. Count von Werdenberg dully listened to his order. When the waiter hurried off after a quiet, "Yes, Your Highness," Werdenberg gave the table a rap. "Ha. Should have known. These scurvy trotters have a nose for rank. Ignored me for the last twenty minutes!"

Miklos commiserated, let Werdenberg down his drink, offered him another. Then suggested a game of cards.

"Think I'll be easy to pick because I've had a few, do you?" Werdenberg smiled slyly. "We'll see, we'll see. Order a bottle."

He won for a time, then occasionally began to drop a hand. After a second bottle arrived, he steadily lost and Miklos politely declined his voucher. "Nothing personal, but I've more need of field labor than money at the moment. Twenty serfs on this round, what do you say?"

Werdenberg put up a show of argument, while in reality he was much relieved. Considering the stakes, twenty of his crow bait peasants was a great bargain. "Done." He rocked back in his chair.

"Also, I'll want a steward for them," added Miklos, pouring another glass of brandy. "I believe you've an ex-artillery sergeant, one Hans Krafft. I saw him work at Neukirchen. Is he still worth a horse or two?"

"All the bull he ever was," Werdenberg swore, his eyes fighting to focus. "Throw him in for a bit more cash."

Miklos waved the waiter to bring paper and pen, the captain and casino steward to witness. "Now, Count Werdenberg"—he smiled benignly—"shall we see just how easy you are to pick?"

Balaton: March 20, 1848

Turnips. Like shriveling elves, they stared at Eliza from the dank depths of the root cellar. From the age of four, she'd detested rhubarb, parsnips, rutabagas, and—vehemently—turnips. Now she ate them every day; whatever good they were supposed to do was certainly overdone. She hauled an apronful upstairs to the kitchen, ignored Anna's customary scolding about carrying too much, and dumped her load into a waiting washtub. Grimly droning, "Ah been workin' on de railroad all de liblong day," Eliza began to scalp turnips. With a bang, the main door blew open; an icy wind gusted into the white-plastered kitchen. "Shut the blasted door!" she yelled.

"Yas'm, Miz Dinah," came a familiar drawl at her back.

She slit her thumb to the bone. Thrusting it into her mouth, she whirled. Then gravely sat down on a churning stool. Miklos was so handsome in his greatcoat and beaver hat that she felt dumpily round and red as one of the turnips. At the pastryboard, the grinning Anna rolled out another sheet of dough.

Miklos looked at Eliza's shapeless, gray wool smock, her woebegone eyes, and plugged thumb and wanted with all his heart to cuddle his little *mamuska* who'd never had a mother. But she'd had a father, and he'd no intention of becoming another. He strode forward, tore a towel, and after gently removing her thumb from her mouth, bandaged it. "Were those, by any chance, your sables the chambermaid was wearing when she answered the door?" he murmured, his back to Anna.

"Airing them," Eliza mumbled back. "She's religious about giving them daily walks."

"Um," he grunted thoughtfully. He studied the bandaged thumb. "And the droning from the drawing room?"

"The alphabet. Originally Ugyar. Surely you remember it?"

"Dimly. I presume you've penned up the peasant children; original Ugyars haven't been sacking around here for two thousand years." He cocked his head and plucked daintily at her wretchedly made smock. "Speaking of sacking, my little potato dumpling . . ."

"Who left me with nothing but weensy-waisted Paris gowns?!"

"I assumed . . ."

"Betsy Ross sewed," she gritted. "I stab fingers." She stuck her wounded thumb under his nose.

He kissed her thumb tenderly, then grabbed her hand before she could smack him and led her out of the kitchen away from Anna's pricked ears. "You must be more forgiving, Eliza. You've been forgiving the peasants their taxes, giving them all sorts of presents like a berserk Lady Bountiful." Firmly, he towed her up the wide, walnut stair.

"MacGregor tattled to you quickly enough . . ."

"Just belatedly doing his job. When I said you spoke for me, I had more in mind a parrot than a corseted, meddling Turgenev."

"I couldn't be stuffed into a corset with a crowbar, and as for meddling, I was merely . . . dusting." She grabbed at the banister and missed. As he hauled her on, she sputtered, "It isn't new plows you Hungarians need, it's *dusting*. You can't even breathe, your skulls are so choked with dust . . ."

"It's not a fistful of feathers you need just now"—he dragged her into the bedroom—"it's kissing."

He kicked the door closed, then administered the remedy. She wriggled and hopped, then as if she were sinking in honey, gradually settled. When his lips at last lifted from hers, she whispered, "It's not so simple. Crackers won't train this parrot."

"No," he murmured. "I've given this parrot a taste for eclairs." His lips found her throat, his fingers found buttons. Eliza found herself going breathless and tried to fight it. Nothing had changed between them except that she'd missed him unbearably and he knew it, was using it with merciless, mesmerizing skill. "What were you doing so long in Budapest?"

He nuzzled a swelling breast. "Ah, did you think it was this? That denied one woman, I might seek another?" Maddeningly, his tongue circled a tender bud. "The nights were lean, Bluebird, and I've no liking for a cinched belt."

"Do you think it's easier for me?!" How could he tease

her about fidelity! For adultery, he had murdered his own brother, his wife . . . Feeling her last control swiftly going, she desperately dragged at his hair. "Do you think it was easier for Loise?"

His head came up as if she'd doused water over it. "Why bring Loise into our bed?"

"You left her here, didn't you?" she countered, tension and pent-up loneliness beginning to seep out of her as if seeking cracks. "Did Loise love Balaton in the wintertime, never miss the gaiety of Budapest and Vienna? Did she love to peel turnips and frolic about this empty house in sacks?" She pulled away from him. "Did she do it night after night as I have, hating to go to an empty bed?" Her tawny eyes looked tormentedly into his. "Are you going to tell me she was happy when she turned to Petyr?"

The weariness of the journey hit Miklos all at once. His shoulders sagged and tiredly, he pulled off his cloak. Burning to see Eliza, he had grown impatient with the slow passenger coach. He'd bought a horse, and for the past hundred miles, ridden overland. He had paused only to sleep and at the edge of the estate, to clean up. Now he felt overdressed, defeated, and cold. Explanation was futile, yet Eliza was so distraught and miserable, he might have been seeing Loise's twin, hearing again their endless quarrels.

The gray light of another beginning snowfall paled his face as he rubbed distractedly at his forehead. The bad memories crowded into his mind like stubborn ghosts. "Loise hated Balaton. She grew up in Vienna. Our parents were friends and we loved one another even as children. Everyone assumed we would marry when Loise turned eighteen." He smiled crookedly. "Only our bodies couldn't wait so long. I became her lover just after her fifteenth birthday. We were both frightened, too young. I hurt her and it was all an awkward mess. After that, she let me make love to her as if she were petting a dog. I always felt she simply meant to be kind and I hated it, yet couldn't stay away.

"After a year or so, I turned to a wanton serf girl.

Loise, hurt, demanded to be noticed, not just by me, but all men. At first, she was a little silly, but then . . . grew clever at gaining attention. Our parents eventually found out what was going on and I was hurried off to the academy at Weiner-Neustadt. A year later, Loise ran away to follow me.''

He moved restlessly about the room. ''Our parents were furious, but had to agree to the marriage. Loise and I were in Vienna until I went on maneuvers. The post was too rough for women, so she came to Balaton.'' With a slight shiver, he peered out at the pale lake. Against its wind-shirred birches and storm-faded, satin sun, the falling snow-flake clusters were coin-sized, hurrying against the house, swirling on across the grand, empty steppes. ''She must have hated the pleasure I took from her body; God knows I often felt like a thief.''

Eliza could not imagine a woman hating Miklos's touch. At times, he could dizzy her just by being in the same room . . . as he was now, when she was trying to fight him with all her strength. The last of the fight ebbed out of her as she saw how wretched he had been in his failed first marriage. ''Perhaps Loise hated only her inability to respond to you''—Eliza hesitated—''yet she looked so happy in her portrait. Was she always like that?''

''You mean before Petyr?'' His eyes were bitter. ''Before she became smitten with a half-grown pup who groaned bad poetry?'' He turned on her. ''Oh, Loise's smile was real enough. She could smile and smile, even when she felt nothing.''

Pityingly, she watched his face. ''And now you even regret being faithful to her, don't you?''

''I won't make that mistake again,'' he breathed. ''I'll have a woman, whether wife or wench, to warm my bed.'' His fingers tangled in her hair. ''Touch me, Eliza,'' he whispered. ''To save both our souls. I'm not made to play the priest.''

She ached to take him to her, but do what she would, there was no making right all that had gone so terribly wrong. In killing Loise and Petyr, Miklos had become Cain; none might take away the mark.

He read her eyes. "When will your virtue become a lie, I wonder," he said harshly. "When will you toss it forth?" He grasped her jaw, hard, so that she flinched. "No, my love. I shall grovel neither today, nor tomorrow."

He left and she wanted to scream. So many lonely nights behind her, so many more to come. Righteousness was wrapped in cold, starched sheets, empty as a Dead Sea plain. Miklos needed her now, as she had once needed him, and she could give him nothing. Except their child. That much she could manage at least.

At dawn, Miklos made inspection of the estates. Like a leaden mask, his hard, bleak face closed her out as if he meant to give her no chance to hurt him again. Stubbornly, Eliza, along with Max, the wolfhound, tagged after him. He was moody and tense with even the serfs he knew well, and particularly intent about checking the number of farm tools useable as weapons. The serfs were put to work on a heavy door and shutters for the manor house and Miklos proposed Eliza learn to use a gun. "As it happens, that's one thing you need not teach me," she informed him. "I've been practicing." Using empty wine bottles in the kitchen yard, she demonstrated admirably with a Colt. 44 from his gun collection.

He nodded grimly. "Not that any skill will be much use if the peasants revolt in my absence."

"Why do you think they'll revolt?" she protested.

"After all you've done for them?" he finished for her. "My love, you are but a ripple on the sea of historical persecution. When the tide begins to rise, neither kings nor princes will stay it."

Over the next few days, Miklos became more of a disciplinarian with the serfs, who were often in trouble with the local magistrates for drinking and brawling. Eliza was surprised to see they were not permitted to speak a word in court for themselves; Miklos did so for them and often acted as judge himself in some cases: cases that might range from murder to disturbing the peace. "Is what you're doing legal?" she demanded as one serf was flogged for manslaughter.

"Technically, no," he answered curtly, "but I'm not likely to let the court tamper with my property, am I?"

While Miklos might be fair, Eliza conceded, he still presumed upon his ability to completely govern the lives of his serfs.

"No school! What do you mean, no school!" Eliza furiously confronted Miklos as he closed the drawing room doors against her outburst. A dozen students craned as far as they dared to hear what was going on. Though the Sztarais' argument was in English, its crux could easily be guessed.

"No school," Miklos repeated firmly. "Though God knows they've as much right to learn as anyone, educating kulaks beyond their station only makes them want what they can't have, and expect freedom overnight." He pulled her away from the door. "Nearly all serf uprisings have occurred where serfs have been allowed beyond their limits and," his voice dropped, "where their masters haven't watched their tongues about politics, particularly on the point of emancipation."

"I won't let you shove them back into docile ignorance," she said flatly. "I gave them my word, made them trust me . . ."

"Trust you?" He laughed shortly as he snatched her sables from the coat rack and propelled her out onto the veranda. Max skittered after them. "They'd sooner trust a badger . . . and a foreign badger at that, among their chickens. They're taking advantage of your ignorance. In spring, if she's inclined, you'll find your chambermaid has 'walked' your sables all the way to Debrecen."

She shook off his hand and nearly lost her balance on the slippery boards. When his other hand shot out to catch her, she slithered out of reach. "You may be right, but I did keep half the others from walking to Kaposvár last month. I've made a start with them . . ."

"And not a bad start," was his surprising admission,

his hands still hovering at his sides in case she took another plunge. "A virtually unprecedented and probably pointless start, but not a bad one."

Her cheeks flushed from the wind, she grabbed at the porch swing chain. "You're not going to go back on the tax agreement, all the other proposals?"

"Not until your sapphire necklace is plucked clean by the good fathers at Saint Andrew's. At that point, I may have no choice."

Her fingers hooked in the chain links, she leaned toward him. "You could stop me from working with the commune."

He smiled wearily. "By ordering MacGregor to gag you and lock you in your room?"

She relaxed somewhat. He looked funny, endearing in his anxiety to keep her and the baby from taking a pratfall. So often, without her knowing it, he must have been poised just so, to keep her safe while she first tried her new legs. The trusting Max hung about Miklos's feet as if glued there, his thinning tail thumping. "No, I suppose a man so often wise and gentle would not do so," she answered softly. Then, seeing him startled, she added, "If only you could have been as understanding with Loise. I think she never would have strayed."

He unhooked her fingers from the links and slowly stroked her palm. "What an exasperating little cat you are. How can you spit at me one moment, then make me want to pet you the next?"

"Perhaps because you're the sort of man a cat is inclined to follow." The stroking sent a shiver down her spine.

His blond lashes flickered over his rueful, amused eyes. "So long as he never picks her up."

"The cat wasn't left much choice in the matter."

He kissed her hand before letting it go. "I suppose not."

She smiled wryly. "Still as cats go, I'm dependable in my fashion."

"That seems to be all I can ask, doesn't it?" He gave

her a gallant bow. "Would you care to accompany me for the morning?"

As they walked the fields with Max, they made plans for Balaton. Years later, Eliza was to remember all the ideas they had that morning; dreams that were to prove all, all impossible because an eagle was already swooping on them. A second eagle followed, and yet a third waited to cut across the ice-bitten sun.

Max began to bark as, like a scuttling beetle, MacGregor hurried toward them across the frozen ground. "Revolution!" He waved Bette's letter from Budapest. "Louis-Napoléon has made himself head of France and revolt has broken out in Austria! The Hungarian Diet is about to declare independence!"

His face bleak, Miklos turned to Eliza. "I must return to Budapest. This madness may be beyond stopping, but perhaps if enough Hungarians cry common sense . . ." Seeing the dismay and fear in her eyes, he grasped her shoulders. "I want to stay, Bluebird. Everything that matters to me is at Balaton, but one day soon, all of it may be lost if I hide here." He brushed back her hair. "As it is, Balaton is no longer safe. You will go to Saint Andrew's until the child is born."

On, no, Eliza decided; however dangerous the situation, she was not about to be penned up in a convent. "Fine," she lied equably. "Saint Andrew's is bound to be warmer than this house."

Next morning, Miklos silently escorted Eliza in the sleigh to the monastery. To conceal her miserable expression, she wrapped her furs to the nose, would have wrapped them to her forehead if she dared. When he lifted her down from the sleigh at Saint Andrew's, he seemed hesitant to let her go, then caught her to him as if he thought he might not see her again. Feeling as if her heart would break, she kissed him.

"Good-bye, Bluebird," he whispered against her lips. Then reluctantly, he released her and jumped into the sleigh. At his whip crack, the horses jumped forward.

Eliza, shivering in the snow that blew off the runners,

plunged her hands into her muff and worriedly watched the sleigh race toward the north with its tremors of war. Here, she had her own small war to fight. As soon as Miklos's sleigh disappeared over the rise toward Budapest, she headed back to Balaton. The cat was left again to her own designs.

Chapter 16

A Fork in the Neck

Balaton: April 5, 1848

Three weeks after Miklos's departure, a ragged band arrived at the manor steps. "Off with you," Anna screeched, waving her broom. "Back to where you came from, filthy vermin!"

"That's rather a long way, Anna," Eliza observed from the door as she recognized three dirty Austrian faces in the group's foreguard: Hans Krafft, his scarf wrapped to his blue eyes; his skinny lieutenant, and the ravished child. "What are you doing here, Sergeant Krafft?" she called, hoping her voice sounded even. They looked more desperate than they had in Austria. Some had rags bound around their extremities. Their hands were black, faces patched, and lips cracked from frostbite. Some tracked blood in the melting spring snow. The eight-year-old was flushed with fever and an implacable determination to survive the worst Eliza and Hungary could deal out.

"We've been won at cards by the prince and ordered here, ma'am," answered Hans in limping Hungarian. Wearily, he eyed her cheap smock and the manor's cracked windows. "I hope you can feed us. We've lost four and the children are ready to drop."

"Hush, you bold . . ." Anna began to sputter.

As her forbidden pupils pressed inquisitive noses against the drawing room windows, Eliza cut Anna off. "I am the

Princess Sztarai and you are all welcome. Please come in."

"Into the house?" screeched Anna.

"Unless there's a warmer place." Eliza waved the children back from the windows.

An hour later, sixteen peasants were wolfing meatless stew and the last root cellar cabbages while their drying clothes hung about their heads in the kitchen. Furious, Anna had yanked down a bunch of drying paprika and grated it into the stew until the Austrians perspired. Hans, his mouth half full of stew, watched with some amusement as Eliza ruthlessly scrubbed down an appalled child. "You appear to be a proper general, ma'am."

"I have a proper army." She knew he had guessed Miklos was away, the manor occupied only by herself and a few servants. What if he and Skin 'n Bones decided to start trouble?

He dropped his spoon into his bowl, then rose and strolled toward her. "Armies are most apt to fall apart in winter."

She wondered skeptically if she could fight him off with a scrub brush.

Hans Krafft halted, towering over her as Skin 'n Bones unwound his long frame from his bench and sauntered close. "Still, you manage."

"I manage," she agreed, brush poised, when Skin 'n Bones paused at her back.

With his fingerless stump, Krafft lifted the child's hair and casually picked out an object with his other hand. "Louse." He selected another. "Now you've a better army, Lady General."

"How so?" She gingerly resumed scrubbing the child's back.

He presented the stump like a hardwon medal. "Experience." The stump peremptorily jabbed at Skin 'n Bones. "Stop hanging around the kitchen and make yourself useful."

Hans Krafft was as good as his word. In the weeks that followed, the new serfs gave no trouble, and even Skin 'n Bones was careful where he stepped. This, however, did not soften the hostility of the Hungarian peasants, who despised Austrians. Due to lack of housing, the Austrians had to settle in the barns until spring thaw. Hans had barely restrained many who had wished to defect along the road to Hungary and such a pathetic reception at Balaton made his persuasion even more unenthusiastically received. For himself, Hans was implacably stoic. With a peasant's skepticism, he viewed Balaton's innovations. "The prince approve this?" he questioned Eliza after she explained the expansion of the smithy.

"Naturally," she replied evenly.

And as if he'd never dreamed of doing otherwise, he went to work in the smithy. Not that the chief smith agreed; his blistering objection was taken up with the commune. Eliza spoke for Hans. "I've seen his work. He's a highly competent smith. Objections must be made on factors other than nationality."

As the few complaints were lame and the commune elders dared not cross her too far, Hans went to work in the smithy and the other Austrians accordingly entered the service of the estate.

Unfortunately, the food shortage soon threatened another mass defection of peasants, both Hungarian and Austrian. When Hans volunteered to take a wagon to Sárbogárd to buy food, the Hungarian commune elders scoffed that he'd founder in crossing the rushing, ice-treacherous rivers, particularly with the sapphire Eliza gave him to pay for the food. "He'll be off to France for wine and trollops," warned Anna, who thought France held nothing but wine and trollops.

"Skin'll go with me," Hans calmly informed Eliza, and Anna had more to say, though Eliza considered privately that Hans knew best in not leaving Skin behind to start trouble.

Two Austrians in charge of their food supply was more than the commune could bear. When the wagon left, the burly smith was aboard. And when the wagon returned ten days later, he and Hans were, if not friends, companionable, and a host of new products emitted from the forge.

Skin and the other Austrians were liked no better than before.

While the men were gone, Eliza and one of the kulak women adept at dyes began devising designs they screened on a bolt of cloth bought from the monastery. Soon their gay prints belied the grimness of the situation at Balaton.

A week after Hans returned, a second wagonload of supplies arrived. A few minutes behind it, a messenger from Sárbogárd trotted in with a letter from Bette.

Miklos thought if you ran short on food, you'd have difficulty with the peasants, so expect a shipment of foodstuffs. The abbot has written to tell him of your returning to Balaton. Needless to say, he's furious and summarily orders you back to the monastery. Knowing you will ignore the order, he is becoming drunk and impossible tonight. In his last sober moments, he wonders, have the Austrian serfs arrived? God 'knows why he cares. Count von Wertenberg is sure to send only rubbish.

Speaking of rubbish, Vanda Bellaria has been seen with Miki at the opera and going to his rooms several times. He's also entertaining a Russian countess who is reputed to have rather bizarre sexual tastes. I'm sorry, my pet, but Miki is a man of strong appetites and little patience. You must either settle your differences with him or settle for very little of a husband. Use your head, if not your heart, in the matter. Bette.

Eliza had known it was coming; still, she felt pain worse than she had thought possible. Miklos had been as good as his warning, and so quickly her heart might have stopped. She couldn't blame him; he wasn't a neuter and she couldn't fend off every female . . .

Before she could fully digest Bette's extraordinary missive, another wagon lumbered up the drive past the departing messenger. A familiar grin dazzled her from the driver's perch.

Her jaw dropped. It was Enzo Rossi. Before she could

protest, he jumped down and swept her into his arms, his greatcoat swinging about them. *"Cara! Dio mio,* I've missed you!" A passionate kiss landed on her mouth.

Toes dangling, she protested, "Enzo, the baby!"

"Italians are experts with babies." He kissed her again. "We make more than anybody!"

Catching Hans's stern eye as he came from the smithy to investigate the visitors, she firmly pushed Enzo away. "I have enough just now, *grazie.*"

"So I see." He beamed at her in her worn, gray smock and knotted shawl. "You look wonderful."

"For once, I'm glad you're such an unabashed liar." Enzo was his debonair self, his muffler wrapped rakishly about his head to romantically imitate an Arab. He looked as out of place at Balaton as a cockatoo, and passing kulaks stared at him. She stuck her chapped hands in her apron pockets. "What are you doing here?"

"I'm in charge of your rescue mission." He went to one of the wagons and shoved back its canvas cover. The wagon was crammed with food: Austrian army issue tins of vegetables and fruit that made Eliza's mouth water, smoked hams and venisons, potatoes and bags of rice, flour, and sugar. Miklos, she saw, had gone to a good deal of trouble to ferret so much food at winter's end, particularly as he must have ill been able to spare the money, plus quartermaster bribes. "A third load is a half mile behind us," Enzo said. "We had trouble getting through. The roads are terrible."

"Is Miki . . . ?" she began hesitantly.

"With us?" Gently, he touched her cheek. "No, *cara,* it will be a long time before you see Miki again."

"Are things worse in Budapest?"

"That depends on how you look at it." He noted Hans's oaklike figure and dour expression. "Come, invite me into the house," he whispered. "That one looks like an executioner."

"He's fond of Miki," she said crisply.

"Once I had a mastiff fond of Miki go for my throat."

"You're in no danger so long as you behave." She waved Hans to get kulaks to help unload the wagons, then led Enzo into the house.

He poured glasses of fiery apricot *barack* after they settled in the study, then, handing her a glass, queried with uncharacteristic bluntness, "Has Aunt Bette's letter arrived?"

Wagering Miklos was unaware Bette had delegated her rescue to Enzo, she took a long draught of the *barack*. "Like your faithful sled dog."

"Miki isn't so faithful, is he?"

"Shall I call Hans to teach you tact?"

He touched his glass to his forehead. "You've acquired the feudal manner, Your Highness." He drank. "It doesn't suit you; none of this does." He gestured toward her middle. "Not even that."

"You said I looked wonderful," she replied evenly.

"We can agree I lied." He came to her and hunkering, took her hand. His own was still cold from the drive. "Now you know everything and you're not happy. You can never be happy with Miki. His women in Budapest are just the beginning. He was faithful to Loise for only a year after their marriage. To be fair, I don't blame him. She was sunlight on ice; her warmth was an illusion . . ."

He pulled up a footstool and sat facing her. "I married you, Eliza. I misled you, then handed you to a man I knew could only make you miserable. Still, I never thought he'd bring you *here*." He looked around in disgust at the silent, severe room.

"Balaton is Miki's home," she said simply. "Where else should we live?"

"Home? Has he been here one month out of four?" His lips curled in anger. "You cannot mean to stay here while he publicly shames you in Budapest!"

"What else can I do?" She patted her protruding stomach. Perhaps Enzo's ludicrous self-righteousness, perhaps her distrust of Bette, made her feel detached. Maybe she was still trying to absorb the shock of Bette's letter. Everything considered, she didn't want to think now. She just wanted to open a tin of peas, carve a slice of ham, and eat and eat. Some time later, when she was dull from stuffing herself, she might be able to think about Miklos without Enzo and so much misery sawing at her vitals.

Enzo was dumbfounded at her apparent placidity. *"Cara,* do you think Miki's normally so indiscreet? I know him well enough. He won't endure another disastrous marriage. After the child is born, he means to get a divorce. He's giving you grounds no court will deny: but whatever cause, your marriage contract gives him the child."

Eliza's last buffers began to sag as he continued, "Sooner or later, he knows you will leave him and try to take the child. That child dictates the future of Balaton."

She stared at him. "Enzo, you're not suggesting I run away with you!"

"I am, indeed." His dark eyes flashed. "I want you to come with me to Italy. Where you will appeal for annulment to the pope on grounds that Miki deliberately blocked your conversion. If you move first, you will likely get an annulment, the child, and a settlement." He smiled engagingly. "At the very least, you will get me."

Bewildered and reeling with the pain of Miklos's infidelity, she laughed unevenly as she pushed out of her chair and moved away from him. He would never understand how much labor and hope she'd put into Balaton, how much it had come to mean to her through its challenge and its people. Balaton was her first real home. A home with a shadow husband. "For how long will I get you, Enzo? A few weeks in Capri, perhaps a jaunt to Deauville if you're not bored with diapers and a shrieking baby?"

Enzo looked insulted. "What do you take me for? I mean to marry you! The child I will treat as my own and we will have seven more."

Eliza couldn't help laughing, then crying until Enzo's face was scarcely recognizable beyond a blurr of tears. He was holding her, she knew, but she could scarcely feel his arms, understand what he was saying to soothe her. "Enzo, you'd have a new mistress with our every child," she protested incoherently. "How can you propose I exchange one Don Juan for another?"

"I do not promise to be perfect, *cara*," he told her with dignity, "but in me you would have a husband who would keep you, your bed, and your children happy." He lifted her chin and the gesture was so like Miklos's, she both wanted to cry again and comfort him. "Don't you love me a little?" He held up thumb and forefinger together. *"Piccolo?"*

She made an effort to smile and nodded. *"Piccolo."* When he beamed, she quickly added, "All the same, I'm not going to run away with you. I must talk to Miki . . . and deliver a baby before deciding anything."

Eliza gave Enzo dinner but she wouldn't let him spend a single night in the house. "Miki would never understand," she said flatly. "You must stay at Saint Andrew's."

His arguments fell on deaf ears. Hans's broad, benign smile as he brought up a saddle horse upon Enzo's departure did nothing for the young Italian's disappointment. As he longingly looked down at her, Enzo's eyes were as reproachful as a stricken spaniel's. "Am I to bed down with priests until the baby's born?"

Firmly, she knotted his muffler against a last spring snow hissing through the twilight sky. "Unless you'd rather return to the fleshpots of Budapest . . ."

"No, no." He mounted quickly, then leaned down to mutter, "But what if Miki returns and won't agree to let you go?"

"Then like Lochinvar, you can kidnap me," she whispered back, "only the baby will have to hang onto the horse's tail."

"Be serious," he reprimanded.

"I've had quite enough seriousness for one day, thank you." She firmly slapped the horse's rump.

As Enzo trotted away, Hans, who had loitered a few feet away to ostensibly refill the trough, dunked a water bucket, then carried it to the porch. Without looking at her, he said quietly, "I think you're about to have trouble with the serfs, Your Highness."

Eliza turned a hard, weary eye on him. "Why choose this particular moment to impart such cheerful news?"

Still not looking at her, he put a cover on the bucket. "The wagon drivers have spread the word of what's happening in Budapest. The kulaks think in a month they'll be dividing up this place for their own and the prince will be hanged or exiled as an Austrian collaborator." His bluff, ruddy face was grim as he turned his mittened hands under his armpits and watched Enzo's dark cape fluttering like a hawk seeking twilight game down the road. Despite the still early evening hour, only a few lights burned in the nearby commune huts. Against the storm-heavy dusk, the huts were silhouetted ragged, black, and permanent as clods of earth turned by a plow. Centuries might move, but the huts, the peasants, with their backs to the wind, would merely shift with the seasons. Now the winds of a new day were upon them, and with eyes to the dictatorial sky, they were listening, listening, sensitive as foxes to the changes in the wind's sound and scent.

Now she knew why Krafft was keeping his back to her. The two of them were probably being watched from the commune windows. She picked up a broom and began to sweep the veranda. "Will the peasants turn to the commune for leaders?"

He wound his ragged, woolen scarf higher about his bearded jaw. "The elders are viewed as puppets of the Sztarai family. They have no choice but to side with you."

"What of your people?"

He went after another bucket, making her wait for his answer while he set it on the veranda. "They've no loyalty for the prince, but like the elders, they're resented. If they want to stay in one piece, they'll have to oppose the Hungarian kulaks."

She shivered, like him, feeling the chill. The storm wind was from the north. "Should I call a commune meeting to calm things?"

Nodding for her to go before him along the walkway to the kitchen, he picked up the buckets. "Wouldn't do any good. More likely set things off." He followed her along the walk. "On the other hand, trying to run will do the same." He eyed her. "They're in a fritz now and don't like foreigners. How long they'll put up with you, I don't know, but that silk-pants wop had best keep his distance."

"From me or from them, my impertinent friend?" she retorted as she held open the kitchen door for him.

"Both," he replied calmly. He headed for the sink as she shut the door. "Behave normally, don't take any guff off the servants. Let 'em think for an instant you're not in control and you won't be." He placed the pails by the sink, found another cover. "Don't try to talk to me; I'll find ways to get to you. With your leave, I'll call on your Italian friend tonight."

She nodded, saw him back out the kitchen door.

"When I tell you to run, run." He clumped off toward the commune. "If I get skewered, don't loll about to say prayers."

Like an owl, Eliza watched the moon that night and stiffened with every sound. Miklos had said he'd seemed to take one horrible turn in life after another. She'd followed him until now she could not see her way out. The baby had never had a choice of route. Grown fond of her lump, she'd be damned if she'd let it end on some blood-thirsty serf's pitchfork. "I didn't start all this mess and neither did you." She patted her lump. "We'll ride it out, though. Just don't count on seven brothers and sisters."

She did ride it out. Four days went by until the tension was palpable. She was afraid to turn her back on a house-maid, but did so pretending she didn't expect a fork in her neck. Alongside serfs who wouldn't meet her eye or met it too boldly, she helped plant timothy and alfalfa as if her back weren't breaking and forked sheep dung as if it were perfumed. At night she locked her door and sat up dressed with a loaded pistol. On the fourth night, she heard a scratch at the door. Perspiration drenched her.

"A horse is waiting at the back door," muttered Hans. "Go now to the priests!"

A horse. She'd almost rather face the mob. She tugged on her cloak even before his running footsteps sounded down the hall. Looking quickly out of the window, she

saw torches bobbing across the fields toward the house and
reconsidered about the horse.

Her mount was waiting as Hans promised: a big bay
gelding he must have stolen; she'd never seen it before.
She had to stretch awkwardly to get her foot into the
stirrup, then bounce to get into the saddle. When the bay
danced nervously, she gave him a tight warning, "Show a
spark of spirit just now and I'll box your silly ears!"

She heard the front door crash in and dug in her heels.
The bay danced sideways. Hans, bless him, must think all
gentlewomen were Galateas. She whacked the horse's rump
with the pistol butt; it discharged and the gelding took off
as if he'd been burnt. Heart in her mouth, Eliza sailed
along through the darkness with furious shrieks welling
behind. "God, I hate sidesaddles," she gritted as the mud
flew in her face and the nag slid and lunged down the
narrow wagon road. "Stay on your sloppy feet, Gluebait!"
Her insults grew more direct as a string of torches snaked
to cut her off. The thoroughly panicked bay, veering from
the fire, headed off the road toward a fence. "I don't
jump, you miserable turd!" she screamed. The horse,
however, did.

Chapter 17

The Test

Saint Andrew's Monastery: April 9, 1848

Eliza had never considered sitting in a priest's lap, but once she got into one, she never would have willingly gotten out of it. For eight miles of staying aboard the gelding after his spine-wrecking leap, Eliza had sworn, wept, and threatened as the panicked animal tore across the countryside. Finally, mud-daubed and bone-wrenched, she half-steered, half-browbeat the exhausted bay to the monastery gates. "Somebody get me off this dungbrain!" she howled. "I want to shoot him for breakfast!"

Instantly, lights lit in stone arched windows and a monk appeared at the wrought iron gates. As he thrust open the gate and hurried to her side, she nodded in dazed approval. "Hurrah. I thought I might have to knock the nag senseless and roll off." With that, she slid down into the monk's arms. The bewildered man collapsed with her atop him.

"Your Highness," he wheezed. "What has happened?!"

"Have you ever heard of Paul Revere?" She wiped at her muddy face with her sleeve.

"Is he French?"

"No, *liberté, égalité, fraternité* is French, and like measles, *c'est arrivé.*"

With nightshirt flapping, Enzo ran out of the cloister just ahead of the abbot. "Eliza!" He knelt on the cobbles,

and as the abbot held up a candle, touched her face.
"You've a bruise from jaw to crown! Did someone hit
you?!" He paused in horror. "Miklos?!"

She shook her head. *"That"*—her finger accused the
frothing bay—"tried to wipe me off on a tree: *several* trees.
My left shin is puffed like a three-day-dead porcupine."

The two men helped her off the monk, who muttered,
"I still don't understand."

"Do tell that good man," she tiredly advised Enzo,
"that we are having a revolution." And then she fainted.

"I shall need a conveyance, Father," Enzo quickly
informed the abbot. "I must see the princess to safety
tonight."

Saint Andrew's: April 11, 1848

Had Miklos arrived at Balaton two days later, he might
have met an abrupt and bloody end; instead, he paused by
the monastery and so only became furious because he
could not give Enzo a thorough thrashing. The storm of his
anger could be heard all over the monastery, which had
not endured such racket since the sack of the Turks.

Eliza, flailing restlessly, was jolted awake. A gray,
sullen sky lurched overhead, and in groggy puzzlement,
she pushed up on her elbows. She felt terrible. She was
lying in a flatbed farm wagon rattling at a reckless rate on
a muddy road she didn't recognize. She did recognize the
driver. "Enzo! What are you doing? Where are we going?"

"Székesfehérvár"—he stumbled over the pronuncia-
tion—"a town just north of the lake. We can stay there
until the baby's born."

"I can't run off to . . . Szeke . . . whatever! Many of
the serfs at Balaton are fighting for their lives! All its
buildings could be burned!"

"Whatever damage has been done is done. This is
Thursday. Even the monks have probably fled to Sárbogárd.
They'll tell the magistrate what's happened; he'll take
some men and put down the insurrection."

"Enzo, those rebel kulaks are like rabid animals. Helpless women and children are there . . . ."

"There's nothing you can do," he said flatly. "You
were lucky to get out alive as it is. The worst should be
over by fall." He clucked to the horses. The wagon bounced
and her hand shifted to her aching back.

"Enzo, I want to go back to the monastery to wait for
Miklos." She was dizzy. No breeze stirred the roadside
beeches; the air was oppressively close.

With an uneasy glance at the clouds, Enzo replied bluntly,
"It's time you understood, Eliza, with Miklos you'll
always come second to Hungary and just now Hungary may
be going on the block. If he intended to be bothered with
family responsibilities, he would have come as soon as he
heard you weren't at the monastery. The sooner we get to
Székesfehérvár, the safer we'll both . . . all be. We'll
cross the river just below town."

Eliza stopped arguing. Her back pain was worsening,
and given the danger, Enzo would not change his mind.
Besides, she had the dull feeling he was right about Miklos.
In all the months Miklos had spent in Budapest, he'd
written few letters: all impersonal, scarcely more than
notes. What was there to say? How's the weather and are
the turnips in? He could hardly discuss the political situation for fear of the letters being intercepted; considering
their differences, anything more intimate was pointless.
Yet, she wondered sadly, couldn't he care a little for the
baby, not as recompense for old wrongs, not as an heir,
but just as . . . their child?

What would happen after the baby's birth? Was she to
be left at Balaton to look after the child? Or be denied
even that? After the delivery, she'd be of little use to
Miklos. He might wish to be rid of her.

Hot, achy, and exhausted, Eliza closed her eyes. Shouldn't
she just let Enzo take charge for the time being? He knew
Miklos far better than she. Both he and Bette said Miklos
had turned to other women. Besides, Miklos would probably think now that she and Enzo were lovers. Only he
won't get my baby, she thought dazedly. He's taught me

how to fight . . . and when I'm not so tired, I'll use his own weapons on him . . .

Praying the wagon would hold together, Enzo quickened its pace down the road. He glanced back, saw Eliza had gone back to sleep. This jostling could cause her to miscarry, but he dared not tarry. Then, a horseman was silhouetted on the crest of a barren hill and he saw what he feared more than pursuing serfs. He lashed the horses to a stumbling run toward the river crossing.

Eliza woke when icy water blasted against her. Bewildered, she clutched the wagon side only to find it collapsing and water rushing through her fingers. The wagon was hurtling down a river choked with thaw-rotten ice and upriver forest debris. "Enzo!" she screamed as a piece of gray ice raked her neck. Through the spray she saw his white face, his dark eyes huge with fear as he scrambled over the plank seat to her. He grasped her reaching hand, then lost it as the wagon whipped around like a matchbox in the current. Sickeningly, her hand slid through his as he hurtled outward into the slashing river rush. His body smashed into the collapsing wagon side, then everything splintered: the wagon, her left side as the boards struck it; all the grim, gray light.

The innkeeper at the inn on the outskirts of Székesfehérvár peered through driving rain at a pair of frightening figures. The ominously tall man was drenched, his face and hands bloodstreaked. The pregnant, young woman he carried was also soaked and bloody; she looked dead. The man's eyes were wild. The innkeeper started to shut the door; a booted foot jammed in it, then he was shouldered aside. "I'm Sztarai. We want a midwife and a room," the stranger ordered curtly. "Be quick and you'll profit; dawdle and I'll feed the stable dogs your kidneys."

Everyone in the district had heard the black tales about Prince Sztarai. Profit or none, the innkeeper wanted nothing more than to see the prince's departing back, but the breadth of that back was impressive. Timidly, he pointed up the stair. "Second room on the right, Your Highness. Will you be wanting dinner?"

Miklos headed for the stair. "Later."

The midwife arrived within the hour, but the Sztarai heir came quicker. Minutes after getting Eliza to bed, Miklos held his dead daughter in his hands and in all the tales told of him, none could have imagined that so black a heart might break. Tiny Anitra Sztarai received her first and last brief bath in her father's tears.

And then, as terribly as a knife twisting in his heart, Miklos realized he was losing Eliza as well. Her skin was ashen; her smock, the bed linen blackening with blood. With shaking hands, Miklos shoved pillows under her legs, then tore linens from the bed for packing to slow the hemorrhage. As if blinding him, the blackness spread. Only once before in his life had he known absolute helplessness: one hand had held a gun, the other . . . emptiness.

He caught Eliza's lax hands to the sides of his face. "Don't go away from me, Eliza. Don't wander away after Anitra." But she was distant with the indifferent preoccupation of the dying. "If you won't follow me any more, I'll follow you," he coaxed. "I don't expect you to love me now, but we mustn't lose each other, don't you see?" Only he couldn't reach her, couldn't protect her, and then he knew the next turn in hell led to Stygian darkness, a silence no living voice could break, a void he must stumble through endlessly alone. Shivering, he wrapped up Anitra and, holding her tightly, lay down beside Eliza. Dully, he waited for all the lively mischief and hot temper, the loneliness and vulnerability and quick passion that was Eliza to go.

"You'd best get away from her, Your Highness," briskly ordered a woman's voice. A broad, ruddy-faced matriarch slapped his shoulder. "If the afterbirth's causing the problem, she's got a chance. Give me the baby, then up and make yourself useful!"

The midwife wrapped Eliza's upper torso in blankets and massaged her abdomen. She had Miklos pour a measure of herbal ergot from her medical pouch down Eliza's throat, then order warming pans from the innkeeper. Finally, stains on the new packing failed to spread. The midwife, Marya, nodded approvingly as Miklos sagged into a chair. "You do well enough with your wits dry. You're not the first who tried to ford too far downstream."

She efficiently covered Eliza. "Best get out of those wet clothes, Prince, or you'll be sicker than . . . this your wife?"

The sharpness of her eyes almost made him smile. "Yes. The Princess Elizabeth." He could read Marya's mind. Titles always sounded important, but Eliza didn't look important; she looked small and shabby and frail. Covered with her blanket, Anitra, who might have been so like Eliza, resembled a tiny, forgotten lump. Only he would never forget . . . and Eliza would never forgive . . .

He glanced up to find Marya was watching him. "Well," she said crisply, "what are you waiting for? Off with the clothes and into bed!" She headed for the door. "I'll be back in a bit."

Thank God the woman not only was competent, but sensitive enough to leave him alone. He felt cold and hollow, as if part of him were missing. Eliza began to shiver again. He pulled off his wet clothes, gently picked up Anitra and cuddled her under the covers with himself and Eliza.

He awoke to hear Eliza coughing. Marya had returned to spread her bulk in the big chair. "I think Her Highness is going to be a very sick young lady," she observed, "but first things first." She nodded to the child. "Will you be burying her here?"

"At Balaton," he said slowly.

She held out her hands. "Then I'd best be getting her ready for her journey."

He made no move to release Anitra.

"You can't keep her here," the midwife said gently. "Your wife will not be getting well overnight and Balaton's nearly a day's ride. Naught can hurt your little one now." She touched the tiny head. "Do you think the Lord pays no mind to the smallest of his angels? Young ones take the most attention.''

He kissed Anitra, wound her fingers about his. ''She's perfect, isn't she?''

''Yes. Just a little too impatient to try life on her own.''

Like her mother, he thought. Slowly he unwound Anitra's fingers and gave her to Marya. ''I'll bury her here. Now. I don't want Eliza to see her . . . like this.''

Marya rocked Anitra. ''Dry clothes are in the bag here. My husband's, if you're not too fussy.''

''Thank you,'' Miklos said simply, ''for everything.''

''Don't thank me yet. Your lady's showing all the bright signs of lung inflammation.''

For the next six days, Miklos was not out of Eliza's room, but she didn't know him from Enzo. She babbled names he didn't recognize—most of them Austrian and Hungarian—but took to be serfs'. She called for him, but never realized he was there. From delirium emerged months of resentment, frustrated longing, and finally defeat. She flailed out at him. ''I'm not going to die . . . all of you, get back! Get your torches back! I'm not going to curl up and die for you, Miki! I'm not going to be thrown away . . . by a man who doesn't want me. I'll . . . walk away. Walk away . . . from all of you, all the way home.''

He held her; for days he held her, until she believed Enzo's arms would always be there.

One morning, she awakened against him and saw she had been wrong. By dawn's uncertain light, Miklos could barely read her expression. She was not afraid, only puzzled, trying to remember what had happened to Enzo. Then she remembered and her face twisted. ''He's dead, isn't he?''

''Probably.''

The grief that welled in her eyes dismayed him, swelled against his own grief. He'd tried to find Enzo after he'd gotten Eliza ashore, but the wagon had dashed to bits in the swollen river; nowhere in its lash of mud and debris had he seen a sign of Enzo. His friend, and like his brother, his betrayer.

"Don't be glad," she said faintly. "He came to help me. I didn't mean to run away with him. The serfs took over and I was just . . . too tired to argue anymore."

His arm tightened about her. "Even about seven children."

Weakening, she was too dazed to understand. "I've been ill? I must have rattled . . ." She murmured something about the baby, then slipped into a heavy sleep. The next morning, she awakened, this time awakening him as well when she put a hand to her stomach and stiffened. "Where's the baby?"

Sleep whistled from Miklos's mind. He'd had a horror of this moment, like a careful actor prepared for it, and now not a single line remained in his head. Only echoes of the pain of Anitra's death hovered in the emptiness that remained after her loss. Now he must cover Eliza with that emptiness like a smothering, terrible cloak. His throat tight, he told her as gently as he could about Anitra.

Before he could react, she clawed at him with a maniac strength he would not have believed possible. "Liar!" she screamed. "What have you done with her?!" She went for his face again, and he felt his cheek rip. Grabbing her wrists, he forced her flat.

"Eliza, she was scarcely more than half term!"

"Premature babies live!" She craned to peer for a cradle in the gloom. "It's possible! Give her to me!" When he didn't let go, she resorted to pleading. "She has to eat. Please, let me nurse her . . ."

"I can't." His voice cracked. "Would to God I could . . . but Anitra's been dead a week. You've had a lung inflammation and you haven't any milk . . ."

"No!" She bucked against him. "No! No, no! You're lying . . . just like you've always lied!"

A sharp knock sounded at the door. "It's me, Marya."

Marya was kind but matter-of-fact as she confirmed Anitra's death. "Lucky you are, Your Highness, not to be lying next to her."

"I don't believe you," Eliza said frantically, then turned in fury again on Miklos. "You've paid her to lie!"

Marya motioned Miklos to the door. "Out with you. She needs to talk to a woman now."

An hour later, Marya called Miklos upstairs again. She met him in the hall corridor outside the room. Her honest face was sober. "You might have married a child, but your wife's a woman now that's lost a child. Her face may be fair and fine, but she'll never be a girl again, so she's twice to grieve and you'll have need of twice your patience."

"What did you say to her?"

Marya smiled sadly. "What a woman who's lost three of her own would say. Death has many faces: cruel and kind and mischievous. I've been both his friend and foe, but I always see him clearest when he comes to play with children."

Eliza had turned her face to the wall. For two days, she didn't move. Miklos had seen only creatures in the wild stay that still. Was it due to her instinct for self-preservation or reversion to the habits of an invalid? How many hours, days, had she laid just so as a child? Fighting hopelessness, searching for reasons to live as one would sift and examine minute grains of sand. In a way, she was fighting for both of them, deciding what was worth preserving in their lives; what, if anything, she was willing to share with him again. He dreaded the guillotine finality of that decision.

Not a tear marked her face when she finally looked at him. "What has happened at Balaton?"

The expressionless question startled him. "I don't know. I hadn't thought to find out."

"How will you recover the estate?"

Puzzled, he watched her. "I'll apply to the magistrate at Sárbogárd, I suppose. Why?"

"I wonder how many lives will be given for a few days of freedom," she said softly. "When will you go for the magistrate?"

"That can keep until you're well enough to travel."

"That should give them a few more days." She smiled enigmatically. "Perhaps they'll be sober enough to fight."

"I should think you'd hate them."

"If a dog is beaten long enough, he can't be blamed for biting."

Sighing, he rose and went to the bed. "Then you hate me. Anitra's dead more because of me than anyone. I could have taken Balaton off your shoulders, controlled the serfs, kept Enzo from talking you into one of his hair-brained schemes . . ."

"I don't hate you," she replied quietly, "and Enzo didn't talk me into anything any more than you could have been sure of restraining the serfs." She described the wild ride to Saint Andrew's and bone-rattling dash to Székesfehérvár. "The baby was bound to miscarry. No one person was to blame. Enzo had as much to do with it as anyone, and if I had stayed where you left me at Saint Andrew's, Anitra would have been safe. I was afraid you might take her and leave me there for good."

His face went bleak. "Whatever you've come to think of me, I'm not that much a monster."

"I knew that when you chose to come not to Balaton but to me," she said softly. "Marya says you saved my life."

He shook his head. "You can thank her for that. Most of the time I didn't know what to do. I just held you."

"Hold me now, please," she whispered. "I miss my lump."

Then in his arms, she wept. He'd never seen her cry and much doubted if anyone else had, for she wasn't any good at it. The tears came unevenly, stubbornly, as if she didn't want to let them go, but their reservoir ran deep and once cracks appeared, the restraints began to crumble. Then his sorrow met hers and he hid his own tears in her hair.

"Miki, don't let's cry anymore," she whispered at last. "Take me back to Balaton. I want to go home."

Only forty-two serfs were left at Balaton when Miklos and the magistrate's men arrived. The rest who had taken part in the uprising had run away to be rounded up over the next three weeks and jailed. Hans was among the loyal survivors that threaded from the forest. Miklos soberly

took his maimed hand. "My wife and child would have
been murdered here but for you. From this day, you are
free. Forty acres of good land will be entitled to you and
your heirs. So long as I am alive, you have my friendship
and protection."

Hans's face glowed with pride. "I'm to be my own man
at last! With my own land!" He crossed himself. "God
bless you, sir! You won't regret it!"

"No, I don't think I will," Miklos replied quietly.

Eliza met Miklos in the courtyard of Saint Andrew's.
His grim face assured ill news of Balaton. "Max is dead."

Eliza nodded sadly. She had known he could not have
survived. "We'll bury him by Anitra."

"Hans is alive," Miklos went on wearily as they walked
under the ivy-clad colonnade, "but the rioters salted the
manor gardens and three of the east fields. The barns and
stable are burned. They would have destroyed more, if the
wine cellar hadn't been more inviting than vandalism."
His frustration exploding, he slapped his riding gloves
viciously against a column. "Don't they ever think beyond
the moment?! That they were ruining property they hoped
to keep for themselves?!"

Wrapping her shawl closer, Eliza looked out at the
monastery's tranquil garden with its budding yellow for-
sythia and crocus. "The kulaks must have known they
could hold Balaton only for the moment. That's why they
drink so much, I think: to forget the futility of their lives.
But Miki"—she took his shoulders—"you said yourself
they keep revolting, more and more of them. Despite her
power, Austria is afraid. To take everything that matters
from people is dangerous, for then they've nothing to lose.
Even your own class is rejecting censorship, repression of
every sort. How much more desperate must the peasants
be to win the simplest of freedoms?"

He touched her cheek. "You're right. To leave a man
nothing *is* dangerous. When I remember how we once
were together, I feel I'm one of those salted fields."

"What of your women in Budapest?" she said softly.

"The monks have probably enjoyed more women of late." His eyes' bleak longing belied his crooked smile. "Not that I've lacked endeavor; I'm fixed on a spitfire with uncommon golden eyes and hair. I simply cannot find another lover to my liking."

"I've the same problem. Among the turnips is not one that resembles you."

They both broke out laughing, and then she was in his arms. Minutes later, she was in his bed. Rediscovering one another was slow delight, their hunger sharp, but held for savoring. Entangled in the long, shining mass of Eliza's hair, their bodies sinuously intertwined with whisperings to the slow, languid measure of their love. They flowed together, became one, as a single, throbbing heart. Enchantment was upon them, its bud grown rich and wild. Enveloped in its bright petals stirred life ebullient and lustrous, with all its poignant miracle. Peace and oblivion came with their passionate joining, then a flowering that sang of recovered joy. The bitter snows had passed; the spring's high freshet spilled clear and clean. Eliza's crow of pleasure was sweet as a flute. During that long, spring afternoon, they lay entwined in each other's arms: a union of souls and bodies tranquil as the newborn sigh of wakening spring across the land. As the afternoon drowsed away, Miklos contentedly ran his hands through Eliza's hair. Like a harpist, he threaded strands that caught the sun's bronze glow as it filtered Lake Balaton's gray, cumulous clouds. Her head moved to follow his hand. "Look, Miki, a rainbow's forming over the lake." She tumbled over him and pointed. "Perhaps our luck's changing."

"My ancestors believed in omens." Drowsily, he stroked her silky bottom. "Their flags were horse's tails, their women captives." He pulled her down on the sheets and his gray eyes lost their sleepiness as they looked deeply into hers. "I didn't give you much choice at Stagshorn, but if I were to let you go now with all the money you want, would you tear off for Paris in the morning?"

"Ask me in the morning." Her hair tumbled about her face, she smiled up at him. "As you don't have any money left, I'll have to collect in another way. We may just have to stay here another day, and another . . ."

"Even if nothing's changed about Loise and Petyr?" he asked quietly.

Her golden eyes were calm. "You didn't murder them."

"As simple as that."

"As simple as this." Locking her fingers behind his neck, she kissed him. "You might have beaten Enzo to a rag if the river hadn't gotten him, but you wouldn't have killed him out of hand; you certainly didn't try to hurt me. I don't think you murdered Loise and Petyr."

He tapped her nose. "You're no angel, so don't get too carried away with forgiveness."

She smiled serenely. "You don't want forgiving; you want loving." She gave his manhood a feather-light caress. "Now about Paris . . ."

They were awakened after midnight by a wan monk who flushed as Miklos stumbled in naked grandeur to the door. "An Austrian emissary from Budapest, Your Highness," stuttered the monk.

The sleep drained from Miklos's brain. "I'm not here."

"I can't tell him that," the monk protested.

"Then I'll tell him." Miklos strode to the window and flung open the shutter. "Miklos Sztarai is not here," he boomed at the messenger beneath the whiplike willows in the courtyard. "Now go and say ten Hail Marys for waking everybody up!"

The messenger didn't budge.

Eliza joined Miklos at the window. "I don't think he believes you, Miki," she observed lightly as she peeked from behind him. "Perhaps it's your lack of a cassock." She hugged his waist. "What do you suppose he wants?"

"I know what he wants. I'm not going."

Her humor went. "Back to Budapest?" Silent, she moved back from the window to gather her silk negligee from the bed.

Miklos turned and pulled her into his arms. "Don't worry. I won't go away again. I'm needed here. Besides, I can't do the Austrians any good in Budapest." He kissed her bare shoulder and eased her toward the bed.

"But they think you can. Kolowrat told you what would happen if you don't work with them." She turned in his hands. "You can be sent back into exile, lose everything."

"I'll write Kolowrat I'm in mourning; it's true enough. He'll have to forget about me."

"But he won't. You're a Hungarian among revolting Hungarians. He'll think only one thing: that you assume you can safely thumb your nose at the Austrian emperor." She put her arms about him. "You must go to Budapest again, if only to make a show of cooperation."

"Will you come with me?" he murmured against her mouth, his hands sliding down her hips.

She sighed wistfully. "I have another month of unfinished work at Balaton."

He stared at her. "You've begun to like turnips?"

"No, cloth printing as they're doing in Sopron. I've already sent hand-printed samples to shops in Budapest for orders to start a cottage factory. Hans is building the machines to hold the blocks we're carving. I'll be safe enough with the troublemakers gone. With so many fields and buildings burned, we need the money."

"The place is in ruins and you want to turn it into a factory," he said bemusedly. "Just what do I do in Budapest with this?" He held his sex at attention. "Carve cogs in it?"

"Well"—she grinned wryly—"you can't very well use it for a crochet hook."

Chapter 18

Guns and Mistresses

Budapest: June 25, 1848

A month later, Eliza traveled to Budapest with finished fabrics to fill their modest orders. The time at Balaton had been busy. The first bolts of cloth had been purchased from the monks on credit; now she hoped to buy cotton thread the same way. Hans had built two looms and four girls were learning to weave. By next month, their efforts might be good enough. The printed chintz had been particularly popular among upholsterers and drapers; she was assured a solid profit even if the dressmakers were uncertain about the folk designs. Eliza wagered rising nationalism would soon favorably make up their minds. She'd written Miklos of her coming but expected no reply due to slow, undependable mails.

As the passenger coach rolled through the Budapest streets, Eliza craned from the window. Nowhere in the world was there a city like Budapest: a vision from a fairy tale. A hodgepodge of turreted ruins and castles, medieval houses, and baroque state buildings were crammed together along the Danube. Jugglers, gypsies, beggars, and bears wandered the lively crowds on cobbled streets vivid with the Hungarian love of bright color. Budapest was a delightful, living summer. Shortly, her fellow passengers, at last forgiving of being crowded by her cloth bolts, began to laugh at her eagerness, both to view the city and see her husband.

When she arrived at his lodging, the hotelier told her Miklos was in parliament for the day, so she went to Bette's. Bette was surprised, but pleased to see her; she was much less pleased with the fabric idea. "Sztarais, merchants? No, dear, it won't do," she declared. "Our family doesn't peddle things of this sort."

"Well, Hilliards *do*. Selling Balaton may be more prestigious, but also far more foolish than selling cloth. You can either loan Miki and me the money we need or pretend you don't know us."

While that settled Bette, the miser of the family, on one score, she was more persuasive on another. "Stay for dinner. I'll send a message to Miklos at his hotel and he can meet us here."

Eliza smiled. "Perhaps another night. Miki and I've not seen each other for a month, remember."

Bette eyed her shrewdly. "My dear, I learned early never to surprise a man who's been living alone."

Ignoring the inference, Eliza took out her reticule, jotted a message in her journal, and tore it out. "Thank you for the dinner invitation, Bette, but if you will kindly forward this note to Miki, I shall be dining with him tonight. Also, if you don't mind, I should like the use of a bedroom to change into something more suitable."

"Give me the note; my coachman will take it." Bette carelessly waved for a servant. "Show the princess to the front guestroom, then call Marie to help her." She smiled tolerantly at Eliza. "This evening isn't the time to meet Miki with cracked nails, is it, my dear?"

Wearing the simple pearl and diamond necklace and topaz gown Miklos had given her at Como, Eliza dismounted the carriage outside his hotel that evening. The gaslight over the baroque main door's ornate arch hazed with his window lights. Life at Balaton might be barren, but Miklos lived well in Budapest. A wry smile curved her lips. He must need to make a show; display was important to his class, just as to American society, even if they had to ruin themselves.

She hurried up the *faux marbre* stair to the upper floor hallway, but hearing voices, slowed some distance from Miklos's door. Suddenly cold, she slowly walked closer, recognized Miklos's voice . . . then, like a stab to the heart, Vanda Bellaria's. The hallway walls pressed in on her. For a moment, she couldn't breathe, the pain was so intense. She took a step; the pain lessened slightly and black emptiness seeped in where the pain had been. Another step and she felt more emptiness. Another. More. Then the acid beginnings of rage. She knocked. Miklos's manservant who answered the door went pale. Noting her eyes' dangerous glitter, he hastily bowed and backed out of her path. Vanda, lounging in seductive, sapphire taffeta on the sofa, was far less surprised than Miklos to see her. Miklos looked as if someone had hit him. "Eliza, what are you doing here?!"

Trust Bette, Eliza thought blackly. Her afternoon's note to Miklos had gone no farther than Bette's rubbish pile.

"Why, *caro*," Vanda drawled, "Eliza has already learned to be a suspicious wife. I think she's about to make a scene." She turned languidly on the sofa toward Miklos. "May I have my wrap, *caro*? The theatre is so much better suited to shrill hysterics."

Eliza picked up Vanda's wineglass and tossed the contents in her lap. Vanda let out a screech. "You were saying?"

Eliza turned expressionlessly to Miklos. The acid was searing away her sight and coherent thought; only blazing pain was left. How could he betray her *now*? They had lost a child, nearly lost Balaton, yet despite everything, found each other again . . . only for him to kill their spring with the frost of more hideous deceit: all for Vanda Bellaria, a callous, self-seeking tramp. "Don't bother with dredging up an explanation this time, Miki." She was surprised her voice was so flat and even, when her heart was splintering. "Since we married, I've fairly choked on all your explanations and lies. Now I'm going to breathe again. I want a divorce."

"I won't give you one," he answered tightly as Vanda furiously pawed with a velvet pillow at her dress.

"I think you will. I've had much more practice than the *contessa* at being embarrassing." She left.

To move in with Bette. "It's the least you can do," Eliza advised Bette furiously. "You stirred up the whole mess." After she left Miklos's hotel, she had done nothing but cry, hot explosions of tears that carried beyond the carriage. Love *was* close to hate and she was being carried by hellish pain into hate. She wanted to be free and whole again, and she also wanted to get even!

"Now, Eliza," countered Bette warily, "you are going to behave?"

"No, indeed," was the wicked reply. "Only *bad* women get divorces."

"You've no need to start bouncing in and out of beds," Bette said quickly. "Jealous males, particularly Miklos, can be a great deal of trouble. If you really want a divorce from Miki, I can show you readily enough how to get it."

"Your idea had better be good, Bette," Eliza retorted. "I was rather looking forward to riding naked through Parliament!"

Politics: not precisely the stuff by which blighted romance is revenged, and yet again, Eliza had to agree with Bette, it was the perfect weapon to prod Miklos into severing the nuptial knot. All she had to do was attend Bette's weekly salons and look interested while such statesmen of the new government as Kossuth, Batthyány, and the increasingly erratic Széchenyi argued politics with one another, aristocrats, tradesmen, and students. She was willing enough: anything to distract from the heartache threatening to overwhelm her. Not only was she tormented by the loss of Miklos, but haunted by the death of Anitra. When she was not promoting fabric sales, she entertained liberal thinkers at breakfast, lunch, and dinner, accompanied them to the opera, theatre, and the Casino. Also, to Miklos's particular irritation, she regularly sat in the public box at Parliament.

Indeed, far from bored with proposals for the shape of a new, Hungarian republic free from Austrian domination, Eliza was fascinated, too much so to remain neutral indefinitely. She suspected her preoccupation with politics was partly due to her hopeless need to forget Miklos, also to make a new life by helping others far more unhappy than herself. She had meant to vindicate the deaths at Balaton by persuading Miklos to free their serfs, but now saw a way to free every kulak in Hungary. Attracting many friends and prospective lovers among Bette's large, political acquaintance, she began to develop and trade opinions.

Her favorite companions were the brilliant young poet, Sándor Petöfi, and his bride of a year, Julia, who was close to her age. When not moving among the brilliant society of Budapest, Eliza spent most of the time with the Petöfis and their student friends drinking wine and debating in cafes and forums. Because she encountered Miklos too often in society, the student circles were a haven where she could relax and put his possible appearance out of her mind. As if he were as angry and betrayed as she, he made no effort to seek her out. At parties, they circulated in very different groups, but she was never at ease when he was near; as a lover, he had been too near once, so much so that he had been able to tear out her heart. More and more, she drifted away from society to the students. For them and many others, Sándor Petöfi's poetry was the intoxicating breath of the new Hungary. Eliza became convinced plodding imperialism was doomed.

Yet, despite the quiet rise of the liberal, reform-minded Batthyany cabinet, she suspected peace would not last. Austria's distraction with its own internal revolution and outbreak of war with Charles Albert in Piedmont-Sardinia unfortunately had been temporary. Charles had made a fairly resolute grab for power, but on July 25, his army had been beaten at Custoza. Now Austria was taking alternately hard and soft lines with Hungary, all the while encouraging factionalism. Rumors of a new emperor circulated.

"Sándor," she told the poet at one of the salons, "we may need weapons here in Budapest before the year's end. If her local revolutionary outbreaks fail, Austria will be free to turn on us."

"Shh." With a quick glance about them, the slight, dark young man caught her arm. Typical of Bette's gatherings, the buff and gold room was full of politicians and not a rosewood chair was empty, scarcely a canapé was left. "Eliza," he said quietly, "some of us think a police spy has been attending the salons. Stiffel, an Austrian ministry secretary friendly to our cause, says Kolowrat has information he must have gotten from your aunt's salons. Two Hungarian parliamentarians have disappeared, both after expressing rabid opposition to Austria in this house." He led her aside to an alcove window seat. "I agree we need weapons, but they're not easily obtained. None of the monarchies will sell us arms."

"My mother will," she said briefly.

"Your *mother?*"

"If you pay in gold, and she'll bite every coin, she'll ship anything you like: Parrott guns, Colts, probably listed as farm tools. Can you get the money?"

"I can't," he said slowly, "but I know a man who can: Vlad Rakoczy."

She tried not to flinch. "Can you trust him?"

"When it comes to fighting Austria, yes." He smiled skeptically. "Beyond that . . ."

When their guests had gone, Eliza told Bette about the police spy suggested by the Austrian, Stiffel. "Someone is tattling; we're just not certain who."

Bette picked up her embroidery and began taking tiny, perfect stitches. "I've never liked needlework." She studied the stitch tension. "Theodor Bakocz."

"What?"

"Bakocz. He speaks Hungarian like a native, except his *r*'s have a faint ring of Austria's western Stiermark. He claims to be an art dealer and certainly knows the masters, but not enough of minor works he'd probably be limited to handling. His hands have a horseman's calluses; enough to be a soldier." She began to stitch precisely again. "Why not drop a little corn and see where he follows?"

So, in conversation with the suspected Bakocz, Sándor's wife, Julia, obligingly dropped a few tasty pellets, in the form of the unwitting Vlad Rakoczy and a fictitious plan to recruit the Rumanian peasantry into a private army. As Rakoczy's courier, Eliza provided the rest of the cob.

Scarcely had Eliza left Bette's house on the appointed evening when her carriage was followed by a green, closed coach. She took no evasive measure, let Bakocz assume she was an unaware amateur. Sándor's friends were stationed along the route to Rakoczy's stone mansion on the city outskirts.

Rakoczy greeted her warily. Eliza liked Vlad less each time she encountered him. He affected a long, velvet theatrical villain's dressing gown of black lined with scarlet; his decrepit house was done completely in gray and scarlet with fifteenth century Venetian and Byzantine furniture. Paintings of the Levant and Russian icons were spottily lit by gold censers. The dark, depressing whole was dulled by dust.

He sensed her curiosity, also her distaste, as he led her to his study. "My great-great-grandfather Ferenc's Turkish mistress collected these pieces during his exile. I confess to more sentiment than liking for her choices." He relieved her of her claret moiré cape and waved her to an overblown settee. "But then you are somewhat familiar with the vicissitudes of exile; one cannot always live as one would like."

Eliza gracefully spread her watered silk skirts like a rich spill of wine. Her emeralds and diamonds were Bette's largest and heavy as a horse collar, but Rakoczy needed to be impressed. "On the contrary, I was for the most part quite happy in Italy and abroad," she assured him, "but then perhaps I am accustomed to making and adapting to unpleasant choices.''

"I regret I had to be the one to force some of those choices.''

You fairly frothed at the chance, you troll, Eliza recalled coolly. "I owe you thanks for that, Your Highness, and I've now found a way to repay you at a handsome profit to myself.'' She explained about the guns. "As agent, I will receive twenty percent of the purchase price. Miki is in no position to pay me a divorce settlement.''

That tidbit, she saw from Rakoczy's satisfied expression, would be all over Budapest in twenty-four hours. No one had been sure previously of her intentions toward Miklos.

"I suggest the arms be transported through Yugoslavia, Piedmont-Sardinia, and areas held by Charles Albert,'' she went on. "If the arms are intercepted by the Italians, they may still eventually be used against Austria. And,'' she added mildly, "Charles will be less likely to shoot the escorting detectives as agents provocateurs, which should relieve the detectives and keep their fees bearable.''

Rakoczy smiled slightly. "All this is intriguing, but who, may I ask, gave you the idea that I could afford to furnish arms to the Hungarian army?'' He gestured to their somber surroundings. "Do I appear rich?''

She rose and wandered about the room, ended at a wall of dusty icons. After peering at them several moments, she said flatly, "The jewels in six of these icons would equip a platoon. The gold candelabra on the table would pay for a pair of field pieces, probably with horses. The rugs, let's say . . .''

"Never mind,'' he interrupted dryly. "I see you have a Hebraic eye.''

Thanks to Mother, Eliza thought, who spent most of her time in other people's houses adding in her head.

"How many guns do you propose,'' asked Rakoczy, "keeping in mind I do not plan to spend the rest of my life sitting on the floor?''

"As you're miserably short of cannon, let's say a bat-

tery of howitzers and two thousand rifles . . . unless you
can afford more.''

"Two thousand! That has to be . . . how much of a
fortune?!''

"Every bit of fifty thousand pounds. Thrones are
expensive.''

His eyes glittered. "Why should Batthyány and his
crowd make me king?''

"Because your great-great-grandfather Ferenc would
have been acclaimed king, had he succeeded in his revolt
against Austria.''

"He was popular,'' Rakoczy said flatly. "I am not.''

"Popularity won't matter if you control the arsenals.''

His eyes narrowed. Her skin prickled as if she were
being watched by a snake. "Do not make me Casca to our
Hungarian Caesars, Princess; I mislike the role. My grandfather was a titan. I need not crawl to power like a
worm.''

No? she thought warily. Even now you're not thinking
to muffle your rattle. "Titans take power,'' she affirmed
boldly. "Will you do less?''

His eyes turned sly. "What I will do is my affair.'' He
began to pace. At length, he turned with new dignity that
made him seem taller than he was. "I will send you a man
I can trust with the gold. Order the guns. Give them all to
Batthyány as my gift. Tell him he may keep control of the
armories. These will be my gifts to Hungary.''

Strangely, Eliza believed he meant what he said, yet
how much of him was charlatan, how much his ancestor's
nobility? And if Vlad Rakoczy had the capacity for greatness, to what end?

Still pondering Rakoczy's puzzle after taking leave of
him, she walked slowly out to her carriage. No sooner had
the coachman handed her into it than she saw she was not
alone. She became stifled by a sudden sensation of heat
and claustrophobia. "Miki! What are you doing here?
How did you . . .''

"This is, after all, my aunt's carriage,'' he murmured.
She couldn't see his face clearly in the shadows, but the

shoulders of his black evening clothes and hat were dusted with flower pollen as if he'd been poking through shrubbery. The carriage started down the drive.

"Well, I happen to have exclusive use of your aunt's carriage for this evening," she retorted, forcing her voice to stay steady. "Please get out." He was sitting too close. Along his thigh and shoulder she felt tension that didn't show in his voice. Eliza was stirred by the old need and longing she hated, but could not subdue. She felt naked, exposed as if he'd abruptly stripped her. She could see his eyes now. Their gray was smoky, brooding. Her nearness disturbed him too, with anger and desire.

Miklos studied the Sztarai emeralds and diamonds that winked from the throat of her cape. She's damned beautiful tonight, he thought grimly. And damned dangerous. "A woman alone shouldn't wear so much jewelry. She might tempt unscrupulous elements." He flicked her swinging earrings and she jerked away. Jealousy and frustration gnawed at him like sullen wolves. "You're dressed as if you're selling something. Did Vlad have the price?"

Her eyes narrowed. "If he did?"

His own turned to gray ice. "Then you've just bought a great deal of trouble."

"Such as?" The taut note in her voice suggested Eliza was beginning to suspect trouble already. The carriage wasn't headed toward Bette's as she'd directed; instead, the driver, skirting the park across from Rakoczy's mansion, turned in the opposite direction to cut down a deserted road through the hills beyond the city.

Sitting back, Miklos eyed her with a dispassion he didn't feel. Would she never believe in herself enough to believe in him? He was sorely tempted to shake her until her jealousy of Bellaria was jarred away. Out of her old insecurities and green-eyed spite, she was inviting destruction as if tossing out notes for tea! "I'm trying to decide whether you came here as bait or something else. You were with Vlad over an hour. During that hour, a man was strangled: Bakocz, the man in the carriage that followed you."

She went pale. "That isn't possible!"

"No? He heard a tale about your being some sort of courier, and now he's a staring corpse in that wood across from Rakoczy's house." He flicked her cape back to caress the curve of her neck. "You should count yourself fortunate; he considered squeezing the truth out of your pretty throat."

She twisted to face him fully. "You can't know that! You're trying to frighten me and you're guessing!"

"Guessing?" He forced his attention from her pale, naked shoulders. In the shadowy coach, his eyes glinted strangely. "I'm Bakocz's contact. Everything he knew about you, he learned from me." As horror filled her eyes, he went on. "It was you who insisted I return to Budapest to play along with the Austrians. Have you any idea what sort of games they're playing here? You've set yourself up as a target. What do you suppose they're going to do when they learn one of their agents was killed drawing a bead on that target?"

She grabbed for the door and he jerked her hand away. "Driver"— he rapped on the mount panel—"to Princess von Schmerling's." When the carriage headed back toward the main road, he continued flatly, "They're going to come after you and they may come after me if they think I warned you or . . . otherwise interfered."

She looked numb. "You mean . . . they might think *you* killed Bakocz?"

"Bravo," he murmured ironically. "So, considering you've dragged my head into a noose along with your own, suppose you explain your business with Rakoczy."

He needs something to trade them, she thought, to get both of us out of this. "We suspected Bakocz was a police spy. I was, as you say, bait to flush him out, but I didn't know he was to be killed." Her tawny eyes held his levelly. "As for Rakoczy, there's really nothing to tell. We merely dreamed up the story for Bakocz. If anyone had to get into trouble . . . well, Vlad is disliked and mistrusted." She glanced out at the passing, house-lined street. She was reasonably safe; they were well into the city. For now, she needed to placate Miklos until the carriage reached Bette's townhouse, so she diverted the subject. "I'm not sure about Vlad. He's a complex man. I feel he's dangerous and yet . . ."

"What story did you give him?"

She was disconcerted. "What?"

"Don't expect me to believe you exchanged small talk for over an hour."

"I asked him whether he can be counted on in a fight. He promised his help." Her eyes lowered. "That makes me feel rather badly about compromising him."

"I can just imagine," Miklos said dryly.

She ignored the barb. "So you see, my so-called spying is at an end. You've nothing more to worry about."

Silently, he stared out at the city streets as if pondering a decision. Finally, the carriage pulled up in front of Bette's door, but when she started quickly to get out, Miklos clamped a hand on her arm. "If you're lying to me, we'll both regret it." His grip tightened until she winced. "Be out of Budapest by morning. I don't care where you go: Italy, France, or England, but leave." He let go her arm and dropped an envelope in her lap. "This should support you for a few months: long enough for this mess to settle. If it doesn't settle, I'll bring you more money when I can get it. We need to discuss more than politics."

She tossed the envelope back. "Keep your money, Miklos. We've nothing to discuss. I've told you what I want, but whether or not you give it to me, I'm not leaving."

"No?" he drawled ominously. "Then perhaps you should know what to expect if you stay." He pulled her to him and his mouth drove down hard on hers.

Eliza was furious. He'd never kissed her this way, put his hands on her this way. She twisted and clawed at him until, with a muttered oath, he tore her claret silk bodice to the waist. She felt his mouth hot against her breasts, his hand thrust between her thighs. She swore at him, jerked at his hair with a muffled cry. "You bastard! You're not going to rape me!"

"I wouldn't dream of it." With apparent calm, Miklos sat up and arranged his clothes. "But as long as you wave temptation in front of my nose, I would be doing less than my conjugal duty not to attempt a reconciliation. Who knows? I might throw myself upon you in Parliament, drag you beneath the tea table at one of your liberal-loving fetes or . . ."—he grinned evilly—"creep into your lonely bed at the full of the moon."

She practically fell out of the carriage. "You stay away from me!"

He clipped shut the carriage door as she scurried up the walk. "Sorry, darling; I just can't help myself!"

Miklos was as good as his word. Glowering at Eliza's male escorts until they thought better of keeping company with the wife of a notorious man, he followed her around the city, and once into the opera powder room. He came to Bette's salons, where his Austrian affiliation killed all political conversation. Conscientious as a tom after a tabby, he leered at Eliza over his teacup until she was tempted to throw her own at him. When an infatuated student heatedly offered to call him out, she assured him her husband's clownish sense of humor did not extend to the dueling field. "Keep it up and I'll take a lover half your age!" she hissed at Miklos through a vase of flowers.

"Go ahead," he purred back. "You'll get more finesse from a baby rabbit."

Two weeks later, the situation became less amusing when Sándor Petőfi accosted her at a National Art Gallery reception. "Have you discussed Stiffel, the Austrian secretary, with anyone?"

"Only Bette, why?"

He drew her away from the crowd down a long hall of paintings. A hundred flat eyes watched them pass. As if displaying a picture, he paused under a painting of the martyrdom of György Dózsa, ill-fated leader of Hungary's

one great serf rebellion. "Stiffel's dead. Strangled like
Bakocz."

Shocked and bewildered, she wheeled on him. "I thought
our people killed Bakocz!"

He snorted. "I don't know who did. Exposure would
have been sufficient. The manner of death is a warning; an
eye for an eye."

Sickened, Eliza looked up at Dózsa, roasting alive on
his red-hot iron mockery of a throne. Miklos was right; it
was getting uglier. But what was his part? If Bakocz had
found out about Stiffel, Miklos might have known about
him as well. He'd thought her Rakoczy tale was thin; had
he found another one with a streak of fat for the Austrians?

The next morning, she moved out of Bette's.

Budapest: September 11, 1848

Two days later, all Budapest knew of the guns. Eliza
couldn't trace the leak. Several people had shared the
secret: Sándor, Julia, others in their rebel group . . . and
Rakoczy himself. Had he vaingloriously boasted to his
"gang" of his contribution to the Hungarian cause? Whatever happened, the wrong person learned not only that
guns were expected, but that they were American. American guns led to considerable discussion in Vienna; fortunately the ministry was unable to put two and two together
as quickly as Miklos.

Fuming, he tried to find Eliza, but she'd grown as deft
at eluding him as he at embarrassing her. Finally, he
traced her to the Pilvax Cafe, a popular students' gathering
place. At first, he didn't see her among the throng in the
smoky room. Spotting Petöfi with several students at a
corner table, he pushed through the crowd. A few students, making crude remarks about his pimping for Austria, jostled him. They soon backed off from a frozen
smile that would have cracked stone.

"*Szervusz*, Sándor," he said quietly as he reached the
table. "Have you seen Eliza?"

"I wouldn't tell you if I had," returned Petöfi calmly. "Neither will anyone else here."

Drumming began to shiver the plank tables. "Sándor, Sándor!" Beer mugs thumped the bar and wineglasses sang. "Sandor, give us 'Talpra Magyar'!"

Petöfi glanced up at Miklos. "Excuse me. They want a poem. I doubt if it will please you; it speaks only to Hungarians."

Miklos smiled imperturbably. "Don't play prima donna with me; I remember when you couldn't string four words together."

Petöfi laughed. "Count them tonight, old man. Like bullets, they're aimed at the heads of you and your kind."

"Men get to be old by learning when to duck, Sándor. How much have you learned lately by listening only to your own voice and everybody telling you how wonderful you are?"

"I used to listen to you; so did a lot of others, until you got too busy ducking to say anything," retorted Petöfi. He jumped up on his table. "See you when the war's over, old man." He looked out at the crowd. "You want 'Talpra Magyar,' children! I give you 'Talpra Magyar'!"

The table banging reached a crescendo, then abruptly hushed as Petöfi spread his hands.

After Petöfi finished, Miklos, barely twenty-eight and a year more than Petöfi, felt old. All the young, exultant faces made him pity and envy the rebels their bright, fragile hopes. He wondered how many of them realized the revolt in Austria was failing.

And then he saw Eliza, her face shining with the rest. She was dressed cheaply like the poorest of the students and he realized why he'd had trouble finding her. He started toward her when the cafe door burst open. A student fought through the crowd.

"The emperor's set his dog on us! In his name, that Croat, Jelačić, has invaded Hungary!"

"We'll show them how we whip down dogs," cried a student at the bar.

"Hang that traitor intermediary, Count Lamberg!" shouted his drinking mate.

Someone began to sing the "Marseillaise," and others joined the rousing chorus. Cheers filled the room. Miklos saw Eliza's face as the cafe crowd poured into the streets; she looked pale and dazed as she was jostled along. He fought to reach her, but she was swept ahead of him. By the time he got to the street, torches were flaring in the darkness, people were spilling from the buildings, and he couldn't see her. The crowd hurtled toward Gellert Hill to find Lamberg. Then he caught a flash of pale hair and saw Eliza knocked against a wall. He pushed toward her, hauled her up before she went down under the press. "Good God, leave me alone!" She tried to pull away from him. "Just stay away from me!"

He threw her over his shoulder and waded through the mob. "Miki, damn you!"

No one paid much attention to her yelling, but a student caught Miklos's name. "It's Sztarai! He's got Eliza! Run the turncoat up with Lambert!"

Before the others realized what was happening and mobbed him, Miklos lunged into an alley. He heard cries behind him, but they were halfhearted, his pursuers still preoccupied with Lambert and unsure of his direction as he cut down another street. He tensely wondered whether Eliza might summon them, but aside from a muffled cry as she grazed a wall, she suffered abduction silently.

Near the river, he banged on a door. A kohl-eyed woman inspected him from a peephole, then quickly admitted him. After checking the street as he dropped Eliza on her feet, she hastily closed the door. "This way. Hurry!" she whispered, then hurried silently down a long, dim hallway. She waved them into a dark room, then stood a moment watching the hallway as if it held as much danger as the street. Then she slipped into the room, locked the door, and lit a wall lamp hung with crystals.

The room was ornate with black-brocaded walls and a huge gilt bed shaped like a griffin. The woman herself was a tall beauty with auburn hair and lozenge-shaped

hazel eyes. She wore a green silk Chinese dress decorated
with water lilies. Disregarding Miklos for a few moments,
she studied Eliza. Her eyes were as unreadable as a cat's.
"Would you care for champagne?" she murmured. "You
will find it in the bucket by the bed. Caviar, butter, and
toast are on the tray. Also a bottle of vodka and a samovar
of tea. A good evening, *monsieur, mademoiselle.*" She
left the room, and a moment later Eliza heard the door
lock.

She whirled on Miklos. "What is this place? Who is
that woman?"

"Swan is an extraordinarily skilled pillow artist. She's
also Russo-Chinese and illegitimate. Any other questions?"

"Yes," she replied curtly. "How do I get out of here?"

He shook his head. "The streets aren't safe tonight."

"It's *you* they want, not me!"

"You could have led them to me," he said quietly.

"I'm after a divorce, not your head on a platter!"

He smiled. "That's forgiving of you. I suppose as heads
go, mine doesn't divide too many ways."

"What do you mean?" she asked warily.

"The American guns. Sooner or later, someone's going
to remember I have a star-striped wife." His hands slid
down her arms to rest on her wrists. "You're not stupid,
Eliza. Until now, the revolution has been peaceful, based
on constitutional law, but you saw what happened tonight.
One moment people wanted poetry, the next they howled
for a man's head. Guns fire bullets, not ideals."

She pulled away. "I don't want bloodshed, but it's coming! Jelačić's invasion proves Austria won't let us have
freedom without a fight! Their power is mostly on paper;
Jelačić's a spearhead to take the brunt off their army."

"Eliza, paper power, treaty power, can be dangerous.
Austria is allied to Russia and if we make too much
trouble, we'll have great Russian bear tracks from east to
west. We can't fight the Croats, Austria, and Russia,
too!"

He poured a pair of vodkas and grimly handed her one.
"Here's to the freedom you hotheads say Hungary must

have, no matter what the cost. To the aristocrats, who
want to regain control of the government, to the middle
class and intelligentsia who await Utopia, to the peasants
who think a little something might trickle down to them.''

He tossed off his glass. ''Who do you think is going to
get this freedom? The peasants? Don't make me laugh.
Your lot, their Utopia?'' His voice grew harsh with disgust
for himself and his class. ''Not if my lot has anything to
say about it, and it's my lot that will be running things in
the same old way once the dust settles.''

''Miki, you may be right,'' she said earnestly. ''God
knows these patterns have recurred often enough in the
world, but we have to try to change them and if we fail,
try again.''

''There is no chance this time, Eliza,'' he replied gravely.
''I must have those guns.''

She took a sip of the vodka to moisten her dry mouth as
she tried to think of how to escape. ''I won't tell you how
to get them.''

''Do you want me to have to persuade Sándor or one of
his friends?''

''Only I know where the guns will arrive. The Pinker-
tons will deliver them only to me.''

His eyes turned bleak. ''That makes things unpleasantly
simple, doesn't it?''

Her spine prickled with creeping fear. ''What do you
mean?''

''Either you tell me where the guns are, or I must make
certain you tell no one else,'' he said huskily.

Vodka seeped from her tilting glass, chilled her shaking
fingers. ''You wouldn't . . . couldn't.''

''I never want to know if I can, Eliza,'' he said tensely.
''For God's sake, *tell me!*''

''I *can't*. All I have left now is Hungary, the country
you gave me. She's become what I live for now, her
dreams.'' She smashed the vodka glass and held it edge
out. ''So you *will* have to kill me, Miklos. Only fair
warning; I don't intend to go like some miserable chicken.''

''You won't,'' he assured her softly. ''You'll explode

like one of Guido's bombs. You've become more woman than that small skin can hold."

"But I was never enough for you, was I?" she murmured.

"Enough?" His voice became husky. "I'll never see your like again, you Circe. Like a will-o'-the-wisp, you'll haunt me through every bend in eternity."

A spark of mischief lit her eyes. "Nothing so gloomy! Murder me, and I'll be damned if I'll keep you company. I'll chase after Enzo and we'll produce those seven little hants."

"So"—his smile twisted slightly as he loomed over her—"even after death, I can never be sure of you. Why must I ever crave women faithless as cats?"

Her own mood turned bitter. "Have you ever given them any choice? Bed Bellaria when you're done here! I don't envy her. Go ahead, kill me and call it noble; forget how expedient being rid of me would be, forget I ran away with another man, that I publicly discarded you."

As he frozenly stared at her, her nerves reached the snapping point. If she was to die, she wanted to be rid of the damned, horrible anticipation! "Enzo and I *were* lovers. I've had others, even Rakoczy, to get money . . ."

Something altered in Miklos's eyes, like gray stone cracking, and Eliza glimpsed the demon that had so long preyed upon his mind. She slashed out as his hands went for her throat, saw blood streak his palm. With an oath, he smashed the broken glass from her hand, then knocked her to the floor. Stung by terror, she rolled away as he grabbed. The cloak tie tore, then the shoulder of her dress ripped in his hand, and frantically she kicked free. She scrambled to her feet and bolted for the window.

"No, don't," Miklos cried roughly and for a crazy instant, she heard fear in his voice. Certain now the window meant freedom, she flung back the curtains and jerked at the sash . . . to stare at the rushing blackness of the Danube River three stories below. Swan's house was set into a steep hillside bordering the river. Muttering a prayer, she flung outward. Then screamed as one of Miklos's hands grabbed her by the hair, the other by the arm.

Swiftly, he hauled her back, kicked the sash closed, and threw her on the bed. She flailed out, the breath slammed out of her lungs as his body came down atop her. Before she could breathe again, his hands closed about her throat, his blood slippery on her skin.

"Lies, lies," he rasped desperately. "Eliza, tell me you're lying!" His grip eased slightly. "Please," he whispered.

"No," she gasped dazedly. Her aching head wouldn't think clearly.

His eyes tormented, he stared down at her. "Those guns. You want me to believe you sold yourself for those damned guns!" Slowly, his hands tightened until his face became a blur. Then somehow, as the darkness thickened, his hands moved to her hair, knotted in it until her faint moan was abruptly cut off by his mouth, hard and hurtful on hers. He kissed her as if he were trying to tear something from her. She felt her cheap, ragged clothing rip, his torn hands moving over her skin, searching, bruising, exciting so that she perversely coveted each moment, each demand on her senses that returned her to the reality of life and the passion he could arouse in her. The roughness of his clothing against her bare flesh baited, roused her to twisting impatience. He wove desire about her until she fought away his clothes to seek him, closed on him until he groaned, twisting over her. Then as she opened to him, he plunged into her as if his sex were a weapon that might destroy and release them both. He thrust until sweat sheened his skin and their bodies arched together in a scalding, fearful craving for life that fountained at its scarlet source. Through that long, fevered night, they sought one another again and again, each one seeking to defeat and drain the other, but never succeeding.

As dawn paled the room, Miklos looked down at Eliza's heavy-lidded eyes and swollen lips. His head drooping with fatigue, he breathed in her ear, "As I seem entirely unable to dispatch you, I will be your keeper until the need for your guns has passed."

"A not altogether unexpected decision."

Her mild tone sparked his suspicion. "If you're thinking of leaving by the window, I'm going to board it up."

"Then I won't leave by the window, or the door, or any other way," Eliza whispered. "I'll wait in bed and weaken your resolution." She might have lost the battle, but she was determined to win the war. Miklos had proven she hadn't gotten him out of her system, that she still craved him as he did her. If they stayed together, they would destroy each other. While something primitive in her craved destruction if that was all she would have of him, she could not turn away from the road she had begun for the sake of the kulaks and frozen children who would be forced to flee so hopelessly again this year, and the next, and the next.

For five weeks, Miklos rarely left her and that bed. It became both their battleground and their haven of insatiable sensuality. Outside their private world, Jelačić became head of government and the liberal Hungarian ministry resigned. And then one fine, early December day, Eliza found the leisurely solitude to pick the door lock with a pickle fork and be gone.

Miklos wasted no time in trying to recover her. With Jelačić in control, he was sure she would immediately leave town. On a hunch, he went to Bette's.

"I don't know how she got in," she told him, "but the wardrobe and jewelry she left here are gone. She must have lowered everything from the bedroom window." Bette's curiosity sharpened. "Why on earth would she go into hiding? Hungarian sympathizers are not being imprisoned."

"Yet." He didn't mention the guns; better if Bette didn't know about them. The guns and disappearance of Eliza had set up too much disquiet among the students. Rumors had run rampant; in one way to Eliza's advantage, for they smokescreened the truth; in another, they assured the guns' existence to Jelačić and the Austrians. Of late, rumor claimed Eliza had paid for more guns than she'd gotten. A wagonload of American weapons had been intercepted by the Austrians at the Italian border;

Austrian spies in Northern Italy reported another two loads
had been confiscated by the Italian army at Merano.
Almost half her shipment was in enemy hands.

Knowing he would go for her neck, she couldn't safely
remain in Hungary, and with the Russians and Germans
hanging revolutionists, she'd probably head for Italy. Given
her audacity, he wondered which she would attempt: a
divorce or stealing her guns back? With her grand affection for horses, she'd travel by carriage and strike snows in
the mountain passes. She might make it; then again . . . if
she tried to return with the guns, she'd bait the devil twice;
that was once too often.

Chapter 19

The Yankee and the Snake

Brenner Pass, Italy: January 20, 1849

Eliza settled peacefully in her fox furs as she sipped schnapps and watched swirling snowflakes enlarge outside her carriage window. The snow was lovely, the stark Dolomites magnificent. Winter travel through Hungary and Austria had been harrowing. To avoid the Austrian authorities, she and her driver had slept and eaten in the carriage. She'd helped pry the carriage out of drifts and endlessly twiddled her thumbs while repairs were made in obscure villages. Life's requirements became simple: she wanted a bath, shampoo, and a personal bonfire. At a Brenner Pass monastery, she'd gotten her scrub with a modified bonfire in her bedroom, which Napoleon had once occupied. She also had been lucky in encountering several Italian officers; one of them, a Colonel Louis Ascoli, was bound with his squadron for Merano, where her guns were stored. Persuading Ascoli and his senior officer to escort her to Merano had been simple.

Ascoli, the handsome Italian colonel, bent from his horse to peer into the carriage. "Comfortable, *Contessa?*"

"Perfectly," she replied in the Hungarian-accented, childish Italian the Italians seemed to find charming. "How could I not be when you and your men have been taking such wonderful care of me?"

He looked as if he might wag his tail. "Ah, *Contessa*, but you allow us to do so little . . .''

As he embarked on his usual round of flattery, she smiled tolerantly. She knew perfectly well what "more" he would enjoy doing. Like Enzo, he was charming and attentive; yet she desired only Miklos. In Budapest, she'd spent most of her time in the company of brilliant men: young and ardent, aging and distinguished. While often fascinated, she'd automatically fended off advances. Miklos had once joked he had spoiled her for eclairs; plain sugar cookies would no longer do. But they would have to do. Life without Miklos was hateful, but life with him was impossible.

During those autumn weeks at Swan's, they'd luxuriated in each other, sought to be satiated and done with one another, but it hadn't worked; when she remembered those afternoons like tawny wines, she wanted him with almost painful sharpness. Even more than his body, she wanted his company and the old, lazy chats, the colors and textures of him, his laughter and haunting Hungarian songs. When he was sad or angry, he never shut her out, but when they were apart, their former closeness never held; it always cracked, leaving misery to cut and scar.

She must end the marriage in Rome before Miklos caught up with her, for if he didn't follow her, he would follow the guns. Whatever happened, she wouldn't go back to him. They hadn't discussed Bellaria; Miklos realized nothing he said on that supremely sore subject would be believed. They had foundered upon too many lies: Bette's and their own to each other. Enzo had died trying to rescue her from that quicksand of lies. She missed him and his shameless, cheerful lechery, now more than ever.

So here she was, trailing across the top of the world with a troop of womanless soldiers, and she was no more good to them than they were to her. Her only loves were two wagonloads of guns filched by the Italian army at Merano, so to Merano she would go. And after that, to Rome.

Army Camp Outside Merano, Italy: February 25, 1849

"*La bella Contessa Veszto!*" Twelve crystal glasses lifted to salute Eliza. "The regiment will be very sorry to lose your delightful company tomorrow, *Contessa*," declared General Bugani, with the droop of his moustache accenting his mournful tone. "We had so hoped we might persuade you to accept our escort to Rome."

As green and gold uniforms closed about her in the command quarters dining room, Eliza smiled inwardly. If Bugani knew what she planned at dawn, he would escort her much less lugubriously to prison. "My travels with the valorous Fourth Cavalry are an adventure I shall never forget, General." Ravishing in diamonds and décolleté apricot velvet, she lifted her glass. "To the gallant Fourth!"

Everyone drank and a cheer went up. "Hurrah, hurrah for the *contessa!*"

"May I add my regrets at losing your company so shortly . . . *Contessa*," murmured a low, horribly familiar voice behind her. Her fingers went lax on her glass, then spasmodically clamped just as champagne began to spill on her dress. She forced herself to turn slowly . . . to stare up into Miklos's mocking gray eyes. He and two Italian officers had just entered the dining room. His face was weathered to dark mahogany; his lips were chapped and cracked, and his blond hair and moustache had grown shaggy. He wore a peasant's tunic, sheepskin jacket, and rough boots; with his fur-banded hat, he could have been taken for a steppes brigand. The way he surveyed her low-cut velvet said he hadn't had a woman in a long while. Sure it would pop out of her throat like a billiard ball, she made no effort to find her voice.

"May I introduce Colonel Miklos Sztarai of the Austrian army, *Contessa?*" put in General Bugani in his same dolorous tone. "Colonel, I have the honor to present the *Contessa* Veszto of Hungary." When Eliza continued to fixedly watch Miklos as if waiting for him to fly to pieces, the general added even more glumly, "Unfortunately, the colonel also takes leave of us at Merano."

She took in the unsmiling lieutenants at Miklos's sides and her voice went again. At her elbow, Colonel Ascoli put in quickly, "Though his accessory escaped, Colonel Sztarai was apprehended while attempting to raid our armory. They were about to drive away with two wagons of new American rifles. Unfortunately, he was out of his customary Austrian uniform and I recognized him. We went to the Weiner-Neustadt Academy together." He smiled apologetically at Miklos. "I took the liberty of inviting Colonel Sztarai to join us at dinner this evening. I hope you don't mind."

"No, of course not," she managed. My God, they were going to execute him as a spy! All because . . . Her eyes narrowed slightly. "May I ask why you wished to raid an armory in peacetime, Colonel?"

"I'm fond of hunting large game, *Contessa*," blandly replied Miklos, pulling off his heavy woolen gloves. The gloves had holes at the knuckles; his hands looked like he'd worked his way over the mountains with an ice ax. "Legend has it," Miklos continued deadpan, "that Hannibal's elephants mated in the snows of the Alps and left offspring to wander."

She eyed him sardonically through her heavy lashes. "So you needed artillery to drop the poor little dears."

Colonel Ascoli laughed. "Miklos has been telling us the same sort of nonsense, but I know him well enough not to bother hanging him by his thumbs. The elephants would only get bigger."

"My dear Colonel Ascoli"—she laid her hand on his arm—"would you mind forsaking your place by me at dinner? I'm dreadfully homesick and as Colonel Sztarai is Hungarian . . ."

Ascoli looked startled, then greatly disappointed. "Why, of course, *Contessa*, if you wish."

Two waiters took their places by the sideboard laden with delicacies and bottles of wine. The head steward bowed to the general, who nodded. "Veal Marsala tonight, I believe. High time we had dinner." The general nodded to Ascoli, then waved his officers to be seated about the table glittering with crystal, porcelain, and silver.

Eliza's hand carefully shifted to Miklos's arm. As they fell in behind General Bugani, she muttered, "You were trying to filch my guns, you sonofabitch!"

"Have a heart," he murmured, handing his sheepskin jacket to an orderly. "After noon tomorrow, I'll be as much a part of history as Hannibal's behemoths."

"One who froze his *losaszt* rutting in the drifts, no doubt." She hoped she sounded unconcerned.

With a tolerant smile, he seated her. "You may have learned the intimacies of Hungarian, but your accent has more pepper than paprika."

"I've had no complaints," she muttered under the racket of the officers' scraping chairs. Glad to be out of tents, the Italians were chatting busily.

"We can't afford complaints." Miklos took his chair.

"*We?*" She shot him a sardonic look.

Under the table, he patted her knee. Undisturbed by her slapping his hand away, he looked hungrily up as the *funghi al pomidoro* was served, then wolfed it as if he hadn't eaten for a week. So much for his dismay at the prospect of being shot.

"You expect *me* to get you out of this?" She jabbed vengefully at a tomato.

Noticing the flush that stained her cheeks, Colonel Ascoli interrupted with a jealous edge, "Pardon me, but didn't I hear you'd remarried recently, Miklos? Quite a beauty, they say. I'm sorry to miss the opportunity to meet her."

"Oh, she's a quiet little thing," Miklos said mischievously as the waiters replaced the *pomidoro* dishes with plates of ricotta-plump cannelloni. "Sweet as cream, never a harsh word."

Simply a lamb, bland as mutton. Eliza guillotined a canelloni.

"Are you acquainted with the *Principessa* Sztarai, *Contessa?*" asked the general.

"Only by reputation," purred Eliza, her eyes feline in candlelight. "She'll make a lovely widow."

"With bells on." Miklos resignedly polished off his Chianti.

"Shall we drink to the *principessa?*" suggested the general.

"Let's not," Miklos demurred as he held out his glass to be refilled. "It would go to her head."

Eliza raised her glass. "Oh, let's do toast, Colonel Sztarai. What's a little more head to her in the morning if you're losing yours by noon?"

The general was bewildered by their gallows humor. "For a Hungarian, Sztarai certainly had no head for liquor," he muttered to Ascoli, "but is the *contessa* drunk as well? I can't tell whether she's flirting with him or carousing on his grave."

"We'll drink to Eliza, then." Adroitly missing a candelabrum, Miklos leaped to the tabletop. "To a true Sztarai," he said gravely. "A brave Hungarian patriot and my only love." He drank, then deftly hurled the glass to smash against the fireplace hearth. He looked down to see Eliza staring up at him, her face white as if he'd struck her.

"The *contessa* to see you, sir," announced Bugani's aide.

Startled, the general leaped into his dressing gown. "Show her in."

Sailing into the room, Eliza held out her hand to be kissed. As Bugani bent over her hand, she spotted his desk. "Thank you for seeing me, General." Praying he was as susceptible as his compatriot, Charles Albert, she let her hand linger in his. "I wanted to thank you privately for your many kindnesses." Then added throatily, "You've no idea, of course, what a relief it is to a woman alone to be under a strong man's protection."

The general blushed with pleasure. "I'm only delighted I can be of service."

"Oh, but you've been heroic." Her fingers fluttered to her throat, let fall her cape. Hastily, he caught it as she drifted toward the desk. "I'm convinced you saved my life." She paused by the desk drawer, then bent over it as

she leaned on the desk to give the general a splendid view
of her cleavage. "How can I ever repay you?"

His eyes widened and as she expected, his attention
dropped to the cape as he wondered where to be rid of it.
Swiftly she tugged at the drawer; it was locked. Shooting a
dismayed, furtive glance up, she sucked in her breath.
General Bugani was standing over her. With his face pink
and perspiring slightly, he was gingerly holding out her
cloak. "You need do nothing, Madame." Misinterpreting
the acute disappointment in her eyes, he gabbled, "Save
perhaps . . . say a prayer for my wife and myself, also our
children at Easter mass. We should be so pleased."

"I . . . should be delighted." Eliza's own face went
pink. Bugani was not like Charles Albert. Her first fum-
bling attempt at extramarital seduction had backfired, even
if she'd never intended to end up in the general's bed. The
poor, embarrassed man was eager to be rid of her. Both
desperate to see it filled, they regarded the dangling cloak.
"But . . . I hope you won't mind granting me one last
favor, sir. I should like . . . to visit Colonel Sztarai." She
floundered for a plausible excuse. "He mentioned a letter
to his wife he wished me to take back to Hungary."

"Oh, gladly, gladly. Just present the letter to me to
review." He flung the red fox cape over her shoulders so
hastily he nearly wrecked her hairdo. Steering her by the
elbow, he propelled her to the door and called for his
aide. "Lieutenant, obtain the key from the provost and
escort the *contessa* to the cell of Colonel Sztarai. Good
evening . . ." She was out the door.

As the aide led her across the square before the commandant's quarters, Eliza gave the key in his hand a
pickpocket's attention. She needed the key, but not the
aide as a witness to a jailbreak. She had to stay on the
good side of the Italians long enough to get her guns.
"That key looks dreadfully heavy, Lieutenant," she
observed hesitantly. "May I see it more closely? It looks just
like the key to a tower room where I used to play in Castle
Veszto."

"I'm sorry, *Contessa*," was the lieutenant's brisk reply. "I cannot surrender this key to a civilian for any reason."

"I promise to be careful with it. Couldn't you, even for a moment?" Just long enough for her to appear to trip and drop the thing in the dark. While he uselessly searched, she would pretend to grow weary and retire, then go alone to the armory storeroom cell.

"Not even for a moment," replied the aide firmly.

Prick, she thought.

A shadow loomed up in the dark. The aide, halting instantly, saluted. Eliza, still intent on the key, nearly stumbled into him.

"Lieutenant, it's long after curfew," growled Colonel Ascoli. "State your business."

After it was stated, Ascoli fixed a narrowing eye on Eliza, who minced behind the aide to evade his inspection. "I'll see to the *contessa*," he dryly said at last. The aide surrendered the key, saluted again, touched his cap to Eliza, and marched off.

Eliza went as still as a cornered chipmunk.

"May I ask your business with Sztarai, *Contessa?*"

She babbled the wife-letter excuse.

"I see," he said in a tone she found disagreeably suspicious. "You realize I must read that letter."

"The general wants his turn first," she retorted pertly, then headed toward the armory. A moment later, his footsteps followed. She breathed again, but with effort. How the devil was she to get that damned, elusive key and be rid of him?

"Somehow I have the feeling you and Miki have met before tonight," murmured Ascoli to the back of her neck after he summoned the jailer at the guarded armory door. The armory was an L-shaped building, with one wing housing the weaponry, the other the stable, part of which was reinforced as a small prison.

"Don't be a shrew, Louis," she retorted mildly as the jailer saluted and waved them into the prison area. Accompanying Ascoli through the dim corridor, she added, "I'm the only Hungarian in town. Why shouldn't the poor wretch ask me to deliver his last words to his wife?'' She stepped daintily about a dry pile of manure.

Ascoli stopped outside a thick, wooden door with a barred peephole. ''Because if I know you're not Hungarian, Miklos damned well does, too.'' He turned to put the key in the lock. ''I think it's time all three of us had a chat.''

Her wits went numb. Without thinking, she grabbed the bar wedged across the neighboring stall and brained him. He turned to stare at her as if the chipmunk from the square had leaped up and bitten his nose. Horrified at his alertness, she whacked him again. Throwing up an arm to ward her off, he let out a loud groan and sagged at the knees. Encouraged, she delivered her best blow at his solar plexus and one more against his descending crown. He went face down in the manure. When he didn't move, she gingerly turned his head so he could breathe.

''Why not sauté him to boot?'' Miklos observed from the cell door peephole. ''He should be tender by now.''

Eliza brandished the bar. ''Go on, be clever! Let me hear just one more bit of that bright wit that got you caught and I'll let those Italians have you for tomorrow's lunch!''

He grinned at the bar. ''Sztarai scallopini?''

She pitched the bar into a hay pile. ''Oh, shut up!''

As she fished under Ascoli for the key, he observed, ''Doesn't this complicate your plans for retrieving the guns?''

''My coachman and I will have those wagons ten miles away by dawn.'' She found the key. ''Only they'll think you're the one who took them. You're going to stop being a damned nuisance and provide a decoy.''

His eyebrows lifted. ''I am?''

With a sweep of furs, she came to the cell door. ''You are, because if you aren't, I'm going to take this key and trot.'' She held up the key. ''I also want an uncontested divorce, Miki.''

His eyes lost their amusement. ''I *don't* want a divorce, Eliza.''

''I *do*,'' she said tightly. ''That toast tonight wasn't fair, but you got what you wanted just as you always have from me. This is the last. You gave me my life; now I give you yours. We're even and it's over." She nodded to the inert Ascoli. "If you agree, my guns go unmolested to the Hungarian army while you trail a scent in the opposite direction."

His face pressed against the bars, he gravely studied her for a moment, then replied expressionlessly, "We've little time for argument, so I agree."

"Word of honor, Miki."

"Cross my heart and hope to die." His voice had an odd intensity, as if he were making the vow before an altar.

She unlocked the door, then warily stepped back as he emerged from the cell. He made no move toward her. Quickly, he caught up the lax Ascoli under the shoulders and dragged him into the cell. She relaxed slightly.

"Come in and shut the door," he muttered. She did so, then puzzled, watched him exchange clothes with Ascoli. The gold-braided jacket hung open from his bare, furred chest as he bound and gagged Ascoli with strips from his shirt. She turned to the door, but before she'd gotten two steps, he'd whirled her back around. His mouth plunged down on hers. Her arms pinned, she kicked and wriggled, but his starving kiss made her feel as if she were drowning in fire. Relentlessly, the old, inevitable power he held over her took sway. Within hours, he might have been shot, and sickeningly, she knew too much of her would have gone with him. Her eyes closed as she whispered, "No . . . I don't . . ."

Then, his mouth stopping hers, he pressed her against the wall, his hands moving under the furs to part her bodice, and the moment he began to caress her breasts, she knew hopelessly she wasn't going to fight. Only Miklos was taking no chances. Holding her wrists with one hand, he gagged her. "Sorry, darling, but you're a noisy lover!" he breathlessly whispered. Then added, "By the way, this is a marvelously seductive dress, what there is of it," before he had her down on his cloak.

With a long sweep of his hand, he swiftly slid her skirts

up to her waist with an urgency that had nothing to do with their being discovered by the guards. His face was pale, his neck corded as he looked down at her pale nakedness, the roses of her breasts, the honey pelt between her slim thighs. Half frightened, she tried to twist from under him, but too late. His hard form arched over her half-clothed body and his mouth roved hot against the straining peaks of her breasts until her arms locked about him. His hands feverishly caressed her flat belly, the inner curves of her thighs, coaxing them to part until she twisted, moaning, then melting to his mouth. When she was wild to be filled, he lifted her hips. His sex drove into her, harder until she gasped, her head arching back as she shuddered with the pounding of his big body into hers, the terrible power of him that shook her, battered her, lifted her to mindless, piercing pleasure. The gag muffled her cry at the violent, shattering tremor of their peak as their battling spirits collided, exploded together. Miklos went limp, his arms spasmodically closing about her.

As the stable's chill reached her bare skin, Eliza began to feel humiliation. God, he was sure of her! And why shouldn't he be sure, when she always responded to him as if she were a whore? Why must he hold her so tightly now as if he couldn't make himself let her go? His nerves, his body, on edge from danger and the prospect of a firing squad, he'd wanted a woman. Just as he'd wolfed his dinner, he'd wolfed her, only he'd taken time to prove just how weak he could make her as revenge for making him chase the guns, for wounding his princely, male pride by leaving him. And now he was kissing her again with all his unbearable certainty of possession. She closed her eyes and forced herself to stay soft in his arms. "Come," he whispered, then rose to help her up.

As soon as his weight left her, she flung to her feet and headed for the door. He hooked her foot. Sprawling head-long, she hit her head on the door rim. As she dropped into blackness, she vaguely hoped a manure pile wasn't waiting at the bottom of it.

Anxiously, Miklos knelt to examine her injury. He found

a bruise above her temple, but her pulse was steady. After quickly fastening most of her clothing, he retrieved Ascoli's cap, snapped it on, and yanked down the brim to shadow his face. He arranged Eliza's arm and cape around his neck to conceal his telltale, fair hair, picked her up, then kicked shut the cell door on his way out.

"Sir!" The guard saluted when Miklos ducked under the stable stanchion. "Is the *contessa* unwell?"

Miklos kept his head low. "Fainted. Went down as if flattened by a board."

"Women," sighed the guard. "Thank God they'll never be in the army."

Miklos spotted Eliza's bearded coachman, Felix, lounging atop a keg in an alley across from the rear of the armory. He appeared to be drunk. Miklos eased Eliza into the back of one of the canvas-covered arms wagons, then waved Felix over. Seeing the Italian uniform, Felix responded reluctantly. His head held tensely despite his drunken weave, he arrived at the wagon where Miklos had deposited his burden. Miklos jabbed a thumb at the fur-wrapped, unconscious Eliza. "Your mistress," he informed Felix, "has had her fill of sunny Italy for the moment. She wishes to be driven home as fast as hell. Presuming we can hitch your coach team fast enough, I'll take this wagon, you take that. Lash the canvas tight. Any questions from the sentries and you've got typhus aboard. Understand?"

A quarter hour later, two wagons rolled northward through the picket lines. Within the hour, they were aboard a heavy log raft Miklos had arranged days earlier and were drifting rapidly downstream. At dawn, the wagons rolled off the raft and by midmorning were well along toward the route to Yugoslavia.

Pursuit was circumvented; Eliza was not. Miklos shortly felt a gun in his neck. "You know what us Yankees do with snakes?"

"Even if the snake isn't poisonous?" he murmured, flicking an appreciative glance back at her still unbuttoned bodice peeping from the parted furs.

"We blow their Judas heads off; that's what we do," Eliza growled, clamping the furs closed.

"Don't worry, I'm keeping our bargain: most of it." He shaded his eyes against the sun slanting through the pines of the narrow valley they were threading. "We're heading into Yugoslavia, then Rumania, where the Hungarian Liberation Army plans to besiege Temesvar so they can fend off the Russians. They've retaken Budapest, but Temesvar will be a hard nut to crack. If it takes long enough, the army will have to face the Austrian *and* Russian armies. Our new emperor, Franz Joseph, has declared Hungary a part of his empire, the constitution unconstitutional, and all Transylvania crown land."

She remembered Franz, that stiff teenager, and his deceptively unimposing mother. "He can't do that!"

"He did it before Christmas. I just didn't want to swell your head." Miklos burrowed down in Ascoli's cloak. He'd wrapped rags over Ascoli's inadequate leather gloves; those rags reminded Eliza her ball dress was insufficient clothing for mountaineering. She crammed her free hand under her sables.

With a chirrup to the horses, Miklos guided them into the tracks of Felix's wagon lumbering ahead up the steep trail. "Now we'll have to fight them all, and we'd better damned well win."

"We?" Her pistol nuzzled his ear.

"I'm taking these guns to the rebels at Temesvar," he said unblinkingly. "I'm even joining your noble zealots. Until I'm dead or Hungary's safe, you're stuck with me, but either way you'll be free. If I live, you get your divorce."

She indignantly reared up in the rattling wagon bed. "Why should I believe you? You lie as regularly as you blink. You haven't the honor of a . . . a . . ."

"Copperhead. They don't precisely blink."

"No, they do it upside down; that's the way you turn everything every time I listen to you." She poked him in the spine. "I'm keeping my gun, so don't get any ideas about blinking sideways."

"Keep it," he said agreeably. "Whatever makes you happy."

"Happy?!" she yelled as the wagon banged a rut. "I really ought to shoot you, Miki!"

Two males and a small female were an inept team for maneuvering heavy wagons through the soggy spring drifts blocking the higher slopes, but slowly they fought over the passes by using trees, horses, and pulleys when the way grew steep or the wagons foundered in the drifts. Every night, Miklos tried to join Eliza in the wagon; every night he was met by her evil-eyed gun against his nose. Both spent many a restless night, but his were passed next to Felix's stolid backside.

By early spring, they were crossing Yugoslavian snow-fields where rotten crevasses added to the peril. Miklos, leaving the coachman and Eliza to drive the wagons, went ahead with a long staff and an ice pick to test the snow before every step.

On the afternoon of the second day beyond Dravograd, Miklos warned the ice was honeycombed, highly treacherous after a week of steady sun. "Center on my tracks." He moved ahead across a tundra of rock and dirty snow. Eliza, in thick woolens rummaged in an Italian border village, came next, to be followed by Felix. The sun took effect on more than the ice. Felix drowsed as his wagon drifted a few feet to the right. As if a giant hand were reaching up to claw out the earth, the snow parted in a roaring churn of breaking ice. Flailing awake, Felix screamed in the wagon rolling to be swallowed into the icy maw.

On her wagon seat, Eliza shivered in horror. The exposed crevasse was so dark and deep she could see nothing of what had been, moments before, half their small convoy. Miklos retraced his tracks back to her. "Get down."

"Why?" She looked at him distractedly. If not precisely her friend, the taciturn, intense Felix had faithfully accompanied her a great distance at risk of his life.

"You're going to work point. The horses are too heavy to trust. A person can cross ice the wagon would crack."

She saw again Felix's white face and startled terror as the ice screamed over him. "Why don't we both walk, lead the horses?"

"We'd all go into a crevasse." He lifted her down, then drew a map in the snow and explained the remaining route to Rumania. "All you've got to do is get to Temesvar before there's no point in going."

Barely listening, she sagged in the snow. "Poor Felix . . . what a horrible death."

"But quick. A bullet's not much faster a killer than a crevasse." Miklos envisioned Felix's long, battering plummet. Why was he bound only to lie to her? He lifted her up, thrust the staff into her hand. "It's up to you, Yank."

She blindly took the stick and stumbled forth.

An hour before sundown, Eliza thrust in the staff for what seemed to be the millionth time and it sank soft. At this time of day, shadows deceptively flattened the snow. She waved Miklos to halt the wagon and turned to plot a new course. The next plant was better, the next solid. She waved him forward. Planted again and stepped forward. Into nothing. The snow angled away in a rush of pouring curds, shoved up her skirts and back. Blue sky opened, narrowed. Something struck her back, stabbed sharply like the old pain. She screamed. Like Felix, Felix, Felix. The staff snapped against her fingers, almost jerked loose, then held. With her free hand, she grabbed, wedged the staff, clamped tight. Then lay on the end of an angled outshoot, with her legs dangling into nothing while the surrounding ice sheared and screeched. Finally, mercifully, it stopped. Clamping her eyes shut, she began to cry. Like an uncontrolled baby, she let tears stream.

"Eliza!"

Miklos's distant voice was sharper, higher than normal. She tried to answer, but her voice came out in a choked wail.

"Stay still! I'm coming!" He didn't sound quite so strange, but she couldn't stop crying.

In moments, she heard crampons being driven into the ice wall. Like the staff jabbing the snow, they went on

endlessly until her hands, then her arms and shoulders,
went numb and ceased to be hers. This sunless hole was
bitter cold. She was hardly aware when her fingers went
slack until her body suddenly dropped and swung by one
frozen hand. She tried to harden her grip, but couldn't feel
the staff. She couldn't even tell when, seconds later, the
staff turned to Miklos's hand. He hauled her up against
him. "Miki," she whispered, "I can't feel anything."

"You don't have to. Just trust me." He looped himself
to the chiton, then swiftly slung a rope about her waist,
another under her armpits. Then inch by inch, he began to
climb the groaning, glass blue wall.

She could hear his labored breathing, the thump of his
heart. "Miki, we're both going to die. You must deliver
the guns. You have to let me drop."

He didn't answer. "Miki, drop me!"

"Hush," was all he rasped.

She stared blankly up at the blue sky a sun away. She
prayed that God, any god, would reach into their terrible
hole and pluck them forth.

And in time, whatever god was listening, did. Miklos
dragged across the jaw of the crevasse and collapsed on its
lip. She lay still bound to him with his heart pounding as if
it would burst under her ear. "Miki," she asked weakly,
"are you all right?"

He didn't respond. Her fear mounted when for another
minute, he didn't speak. Then he rolled over and kissed
her. She was too relieved to fight him off. Only the kiss
went on, as if he were trying to force himself into her. In
another breath, the witchery rose, the craving he would
always excite. She tried to hit him with the unfeeling clubs
of her hands. "Stop it, Miki! For God's sake, let me go!"

His face lifted; it was raw from the ice face, raw with
need and yearning. "No," she cried like a pleading, desperate child, "don't touch me any more. You always end
by hurting me . . . I never want to see you again!"

His face altered as if she'd slashed him with a whip.
"So I've taught you to fear me as much as Loise did," he

said roughly, "and Petyr. God grant I never see fear in my child's eyes."

She went white. "Why say that? Anitra's dead."

His beard and moustache frozen from his struggle to breathe in the crevasse, he dragged her to her feet. "So you still mean to trade lie for lie, child for child"—his grip tightened on her arms—"only I'm not willing to deal so easily. My price is higher than you may like, Eliza. You want a divorce; I want the baby you're carrying."

Futilely, she tried to pull away. "I'm not pregnant!"

"The Merano prison was your time, Eliza. You've been first up every morning, so you can throw up."

She knew lying was no use. He'd seen her pregnant before and he'd probably contrived to get her that way again. Perversely, it hadn't happened at Swan's. "I'll never give you my baby," she said flatly.

"Then hope I die at Temesvar." He let her go so abruptly she almost fell in the sun-red snow. "The baby's mine as much as yours. I'll give you anything else in the settlement, but not the child."

"You haven't got anything else!"

"Balaton."

She was incredulous. "You'd sell Balaton to pay me for the baby!" And she'd once thought all he wanted was an heir. He looked like a wild man, his hair and beard matted, his face hard and distorted with pain and resolve. "I'm sorry, Miklos," she said quietly. "Deeply sorry, but there is no way under heaven I will give you this child."

"You've forgotten it's not heaven that watches over me; I'll play the devil's game if I must." His face twisted. "I need to love, be loved! Would you take everything from me?" He clenched his hand before her face. "You may get away, change your name, but I'll follow you the rest of my days, if need be. By contract, the child is legally mine . . ."

She was sickened as she listened to him. He would be ruthless when fighting for what he felt was his own. She'd never wanted to hurt him like this, but she would have to fight him in the same way. How easily she could appear defeated now. "Perhaps I can't win," she said slowly. "Still, I may need time to get used to that idea."

A glimmer of compassion and bitter irony touched his eyes. "The lie indirect again. Lies have pulled us down, yet we still pile them one on one as if they were our only way up."

He picked up the staff. "From now on, we'll walk point together . . . everywhere together until the baby's born. We'll be as inseparable as lovers."

Chapter 20

Winter in August

Temesvar, Rumania: June 14, 1849

"Prince and Princess Sztarai?" The picket stared at the two bedraggled peasants who peered apathetically down at him from the wagon seat.

"No, Humpty Dumpty and his trull." Eliza scratched among her dirty rags. The furs had been sold in Yugoslavia.

The picket hurriedly notified his commandant.

The Sztarai wagon drove into camp amid cheers. Rakoczy ran from the crowd of shouting, motley soldiers to help Eliza down. "You *did* it and none too soon! Things are going slowly here. Every gun will be worth its weight in gold." Challengingly, he looked up at Miklos's bearded face, wrapped in its ragged scarf. "And every man as well."

"Both the guns and I would be at the bottom of a crevasse but for Miklos," Eliza said bluntly. She scanned the grim stone walls of the city of Temesvar. The place was ancient, medieval, depressing . . . and after months of Hungarian siege, intact.

Rakoczy held up his hand to Miklos. "Then the prodigal has returned in earnest. Welcome home, brother."

More cheers went up as Miklos briefly shook his hand. "We'll win or all hang together, brothers!"

The crowd parted to allow General Görgey to greet the Sztarais. He was barely thirty, trim and energetic. The temperamental, bearded Kossuth, handsome in his fifties, was just behind him. Practically purring, Rakoczy prowled with them about the gun wagon.

"Good work!" declared Görgey as he inspected the guns.

"A superhuman feat, I'd say!" Kossuth bowed to Eliza. "Hungary owes you and your husband a great debt, Your Highness. If every man of us had your courage, we could stand against any army on earth." Impulsively, he lifted off his Order of the Double Eagle and placed it about her neck. "I should be honored if you would consent to wear this until Sztarai valor may be properly rewarded before our victorious forces." As Eliza thanked him, the cheers rose to a howl.

"Unfortunately, Princess," said General Görgey with a chuckle, "I cannot with any responsibility allow you to continue as Joan of Arc. Your husband will see you to safety in the nearby town of Vilagos." He gave Miklos a knowing smile. "Just see you're back by reveille for morning review, Colonel."

Eliza slid Miklos a sly, triumphant glance. Let him keep track of her now he was in the army! Ten minutes after he left her in Vilagos, she'd head back to Italy.

Miklos had no difficulty reading her mind. She didn't like his complacent expression.

No sooner were they shown to a tent to clean up than she whirled to inform him she'd not be locked in some attic in Vilagos. Pouring wine, Miklos mildly agreed the idea was out of the question, particularly as she'd likely be out like a ferret. He handed her a glass. "I can't chance your wandering across country before an advancing army, particularly Haynau's."

Eliza took a sturdy swig to calm down. "So what are you going to do?"

"I've already done it."

Shortly, he emerged from the tent with Eliza limp in his arms. "She's fainted . . . fatigue and emotion, I'm afraid," he explained gently to General Görgey as he installed her in the waiting carriage.

* * *

"Where's my hair!" shrieked Eliza, staring in horror at the short, dark brown crop that was left of it. Bolting upright on the bed, she pulled futilely at matching hair wisps on her upper lip; tepid a display as her new mustache was, it wouldn't uproot, thanks to fresh glue. She made a wild grab for Miklos. He dodged just out of reach, a bottle of dye in his hand.

"Like to view the back, Princess?" Hans Krafft, who'd waited weeks in their cheap, Vilagos inn room for Miklos's arrival, obligingly held out a hand mirror. "Have a look at your cadet uniform. The colonel's old one tailored to a pip!"

"You planned this before you came after me in Italy, you miserable . . ."

The mirror went flying to just miss Miklos's head. He grabbed it in midair. "Now, now, we don't want a bout of bad luck, do we?"

"*We* will kill you with our bare hands!" She dived for him.

He grabbed her about the waist and tossed her back on the bed. "No point raising a fuss, Cadet. What's done's done." He tried not to think of her soft, butchered hair falling through his fingers as he'd cut it off. "I hope you remember how to ride a horse."

"You might as well substitute a hippo," she retorted. "I'm not going back to Temesvar. If you force me, I'll tell General Görgey about this whole farce."

He waved Hans from the room, then sat on a table, his long legs dangling. His own hair and mustache had been neatly trimmed. He'd had a shave and a bath and wore an ill-fitted uniform. "Why didn't you tell Görgey yesterday?"

"Because you got me and those guns out of Italy. Also, they need you." Her eyes narrowed. "But I'm fighting for my child, Miki. If you push me, I'll go for your jugular." She got off the bed. "Now, give me something to get this silly mustache off."

"Sorry, *Bluebird*, but so long as I serve Hungary, so will you"—he laughed softly at her thickened waist—"at

least until you round into too much of a pear." Then his
eyes cooled. "Give the game away and Hans, Bette, all her
connections and lawyers will be on your neck to claim the
family heir."

"For God's sake, Miklos, think of the child!"

"I am thinking of the child. I haven't joined the rebels
just to defend Hungary, but you, and my name, and my
child. I can never make the world forget what I did, but
after Temesvar, I can make it stop pointing. Here, I struggle for life, but you, despite your courage, still play at it
and avoid commitment to anything that might hurt you."
He rose from the table and grasped her shoulders. "Eliza,
I won't surrender my child to a mother who runs."

"I didn't run! I was driven away by lies and betrayal!"

"No," he said softly. "I never took Bellaria or any
other woman to bed after Como. You never asked to hear
my side because you cared more for me as a crutch than a
man. When you thought you couldn't trust the crutch, you
flung it away. Only you're not ready to walk, Eliza; you're
still a cripple trying to run, usually in the wrong direction."

Tears of frustrated rage and misery welled in Eliza. "I
did care . . . for you." She swiped savagely at her eyes.
"Why do you suppose I saved you from a firing squad?"

"I admit I hoped you were then persuaded by more than
duty." He grimaced. "At the crevasse, I learned differ-
ently. In your fashion, you're the most loyal creature in
the world, but I've never been able to lure you . . . or
bully you, as you say, into loving me. Once, I thought
. . . but never mind." He picked up a military cloak from
the bed. "Don't feel too badly. Loise didn't love me.
Vanda certainly doesn't." He dropped the cloak about her
shoulders. "It's a lack I have, like Hans's missing fingers." His lips brushed her bare nape, lingered. "Perhaps
it takes one cripple to understand another."

Temesvar: August 8, 1849

Miklos didn't keep Hans with them at camp, so Eliza
couldn't solve her problem by turning them both over to

the general. She was introduced as Miklos's aide, whom he'd run across in Vilagos. "You're Clive Farrow," he informed her, "younger brother of a schoolmate of mine, and you went to Sandhurst as I did. You're a liberal idealist come to serve the cause. Long live Lafayette."

So Eliza entered the army. Immediately, she won the nickname of Grimsby, for she rarely spoke and never smiled. After Miklos added thick, wire-rimmed spectacles to her disguise, she resembled a tiny, myopic bird; her head was always moving either to focus the spectacles or detect suspicion among the officers, many of whom she'd entertained in Budapest.

Miklos foiled most difficulties by keeping her at his elbow. He also confined her to clerical duties during the army's monotonous, futile assaults on Temesvar. The throaty, nervous croak that was her effort at a masculine vocal pitch often made her brief replies incomprehensible, so most of the officers gave up talking to her and directed their conversation to Miklos. The offensive exception was Colonel Bekes, the senior surgeon, who took a buffoon's delight in "making a man" of her. Upon her ventures into the mess tent, Bekes's backslaps sent her reeling, and his vilely obscene anecdotes turned her scarlet until Miklos quietly took him aside and invited him to a thoroughly "manly" thrashing. Thereafter, Colonel Bekes's baiting continued, but at an ignorable distance.

Miklos seemed lighthearted despite the army's deteriorating situation. Indecision and bickering over government and military policy had split their leaders. Kossuth was a mixed, volatile genius. Görgey was a patient, practical technician with little use for Kossuth's devisive prejudices. Their rift widened daily.

Temesvar baited the army too long, making the outlook grim. A large Russian force under General Paskevich advanced from the north, an Austrian army under General Haynau from the west. By early August, the armies converging on Temesvar poised for conflict. On the eve of battle, the horizon glittered with enemy campfires as if it lay in the path of a malevolent dragon.

When Eliza commented on Miklos's lack of concern, he explained, "I may retrieve some portion of my honor tomorrow. I'm part of Hungary's throw for all or nothing. If it's all, I'll share the magnificent possibilities for her future; if the die turns up nothing, I'll never live to see it."

Despite the late summer heat concentrated in their worn out tent, Eliza was cold. No matter how hot the weather, Miklos never loosened a uniform button; outside the tent, he insisted she maintain the same military decorum. Without being asked, he'd strung a blanket on a cord between their cots and during the past, sweltering weeks, they had maintained the lonely separation begun in Italy. Now Eliza sharply feared that separation might be made lethally permanent. She'd never accepted either the possibility of losing or his being killed. Why did she want so desperately never to see him again, yet could in no way face the idea of his ceasing to exist, of going forever beyond her reach?

Misreading her stiff, distant expression, Miklos murmured wryly, "I can understand your not sharing my equanimity. After all, Hungary's independence may cost you your own until the baby's born. Cost you the baby as well." He stood looking down at her, huddled on her camp stool. "I'm sorry, Eliza. Hungary owes you, perhaps as much as anyone, her chance for freedom. You don't deserve to be rewarded this way." He gently ruffled her shorn hair. "How you must wish me dead." He hunkered down to thoughtfully study her face. "Shall I die for you, my love?"

She whitened at the possibility of his seriousness. "Stop it, Miki! Stop baiting me!"

He smiled crookedly. "I'm not, believe me. I've never meant to make you unhappy, yet I've done nothing else. If I thought you would stop running, Bluebird . . . there would be no more lies. Tomorrow, I could show you the truth in a way you could accept. You would have to learn to walk alone, but perhaps one day you might find happiness."

"You're wrong," she cried. "I want the baby but I don't want you dead! I don't want you to do anything stupid!"

"I won't do anything stupid," he said softly. "I shall be very wise indeed, as I was wise to love you."

She tried to read his eyes through her blurred spectacles. "Don't make me believe you now, Miki," she whispered wretchedly. "Be kind and go on lying to me as you always have."

He shook his head. "You're not a child any more. You've lost one baby, but you'll soon bear another that will expect as much from you as you once expected from me. You'll find only God can answer for so much." He rested his hand on her rounded stomach. "All quiet within . . . I'd go to the devil happy to feel a sign of life. Innocence."

She put her hand over his. "You may not lose tomorrow, Miki."

"No . . . even at worst, not everything. And I may win far more than a battle." He smiled gaily like a boy in prospect of being given his first puppy. "But you've a part to play as well. You're to stay in the tent tomorrow." His smile became impish. "Eat a turnip to produce a lovely case of morning sickness. Shortly after I've left with the army, Hans will take you to a sheltered vantage of the battlefield. If the Hungarian center falters or curls up, you're to both immediately leave for Vilagos. If we win . . . save the first dance for me at the victory celebration."

She recalled the first time they'd danced to the balalaika. She hadn't known how to dance until he'd patiently taught her, as he had almost everything else. His closeness seemed unbearable. "I'd like to go to bed now," she murmured. "It's been a long day."

"Of course," he said quietly and left her to her toilet. As she undressed, she could see his cigar glowing like one of the stars outside the tent. The cigar lowered as he watched her. He was part of the blackness, as if he wasn't

really there, yet she could almost feel him touch her. If she
reached out to him now, he *would* touch her and then . . .
then he would win everything. He always won and in the
end, she always lost.

She pulled the nightshirt over her head and went to bed.

She lay awake a long time, but didn't hear Miklos come
back into the tent. His cigar was gone from the collection
of stars. She watched the stars, as if their cool, blue,
distant campfires were those of another waiting army. In
the distance lilted a sad *balalaika*. A Russian player, she
thought, but perhaps a Hungarian; perhaps Miki. She touched
her face; it was wet. Ah, Miki, your song has so much the
sound of tears, my love.

Like the night wind, Sándor Petöfi's voice whispered,
"Talpra Magyar" over the *balalaika*. Across the empty
snow drifted dancers silent as ghosts. The wind swept
away Sándor's voice, sifted the snow high. Alone, Eliza
moved among the dancers, heard the icy wind's violins
echo the *balalaika*. I promised this dance to Miki, she
called to the wind, but her voice had only the sound of a
sigh. The dancers passed through her, dwindled into wraiths
of blowing snow, leaving her alone in the moonless, icy
night. Miki, Miki.

She whirled as on the white, stark plain a tramp of feet
cleaved the hiss of the wind, mounted to thunder. The
wind was sheared with screams. The snow seeped scarlet.
Bodies were half buried in drifts gathering with unnatural
swiftness. A few lone figures stood in gray, stone col-
umns; none moved, none were Miklos. Terrified, she began to run, then to paw the snow. She uncovered three
men she knew: all dead. Desperately, she flung over one
body after another. Sándor's muffler trailed across the
snow, but when she touched it, slithered away as if alive
into the gathering fog. "Miki!" she shrieked in panic.
"Miki!"

Then she felt his arms go around her, his body real and
strong and alive against hers. She locked her arms about
his neck. "Miki, you mustn't go tomorrow! Stay with me.

Please . . . they were all dead. I couldn't find you anywhere!''

"Shh, don't cry," he whispered. "I'm here, darling. Tomorrow's far away."

"No, Miki, you mustn't fight! You won't come back," she pleaded. "I found Sándor's scarf, but he was gone"—her voice broke—"so many of them gone!" Bleakly, she clung to him. "My God, we've no time left, Miki. What have I done?"

"The fault's not yours alone; we've both squandered more than we ought"—he gently brushed his fingers across her mustache—"but we've had fun, too. Remember Charles Albert under the bed?"

"That was fun?" she replied weakly, burying her head against his open tunic collar.

"I thought so, once I decided not to wring his neck."

"And mine."

"I could never quite bring myself to beat you, though you often richly deserved it," he said lightly. "Kisses were more pleasant, but rarely improved your behavior."

"Suppose you kiss me now," she said softly.

"You're wearing a mustache, sweet," he teased. "I'm not quite sure how to deal with that."

"Then take if off."

Tentatively, he tugged at the bit of fur. It gave. Gently, he stripped it off and kissed her with slow, soft hunger.

"Take everything off me," she whispered against his lips. In moments, he'd put the nightgown and his uniform from between them and buried his face in her throat. "When I cared little if I took a sow for a wife, the fates sent me an innocent, golden-eyed Circe." His mouth covered hers, teasing her lips apart; his tongue probed, darted, excited, until she moaned. "Only now you are no child," he breathed, caressing her breasts, shaping their soft, aching weight to his hands, to his mouth.

Shivering with desire, Eliza clasped him closer, craving the heat of him, the long, supple muscles moving under his skin as he parted her thighs. Rough-soft, his tongue darted into her, flicked the tiny, burning bud, then drove

deep. With a muffled cry, she writhed against him. "Miki,
please . . . now!"

He pressed her thighs wider, slowly sliding his swollen
sex against her liquid softness. Her body arched like a
waterfall as he thrust into her, the size of him sweet, wild
torture, the swirl and drive of his hips spinning her down
into a deepening whirlpool of lights like flung torches. She
locked to him, felt a tremor run through his body. His
head buried in her neck, he drove into her and the whirling,
trident net of torchlight wrapped them to blaze in the
dazzling snare of love and desire.

For a long while, Miklos held her, then thinking her
asleep, eased away from the cot. His fair head inclined to
clear the tent flap, he looked out at the scattered guard
fires covering the hills. The stars were beginning to pale;
dawn was only a little time away. Silently, Eliza went to
him, laid her head against his back. He turned to envelope
her in his arms. Close against his warm nakedness, she
lifted her head. "Let me go with you tomorrow. No one
will know."

"I would know. I'd end by defending you rather than
Hungary." He nuzzled her hair, then tipped her chin up.
"You're not going to do anything silly, are you?"

Eliza laughed with a humor she didn't feel. "What
could be sillier than a soldier malingering with morning
sickness?" Laying her head against his chest, she stroked
him, memorizing his textures, his scars, the thick chest fur
that sifted to a fine down of gold across his flat stomach
and thighs. All, all to remember until the snowdrifts covered her own face and mercifully stopped her aching heart.

She slid her fingers lightly over his sex, her lips curving
at his quick response. She cupped the weight of him, then
closing her eyes, caressed the sheathing of his magnificent
virility. So exquisite a containment for such power, such
delight. She caught her breath as his fingers gently probed
between her thighs, dipped deeper to find a welling moisture.

Miklos wondered if the extent to which she often tried
his mental and physical control dawned on Eliza. Like a
careless kitten she teased him, sank her claws in him,

aroused him. Somehow, despite their fights, she always took him for granted. Loise had been too much the other way, always preoccupied with what he might be thinking. Secrets he might be keeping from her. Eliza was bright, uninhibited, natural. Greedy in bed; greedy out of it; expecting everything, yet apparently satisfied with whatever she got. Until he'd begun to give her only misery.

Now she was toying with his body almost innocently, trying unhappily to imagine his nonexistence, examining him for proof of life, as it were. And found it quickly enough. She couldn't comprehend how starved he was for her. Having her once merely tantalized his desire. Sometimes the challenge, the energy of her almost crazed him. Just now, her idle exploration made his belly knot.

Silently, Miklos tugged at the tent flap and they were once again in warm darkness. He lifted her, then lowered her upon him, massaging her to slowly encompass his length. This might be his last chance to love her; he wanted to make it last. Wrapping her legs about his hips, he began to thrust easily, moving her on him until her head arched back. With her bound tightly to him, he knelt, eased her onto the carpet until she lay with pelvis lifted between his thighs. His hands roamed her breasts, her belly, first gently, like the slow slide of his sex within her. She sought him. As lissome as a willow flowing with him, she invited him.

This time he loved her in both greeting and farewell to the Eliza she must become after the dawn. To love her had always been so easy, so irresistible. Let there be sleep after death, he prayed as he felt again her warmth, her passion. Let me not be lonely for her. Let my desire be as ashes, my heart as a stone lost in a dark river. Eliza, Eliza. He felt her desire welling, higher, swirling as if it had entered turbulent water, rushing, rushing to a high, singing crest. He soared, taking her weightlessly with him into the airborne spume of diamonds flung against the rising sun.

Then the sun became dawn, gray and terrible as a saber slash.

Chapter 21

The Saber Dawn

Temesvar: August 9, 1849

Trapped in the tent by pseudo-illness and Hans, who
arrived virtually with the dawn, Eliza couldn't watch Miklos
ride out with his regiment. Dismally sitting on the cot, she
listened to the creak of leather and shuffle of departing
troops outside. Aside from her two field pieces, scant
artillery passed the tent.

Some time after the sounds ceased, Hans looked outside
the tent. "All clear except for a few pickets. Time to go."
He glanced over his shoulder. "Best slump on your horse.
No need to give the pickets suspicions about malingering.
The surgeon was giving you enough of a walleye this
morning."

Her ears pricked. "Did you say 'horse'?"

"One of our new brood mares," he said proudly. "A
real fire-eater fit for a Valkyrie."

The mare was as frisky as promised, and within a lively
twenty-minute ride, Eliza and Hans reached the hilltop
vantage Miklos had named. Hans slid a telescope from his
saddlebag and surveyed the field. The August morning sun
hazed the hills, whitened the sky as if with coming snow.
It glinted on rifle stocks, flashed on sabers and bayonets.
The battle had already begun. Men moved like ranks of
ants: some quick, some slow, some crushed and unmoving. The Russians were mostly in green, the Austrians in

blue, the outnumbered Hungarians in motley with arm
bands. "Where's Miki's regiment?" Eliza asked.

Hans handed her the telescope. "Dead center. Most of
your American guns are there because if his outfit breaks,
Hungary can say good-bye to the regiment and her
independence."

Good-bye altogether, Eliza thought, focusing the telescope. Sickeningly, she realized the Hungarians were
outnumbered far more than she could have imagined. Smoke
puffs swelled across the field as cannon recoiled, their
trails gouging scars across the ground. Austrian and Russian artillery pounded the Hungarian lines into gouts of red
dust.

Her hands perspiring on the telescope, she scoured the
center for signs of Miklos's dappled gray charger. About
the field, smoke lay in clumps like dirty tufts of cotton.
She spied the dappled gray in the thrashing mass, then the
struggle knotted and she lost sight of it. A chunk blew out
of the knot where it bound the Austrian line. Minutes later,
a Russian battery found its range and chewed out another
segment; the knot writhed like a beheaded snake. Two
Austrian cavalry squadrons pelted from around a small
hill, paused a moment to dress line, then charged, driving
deep into the Hungarian line. A wild melee churned, split,
as the Austrian horses broke through the Hungarians and
circled behind them. "Now," muttered Hans dully. "We
leave now, Princess."

Eliza tossed him the telescope. Giving the mare an
awkward thump in the ribs, she headed breakneck down
the hill toward the collapsing Hungarian line. With an
oath, then a wild, warrior yell, Hans gave his horse's rump
a whack with the telescope and pounded after her. Eliza
heard him close on her. He was shouting something. Thinking he meant her to turn back, she spurred the mare. She
heard clear swearing then. Just as she neared the Hungarian
line, Hans caught up. Leaning from his saddle, he thrust
out a Colt pistol. "Take it!" She grabbed it, then yelped
when the mare took a ditch and her neck whiplashed.

As the line of infantry coiled around Eliza, dirt and rock

sprayed into her face from another twelve-pound shell
slamming the earth. A saber-wielding Russian slashed
toward her leg and without thinking, Eliza shot him in the
face. A scarlet cavity cratered his features as he went over
his horse's rump and she gagged, twisting the mare away
to scramble across the breastworks through the battering
men. The mass thickened. Slipping in blood and bodies,
the mare nearly went down, and gave an Austrian a chance
to move in with a bayonet. Guarding her rear, Hans smashed
his rifle down on the bayonet, then rammed the stock into
the man's skull. "Thank you, Sergeant Krafft!" Eliza
yelled as the mare dodged the body.

Then she saw Miklos. His shako was gone; his left arm
and side were scarlet from shoulder to wrist with his hand
useless on the reins. Guiding the gray with his knees, he
hacked with his saber at three Austrian Hussars. As he cut
down one, another hamstrung his charger. The gray
screamed, his hindquarters dropping. Eliza spurred forward, saw a Russian infantryman run up the earthwork to
draw a bead on Miklos as he swung a leg over the pommel
to dismount. She fired, missed as her mare misstepped,
but came close enough to make the Russian flinch and
swing toward her. He took her second shot in the chest.

Looking again for Miklos, Eliza saw the pale flash of
his saber. Heeding his caution against distracting him, she
curbed the impulse to close in and shoot the Austrian
Hussar hacking at him. Shielding his head, a Russian
ducked under her mare's neck, darted a glance up as he
wheeled to defend himself. Seeing her opponent was as
young and white-faced as herself, she hesitated. His panic
welled over. Lifting his saber too high, he charged. Just as
Hans's bullet found him in the throat, a sharp blow to
Eliza's head flung her sideways off her horse. The ground
came up hard, but she didn't feel it, didn't notice Hans
swiftly dismount to smear his face with the dead Russian's
blood, then fall atop her. She didn't see the knot break and
the Hungarian force overwhelmed. Miklos cut down.

Eliza awoke in darkness amid sighs of wind and death.

Something clammy covered her face; with a startled groan, she tried to knock it away.

"Be quiet," came a hissing whisper, "or you'll get us both bayoneted!"

Her eyelids fluttered, then slowly she focused on Hans's blood-smeared face. He held her still as she stiffened. "Don't worry, I'm not hurt and your skull is just grazed. Try to collect your wits. Haynau's damned infantry is dispatching the wounded. Let me know as soon as you can stand and I'll see if I can get us out of here."

Registering his anxiety, she turned her head. Fifty yards off, dim Austrian silhouettes moved over earth blanketed by dead and wounded. Occasionally, one jabbed his bayonet downward with the dispassion of one spearing refuse. Gradually, they threaded away. "Where's Miki?" she demanded tensely.

He was silent a long moment. "I don't know. His regiment was surrounded. If he's all right, he's a prisoner. If not"—he nodded dully at the carnage about them.

Wincing, she sat up. Her head felt like two, separated by an ax. "We have to find him."

He let out a breath, then hauled her up by the arms. "That's insane." With a grip like steel, he dragged her toward the oak grove below the hill where they'd watched the battle begin.

Eliza wrenched at his hands. "I won't go without him."

"You can't find him in the dark! Thousands of bodies are out here!"

"I'm staying!"

Abruptly, Hans let her go. "Stay then. Get killed!" With a nervous scan of the circling Austrian ghoul patrol, he ran for the oaks.

Dropping down to her belly to skirt the patrol, Eliza began to crawl through the bodies strewn over the field. Acrid smoke hung over everything, and before she started, she knew she wouldn't find him. He was lost in these drifts of dead and dying like the snow piled cold and nerveless in her nightmare, only in the dream, the bodies had faces, limbs, entrails. The artillery concentration on this part of the line had mauled it; here she found stiffening parts of men like bloody, scattered puzzles. In the dream, the wounded had cried out silently; here they made noises like butchered animals. Her hands and underside grew slippery and unspeakable.

She began to loathe them all, living and dead, particularly the professional soldiers. Having once breathed this stench, how could they fight, lure each other into battle with poetry and flags? She had been as guilty as any of them. Miklos hadn't wanted this fight; he'd been driven to it. How many in these dead armies were like him, here because they believed they had to be? Because they would be worse than dead if they refused to fight?

Frantic, Eliza risked searching within a few yards of the patrol. Hearing the rustle of her advance along an earthwork, an Austrian sergeant wheeled, his bayonet poised. Her heart pounding, she froze, burrowed against a body. With a sickening sound, the bayonet rammed down, poised again. Holding her breath, she waited for her heart to explode. The point inched over her ear, trailed over the bodies . . . went about its business.

Her eyes opened. And looked into Miklos's silent face. She almost screamed. From crown to hairline a saber had sliced his scalp to bare bone and his face was nearly blackened by seeping blood. She forced herself not to move, to wait until the patrol drifted further down the earthworks. Furtively, she felt for Miklos's heart. Inside his tunic, she found blood and silence. No, her mind shrieked, I don't believe it! He can't be dead! Not Miklos, who was more alive than any three men she'd ever known! She placed her ear against his heart. Nothing, nothing!

A hand grabbed at her scruff, jerked her half up. "Is he alive?" muttered a blunt figure in Austrian uniform.

"Hans! Oh, God, I don't know!" she whispered wildly. "I can't find his heartbeat!"

He thrust her toward an Austrian corpse. "Strip that body of its tunic and put it on!" He dropped by Miklos to feel his temple and wrist, then stripped another Austrian.

Eliza's fingers stopped, shook on the enemy tunic she was buttoning. "Is he alive?"

"I'm not sure . . . forget the rest of that and help me with him." Together, with Hans's back blocking the view of the nearest patrolling soldier, they got Miklos into the new tunic. The soldier saw two crouching Austrians, but assuming they'd paused to rifle the dead, he wandered on his grisly way.

But as Eliza helped Hans drag Miklos toward the trees, the soldier halted. "Hey! What are you doing? Our surgeon's tent is that way!"

In that moment, Miklos was repaid for giving hope to a crippled serf. "Want to take a leak first," Hans called in German. "Bad luck to piss on the dead."

With a sardonic laugh, the patrol waved them on to the wood.

In the wood, Hans ripped off his shirt to bandage Miklos as best he could, then heaved him aboard his horse and climbed up behind him. Eliza mounted the horse he'd caught for her. It was tottering from exhaustion and fright and she pityingly patted it with something like friendliness.

"The password through the Austrian pickets is Croatia," muttered Hans, "but better hope we don't stumble into any Russians."

"Where are we headed?"

"Vilagos. Görgey and what's left of the army have retreated there. They won't be much protection for long, but we can at least find a surgeon and get a few meals." He clucked to the horse. "Now, don't make another sound until we clear our own pickets."

Eliza didn't, even though they were stopped twice by the Austrians and her horse collapsed partway to Vilagos. Both of them were required to carry Miklos into the shed of wounded outside the surgical tent set up for the shreds of the mangled army. Most of the men in the tent had reached Vilagos on their own feet, and Miklos was among the most critically hurt. Under the wasted, yellow glow of an oil lantern, they found a saber slash to his left shoulder and hand, a bullet hole in the right ribs, and among

smaller ones, a large shrapnel tear in his right groin and
thigh. The bayonet that sought Eliza had found Miklos in
the back. In the dark wood, Hans had missed most of the
wounds. Under the Austrian jacket, Miklos's sodden uniform was unidentifiable. *"Mein Gott,* no wonder they left
him for dead," muttered Hans. "He damned well ought to
be."

With a soft, shaky laugh, Eliza sat back on her heels.
"But he isn't. For once, he was wrong. If he's alive now,
nothing short of old age will kill him."

Hans, dubiously glancing at the blood-soaked breeches
he was cutting off Miklos, said nothing.

Eliza, her nerves flayed and restive, instantly guessed at
Hans's reservation. Rocking on her heels, she uneasily
watched him fling scraps of cloth into the soiled straw.
Wounds shrouded by darkness were one thing; raw, under
the light, they were another. She'd never seen so much
blood. Miklos seemed inhuman. Unbearable. Her own
ignorance and inadequacy were unbearable. He'd been
accurate, calling her a cripple. Fear was returning to twist
her mind and body into paralysis. Terror that he might be
dead was becoming terror because he was not, that he
would yet die and she would have to watch, unable to do
anything to prevent it. Desperate both to do something and
be away, she leaped to her feet. "Stay with him. I'm
going after water and bandages."

But she was allowed no escape. At the surgery, she was
told the wrecked army had only two surgeons. No one
knew when they would get to Colonel Sztarai. Bandages
could not be spared; water she would have to find in the
town. "Blankets?" Eliza persisted hopelessly, knowing
where there were no bandages, there could be little else.
With an impatient shake of his head, the corpsman went
back into the surgery tent, leaving her a glimpse of the
scarlet, screaming hell inside. Beginning to shake uncontrollably, she sat in the dirt outside the tent. Oblivious to
the dull stares of men slumped by the nearby campfires,
she locked her arms about her knees to still her limbs.

"Get up!" she hissed between clenched teeth to herself. "Get up, you squeamish little toad!"

A boot in her rump sharply lifted her into the air. She scrambled to avoid pitching on her face. "Snivel somewhere else, you pipsqueak, and stop blocking the orderlies!" By the light of the open surgery tent, she recognized the red, beefy face of Bekes, the senior surgeon. He had the reputation for amputating anything that defied his limited skill.

Hardly thinking, Eliza raced toward Vilagos's square to knock on house doors. Suspicious of looters among the defeated troops, no one answered. At last, a burly householder opened up and shoved a fowling piece in her face. "Get away from here," he snarled, "or I'll blow your head off!"

Her heart in her throat, Eliza blurted out what she needed. When the door started to slam, she dug in her tunic for her wedding ring.

Hans looked up as Eliza dumped blankets, petticoats, linen handkerchiefs, and three bottles of liquor beside him. "What did you do, rob the bishop?"

She laughed shortly. "If he was a bishop, the world's in a bad way."

"So's the prince," was his dour reply. "If those surgeons don't get to him soon, he's not going to have enough blood in him to fill a spoon."

They bathed Miklos and reapplied tourniquets. Time inched; still no orderlies came for him. Near dawn, he stirred, his lips moving as if he were speaking to someone. He smiled, but then the smile twisted terribly and Eliza saw his eyes open, startled by sharply rising pain from the Caemerian, unfeeling, half world where his body had retreated to gauge its damage. His fingers curled about hers, tightened painfully. "Eliza." His whisper sounded unsure of still creating words.

Miklos tried to think why he hurt so, then why he wanted Eliza gone, yet wanted her here. The pain kept climbing. He tried to take her hand, but it was like his saber, too slippery to hold, too heavy to lift. His tormented

mind scratched out visions of battle smoke filled with
twisting metal that carved him like a hasty, careless butcher.
Until he'd slashed back at a falling saber, screamed as its
terrible blow struck him in the side. Unthinking, he grabbed
at it as if fending off a wasp, but its poison was blackening
his brain already dulled by the saber cut, mocking his
nerveless, flailing limbs as if he were an insect ready for
devouring.

Why was Eliza here with that foolish mustache? She
should have been in Italy. Having her divorce and the baby
. . . only she wouldn't need the divorce now. All she had
to do was wait . . . he passionately wanted her to wait,
only she mustn't. "Go," he managed to croak. "Just not
Enzo."

She was watching him strangely and he tried to make
her comprehend the coming horror. "Wasps . . ." When
she didn't understand, he became desperate. "Haynau and
his wasps . . . go . . ." She still didn't understand, but he
saw Hans did.

"Don't worry," Hans said quietly. He looked up to see
orderlies coming toward them. "I'll take her as soon as the
surgeons have had a look at you."

"Not Bekes." Miklos's hand convulsed on Eliza's as
the orderlies bent over him.

Eliza put a protective arm over his chest. "Who's going
to operate?"

The orderlies looked at each other. "We don't know,"
one mumbled hastily and started to hook his hands under
Miklos's shoulders. When Hans moved to knock his hands
away, the other orderly pulled a pistol.

Miklos's gray eyes were stark, his lucidity wandering.
"Eliza, don't take your revenge this way," he whispered
desperately. "Don't let Bekes butcher me!"

Ignoring the leveled pistol, she got to her feet. "I'll see
to Bekes. Hans, help them carry him." She strode past the
orderlies to the surgical tent, briskly saluted the guard.
"Princess Sztarai to see Colonel Bekes." When the guard
merely stared at her, she started to brush by him. The rifle
slapped down to bar her path.

"What's going on?" bellowed Bekes, shoving back the tent flap. "Where's Sztarai?"

"Here." She moved aside to let the bearers carry Miklos into the tent. He struggled feebly as they laid him on the gory table. Using Bekes as a shield from the sentry, Eliza swiftly stepped into the tent. Kalosca, the junior surgeon, was finishing work on an officer she recognized at a second surgery table; the sight made her gorge rise. The smell of carbolic, the sight of the instruments, the pain and terror of her childhood operations, all nightmarishly blurred. With voices buzzing in her ears, she swayed dizzily.

Bekes glanced over Miklos. "That leg'll have to come off at the hip." He picked up the saw and waved his other hand at Eliza. "You, out." Dimly, Eliza heard Bekes. She was sick, sick . . . must have air, get away . . . The orderlies clamped down on Miklos.

"Eliza," Miklos whispered, unable to see her for the men about him. His eyes darkened like those of a trapped animal in a blackening pit. "Please . . ."

His neck corded as the orderly, thinking him delirious, soothed, "Now, now, your lady's gone. The doctor'll fix you right up."

She'd gone. And in that betrayal, Miklos found the last, obliterating reach of despair.

"He's out," the orderly reported to Bekes. "You can begin, sir."

Eliza's head lifted. Her palms pressed her temples to shut out the buzzing. Begin . . . no . . . Bekes mustn't touch Miki! "I beg your pardon, Colonel Bekes," she said faintly, trying to seem steady on her feet. "But you may not begin. My husband will be Captain Kalosca's patient."

"What impertinent nonsense!" Bekes turned like a baited bull. "I told you to get out!"

Kalosca, hearing his name, and possibly his career, thrown into the breech, looked up to see what was going on.

"Do not presume to give me orders, sir. I am Princess Sztarai." Eliza carefully, regally drew herself up before Bekes. Both surgeons started in shocked recognition as she

stripped off her mustache. "Modesty forbids I display
further proof, gentlemen." Unable to resist, she held out
her hand for Bekes to kiss. His jaw slack, he reluctantly
did so with a bloody hand. She inclined her head to
Captain Kalosca. "Captain Kalosca is our family physician."

Bekes gave Kalosca a hard stare. Deadpan, Kalosca
nodded. "Captain Kalosca is occupied," Bekes blustered.

"Then we will wait." Eliza waved a peremptory hand
to the orderlies. "Please remove my husband to the fresh
air outside the surgery."

Bekes longed to fly into an indignant rage, then he
longed to order his subordinate to prolong his current
surgery until Miklos Sztarai croaked, but noting the evil,
warning look in the princess's eye, grudgingly thought
better of it.

All the same, when Captain Kalosca began Miklos's
surgery, Eliza was present to make certain Colonel Bekes
did not "assist".

Hans, wearily waiting in a shed crammed with wounded,
roused to see Eliza's strained, white face as she followed
the orderlies carrying Miklos, swathed in blood-soaked
bandages. After the orderlies left, Hans pressed a cracked
cup into her hand. "I saved some water for tea." He
watched her gratefully sip the tea, then added, "We have
to leave Vilagos when you finish."

Her head jerked up. "Miklos mustn't be moved!"

"What do you know of Haynau?" he asked quietly.

"He's an Austrian general; why?"

"He's also a clever madman. The Austrians leash him
like a killer dog unless they want killing. Your Hungarians
have made them look like asses and now they want your
backbones broken so you don't get up again. Haynau's got
just the teeth for the job. That's why Görgey retreated
here. He prefers to surrender to the Russians." He nodded
at Miklos's bloodless face. "Haynau'll slaughter every
wounded man, hang every Austrian-trained officer as a
traitor."

Chapter 22

A Howl Across the Land

Szeged, Hungary: August 13, 1849

Under a sweltering sun, Eliza, dressed like a peasant boy, drowsed fitfully in the saddle as they trailed along the road from Temesvar across the Yugoslavian border into Hungary. Black flies persistently settled on her perspiration-soaked shirt, but after three days and nights without sleep, she was past trying to fend them off. For nearly fifty miles, she'd watched Miklos burning with fever and wild with pain from his litter jostling over the ruts. On roads streaming with refugees fleeing the Austrians, laments would rise to fill the air, then recede in a wave, fade to groans and muted wails.

All kinds of rumors drifted from the north, but truth trickled with them. Kossuth had ceded the government to Görgey and fled. Görgey had surrendered to the Russians at Vilagos and Haynau's hounds were loosed. Hangings of prisoners were rampant; villages were ravaged. Death howled across the land.

Miklos was oblivious, a scorched, bare shell. He'd not regained consciousness after surgery. Most of the time, he tossed and muttered in garbled Hungarian too rapid for Eliza to understand; she was too exhausted to try. A few miles up the road, she drowsed and fell off her horse. She awoke to find Hans had settled them in a barn whose owners had fled. Nearly twenty other refugees were hud-

dled miserably in its stalls and loft; most were asleep.
Hans, sitting propped up against their stall, blinked drowsily. "Are you awake now?" he asked.

"I'm awake now."

"Good." He went to sleep.

Eliza crawled across the stall to feel Miklos's forehead;
it was dry, hotter than on the road. She went to look for
water. The trough outside the barn was empty, but the
farmhouse well yielded a bucketful. She returned to find
everyone asleep except a peasant stealthily going through
Miklos's pockets. As a visible gun was too dangerous,
Hans had gotten her a knife; she promptly jabbed it into
the back of the peasant's neck. He froze. "All right, drop
your breeches," she ordered. He didn't move, probably
disbelieving what he heard. Her next jab drew blood. The
peasant fumbled for the cord that held up his breeches.
Minutes later, he was trussed. "When your friends wake
up, you can leave," Eliza informed him, "but try
anything and I'll whack your pecker off." Mournfully, he
settled into the straw.

Although the would-be bandit looked cowed and incurious, Eliza didn't trust him. Like herself and Hans, Miklos
was raggedly dressed, but even ill and unshaven, he didn't
look like a peasant. He had a face and body shaped by
command, discipline, and centuries of breeding.

After the peasant readily departed with his companions
and other refugees at first light, she and Hans decided to
risk lingering an hour or two to give Miklos more rest.
They would then cut west away from Szeged to avoid the
main road, bound to draw pursuing Austrian patrols. With
Hans mounting watch in the loft, Eliza was glad the
refugees had left, glad of the silence.

As she dipped a cold compress to bathe Miklos, one
thing made her sad and uneasy. Not once in his delirium
had he called for her. In his own way, Miklos had deserted
her again . . . or did he feel she had deserted him? Didn't
he know she'd helped get him off the battlefield, kept him
from Colonel Bekes?

Then, horribly, she wondered if he *did* know. He'd been

unconscious until just before surgery, then mostly out of his head. If he'd fainted again before the surgeons had been exchanged, he might believe she'd left him to Bekes. Left him altogether.

In the gathering heat of the barn, she suddenly felt icy, the cold uneasiness and uncertainty she had been fighting taking a fearsome shape. For months she'd been running from Miklos, but if she didn't find him now . . . if he died, she would have no reason to run anymore. No reason for anything. Even the child he had given her would not fill her life as he had done. For a short time, she would be that child's axis, but she would lack half her own center: Miklos's steadiness and wisdom and tenderness.

Tears filled her eyes. "Why couldn't you see I *really* loved you?" she whispered. "You said yourself I was a starved cat. I was always wrapping around your ankles, asking to be petted. Scratching so you'd notice me." She touched his broken face. "I suppose you were as leery as I was. Afraid of having another faithless woman throw love back in your teeth. But you don't have to be afraid." She put her lips to his ear. "Hear me. I love you. *Love* you."

Drenched in perspiration, he'd stopped raving, was still now as he'd been in the surgery shed. Her fear becoming monstrous, she began to shake. She changed the compresses again, and for a half hour he didn't move. She lay down in the straw with him. "I love you," she railed miserably. "I *love you*, damn you. Don't just lie here like a great lump! Rise and *walk!*"

"For once in your life," came a faint, bemused whisper, "be . . . reasonable."

"Miki!" she shrieked, whirling up and clutching him. "You heard me!"

He winced. "No, no . . . quite deaf, really."

"Well"—she kissed him thoroughly, then yelled softly in his other ear—"I love you! Are you too deaf to hear that?!"

"Ay?"

Happily, she kissed him again several times until he seemed to get the message.

"Glad to see me?" he rasped.

She patted his cheek fondly. "My very own troll."

"Trolls only stamp and yowl because they want to be fussed over." His hand tightened on hers. "Tell me . . ."

"What?"

"Must I have a relapse . . . to worm a fond word out of you again?"

"I adore you," she said softly. "Is that fond enough?" Then the full implication of what he'd said registered. She sat up. "How long have you been conscious?"

"Long enough to . . . make sure you were really cooing adorable things in my ear. I was sure . . . when the cooing turned truculent." Laughing, she laid her head on his shoulder. After he drifted off again, she eased away to make gruel to build his strength.

No sooner had she gotten to her feet when Hans urgently called down from the loft, "An Austrian patrol is coming down the lane. Get the prince under the straw, then come up here."

At the urgent note in his voice, Eliza didn't argue. A minute later at his side, she lay peering from the upper feed door down at the barnyard. Three Austrian soldiers trotted into the yard. Spotting the two horses nudging the fence, they split to skirt the paddock. Hans slipped her a pistol, then motioned her to move to the top of the loft ladder just over Miklos's stall. One Austrian returned from investigating the rear and shook his head at the other two. Cautiously, he entered the barn's front door. The tallest of the three followed to cover him with a pair of pistols as he checked all the dark corners. "Nothing," he finally announced.

The one at the door spat into the straw. "Use the bayonet. That peasant wasn't lying about the horses and cavalry saddle. We've likely got soldiers. Rolf," he called. "Round up the nags." He started prodding the straw on one side of the barn while the first soldier took the other side. Number one got to Miklos's stall, poised to jab. With a hearty shove, Eliza dropped a feed sack on his head. He flattened.

The other one came running, yelling to his companion outside, "They're in the loft!" At the moment he put a foot on the ladder, he got a feed sack in the face. Hans dropped on the soldier riding through the barn door. In a split second, the soldier's throat was slit; Hans was off the horse before the body fell. Eliza slid down the ladder to the man stirring under the feed sack and clubbed him with the butt of her knife haft.

Within the quarter hour, Hans and Eliza had the travois rerigged with Miklos aboard, the soldiers' blankets and rations confiscated. Leaving the surviving soldier trussed for the mercies of the next band of beleaguered, vengeful refugees, they were off again to Balaton. Miklos slept peacefully through it all.

Balaton: September 28, 1849

They took a month to reach Balaton, but once there, dared not use the house. Though the serfs had fled before the invaders and the estate was deserted, they never knew when locals, refugees, or enemy patrols might come snooping. They all moved into Hans's small hut, isolated near the estate's northwest boundary. Miklos, only half healed, was quiet, pale, and constantly tired. He tried to manage for himself as much as possible but had to soon abandon any idea of helping dig for potatoes and turnips they were trying to get out of the ground before first freeze.

They could take little from the house to make the cottage more comfortable, for everything portable had been stolen by the departing serfs. Sometimes, Miklos and Eliza went to the house for privacy to make love. Spreading Miklos's army cloak on the bare floor, they lay together urgently, unsure if at any moment they would be torn apart by an enemy gun butt smashing in the door. Sometimes they wandered through the deserted house, and on one such afternoon, discovered Petyr's portrait had been defaced; the one of Loise was gone. "One of the kulaks

probably thought she was just a pretty, laughing girl,"
said Miklos quietly. "She could always bring sunlight to
strangers." He took Eliza's arm, then the stick he used for
a cane. "Let's get out of here."

They walked toward the lake until Miklos eased down
on a rock to rest his aching leg. Dry beech leaves filtered
down on their shoulders, flipped and scattered in the wind
off the slate gray water. Behind them, the house was also
gray, peeled by the gypsy weather. Its trees were nearly as
bare as those about the lake.

"You miss Loise." Eliza knelt among the leaves and
put her arms about Miklos's waist.

He threaded his fingers through the fair hair at her
temples. For a moment, remembering, he stared out at the
lake like a blind man trying to comprehend a mirror. "I
thought she would tear my heart apart, but when I found
her with Petyr, I hated her. He had a gun. I was crazy
enough to try to take it; the gun twisted. Then I hated her
enough to kill, Eliza. That's what she saw in my eyes after
that bullet went through Petyr's throat. That's why she
threw herself out of the window. I might as well have shot
her."

She laid her head on his knee. "Do you still hate her,
after all this time?"

"No, I suppose I pity her more than anything. Affairs
didn't make her happy; she never spent much time with a
lover before going to the next. Then she went for Petyr,
whom I loved . . ." He faltered and Eliza's arms tightened
about him.

"Ironically, this time I found out from Rakoczy. Like
many romantic women, she thought he was a psychic and
told him her secrets." He laughed shortly. "Blackmail is
where Rakoczy got most of the money he used to pay for
your guns. He'd lead a woman on, listen sympathetically
to her every confession, and keep every secret until he had
something vile enough to ruin her; that way she couldn't
expose him. You got none of the Sztarai hereditary jewels:
only the simple pieces Loise couldn't sell for much. When
I found the major pieces missing, I traced them through a

royal jeweler to Rakoczy. He'd sold most of the pieces, but I pried the last back from him. In revenge, he told me about Loise and Petyr.

"That's when I went to the inn off the wine gardens where Petyr entertained women . . . and found them together. Loise went through the window half dressed; only a two story fall . . . but it broke her neck. In the scandal that followed, the city children made up a song about her.

"Loise, Loise, soiled, lovely dove,
Will you die for pleasure or will you die for love . . .

"In the streets, they'd follow me about singing it."
She touched his cheek. "They're not singing it now; they've other things to think about. Hungary is hard-strained to deal with today."

Gravely, Miklos looked at the barren fields beginning to clump with scrub. "And tomorrow belongs to Austria."

She peered sharply into his face. "Miki, even if Balaton is confiscated, a wide world lies beyond it. We don't have to stay . . ."

"My world is here, Eliza. My heritage, my people. I've lived in exile"—he paused, touching her cheek regretfully, tenderly, as he had the last, stubborn, lovely roses in the manor's wasted garden—"but I'll die here as Batthyány and so many died at Arad."

"What are you saying?" she whispered in horror. Death was sweeping upon them on the wings of defeat and despair. She mustn't give up! Miklos mustn't! "Life doesn't stop at the borders of Hungary! It isn't tradition!" She shook him. "The fighting didn't end at Temesvar. *We* didn't end!"

"*You* didn't end." He smiled gently. "You're not a cripple now, Eliza." He ironically waved his cane. "I'm no longer your crutch; you'll never need me again." Fiercely, he caught her face between his hands. "I didn't lose everything at Temesvar. *You* won and part of your victory was mine. When the time comes, I will stay at Balaton and you will leave . . . and live. And for that"—he kissed her harshly as if his heart were cracking—"I will love you even more than I do now . . . although, I wonder how that can be. For so long you've been my heart, my *reason* to be," he whispered roughly against her mouth. "So sweet and blinding a sunrise, I think no matter what happens, I shall never see the dark again." Then he lurched to his feet and hobbled away across the fields.

Slowly, Eliza sat down in the dry, barren earth to let its black dirt crumble through her fingers. A tiny spot darkened, moistened the dirt with the first of tears that came, desolate and furious. You were right, Bette. He doesn't know how to lose. And, come hell or the Austrians, I'm not going to let him lose like this!

In that same hour she left for Budapest.

Budapest: December 2, 1849

Budapest, that enchanting, feminine city, had become a stranger to Eliza. The music of its streets was silent, the sprightly flavors of its atmosphere muted. Curtains were pulled, many shops closed, only a few barges drifted on the river. She felt like flinging red paprika over the city roofs to make everyone sneeze, return sound and life. Instead, everywhere were posted Austrian troops whose marching footsteps echoed through the winding narrow streets and cannon rumbled on Gellert Hill.

Strangely, Bette's townhouse was one of the few places that seemed no different. Carriages were pulled up before the house, horses tethered near the gate. The sight of all the Austrian orderlies hanging about made Eliza uneasy. What if the house had been commandeered by an Austrian officer? Unsure of being recognized, Eliza edged down her bonnet veil. Julia Petöfi had given her a dark blue silk dress and cape with secret pockets as a disguise. "Sándor liked this dress," Julia had said tightly. "He won't see it again."

With a chill, Eliza remembered Sándor's snaking scarf from her dream. "He didn't come back."

"I don't even know where he's buried. Some mass

grave on the field at Segesvár, they tell me. He was killed in July, a month before the end." Julia's mouth twisted.

"Perhaps where his body has gone doesn't matter so much, Julia." Eliza sadly took her hand. "Sándor has left his soul behind. He'll always be young, part of the dreams of Hungary." Her hand tightened. "You aren't alone. Women are weeping all over Hungary, and as if that weren't enough, the living are shriveled by despair. Miklos envies Sándor. He could leave but he's waiting for the Austrians to come to Balaton."

"He's Hungarian," Julia said simply, sadly.

"But I'm not," replied Eliza slowly. "I'm a pigheaded American Yankee . . . and I've just begun to fight."

"Contessa Elisa Rossi, Your Highness." Bette's butler raised his eyebrows significantly at his mistress. He stepped aside to admit the young woman dressed in mourning.

"Close the door, Schmidt." Bette sighed as she surveyed Eliza. *"Mein Gott. Contessa* Rossi. Enzo would turn in his grave. And where did you get that dress . . . Rakoczy's mumbo jumbo trunk?"

"Rakoczy's alive?"

"You can't kill a vampire. His house has been closed since Budapest was retaken by our Austrian friends. Nobody wants such a horror for the occupation. A few nights ago, a light was signaling in one of the upper windows. Soldiers searched. Nothing." With a grim smile, she flicked her drapes closed lest her outlaw guest belatedly be recognized by the orderlies on the street. "Vlad's there, all right. All the Rakoczys were fascinated by secrecy. That wreck of a place probably has more false walls and priests' holes than a rabbit warren has tunnels. Mark my words, Vlad and his pack are up to something. Rumor claims he's gathering insurgents in the north." She waved to a chair and rang the servant bell. "But sit down. Have some tea and tell me why you're here. How is Miki?"

"He needs help: I had thought to get it from you." Eliza ironically inclined her head toward the adjoining rooms filled with Austrian officers. "Considering your current vogue in guests, you may be able to give it."

Bette spread her hands helplessly. "I'm virtually a prisoner in my own home, as much governed by the Austrians as anyone."

Eliza's head slowly, deliberately rotated. After leaving Julia, she'd done some hard thinking about Bette von Schmerling. Neither Bette nor her diamonds displayed a single dent from the devastation surrounding them. "You're Austrian at heart, Bette, and your house is full of Austrians."

"That makes no difference. You may remember my salons in '48 and '49?" Schmidt knocked. She gave orders for tea, then dismissed him.

"I remember the salons, but the Austrians apparently don't," drawled Eliza, "and at long last, I'm beginning to understand why."

Bette took up her needlework. "Then you understand more than I, my dear."

"You were stitching on that piece when you told me about Bakocz, the police spy. Very astute. He was quite guilty."

Bette began to stitch. "Yes, he was, wasn't he?"

"And a bit clumsy; enough so that he would have been caught eventually, under less manageable circumstances . . . and then he would have told about you."

"Me?"

"He was your contact with Kolowrat, wasn't he? So you betrayed him to draw attention away from the obvious conclusion, then had him killed by his own people. The salons were a perfect way to gauge Hungarian politics, pick up secrets. Only he was also Miki's contact, and things got complicated. You weren't sure just how far Miki would go along with the Austrians, but if he crossed them, you'd be in trouble, too. Then you might lose everything: your Austrian lands, this house, Balaton."

She watched Bette's neat, steady stitching. "That's where I came in. Why you chose me as Miki's bride in the beginning. The revolutions were about to explode. I was a naive American with liberal inclinations. I was rash, impulsive. While I looked like Loise, I was vulnerable, a waif that you knew Miki wouldn't abandon, whether driven by duty or guilt over Loise, and either way, you'd win. I'd docilely behave; Miki with his conservative politics would be reinstated with Austria. Or I'd misbehave and meddle with the liberals . . . when you suspected Miki's Hungarian sympathies were too strong and our marriage was too unstable, you suggested I do just that, remember? I'd even swear you set up that whole love tryst with Vanda Bellaria. Miki never got that note I wrote, did he?"

"You've got a vivid imagination, but then Miki wouldn't have tolerated a dull wife." Schmidt returned with tea, poured and left.

Eliza didn't touch her cup. "You thought the more I became involved with revolutionaries, the less sympathetic Miki would be to them, the more loyal to Austria. But if Miki seemed inclined to cross the Austrians, you could throw him to the wolves by drawing their suspicions to him through me. No matter what happened, you'd be uninvolved and Balaton would stay in the family. That's really all you cared about: Balaton. If you had let Miki die in Vienna, you'd have lost it."

Bette's head lifted, her eyes weary, filled with sadness. "Not bad, only you're very wrong in two elements: I care very much for Miki; he's the son I never had. Kolowrat demanded insurance that Miki would be useful to him; I gave him that insurance. I wanted Miki to survive what Loise did to him, wanted him to have Balaton, a wife, children. Crude as you were, you'd have been good for him. You *were* good for him. You'd have stuck through almost anything because you needed him. But I didn't foresee Rakoczy's venting his spite at Stagshorn and your having more scruples than I suspected. I left you alone at Balaton to make or break you. When you came to Budapest, I knew that you, as an American, would inevitably be attracted to Kossuth and his crowd. I had to direct you as a weapon one way or another, but at that point, I didn't pay sufficient note to your family business, including your access to guns."

Bette sipped her tea. "I'm genuinely quite sorry, but you see I can do nothing for Miki now. He's been twice ruined by a woman. He made his choice before God and his emperor. He must leave Hungary. Of the two hundred officers of the Hungarian army, Haynau has sentenced half to death, half to twenty years in prison. In time, things will settle, but even so, the emperor will never permit Miki to remain at large." She set her Meissen cup down. "If you love him, persuade him to leave."

"I do love him, but he won't leave."

For the first time in memory, Bette looked her age. "No . . . I didn't think he would." She sat silent for several minutes, then rested her head on the back of her chair. "What will you do?"

Eliza rose and went to the door. "I'm afraid I don't know how to lose, either."

As she passed through the corridor outside the drawing room, Schmidt passed her to confer with Bette, and she expected Bette to summon guards to stop her. Quickly, she left the house, but near the corner, heard footsteps behind her in the street. Her hand closing on the pistol in her cloak pocket, she turned to see Schmidt. "Wait, please . . . Countess. The princess wishes me to give you this." He held out a black box.

"A bomb?" Eliza asked skeptically.

He smiled. "I think not."

She accepted it. After watching him return to the house, she walked toward the river. On the bank under a rank of lindens, she opened the box. In it were Bette's fabled champagne diamond tiara and a card. "For Princess Eliza, my worthy adversary and formidable friend."

So at last, with Bette's approval, she was an authentic princess. Bette knew she would never wear the tiara: as she was also an authentic shopkeeper's daughter, she would sell it. In Paris, if possible. The Hungarian and Austrian markets were presently glutted with jewels.

Only the chances of seeing Paris again were nil. She had scarcely enough money to return to Balaton. Unless . . . She appraised the jewels' champagne bubble cluster. So vampires never die, do they? I wonder just what their methods are?

As night fell, Eliza watched Rakoczy's mansion. No sign of life stirred behind those shuttered windows. Outside the piked fence surrounding the pine- and willow-scattered park, a curfew patrol passed every forty-five minutes. Unmoving in a stand of firs, she waited another hour. The night was growing chill: snow was in the air. She wondered if the potatoes and turnips were in at Balaton. Whether Miklos, in his preoccupation with Hungary's terrible defeat, had much missed her absence. She missed him. She might be able to stand on her own two feet now as he said, but to her those feet, some indefinable part of her, had been amputated.

Noticing the moon rising, Eliza edged back into the shadows. Not a bird, not a squirrel had explored Rakoczy's silent park at twilight. Undisturbed, ripe cones mounded among the tawny needles beneath its pines and webs of dry chrysanthemum shocks thrust from neglected flowerbeds. The iron gate, its lock smashed by Austrian gun stocks, was propped askew. Slipping her hood up closer about her face, Eliza surveyed the avenue before the house. The patrol had passed a quarter of an hour ago; everything looked deserted. Quickly, she went to the gate, and with a shove of her shoulder against the fretwork, eased it off its prop, then reclosed it. A few snowflakes sifted across the open drive. Keeping to its shadowing willows, she reached the main door, but found it locked. She went around to the terrazzo side veranda, and taking the tiara from her reticule, slit an opening in a portico window, reached in, and undid the door lock.

Once inside, Eliza waited to see if anyone would respond to the clink of falling glass. The house interior was far less unattractive by moonlight. As her eyes adjusted to the change in light, only shapes, their garish colors obscured, were revealed with a curious, striking rhythm in the near darkness.

Taking care to keep to the carpets, she explored the

lower floor. After the curfew patrol passed again, the
silence of the house was breathless, as if waiting for
something. She felt her way up the pitch-black servant
stair behind the kitchen. On the first landing, she caught
for a fleeting instant a possible, faint echo of voices from
an upper floor. She went higher, but only the creak of the
bare stairs disturbed the stillness . . . and whoever might
have been talking.

At last, she reached a webby attic. Mouse and rat tracks
marked the dusty floor; with minute rustlings, rodents fled
into piles of rolled up, rotting oriental rugs and tapestries.
Halfway down a stack of unused furniture, the moonlight
glinted on a slanting pair of eyes. Eliza sucked in her
breath. Unwinking, the eyes watched her. She inched
forward. "Who's there?"

She heard a soft thud. The eyes disappeared, leaving
only a glimpse of an uncoiling, snakelike shape.

A cat, she realized in limp relief. A forgotten pet or
stray, perhaps; but perhaps not. "Rakoczy?" Nothing. She
restlessly fingered the reticule, then wondering if she were
watched, headed back to the servants' stair. On the stair,
she tied the reticule with the tiara about her waist, then
pulled the cloak over it. If Rakoczy were here, he probably
wouldn't be much interested in bargaining for jewels,
considering the market glut, but he might have no com-
punction about relieving her of them for later sale abroad.
At best, dealing with Rakoczy would be tricky. *If* she
could find him. She was beginning to have doubts.

On the mezzanine floor, she softly called Rakoczy's
name in every bedroom, without response.

Upon fruitlessly trying the huge, master bedroom, she
sat down to rest. The baby was growing too heavy to
tolerate all this adventuring . . . and needless to say,
staircases. With her feet tucked under her cloak, she settled deeper in the chair. She might as well spend the night
here; she could afford little else and looking for an inn
after curfew was dangerous. She could better explore the
place by daylight if she took care to keep away from the
windows. The huge, empty house itself made her less edgy

than it might once have done. Living in Balaton's barren, field-mouse-infested dacha had stabilized her nerves. Also sharpened her ears.

Beginning to drowse after a time, Eliza heard something: a smooth movement, an oiled movement in a house that looked as if no one had attended a hinge in years. The back of her neck prickled as from the wall near the fireplace advanced the cat, smoothly, about waist high. In no way under heaven could he be touching the floor. A moment later, she saw he was supported by a cloaked figure. A deep hood obscured the face. Noticing her, the figure halted like a slight wind that had died.

In the alcove, a second cloaked figure appeared. With a flicker of relief, Eliza recognized Rakoczy's startled, ugly features and distorted shape. Upon seeing her, he almost collided with the cat bearer. She wondered how anyone could think him a mystic.

Warned by Rakoczy's stumble, a third cloaked figure halted in the secret arras. With a mixture of reluctance and shy pleasure sparring on his face, Rakoczy loped forward. "Princess! So it *is* you!" He caught her hand to his lips. "I envy Kossuth having a medal to pin at your breast. No one is more a hero of our glorious revolution."

As he talked on, Eliza experienced again the old, uneven reaction to him: of being both charmed and repelled. Tonight his verbal tenses rather than his looks and manner were the jarring note; he seemed not to have accepted, even noticed Hungary's defeat. "Miklos," he asked eagerly. "How is he?"

"Well, at the moment," she replied, "he's the reason for this visit. May we speak privately?"

He smiled. "Fear nothing from my friends; they are perfectly discreet. Indeed, one of them you may be pleased to see again." His voice held a faint, taunting note she sensed was not meant for her. The taller figure in the arras stiffened, became very still. Then, slowly came forward, removed its hood.

Eliza's eyes widened in shock and pity. The left side of the face had been sheared away to crushed, flattened bone.

Its ruined eye was covered by a silver metal patch on which a jeweled, enameled eye glittered as if sharply noting her appalled reaction. "Enzo!" she murmured. "We thought you dead."

"The doctors believe I've a year or so before bone splinters needle that far into my brain." At Enzo's ironic rasp, Eliza had another start. Not only his looks, but his voice had been ruined by his being battered against the river rocks. "At that time, I shall either die or go mad," he added dryly, "but meanwhile, Prince Rakoczy very kindly provides me with morphine . . . and privacy."

Enzo was already dead, Eliza saw sadly. In place of his gaiety, beauty, and charm, only an embittered wreck remained; morphine addiction was rapidly destroying that.

"Perhaps we should allow Princess Sztarai to convey the nature of her errand," Rakoczy interrupted smoothly. He turned to the person stroking the cat as if inquiring whether an introduction was in order. The hand ceased stroking, gave a negligent, negative wave. Rakoczy turned back to Eliza. "How may I serve you, Princess?"

"Is it true you're regrouping a band of insurgents?"

His eyes slid to Enzo, then back to her. "In my Zemplar Mountains, yes. But why . . . ?"

"Miki and I wish to join you." His group offered a temporary haven for Miklos, and in the inevitable end, a way to die fighting honorably as he wanted, rather than to wait like a trapped, toothless wolf at Balaton.

Rakoczy spread his hands expansively. "My dear Princess, you are more than welcome, but Prince Miklos regretfully"—his hands closed—"is another matter. I doubt if he could accustom himself to my orders and as you may know, we have old differences."

"If you wish to one day rule Hungary, Your Highness, you must rule many men, differences or no." She let that challenge sink into his pride. "Also, you need weapons."

His eyes lit. "You can get more?"

"Probably. The important point is . . . I can give you weapons now. Görgey rounded up the American arms before the surrender and shipped them to a safe place. I know where that place is." Thanks to Julia Petöfi.

"You must tell me."

"Better still, I can show you. It isn't far. But first, I want your word of honor that you'll accept Miki and treat him well."

"You have my word," he said slowly, "so long as he agrees to my command."

"Perhaps you can suggest a way to persuade him?"

"Many ways . . . on the way to the guns."

Chapter 23

Heartbeat in the Crypt

They left that night. Three Rakoczy "friends" brought a coach just before midnight. Timing Austrian patrols and sentries like clockwork, they were shortly well beyond the city. The dilapidated coach was a baroque antique, its scarlet upholstery badly stuffed. Eliza shifted uncomfortably as the coach rattled along. The hooded "friend" with the cat was on the far side of the coach, but by moonlight Eliza perceived that the richly ringed hands belonged to a woman: a mute perhaps, one of Rakoczy's acquired, maimed collection like Enzo, for she never spoke. Rakoczy was exuberantly loquacious. "So many times you've been an angel to Hungary, Princess! How Ferenc Rakoczy would have admired you."

Eliza realized with something of a start that this was not merely flattery; he really liked her. "I wish I could have met him."

"Greatness came easily to him; it does to some men"—he thoughtfully stroked his fur lap robe—"like Miklos. Everyone said he was a natural leader, born for magnificent feats. Up until the tragedy of his wife and her lover, he didn't disappoint them, whereas"—he brushed the fur against the grain—"I disappointed everybody." He gestured to his outsized head; his heavy-shouldered, spindly frame. "This face . . . this body: hardly the popular image of a noble, conquering prince. But I've a good mind." He tapped his skull. "I might have excelled in academia had I been able to concentrate; only so much, so *much* was always going through my mind. At times I would become completely exhausted. Everything would leave me for a time, including the simplest things my tutor had taught me. Even now I go along for days sometimes in a trance-like manner, until everything comes back. Other things come back as well, only they rarely make sense, are often nightmarish, as though during those days I've lived another life." He hesitated. "Does Miklos ever . . . forget?"

She thought of Miklos screaming into the wind at Como. "No, I think not."

Rakoczy's face twisted strangely. "I suppose even the blessed of the gods should be tempered by a few difficulties. Miklos was tried more severely than most. I'm sure he was most comforted to have found you."

Wondering how much Rakoczy knew about her marriage, Eliza flicked a glance at Enzo. Enzo wasn't looking at her. He seemed listless, unconcerned, and she wondered if he might have taken morphine just before leaving Budapest.

"Shall I tell you about that persuasion we were discussing?" Rakoczy ventured.

"Yes, of course."

"The key to Miklos is quite simple, yet very complex. As was Loise. On the surface, she was not a complicated creature, merely a gay, winning girl who in her soul was wholly serious. At eight, she fell in love with Miklos Sztarai, and was faithful to that love until her death. I know." His eyes glittered. "She told me everything."

"How could she love Miki, yet consistently betray him?"

"Both physically and mentally, she was far too much in awe of him, could . . . enjoy as lovers only men more malleable. Unfortunately, she loved only him. Wishing to make him jealous, she always saw that he found out about her liaisons. She was caught in her own web as matters grew complicated, Miklos alienated.

"His brother, Petyr, discovering her difficulties, tried to help her, but their conspiracy declined into an affair. As Petyr was the closest substitute Loise could find for Miklos, she loved him, was happiest with him. Ironically, unlike so many occasions when she made 'mistakes' with Miklos, the only fly in the ointment was Miklos's finding out. She knew an affair with Petyr would mean the end between them. As for Petyr, I think he would rather have died than have his brother know of his betrayal.''

The possible truth of the gun struggle flickered across Eliza's mind. Had Petyr turned the gun on himself?

''Only Miklos and God know what happened in that inn room. Quite frankly, I think he was telling the truth about not throwing Loise from the window.''

''If you knew all this, why did you infer at Stagshorn that he'd killed them?''

For a moment, he didn't answer, then said bitterly, ''The two of you were happy. I didn't think he should be forgiven everything. Loise had been so lovely, so unhappy . . .''

''You loved her, didn't you?''

''What matter?'' he retorted. ''She never looked at me. Only Miklos, who had seduced her at fifteen!''

''Seduction requires two . . . doesn't it?''

''Yes, two,'' he said harshly. ''Enzo was seductive once. Now he and I are *two* . . . of a kind.''

A bejeweled hand moved consolingly, perhaps in warning, to Rakoczy's arm. Too late, for Eliza began to realize her dreadful mistake in expecting sanctuary for Miklos from Rakoczy. Rakoczy was an ever-changing reflection of truth and lies, admiration . . . and hatred of Miklos. Under the circumstances, he was supposed to be wooing her cooperation, but his growing lack of control suggested more than his usual erraticism. Also, the hand soothingly stroking his arm was becoming wickedly familiar. It was faintly multicolored on the thumb and first two fingers; their tiny fingerprint crevices were traced with black. Women who wore emeralds, rubies, and diamonds to the knuckles didn't usually make their livings as painters . . . printers . . . assassins. Bianca. She was sitting two feet from Bianca Sidoro.

''We had great plans for Hungary,'' Rakoczy was running on, faltering a trifle in realization he'd said too much.

"Yes, I can imagine," Eliza replied evenly. Plans of murder, terrorism: all bloody and futile and fatal.

We're done, Miki, she thought bleakly. Our last chance is gone and I've given these monsters guns to spread more horror than Haynau.

Two hours after midnight they reached a range of lime-stone caverns north of the city used as wine cellars. Their white skulls scattered among low-lying hills. "Which one?" asked Rakoczy.

She told him. The truth, that it might soon blind him: all of them. With a light even she would not survive. Under her cape, the baby fluttered and wretchedly she touched her stomach. God forgive me, I must trade your sweet life for a thousand. Now she fully understood why Miklos had been unable to stay with her and Anitra during that long winter at Balaton; he'd had no choice, as she had no choice now. If only she could see him one last time . . . but it was better this way. For the time he had left, he could go on thinking she and the baby were safe.

She felt Enzo's good eye on her as they dismounted the coach among white boulders. The companions' torches led to the cave, their lights like crawling segments of an infernal serpent. Walking beside Eliza on the winding path, Enzo sounded completely lucid as he commented, "This should be an exciting moment for you as well as Vlad. You've gotten what you wanted for Miki . . . only you don't look altogether pleased."

She indicated Rakoczy's stunted, powerful back ahead of them. "Do you trust him? After all, he might have loved Loise, but he still blackmailed her."

"That was out of spite, I think. He resented what he couldn't have." Enzo took her arm as the way grew steep. "I understand him now better than I once did." Noticing she was breathless despite the brevity of the path, he wondered whether it was due to pregnancy or nervousness. "Vlad respects you. You've little to fear if you humor him."

"He's quite mad, isn't he?"

"Oh, yes. Having second thoughts?"

"A bit late for that." With reflections dancing eerily on the rocks, the torches neared the cave. Her grasp tightened on his arm as she looked up at Enzo. In the moonlight, his hooded eye was remote as a cold, distant star. "I do deeply regret the river accident, Enzo. You were only trying to help."

"Help? Bette sent me to destroy your marriage. Instead, I helped glue you and Miki quite nicely back together." He smiled sardonically. "If I'd had any sense, I should have run off with you to the South Seas the moment I married you."

She laughed. "But then you would have been *married*, Enzo."

"Yes . . . instead of clinging to the last scraps of my pathetic life"—he glanced at the slight mound under her cape—"I might have created life."

"You probably have, *Signor* Don Juan. Easily those seven *bambini*, don't you think?"

For the first time, he laughed without constraint. With the marred part of his face away from her, he seemed almost like the old Enzo.

They arrived at the cave. The snow white, mold-crusted dripstone just cleared Enzo's head. After Rakoczy's three "companions" pounded torch brackets into the soft limestone, they shortly had light. While Rakoczy went into euphorics over the weapons and ammunition boxes piled on the cavern floor, Eliza estimated the height of the nearest torch bracket; she couldn't reach it. Bianca walked about the cavern inspecting the weapons, the ball and powder kegs, the cartridge cases. She murmured something to Rakoczy and Eliza tensely wondered if she'd noticed more than the guns. But no, Rakoczy was still prancing.

She edged past the indifferent Enzo to the ammunition nearest the middle torch, then sharply scanned the cave floor. For a moment, she saw nothing, then traced a slender line snaking across the dusty floor. After a cautious scuff at the spot where the line ended, she found the fuse; it had pulled away from its putty anchor to a powder keg. Possibly one of the "companions" had unknowingly dislodged it. Seeing the others preoccupied, she quickly stooped, recovered the fuse, then pushed it back into the keg.

"What are you doing?" Bianca's voice came sharp, undisguised.

Eliza's head snapped up. "I dropped my wedding ring."

"Basta! You don't wear one. I noticed it missing in the coach."

Eliza's heart sank. She'd sold the ring when she was masquerading as Miklos's aide. A woman with Bianca's love of jewelry would have noticed her lack of it.

Bianca flipped back her hood. Her hair was sleeked back in a ruby-studded snood: her dark brows were satanic in the hard, ivory mask of her face. "She knows, Rakoczy. She's just playing games with us. You may as well shoot her."

Enzo's macabre, magnificent eyes turned on Eliza and Rakoczy halted his capering. "Don't be absurd! Why shoot her?!"

"Because I know her much better than you. She'll balk at the methods we'll have to use to be rid of the Austrians. She'll betray us."

"Nonsense! Princess Sztarai has proven her worth to Hungary. Why, already she's . . ."

Bianca cut him off. "Already she's up to something. I smell it." As she started forward, Enzo moved quickly ahead of her.

With a quick glance, he took in the rigged powder keg and turned. Putting his hands on his hips, he fanned his cloak to block the view of the fuse. "Bianca, you're jealous. You've had few peers in your profession. Isn't it time you recognized another?"

"I'll tell you what I recognize," Bianca said coldly. "Miklos Sztarai killed my husband in London. Thanks to this little beast, Iron Nicholas was alive to send troops to overwhelm you Hungarians."

Seeing Rakoczy's eyes narrow in suspicion, Eliza protested, "Surely, Prince, you cannot countenance the murder of legitimate regents. You'll soon be one yourself!"

"I am prepared to do whatever I must to become regent," he said tersely. "My line, more than anyone's, has that right. Franz Joseph, who claims the throne of Hungary in my stead, is an unlawful usurper. I shall treat him as a criminal along with his accomplices whether they actively serve him or benignly tolerate him." His black eyes glinted dangerously. "I must know, Princess, where you and your husband stand."

"With Hungary, Your Highness," Eliza said steadily.

"She's evading the issue," Bianca snapped. She drew her stiletto. "Move aside, Enzo. If I prick that baby, she'll soon give a straight answer."

"You cannot allow this, Your Highness!" protested Enzo.

"Regretfully," said Rakoczy slowly, "I have no choice."

Eliza made a grab for the torch, but Enzo was there before her and shoved her aside. "Run!" he hissed. "Run!"

Eliza bolted as he swiped the torch at Bianca's face. Bianca screamed. Her arm before her burnt face, she stumbled back, then with a shriek of rage and vengeance, lunged forward. The stiletto sank into Enzo's chest as he touched the torch to the fuse. She jerked out the knife to stab again, but with a gasp of pain, he grabbed her wrist and flung her against the ammunition crates. Two of Rakoczy's minions hurried to overwhelm him as the third scrabbled to find the fuse buried in the dirt. Rakoczy, blind with rage, went after Eliza.

Eliza heard the scuffle, heard his running footsteps in the narrow corridor of the cave. Leaden with the weight of the baby, she stumbled through the darkness. Suddenly, moonlight broke over her in a flood. Scrambling down the path, she heard a grating slide of rock as Rakoczy slipped. A small rock slide tumbled behind her; more rock fell, but he didn't fall with it. Undeterred, he hurried after her again. The way down was appallingly quicker than the way up.

Panting, she reached the coach. "Rats!" She scrambled

up beside the coachman. "The cave's infested with rats!"
When he predictably gawked toward the cave, she swatted
him on the crown with her pistol butt and shoved him off
the seat.

Her hands slippery with perspiration, Eliza fumbled with
the thick reins. Four horses and she could scarcely handle
one! Then Rakoczy's gnomish face glinted in the moonlight as he grabbed at her skirt. At her screech, the team
bolted.

Snarling, Rakoczy headed back toward the cave. At that
moment, his relieved cohort pulled the fuse from the powder keg; it was the wrong one. In a shower of flying
emeralds, rubies, and an enameled eye, the cave blew.

Mercifully, in the miles back to Budapest, the horses
wore out, but Eliza, once thinking she heard pursuing
hoofbeats, kept them moving at a steady pace. She wept
for Enzo. He'd wanted that last pathetic scrap he called his
life. He'd clung to it, comtemplated doing unspeakable
things for it, yet flung it away to save her and the baby.
For Enzo, she prayed the angels were lovely and lovable.

Fearing a wreck as well as an Austrian patrol, Eliza
drove as far as she dared into the city. In Vizivaros, at the
foot of Gellert Hill, she abandoned the coach, but then
stood bewildered, unsure of where to go. Julia Petöfi's?
Too far. An inn? Too many questions at this hour. Then
she saw Saint Mattias Cathedral just up the Hill; if it were
unbarred, she could wait there until dawn, then take a
passenger coach. But to where?

Out of breath, she labored up the cobbled hill. Though
she saw no one, she had the uneasy impression of being
followed. Finally, she crept into the cathedral. Except for
the distant altar aglow with stained glass and gold, Mattias's
gothic vault was as gray and skeletal as a carefully arranged arc of bones.

The church was not empty. A great slab trapdoor gaped
open before the altar. Between the altar and trapdoor was a
handsome black and gold coffin. Eliza shrank back into
the shadows. A hand closed on her shoulder and she
started violently.

"May I help you, my child?" A mild, middle-aged priest stood beside her.

"I have no place to go," she said simply.

He glanced down at her pregnancy. "Many have been unfortunate in the war. Would you like something to eat?"

She liked him. He only asked the questions that counted. "Yes, please. I'm ravenous . . . but I can pay . . ."

"Another time, if you like. For now, keep your money against more difficult times. Will you accompany me?"

"Thank you." Breathing a sigh of relief, she followed him along a pillared side aisle. Perhaps with food and hot tea in her stomach she could gather her wits. Then the priest dropped like a stone. She screamed and ducked as a heavy candlestick sliced at her skull.

Rakoczy lunged at her from behind a column. "You traitress bitch! Now you've made me kill a priest!"

In fear and fury, Eliza scrambled over the altar railing. "You miserable . . . if you really killed that good old man, you deserve to roast in hell!"

He made a grab over the railing and she dodged. "Will you add blasphemy to murder? I've taken sanctuary in the holiest heart of the church . . ."

He hesitated. "Let it be!" she pressed. "You would have drowned Hungary in blood to no purpose with those guns! For every Austrian you killed, ten would have been sent to avenge him. What point to be king of the dead?"

"What point to caper for my lessers? What point to *this?*" He swept his hand down his misshapen length. "To Hungary's defeats, time after time after time? We came so close and you gave so much . . . *Why?* Why do you betray us now?" When she started to answer, he overran her. "Our world has been driven to madness, the best of men, like Széchenyi, reduced to spewing gibberish. We've no choice but to do evil, become demons to fight back demons. There is no respite; nothing is sacred." His black, maniac eyes fixed on hers, he climbed like a clumsily adroit ape over the rail. She pulled her pistol and he laughed ironically. "You see? Even you will defile what you revere."

Eliza retreated as he took another step. "Get back."
Then, as if plucked by one of the demons Rakoczy described, her hem caught on the altar step to throw her off
balance.

In an instant, Rakoczy wrenched away the gun and
caught her by the wrist. "Come, I'll show you the real
altar of this place." With inflexible, unexpected strength,
he dragged her to the open slab, then shoved her down the
stone stairway beneath it. A candle in a niche feebly
revealed damp, musty stone walls and huge catafalques,
some with carved effigies of their occupants. Glass reliquary cases were grouped along the walls.

He seized the candle and dragged her to one of the cases
where reposed the gruesome hand of Saint Stephan. "Here
lie the greatest rulers and martyrs of Hungary. Here *I* shall
lie." He waved the candle about the catafalques. *"This* is
history, inevitably a realm of the dead! For the living
remains the pursuit of glory. Glory, which once held, once
come to this, cannot be usurped. *Glory,* not ignominy, is
the key to this hallowed place! Before I die, Hungary and
all her enemies shall know my name . . ."

"And hurl you to the dogs!" she spat.

His face twisted in rage. "You vile Cassandra, choke on
your apocryphal cant!" His free hand closed on her throat
and she beat at his face. Suddenly, he was ripped away
and the candle smashed into darkness. Flinging herself
behind a catafalque, Eliza heard pants, muffled growls as
if terrible beasts struggled, battered against the walls in the
blackness of the crypt. Then, horribly, bones ground,
snapped. There was silence. She scarcely dared breathe,
far less breathe a name. Then she heard a body being
dragged away up the crypt stair.

After a few minutes, out of curiosity and dread of being
closed in the crypt, she hesitantly followed. In the cathedral, only a bloody streak was to be seen leading toward a
side door to the outside. She followed the streak, eased
open the door. Snow sifted on the hillside cobbles and a
sprawled black, broken shape: Rakoczy, flung to the dogs.

But who . . . ? Then she heard a tramp of feet from the

direction of the fortress. An Austrian squad was advancing toward the cathedral. Whoever killed Rakoczy must have seen them and fled. The squadron would find Rakoczy and search the cathedral. They would find the priest. And then . . .

Heart pounding, she retreated back into the church. Where to hide? Where to hide in this barren place? Hoping to elude the Austrians among the catafalques, she started back to the crypt, only to hear voices as Rakoczy's body was spotted. No time! She ran to the coffin, and taking a deep breath, flung back the lid. Then almost screamed in horror, for silent in the coffin lay Miklos.

Catching a handle, she reeled. Austrians . . . the baby . . . Shaking uncontrollably, trying to fight off shock and hysteria, she forced herself to climb awkwardly into the coffin. Clamping her eyes shut, she closed the lid. Then bawled.

An arm tightened about her consolingly. "There, there . . . I'm not stiff yet." Fortunately, the other hand was available to cover her mouth, for she *did* scream then. "Good Lord," the body muttered tensely, "be quiet, little girl, and I'll give you a cookie."

"Umph, mumph!" Eliza let out two more flagging bleats and resigned herself to mere shivers.

The Austrians combed the church with exhausting thoroughness. Upon being revived, the priest had wit enough to seat himself on the steps before the coffin and moan, thereby drowning out any protests the coffin's occupants might make for lack of air: a problem Miklos and Eliza were beginning to find dire.

To hasten matters along, the priest baldly confessed to murder, happily motivated by Rakoczy's attacking him with a candlestick. Father Martin had presumably put up a mighty struggle and cast Rakoczy out into the snow before staggering back into the cathedral "to say a mass for the poor fellow," where he unfortunately collapsed.

"Out to steal the candlestick, would you say?" demanded the young Austrian lieutenant.

"I'm not sure of that at all. I shouldn't want to blacken anyone's character," mildly protested Father Martin.

The burly sergeant studied the priest's frail hands. "You must have been fearsome angry to break the man's neck."

"I've a frightful temper," the priest murmured penitently. Then added in a wry tone, "I daresay Our Meek Lord will exact a very severe penance for this one."

The lieutenant patted his shoulder. "Don't feel too badly, Father. The fellow richly deserved what he got. Now I'd better be turning in my report, and as you've got that mass to say . . . good night, Father."

"*Pax vobiscum*," the priest replied benignly.

"The Lord works in marvelous ways, eh, Sergeant?" commented the lieutenant upon leaving the cathedral.

The sergeant let out an age-old grunt of skepticism.

"It's all right; the patrol's gone now," said Father Martin as he raised the coffin lid.

Numbly, Eliza gazed up at him. "Spare a prayer, Father; so am I."

Miklos dug her in the ribs. "Don't be blasphemous, sweet. You're going to need all the help you can wheedle to get out of Hungary." He sat up, pushing her with him like a ventriloquist's limp dummy.

"I'm not going anywhere until I'm good and ready . . ." Eliza twisted to look at him. "By the way, why are you laid out like Uncle Ned?"

He vaulted out of the coffin. "It's a long story."

The priest pointed his forefinger downward. "Explain to her in the crypt, please. I've preparations to make before anyone goes anywhere now that the Austrians have set a watch about the church." He handed Eliza out of the coffin.

Miklos took her hand. "Come along, darling. Some penitent may decide to bend the Lord's ear at an unreasonable hour."

Once down in the crypt, Miklos relit the candle and stuck it on a skull disengaged from its nether regions in the scuffle with Rakoczy. "I got into that coffin"—he planted the skull atop a reliquary case—"by chasing you all over the countryside. Between Julia and Bette, I was able to put two and two together."

"You went to Bette's? With all those Austrians around?"

"She *is* chummy with them now, isn't she?" He lay down on a catafalque, propped his head on his arms. "Actually, I didn't go into the house. I invaded her carriage during the afternoon ride. Relieved not to be strangled, she was very cooperative, but I still had a devil of a time catching up with you. In the end, I followed Rakoczy. He'd cornered you in the crypt by the time I caught up." He eyed her tenderly. "You really shouldn't make lunatics mad, darling. They're apt to twist your head off."

"I suppose you only gave Rakoczy's neck a tweak, Goody Two Shoes."

"A fleeting impulse. If I'd thought, I'd have torn him limb from limb."

She ruffled his hair. "I'm glad you showed some restraint. I've still a touch of morning sickness. Pieces of Rakoczy flying about might have obliged me to make a mess on your illustrious kings and queens." Her hand stilled in his hair. "Did you hear anything I said to Rakoczy down here?"

"About Hungary being a kingdom of the dead? Yes."

From overhead came a grating sound; Eliza shivered as Father Martin sealed the slab. Miklos blew out the candle. The crypt became blacker than Rakoczy's mind. "This isn't altogether a grave, you know," Eliza murmured as she stretched out beside Miklos in the darkness. "Here we lie: Prince Miklos, the last of the Sztarais; his princess and his heir, in the womb of Hungary's history. People, no matter how evil or heroic, die; only memories live. Hungary's memories are here now. The cries of Magyar horsemen free on the steppes, Stephan the Martyr defying the Turks, Ferenc and Vlad Rakoczy promising freedom; Petöfi, Batthyány. All like you: mad Hungarians. They exhausted life, lived and screamed it to the last breath. They're immortal, unforgettable; in that sense, this crypt isn't a grave at all, but a birthplace.'' She lay his hand on her womb. "Can you feel our baby's heartbeat?''

"I love you, and yes, like my own, I feel it,'' Miklos replied softly.

"It is your own, my love. Will you die Hungarian and give only more blackness to this place . . . or live Hungarian and give her hope?'' She held his hand tightly to her womb. *"This* is Hungary's tomorrow, your tomorrow. Our children's children can give her centuries of hope. History, memories will teach her.''

"And you will, I think, teach me.'' He kissed her so sweetly she was afraid to let him go. Afraid when the crypt opened the past would hold him fast.

"Miki, Julia says Kossuth has found asylum in London. He plans an international tour to tell the world what has happened to Hungary, that human rights can no longer be denied, even in defeat. I want to join him. I still owe a debt to Hungary. She gave me you, gave me children and a home. I love you better than life, but I mean to *live*, with or without you.'' She laid her head on his shoulder. "Just this once, won't you follow the cat?''

He stroked her face. "What do you think I've been doing, since you ran off without even saying good-bye? I sat out in that field at Balaton where I last saw you with the tears streaking the dirt on your face. I threw that dirt to the four winds; it only blew back in my face. All that was left of you was dirt with tears in it. At that moment, not at Temesvar, I knew what death was. It has no golden eyes, no mischief, no passion. It doesn't make me crazy with anger and loss and longing It will never give me love and children.'' He kissed her deeply as if some part of him had been drowning before that kiss. "I'll go anywhere you like, cat. Just wrap yourself around my neck.''

She laughed softly. "I'd like to wrap around more than that, if you wouldn't mind risking a shock to the good priest.''

"You heard him,'' he murmured against her mouth. "He's busy.''

"Do you know, we've never gone to church together,''

Eliza murmured after the dust settled. "I finally feel married."

No rice was flung after the Sztarais' coffin as it departed the cathedral in a procession of priests and hired mourners; however, an hour later, an oddly exuberant cheer did go up in a walled cemetery outside of town.

And the following day, Princess Eliza, twirling a tiara and trailing a prince, rode off into the western sunset.

Epilogue

No Fried Eggs

Seattle, Washington: September 2, 1854

For American purposes, the sun sets in Seattle, where Eliza, Miklos, and two-year-old Paul settled after leaving Kossuth's touring train in Denver. "We were homesick for mountains," said Miklos upon being questioned by the Seattle press three years later. "Several hundred miles of Kansas made us impetuous. In Seattle, one runs out of mountains, so we stopped."

The reporters ogled the magnificent Sztarai mansion through open ballroom doors where glittered Seattle and San Francisco society. Over the crowd hung Stubbs's full-length portrait of Eliza. Rock crystal chandeliers from Poland glowed from the cream and gold latticework ceiling and Italian parquetry gleamed beneath a mass of dancers gaily prancing the "Turkey Trot." "For people who rode out of Budapest in a coffin, you and the princess seem to have ended right side up," one reporter commented. "That due to your textile factories, Your Highness?"

"Indeed, we owe a great deal to our company vice-president, Hans Krafft, for the success of our enterprise; however"—Miklos grinned—"most of the credit goes to my wife."

"How so, sir?"

He waved to a servant who went to fetch Eliza. "You must ask her."

Eliza stepped through the ballroom doors. The reporters ogled even more. She was a whisper of cream, French silk, and two million dollars in diamonds. "Gentlemen."

Lacing his arm through hers, Miklos told her what they wanted to know. Eliza laughed. "My mama, with Yankee thrift, used to collect string. I collect diamonds."

"But, Your Highness," said a reporter mockingly, "surely you don't just find them lying around."

"It's true this tiara was a present"—she waved gaily at her champagne tiara—"but the rest were . . . just lying around." In fact, they'd been scattered from Rakoczy's pockets all over the crypt floor of Saint Stephan's. If she hadn't slipped on one . . .

"Your Highness . . ."

"Please, Americans don't use titles, and I *am* an American."

"Question is," said the skeptic, "are you a *real* princess?"

"Would you care to have a closer look, sir?"

He leered forward. Adroitly, Eliza removed his spectacles. With her ring, she scratched *P* on one lens, *E* on the other. "You see." She smiled sweetly. "As real as these glass rocks."

"And now, gentlemen"—Miklos headed his princess firmly out the door—"if you will excuse us. My wife has promised me the mazurka."

Deftly, he whirled her into the throng of dancers in the ballroom. "Happy, Princess?"

"Very." Her golden eyes were full of light. "Was it worth it, Prince?"

Before he could answer, two small, nightshirted figures scuttled on all fours through the crowd. Lifting his arms to his mother, the taller hopped up and down. "I want to dance!"

As everyone laughed, the smaller threw herself at her father's knees. "Ants, ants!"

Miklos popped two-year-old, blond Sonja atop his shoulders, then five-year-old Sándor grabbed his and Eliza's hands. Off they bounced to the mazurka. "Coming to America, worth it?" Eliza called over the music to Miklos.

"I'm not sure. Running a commercial empire's fascinating enough, but you haven't given me a dozen babies yet."

"Wait a minute!" She gave him a mock grimace as squealing Sonja clutched his hair. "I only promised seven!"

"Well?"

"Well . . . you goat," she purred slyly, "the doctor thinks I'm having twins this time. I have the maddest craving for raw turnips."

Sándor soberly scrutinized his dazed father. "If you don't want any more babies, just cook the eggs."

Miklos steadied, then grinned beatifically at Eliza. "Oh, the more babies, the merrier, only . . . I seem to have the maddest craving for raw turnips."

Sándor made a face at his dreamy-eyed parents. "You both can have mine. Come on, let's dance." When they continued to gaze at each other, Sándor resignedly trotted off to a splendid looking Nòb Hill matron. After making a bow, he flashed his most engaging smile. With a laugh, she curtsyed, caught up her skirt, and off they promenaded.

Gazing after her audacious son, Eliza linked her arm through Miklos's. "Is America ready for another Sztarai, do you think?"

He laughed. "I doubt it. A Magyar's more unmanageable than a wild Indian . . . unless he comes up against a Yankee Eliza."

"Then come up against me, you crazy Hungarian." Lingeringly, he kissed her, then yelped as his small daughter demanded a share of his attention.

Eliza tugged his head back down. "Don't nip your father's ears, Sonja. You'll have your own prince before you know it."